Blood And Magic

ROYAL BASTARDS MC: HELENA, MT
BOOK TWO

JENA DOYLE

DIRTY WORDS PUBLISHING LLC

Copyright © 2025 by Jena Doyle

All rights reserved.

No part of this book may be reproduced in any form or by any electronic or mechanical means, including information storage and retrieval systems, without written permission from the author, except for the use of brief quotations in a book review.

This author takes a firm stance against the use of generative artificial intelligence. No part of this work may be used to train, teach, or assist in any large language models. No part of this work was created using AI.

Line Editing: Misha Robinson at Verity Ink Editorial.

Cover Design: Crimson Syn at Synful Ink.

For you, dear reader. Sometimes, leaping before you look is the only way you'll ever jump. Enjoy.

Royal Bastards MC
Series Seventh Run

Barbara Nolan : Saving Blood
Katherine C. Kelly : One Night with the Biker
Nicole James : Paying the Price
Quinn Slater : Total Carnage
Elizabeth N. Harris: Soul
Verlene Landon : Infected by Virus
Crimson Syn : Tick Tock, Boom!
AJ Downey : Iron Hearts
J. Lynn Lombard : Trigger's Temptation
Letha Gene : Tater
K.L. Ramsey : Reacher's Ride or Die
Roux Cantrell : Hot As Hell
Heather Dahlgren : Surge Attack
JA Lafrance : Closing on Lynx
Ciara St. James : Tyrant's Salvation
Chelle C. Craze & Eli Abbott : SAC-RIFICE
Emma Creed : Wild Card
Posey Parks : Ruthless Obsession
April D. Berry : Defended by Bama
Shannon Youngblood : Kingdon and Kourt

Jena Doyle: Blood and Magic
Angera Allen: Next Level
Kristine Dugger : Another Life
J.A. Collard :High Stakes
Maria Vickers
Claire Shaw : Malice
Kathleen Kelly : Justice
Rae. B. Lake : Rage and Paradise
Kyla Orinick : Scorching Faith
Lila Grey: The Bastard's Lily
Kris Anne Dean : Ravaged and Ruined
Dani Rene : Blaze
Nicola Jane : Bully's Darkness
Elise Gedicke : Deadly Aloha
Thetta James : Nightmare's Battle
Elle Boon : Royally Hidden
D. Williams : Raising Cable

Royal Bastards MC Facebook Group - https://www.facebook.com/groups/royalbastardsmc/
Website- https://www.royalbastardsmc.com/

Royal Bastards Code

PROTECT: The club and your brothers come before anything else, and must be protected at all costs. **CLUB** is **FAMILY**.

RESPECT: Earn it & Give it. Respect club law. Respect the patch. Respect your brothers. Disrespect a member and there will be hell to pay.

HONOR: Being patched in is an honor, not a right. Your colors are sacred, not to be left alone, and **NEVER** let them touch the ground.

OL' LADIES: Never disrespect a member's or brother's Ol'Lady. **PERIOD.**

CHURCH is **MANDATORY.**

LOYALTY: Takes precedence over all, including well-being.

HONESTY: Never **LIE, CHEAT,** or **STEAL** from another member or the club.

TERRITORY: You are to respect your brother's property and follow their Chapter's club rules.

TRUST: Years to earn it...seconds to lose it.

NEVER RIDE OFF: Brothers do not abandon their family.

I'd never given much thought to dying.

My mother passed when I was six, and though I understood all things must come to an end, I didn't fully comprehend the precarious tightrope upon which we mortals walked until the Grim Reaper gave mine a good shake.

"Do you think Percy will retaliate?" my twin, Ava, asked from across the dining room. She pushed salad around on her plate, her eyebrows scrunched together in a scowl.

"I don't see how he can," I replied. "Guin and Sol have him backed into a corner. Even if he comes out swinging, there isn't much he can use to his advantage."

Ava nodded and glanced back at her food, but neither of us had an appetite.

Our father, Uther Vanderbilt, had finally succumbed to cancer mere months ago, and in a move we all should have seen coming, our despicable elder brother, Percy, had made a play for the family business. We were the Vanderbilts, the wealthiest and most powerful family in Helena, Montana. In order of birth, Ava and I were smack in the middle: Guinevere, Percy, and Liam on one side, Isolde and

Galahad on the other. We owned over five thousand acres of land where we raised cattle and trained horses, and that said nothing of the wind turbines and natural gas companies we used to sell energy back to the national grid. Our grandparents had made us wealthy, but my father had turned it into an empire.

"Do you think the Royal Bastards will help us?" I asked, bringing my sister's gaze back up to me.

She shrugged. "Sol seemed pretty sure."

Our family and the Royal Bastards had been enemies for years. A land dispute had started it, but the feud escalated when my mother died on their property and my father blamed them for it. He said the Bastards ripped her to pieces, leaving nothing but a bloody patch in the snow. We never found her body.

After Father died, Percy stepped in to take over, and our ranch hands left us, refusing to work for that spineless coward. I didn't blame them. Percy had always had more ego than brains, and he'd never once worked the ranch. Why would they respect him? This had put our dear brother in the frustrating position of having to make a deal with one of the local motorcycle clubs, the Bloody Scorpions. In exchange for our sister's hand in marriage, the president offered his men to help us.

Isolde, whom we affectionately called Sol, had taken a drunken sojourner into the mountains and returned with a lover named Orion from a rival motorcycle gang, complete with the entire Royal Bastards crew behind him. Ava and I had helped her hatch a devilish scheme to bring our dear brother back down to earth, and when he realized he'd been outmaneuvered, he'd sulked off to greener pastures.

It had been hilarious to watch his precious plans crumble around him. I absolutely loathed what he'd done, so I was thrilled to see him sink so low. That had been a few days ago, and none of us had heard from him since.

"I'm not sure I believe Sol when she says they're not responsible for our mother," Ava said. "There's something wrong with them, something off."

"I agree." I sipped my wine, choking back the Cab Sauv despite how much I loved dry reds. The thought of the Bastards always set me on edge. Rumors circulated through Helena that they were vicious beasts that turned into animals on the full moon. It was small-minded folklore, of course. Shapeshifters didn't exist. "Sol seems different now, too. Doesn't she?"

Ava nodded. "Definitely. I don't know what happened to her at that cabin with the Bastards, but—"

"It's her eyes," I said. "I look into them now and see something else staring out at me."

Sol was only eighteen months younger than Ava and me, by all rights our Irish triplet. We were best friends, the three of us. No one else could be trusted, no one who wasn't family. I'd tried to have friends, of course, and I'd even made a few at boarding school. But money corrupted everything it touched, and I could never be sure if they really liked me or my daddy's wallet.

"It was like when Guin started dating that ranch hand. What was his name?" Ava narrowed her blue eyes in concentration.

"Van," I said, recalling the tall, attractive biker with sandy blond hair and dark brown eyes who used to smile at me from under a cowboy hat. "Beautiful Van."

"Right." Ava laughed, drinking her glass of wine. "Of course, you'd remember his name."

I balked and feigned offense. "What's that supposed to mean?"

"Despite being genetically identical, I fear our taste in partners is quite the opposite." She smirked and let out another loud giggle.

"Precisely," I agreed. "I'm a hot-blooded woman, and you're a frigid prude."

She dropped her jaw, half insulted, half laughing, and threw her napkin across the table at me. "Just because I don't screw anyone with a pulse doesn't mean I'm a prude."

"I'm not shaming you," I said, attempting to ease her ire, but a strange tightness in my chest stopped me. My lungs seized, my stomach lurching as a sudden wave of anguish shot down my torso and up my throat. I couldn't breathe. I couldn't think.

Panicking, I clutched at my sternum and gasped for air.

"Mae?" Ava said, pushing to her feet. She scrambled over to my side of the table just as I lurched to the ground. My vision blackened, the world going blurry, my head both light and the weight of an anvil.

The last coherent thing I saw was my sister's frightened stare, a replica of my own, and then the world went dark.

Dying was a peculiar thing, truly. There was no bright white light or angels calling me home to heaven. I thought I might see my mother or father, or perhaps our grandparents, but there was none of that, either—just the tragic droll of nothingness. Eternity of darkness. End of story. Good night.

I woke up with a gasp, electric currents shooting through my body as my back arched off the ground.

"Mae?" said a deep, dusky voice. Bright light flashed through each one of my eyes, and I winced against the splitting pain in my skull. "She's coming back around."

The EMT barked orders at other people around him, but I focused on the ceiling of my family's dining room. A crowd of people surrounded me: staff, paramedics, my sister.

"What happened?" I croaked.

No one answered as I was lifted onto a stretcher and shuttled out of the house. It was only on the ambulance ride to the hospital that I learned I had collapsed and banged my head on the nineteenth-century table on my way down. My heart had stopped, and if it hadn't been for Ava's quick thinking and immediate CPR, they wouldn't have been able to resuscitate me.

Stopped?

What do they mean stopped?

I never got an answer. The doctors at the emergency department ran as many tests as they could and arrived at no concrete conclusions. I didn't have any heart defects, and other than this one incident, there was no indication of illness, genetic or sudden onset. They referred me to a cardiologist, who was as stunned as the other doctors.

Aside from a cracked rib and the scar on my forehead, I'd managed to walk away from death with barely a hair out of place. I had access to the best doctors money could afford. I'd been shuttled to Johns Hopkins and the Cleveland Clinic. I'd flown halfway around the world and back, only for the world's greatest minds to tell me they had no idea what happened or if it would happen again. In the end, they put me on medication to help maintain the electrical current of my heart and said they'd see me again in six months.

"You're okay now," Ava said, gripping my hand on the last flight home. She'd been by my side through it all, through the tests and the endless poking and prodding. She'd been a guinea pig in her own way. As my genetic twin, they could compare our bodies to each other to search for any mutations. But nothing ever came. "You'll be okay now."

I nodded and gripped her hand, giving her a tight grin I hoped was reassuring. But as I stared out the window of the private jet at the twinkling lights below, I vibrated with a hollowness I'd never felt before. It was more than medical exhaustion, more than any doctor or specialist could tell me. It grew into a nagging emptiness in my soul—rotten, dark, and all-consuming.

I hungered for something...I didn't know what. I only knew I had to find it. This yearning clawed at my insides like razors slicing open my veins, making me restless and jittery. My heart ached for the unknown, and until I submitted, I couldn't guarantee I would be okay ever again.

That emptiness stayed with me through winter and into spring. I went back to work at Vanderbilt Enterprises as director of operations, a job I'd been given by my father shortly after graduating from Harvard.

I hate this, I thought as I sat in a leadership meeting about upcoming strategic priorities.

"If we have any hope of remaining in the top five energy producers in Montana, we'll need to increase our operational efficiency by at least thirty percent," said one of our vice presidents.

I blinked against the monotonous corporate speak. This meeting had gone on for two hours longer than necessary, and I should care about the direction the company planned to take, but I wondered if anyone even gave a shit I was here.

I didn't add much value, aside from schmoozing with people who secretly gossiped about me being a nepo baby behind my back while brownnosing to my face. Vanderbilt Enterprises had once been my safety net, the one thing I always knew I would do. Now I dreaded walking into the building.

I rubbed my temples and tried to focus on the metrics on the television in front of me, but what was the point, truly? In the end, none of this mattered.

Death was a tricky thing. It put a lot into perspective. Like how long I'd spent doing things because my father expected me to. Or how much I'd lived in the giant shadow of my sisters. I wasn't as smart as Ava; she'd graduated from Harvard Law. I wasn't as ruthless as Guin; she'd become the heir apparent. And I wasn't nearly as loved by the Vanderbilt patriarch as Sol; she'd been allowed to do whatever she wanted after college.

With this new lease on life, I was determined to find my purpose, to feel alive in all its splendid glory, no matter what that entailed.

NOW

"I can't believe you're going to be gone for two whole months," Ava said, pouting at Sol. "Are you sure you can't take us with you?"

Our youngest sister laughed and wrapped an arm around Ava's shoulders. "Trust me. You don't want to go on this trip."

"Bali would be wonderful," Ava said. "I don't have to spend time with you and your fiancé, Mr. Grumpy Gills."

"Ugh," Guin cut in, twisting her hair into a pin curl before securing it with a bobby pin. "They're ridiculously disgusting together. It's intolerable being in the same room as them."

Sol narrowed playful eyes at her and stuck out her tongue, reminding me so much of the younger version of herself. I sat in a corner, sketching them in my notepad while we gossiped and de-stressed from the week's wedding planning events. I could have wasted hundreds on a gift, but Orion spoiled Sol with whatever she wanted, and God knew she already had everything she could need. Instead, I'd decided to give her a series of portraits commemorating her big day and the moments leading up to it. It was more personal, and she'd appreciate the intimacy in it.

Tonight was a sisters' bonding sleepover. Tomorrow would be the rehearsal, culminating in the big moment the day after.

"I still can't believe you're getting married to him," Ava said, turning to our eldest sister. "You're okay with this?"

I didn't honestly expect Guin to disagree. In the six months since Sol met Orion, Guin had gotten close with the Royal Bastards, too. She had an "understanding" with their president, Kodiak…whatever that meant. Neither she nor Sol had been particularly forthcoming about how we'd gone from hating the Bastards to welcoming them into the family within a matter of weeks.

All they would say was they didn't believe the Bastards had killed our mother, and we needed them to survive. They had gotten us through the winter, and without their help, our company would have tanked when the ranch hands walked. No one had heard from Percy or the Bloody Scorpions in months. The RBMC had stepped up, but that didn't mean I had to like it. And now Sol was *marrying* one of them?

"Sol is as hardheaded as the rest of us," Guin explained. "There's no telling any Vanderbilt what they can or can't do. If she wants to marry Mr. Tall, Dark, and Grumpy from the wrong side of the Missouri River, who are we to stop her?"

"Hey!" Sol brushed wisps of her ginger hair from her face before rubbing in moisturizer. "He's not as grumpy as he used to be. And in two days, he'll be your brother-in-law."

"Not by choice," Guin said quickly.

"Who would have thought our *baby* sister would be the first to walk down the aisle?" Ava shook her head and laughed.

"I hope you didn't think it would be me," Guin said. "I'd rather chew off my own foot."

"Romantic," Ava added. "No, I just thought...well...maybe me or Mae would have gone first." My twin met my gaze. "Do you still talk to Zachary?"

I winced at the thought of my former friend with benefits and shook my head, softening a dark shadow around my sketch of Sol with my finger. I'd have graphite smudges on my hands for days, but that was par for the course. "No. Very much no."

"Pity," she said. "I thought he liked you."

"Well, he ended up marrying a Kennedy, so I doubt he thinks of me at all anymore."

"Okay, back on task," Sol said, grabbing her phone. "We'll be gone from June into July." She went through all of the ranch activities that would need to be done in those weeks. Since the Vanderbilts had made a tentative truce with the Bastards, they'd agreed to help us maintain what our father had built. Orion had taken on the lead rancher role until things were more stable.

Surprising everyone, she had become his right hand. She managed the horses and drew up plans for the cattle, even while maintaining her corporate position on the board.

"Mae, you're still okay with stepping in, right?"

I nodded, reminding myself I could do hard things. I'd grown up on this ranch, after all. Just because I'd gotten a business degree and spent most of my time in an office didn't mean I couldn't return to my roots. Despite having a special connection to my favorite horse, Molly, I'd never really worked the ranch. Father had always hired help for that. But I could shout out orders well enough, and I'd been cleared from my day job to work remotely for the duration.

"I'll be in Europe for that international trade alliance conference," Ava said. "And then I'm doing a networking tour. I'll be gone until August."

My heart ached at the thought of being separated from my twin for so long. Of course, we'd spent time apart before, and we did our best to distinguish ourselves at boarding school and college. But no one knew me the way Ava did, and the notion of two long months away from her formed a pit in my gut nearly the size of Jupiter.

"I'll be in Bozeman for most of it," Guin added. "If you need help, call me. I'm only an hour away."

"I'll be fine," I said. "The Bastards are sending someone to replace Orion, right?"

Sol nodded. "That's the agreement."

"I'm sure whoever that is will know what they're doing," I said. "Besides, we're not losing our ranch hands this time. They've got a well-oiled machine going out there. I'm here more as a supervisor anyway. A face to put on the family name."

"How are you feeling these days?" Sol asked, her eyes full of genuine concern. Since my near-death experience six months ago, I hadn't had so much as a fainting spell. But something still wasn't right. That hollowness had taken hold deep in my soul, my body yearning for something tangible. I just didn't know what it was.

I'd tried a variety of activities to fill it: skydiving, base jumping, heli-skiing. Aside from a massive adrenaline rush and a few new hobbies, it didn't bring me what I was after. My sisters had called it reckless, but I didn't want to squander my new lease on life.

"Okay," I said, trying to keep a poker face.

Sol glanced at Guin, a quick exchange between them that made me curious.

"No headaches or body chills?" Guin said, securing another pin.

"Why do you ask?" Now that they mentioned it, I'd had a twinge between the eyes for the last few days, but I chalked it up to allergies and the stress of a job that didn't truly satisfy.

"Just trying to make sure you're not about to drop dead on us again," Guin said.

"Well, the last time that happened, I had no warning whatsoever." I accentuated a curl on Sol's shoulders and tilted my head to the side, admiring my work. Her nose wasn't quite right, so I took an eraser to the lines on her face and started over.

Again, Sol looked at Guin, who raised her eyebrows once as if to say, "Who knows?"

I glanced at my twin, sending my own mental message.

What are they hiding?

"What's with the secret glances?" Ava said.

I didn't like being kept in the dark. The only two who were allowed to share telepathic communication were Ava and me, and we had identical DNA. Our neural synapses had been formed together in the same amniotic sac. Ergo, we were entitled.

"What? Can't sisters be worried about their family?" Guin rolled her eyes and returned to the vanity mirror, placing another pin curl in her hair. "God forbid."

After our mother died, Guin had stepped into the role of matriarch. She kept the rest of us in line and protected us from the extent of our wicked family. But she never lied to us, not about something important. To see her go from hating the Bastards to welcoming them with a rapidly decreasing frost made me curious.

Ava glanced back at me. *They're definitely hiding something.*

Agreed, I mentally replied.

"You'll let me know if you start feeling different, right?" Guin said. "Both of you?"

"Different how?" Ava asked, narrowing her gaze.

"Just...*different,*" Sol said, glancing at her phone again. I could have sworn her eyes changed to amber and back to green, but perhaps I'd imagined it. After all, no one's eyes changed colors like that, and she'd inherited the same emerald irises as our mother. Ava and I, along with Galahad and Liam, had gotten our father's dark coloring. "Anyway, the rehearsal is tomorrow. Everyone will be here except for Van."

The mention of my childhood crush got my attention, and I snapped my gaze to my sister.

"Why not?" Guin asked. "He's a groomsman. He can't miss the rehearsal."

"He said he had a conflict," Sol said. "Orion told me to drop the issue, so I didn't argue."

"Well, the show must go on, I suppose," Guin said, looking at me before returning to her hair prep.

"Are you sure you don't want a bachelorette party?" Ava said. "We still have time. We could take the family jet anywhere. Atlantic City. Vegas." She gasped as if an idea had just occurred to her. "Monaco."

Sol laughed and shook her head. "No. There's no reason to aggravate my betrothed any more than I already have by insisting we spend the night before the wedding apart."

"I'm surprised he let you out of his sight," Guin said. "Bastards are notoriously territorial."

"Speaking of Van," I said, clearing my throat. "Are you two still together?"

Guin snorted and shook her head. "Heavens, no. As I said, there's no man with hands big enough to carry my crown, and I like it that way."

Sol giggled.

"What?" Guin balked and stared at our youngest sister.

"Nothing," Sol said. "Nothing at all."

Guin returned her forest-green eyes to me with narrowed inspection. "Why do you ask?"

I pretended like my interest in the Bastard was purely professional. He'd worked the ranch in his early twenties, back when I was just starting to go through puberty. He and Guin had been...friends? Friends with benefits? A hearty teenage fling? With her, it was difficult to tell. She treated boyfriends with the same apathetic disinterest as she did strangers.

In the deepest, darkest recesses of my poor pathetic heart, I'd admit I had a teeny tiny crush on him when he worked here. Most of the day workers ignored us or acted like my father might shoot their eyes out for even glancing in our direction. But Van had been nice... decent...dare I say, flirty?

But then he'd left and joined the Royal Bastards and became our enemy. Except now they weren't enemies, and the lines were so blurred, I didn't know how I was supposed to feel anymore. I hadn't seen Van since I was a little girl, but the thought of his bright brown eyes and big smile sent a shiver down my spine, pooling in my lower stomach.

I was twelve years younger than him, barely more than knees, elbows, and braces at the time. But he *saw* me, and growing up in Guin's massive shadow meant not many people did. He'd been a part of my sexual awakening, and if I happened to have a preference for blondes, well, could anyone honestly blame me?

At such a tender age, he'd made an impression.

"Just curious," I said in answer to my sister's question. Shrugging and ignoring the steady thump of my heart as it pounded against my ribs, I kept my gaze fixed on my drawing. The mere thought of Van set my pulse skyrocketing for no obvious reason. I decided it was the remnants of an early girlhood fascination and let it go.

But my question had gotten Ava's attention, and she raised an eyebrow at me.

I ignored that, too.

Sol went through the rest of the wedding plans, and when it was over, we gathered around our family table for dinner.

For the entire night, I tried to hide my relief at hearing that Guin and Van weren't together, even as it mixed with an excited trepidation of seeing Van again after all these years.

CHAPTER 2

Vermillion

L iving was bullshit.

I didn't use to think that, but ever since I'd died and come back to life, finding joy in the mundane had become an impossible task.

"Your heart sounds good," my sister, Morwyn, said, pressing the stethoscope to my chest. "Lungs are fine. You're completely healthy."

I didn't feel healthy. Hell, I barely felt anything anymore. I'd say I was depressed, but such a minuscule term didn't cover it.

Last November, the bloodsucking vampires, aka the Bloody Scorpions MC, had abducted Sol in retaliation for her mating to Orion. If there was one thing all shifters hated, it was a nasty vampire nest close to our homestead. And fucking with one person's mate meant the entire weight of the pack came with a vengeance. We went after her, and in the process, I took two sets of fangs straight to the neck.

It had taken all the magic in the pack to bring me back to life. Or, at least, they'd managed to get my heart beating again. But knowing there was nothing on the other side, no heavenly gates and no ancestors waiting for me, put things in a different perspective. I should have been grateful to have every damned day on this great earth, but things were different now.

I was different now.

My wolf had died and come back darker...angrier...more willing to snarl and tear into someone.

"Good," I said, hopping off the table to put my shirt back on. "Clean bill of health. You can stop annoying me with your relentless questions."

Morwyn rolled her eyes. As a fully trained medical doctor and the pack's resident healer, she saw with more than just her eyes. She had a special connection to the alpha that allowed her unfettered access to the magical ties between us. When someone joined the pack, they made a blood bond to Kodiak, and through that supernatural tie, Morwyn could channel her energy at will to heal us.

It was this energy that had brought me back to life.

"Mill," she said, her features softening, reminding me of our mother. "I'm worried about you. Caelum says you're not eating. You're losing weight."

I scoffed and rubbed a hand over my face. "Our little brother is too busy fucking his way through the homestead to know what I'm doing."

"You look like hell, big brother." She crossed her arms, her brown curly hair sticking out at odd angles around her head. "It took you nearly fifteen minutes to change last moon."

I'd been a member of the Helena, Montana shifter pack my entire life, and eight years ago, I'd been patched into the council...officially made a member of the Royal Bastards MC. We weren't like shifters from fairy tales, unless you count the fucked-up German ones. We only turned once a month, when the call of the full moon activated the magic in our blood and forced us to change. We couldn't turn into our furry counterparts at will, nor would we want to. The shift was painful and difficult and took upward of five minutes for a normal shifter to fully complete. We could accomplish partial changes at will: growing claws, extending our fangs, and letting the inner beast take over our vision. But a complete transformation took place only once a month.

The lore was true about one thing, though. We hated vampires with a bloodthirsty passion, and in Montana, any vampire that passed through became part of the Bloody Scorpions. They ran the territory to the east of the Missouri, and up until six months ago, they'd been in league with the Vanderbilts. Those rich motherfuckers had bought up everything to the south and west, damn near controlling the entire state.

"I'm fine," I said, trying (and failing) to keep my tone light. It came out more in a snarl than I'd intended. I cleared my throat and tried again. "I'm fine."

"Look, I've been doing some research." She glanced down at the ground and rubbed a hand over her neck. "I don't know how we brought you back, and I'm worried we might have done lasting damage."

Yeah, no shit.

Everyone had moments that marked a definitive before and after. Mine was that night. Before, I'd been fun. Jovial. Generally happy with my life and those in it. I loved being a part of the pack, and I loved everyone in it like family. Our parents had died during a Scorpion raid on RBMC territory, so I'd been in charge of my little sister and brother ever since. I took that responsibility seriously.

After? Temper meet short fuse. Anything could set me off and routinely did. I snarled at cubs and later regretted it. I'd had to take a two-week probation from patrol because I'd pissed off our sergeant at arms, Moose, by punching another male when he'd gotten too close to a female who didn't want his attention.

I mean, what was the fucking point of any of this?

We were born. We lived meaningless lives. And then we died. The end.

"I'm fine," I growled, my wolf perilously close to the surface. I felt the shift in my eyes, my canines extending, my fingernails turning into sharp points capable of slicing and dicing.

"Don't take that tone with me," she said, putting her hands on her hips, her own wolf glaring at me from behind her gaze. "With one word, I could have you on house arrest. You're already skating on thin ice with Kodiak. You want to stomp on that crack?"

I grumbled and took a deep breath, trying to calm the rising tide of fury in my gut.

"We're worried about you, Van," she said, using my legal name, the one she'd been calling me since we were children. "We love you."

"I don't need you to worry about me," I said, recognizing the signs of exhaustion in her face. She had nearly wiped herself out to bring me back, and in the time since, she hadn't recuperated. "When are you taking a vacation, huh?"

"Don't change the subject." She sighed and shook her head. "I need you to be honest with me. What else are you noticing?"

The utter frustration with literally everyone and everything. The urge to hunt down every fucking vampire I could until the world overflowed with their wretched, decaying blood. An overwhelming emptiness in my soul that nothing and no one could fill.

I was a zombie, and she'd made me this way.

She should have let me die. They all should have let me die.

I pushed my thumb and forefinger into my eyes, tired of this conversation and her incessant prodding. If I told her half of the things I had been experiencing, she'd slam me in the holding cell and dissect me like a science experiment. No other shifter we'd ever heard of had been dead as long as me and brought back by magic.

It bordered too close to things I didn't want to think of.

"Wyn," I said, putting my hands on my hips. "Our vice president is marrying a Vanderbilt tomorrow. Marx, the king of crusty undead bloodsuckers, is still on the run. I've got no clues about where to look for him." As the pack's tech guru, it was on me to find him, but the fucker was a Goddamned ghost. "Half the pack is pissed about Kodiak's alliance with Guin, and our brother spent three days stuck in a cave with my best friend's sister. Don't you think there are bigger issues to worry about?"

She scowled. "I'll add delusional apathy to the list of symptoms."

"Let. This. Go." I said the words through clenched teeth, hoping she'd get the picture.

"No." Morwyn turned to her notes and jotted down something undoubtedly incriminating that would only piss me off more.

She was as stubborn as I was, and if she weren't my dearest little sister, I'd already have snarled loud enough to send her scampering to Kodiak with her tail between her legs. As it was, she wasn't scared of me and never would be. As much as my wolf hated everyone and everything else, I would never hurt my siblings. Never.

"If I did something while healing you, I need to fix it."

The urge to bite her head off nearly overwhelmed me, but just then, my only friend and fellow RBMC member, Fenris, stuck his head in.

"Hey, buddy," he said. "I thought I heard your dulcet tones."

"The doc is trying to patch me back together like Humpty Dumpty." I grabbed my cut and stuffed my arms into the leather before heaving it onto my shoulders.

"Good," Fenris said, running a hand through his dark curly hair before stepping inside and smiling at my sister. "Someone needs to."

She glanced at him and raised an eyebrow. "Fenris."

"Morwyn." He grinned. She rolled her eyes and returned to her paperwork, clearly not amused. Perhaps I should have been more concerned about Fenris's blatant flirtation, but she'd never given him the time of day, which was a good thing. Fenris had never been serious about anyone or anything, except his younger sister, Lyra. And maybe me.

"What are you doing here?" I asked. "Is Lyra—"

"She's fine," he said. "Being stuck in a cave with your brother was barely a blip on her radar."

At the last new moon mating ceremony, she'd snuck off pack territory in a terrible storm and gotten stuck in a cave with Caelum when a tree collapsed in front of the opening. They'd been there for three days before Kodiak could find them. Other than reeking like sex, dirt, and earth, they'd emerged mostly unscathed. As long as

Caelum kept himself out of trouble, I tried to stay out of his personal shit.

Unlike Fenris, Lyra was a mountain lion shifter, one of the over ten different types of shifters in the pack. Some were prey animals, some were predators, but Kodiak didn't believe in speciesism, nor would he tolerate prejudice based on the status of one's parents. Half-breed, pure-breed, none of that shit mattered to him. But old stereotypes died hard, and for beasts like Lyra, where one parent was human and one was shifter, being a member of a smaller group made life that much harder.

"Kodiak's looking for you," he said. "Something about needing a Bastard to watch over Vanderbilt Ranch while Orion's on his honeymoon."

I narrowed my eyes. "He wants me to do it?"

Fenris shrugged and shoved his hands in his pockets. "Moose has to play second while Orion's gone. Ruby is on shift at the Fiver, and Serpent's taking almost everyone else on that run to the Washington chapter."

Fuck.

I glanced back at my sister. "We're done here."

"Sure," she said. I turned to leave, but she grabbed my arm to stop me. "I need to see you back after the next moon."

"Right," I answered, knowing I had no intention of doing that. Whatever had been done to me had no prognosis. I'd just have to wait it out until I eventually recovered or wasted away.

I followed Fenris through the underground tunnels connecting our homestead buildings. He rambled about the upcoming shipment and how he'd volunteered to help out at Vanderbilt Ranch, especially when he found out I'd been volun-told to run things.

"You're gonna need me," he said. "They've got a lot of land and more cattle than I've ever handled before."

While he talked, I thought about what I'd say to Kodiak and if there was any way to get out of this. I had to find Marx. I had to clean up this fucking mess before he came back for more blood. If I knew anything about those bloodsucking pricks, they wouldn't let something like this go. We'd attacked them, stolen the president's fiancée, and killed half their nest. He'd be back, and we'd have to be ready.

Once upon a time, we used to have bad blood with the Vanderbilts, too. Uther Vanderbilt thought the Bastards had killed his wife, so he made a deal with the Scorpions to send them into pack territory during a full moon. They took out nearly two dozen males, females, and children, our parents included, before the previous alpha was able to stop them.

It had been this rage that sent me to Vanderbilt Ranch all those years ago.

I thought I could get revenge. I thought I could infiltrate them, learn their secrets, and report back to Kodiak. I'd never counted on developing a friendship with Guin Vanderbilt. I'd never guessed she'd turn out to be a shifter, too. I'd spent two summers with their family before coming home with a whole host of new problems to keep me up at night.

Then, six months ago, Sol crashed her SUV on Bastard territory and was rescued by Orion. While stuck at Fiver Cabin with the veep, Lycan, and Poe, she'd gone through the transition—a painful process where the shifter magic activated inside a human, a kind of second adolescence. Pack children couldn't shift; the magic would be too strong and overwhelm them, potentially killing them. It was only when a shifter reached their early to mid-twenties that their preternatural side took root, and they needed another shifter to help them through it, to lie with them and give them their magic in blood, saliva, and seed.

I'd been the one who helped Guin. Orion had helped Sol. Now, they both turned into a fox every full moon with the rest of the pack. When it was just Guin, she changed on her own on Vanderbilt property. Now that it was the two of them, I didn't know how they kept it from the rest of their siblings. But that wasn't my problem.

Once that mating had been sealed, Kodiak struck up a stupid deal for a reciprocal work share. We helped them with their land, they injected our homestead with cash, and never two nicer bedfellows did such former enemies make.

"Anyway," Fenris said when we got to Kodiak's office. "You're the right guy for the job. It'll be good for you to get out of the den and back out on the pasture. And I'll be there to help you."

I nodded but didn't acknowledge how much I disagreed with him. He clapped me on the shoulder and turned to walk away. Taking a deep breath, I steeled myself against the onslaught I was about to face before knocking twice on Kodiak's door and waiting for his reply.

When I walked inside, the alpha sat behind his desk, writing on a piece of paper. At six-six and well over two hundred fifty pounds of muscle, he made the furniture look like a tea set for a little girl. That was how he'd gotten his road name. He was bigger than a grizzly as a wolf and damn near as terrifying in both forms.

"Vermillion," he said, glancing up with a smile as he gestured to the seat in front of him.

I took a deep breath and sat as I tried to unclench my muscles. Working at Vanderbilt Ranch wouldn't be hard, not even close to a stint up at Fiver Cabin. That tiny fucking shack was in the middle of nowhere on top of a mountain. Why we hung on to it, I'd never know.

"You wanted to see me?" I cleared my throat and met the alpha's gaze. Because he was so connected to all of us, he saw through me. His typically brown eyes were flecked with red when his beast was close to the surface, and now, both of them read me like a book.

"How are you doing?" Placing his elbows on the sides of his chair, he steepled his fingers in front of his mouth, awaiting my answer.

"Fine," I said. Not technically a lie, even if it wasn't the entire truth.

"You look…" His incendiary gaze swept over me, from my dirty blond hair down to my shitkickers and back up again. "Tired."

A million retorts bounced around in my head, each one more petulant than the last. But I didn't say any of them. Kodiak wouldn't put up with it anyway, and I didn't feel like adding an ass-beating to my itinerary.

"Are you sleeping?" He raised an eyebrow.

"C'mon, Prez," I said. "I already got the grill from my sister. Do we have to go through the formalities? You need me to take over Vanderbilt Ranch."

Kodiak pursed his lips. "That's right, I do. With Orion leaving for his honeymoon and half the damn council on a run, you're my best option. You used to moonlight there in your early twenties, right?"

I nodded, ignoring the lump in my chest at the thought of returning to my old stomping grounds. I didn't know why. Guin and I had left things on friendly terms. She'd even helped bring me back to life last November. Something about venturing back into quasi-enemy territory set my teeth on edge and had my wolf stretching in preparation for a fight.

"So it shouldn't be too much of an issue to take things over from Orion for a few weeks." He phrased it like a statement rather than a question.

"No," I replied. "I'm happy to help."

Kodiak narrowed his eyes. "Are you?"

"Sure." I coughed to clear my throat and tensed to keep myself from squirming under his stare. I was a dominant wolf, high ranking in the pack. But the alpha was alpha for a reason. The only one who could come close to matching him was Orion, and even then, Kodiak could pummel him in minutes.

The alpha drummed his fingers on the table before tilting his head. "How's your temper these days?"'

"Between you and Morwyn, I can't catch a Goddamned break." I pinched the bridge of my nose. "If I say fine, are you gonna believe me?"

"A year ago, you woulda come into my office, laughing about some stupid thing Fenris did or complaining about your idiot little brother." Kodiak stood and walked around his desk, leaning against the front of it before crossing his arms. "Now, I don't remember the last time I've seen you smile."

"A year ago, I didn't die and come back to life," I cut in.

"Are you suggesting that changed you so fundamentally that you've become unrecognizable?"

I didn't know, and I had no good answers, so I stayed silent.

"I'm worried about you," he said. "Fenris, Morwyn, we all are."

This interrogation, alongside this morning's appointment with my sister, had tested my patience to the breaking point.

Can't a guy deal with his own shit?

"I'm—"

"If you say fine one more time, so help me..." Kodiak growled, and I lifted my gaze to his, holding it for only a moment before dropping it again.

"What do you want me to say?"

"How you really feel," he said. "Fuck, brother. You died. You were brought back to life with magic. You're not an idiot. You know what that sounds like."

Vampire.

It wasn't the first time the thought had occurred to me. The Bloody Scorpions were so vile because their magic had been polluted, warped, and mutated by necromancy. It wasn't natural. Shifters, on the other hand, our magic came from the earth. It was part of the reason we lived in rural Montana, out in Big Sky country. We were so deeply connected to nature that separating from it would stifle our wild sides until they turned feral.

The last alpha had gone rabid after losing his mate during the raid. Kodiak had to put him down for the sake of the pack. I had no desire to relive that experience.

"Let me ask a different way." Kodiak cleared his throat and leaned closer to me. "Are you sucking blood?"

"Man, fuck off," I snapped. "I'm not a Scorpion."

"No?" He raised his eyebrows, seemingly surprised. "Then stop pulling away from the people who love you. Morwyn wants to help you. *I* want to help you."

I didn't like to be reprimanded, not by my sister and not by the alpha. Both were humiliating in their own ways.

"If you won't talk to me or our trained healer, then talk to Fenris. Talk to Caelum or Moose or a fucking therapist; I don't care. Bottling it up is only going to make you explode."

I nodded once, and in the deafening silence afterward, I scrambled for a way to get out of there. "When do you need me at Vanderbilt?"

Kodiak sighed and straightened, moving back behind his desk again to sit before shuffling through some papers. "The day after the wedding."

Two days.

"Okay," I agreed, pushing to my feet. "Is that all?"

He shifted his shoulders. "Give me an update on the Scorpions."

I ran through the latest status on Marx and whoever he'd been able to salvage from the wreckage of his nest. We'd wiped out a lot of them, but even more got away.

"I've got facial recognition running nationwide," I said. "It's a lot of ground to cover. He set off a ping out near Crow Res three weeks ago, but he's been quiet after that."

Kodiak nodded. "You think he's regrouping?"

"He'd be stupid not to. He still thinks of Sol as his." Even though she wasn't my mate, she was pack, and I didn't like the thought of some undead fucker laying claim to her. She belonged to Orion. She belonged to us. "We never found her brother's body."

After everything went down with Sol, her eldest brother, Percy, ran to Marx for safety. Sol said the Scorpions had turned him into one of them. Once we saved her, we rounded up the corpses to burn them, ensuring they didn't heal themselves and reanimate. Guin had been certain he wasn't among them, which meant he'd escaped and still walked with the undead.

"So Marx has someone who knows the ins and outs of Vanderbilt Ranch," I said. "Not to mention leverage to pull with the siblings."

"I don't think we need to worry about Sol or Guin," Kodiak replied. "But Liam may be a problem."

I couldn't disagree.

"Keep an eye on him," the alpha continued. "Guin will be handling most of the business in Bozeman while Sol is away, and Lycan is escorting Ava on her business trip to Paris. Which means Maeve will be there alone."

I nodded, hearing what he wasn't saying as much as what he was. I wouldn't just be there to run things while Orion was out of town. I'd be playing bodyguard, too, which was fine with me. If any Scorpions came sniffing around, I'd give them a taste of their own bullshit. I'd been antsy for revenge since I died.

"Here's the operating plan." Kodiak handed me a stack of papers. "And it goes without saying...don't fuck with the Vanderbilt, alright?"

I snorted. "That won't be a problem."

"I'm serious," he said. "The last thing I need is Guinevere dragging her Louboutins in here to bitch me out about another one of my brothers putting their paws where they don't belong."

The visual made me laugh, and I covered my mouth to hide it from a clearly displeased alpha. No one talked to Kodiak the way Guin did and got away with it, and maybe that was because she wasn't *officially* part of the pack. She changed with us at the full moon and came to *some* pack meetings, but she hadn't made an oath to the alpha. Nor had she cut her hand and sealed the blood bond. I'd never ask her about it, but Sol indicated Guin preferred to be a lone fox. That would only go so far with Kodiak, and I secretly begged to be a fly on the wall when they finally had that confrontation. They'd been known to have shouting matches that could be heard halfway across the homestead.

"I don't know, Prez," I said. "I think you like it when the eldest Vanderbilt gets all hot and bothered."

He snapped his gaze up, features twisted into an angry scowl. "Was that a joke?"

I couldn't help my shit-eating grin. Years ago, Kodiak's wife had tragically died in a car accident caused by the Scorpions, leaving him with two little girls. It was part of the reason we hated them all so much. Since then, he'd insisted Kendra would have been his mate had she lived, and he gave up on the whole dating scene in general. But most of us suspected that was bullshit. If she *were* his mate, his wolf wouldn't have been able to live without her. Kodiak would have gone rabid just like our previous alpha. Orion would have had to put him down or die trying. Being that he remained the most competent man I knew, Kodiak could (and should) mate someone else. My money was on the eldest ginger Vanderbilt.

"Get out of my office," he said.

Shaking my head at how blind he was choosing to be, I turned to leave.

But he called out to me as soon as my hand hit the door handle.

"Will I see you at the rehearsal tonight?" he asked.

"I've got patrol," I said. "But Lycan promised to fill me in. I'll be there tomorrow."

Kodiak nodded. "Have a nice night, Mill."

"Yeah. You too, Prez." I left him with his thoughts and headed back to my cabin to prepare for my perimeter run. On the way, I stopped by my little brother's room in the dorm to check on him and let him know I wouldn't be around tonight if he needed anything. At twenty-five, Caelum was only two years out of his transition and acting like it. He ran through the females in his age group like he'd just discovered his dick and couldn't wait to show everyone. I tried not to slut-shame him, even if I'd never been the same way.

The pack had a more liberal approach to sex than the rest of society. As beings that regularly got naked together each month to shift into our animal alter-egos and fought off attacks from an enemy herd of vampires, fucking around seemed like the least of our worries. The camaraderie it created kept the pack strong.

But I found I could never really get into it with anyone else. I'd had a few flings when I was younger, but nothing substantial, and nothing that held my interest for longer than a night.

I knocked twice, raising an eyebrow when bangs and hushed shifting echoed from the other side. The door opened, and a miniature version of myself peeked around the corner, naked from the waist up, purposely hiding what was going on below that.

"Hey," he said, doing his best to play it casual.

The reek of sex, sweat, and sin wafted out of the room, and I winced, taking a step back. Then, I recognized the female's scent and sighed.

Lyra. Fenris's little sister.

Whatever. Not my circus.

"What's up?" Caelum asked, running a hand through his blond hair, nearly the same shade as mine.

"I'm going out on patrol tonight," I told him. "Tomorrow, I'm heading to Vanderbilt Ranch." I filled him in on the next two months and what Kodiak had required of me. "Wyn will still be around if you need anything."

Caelum nodded and glanced behind him before disappearing for a moment and returning with a towel wrapped around his waist. He stepped out into the hallway and shut the door behind him.

"Two months, huh?" He whistled. "You gonna be okay that long on Vanderbilt territory?"

"I've done it before," I said.

"Yeah, but that was then." He raised his eyebrows as if to add, *"Before we knew about Sol and Guin."*

Technically, I had known about Guin the whole time, but *he* didn't know that.

"Don't piss off Moose," I said. "And don't go running off with Kai and Nix and get into all kinds of stupid, okay?"

Those two idiots were the ringleaders of Caelum's age group. Kai had been born with the scent of an alpha on him, and one day, he'd branch off to form his own pack, possibly taking some of his age group with him. Kodiak would never begrudge him such a thing. It was the natural order. If he didn't, we'd grow too large to contain everyone, and an overcrowded pack was a powder keg waiting to explode.

Caelum rolled his eyes. "Like you're the one to talk. Don't go dying on us again, okay?"

I tsked through my teeth and rubbed a hand over his messy hair, ignoring his fraternal jape. Then I nodded toward the door. "So you and Lyra, huh?"

"Shhhhh." He glanced around to make sure no one else had heard me. "Keep that to yourself, brother. It's not like that."

"Oh?" I bit back my surprise. "I thought you two hated each other. I thought the three days you spent stuck in a cave together were the worst time of your life."

He blew out a disbelieving breath and shook his head. "It was."

"It doesn't smell like it."

Objectively, Caelum had always been a good-looking kid. The women flocked to him, especially because he was a wolf and came from a dominant bloodline.

"She's not my mate, if that's what you're getting at."

I held my hands up to say I meant nothing by it. "Just play it safe, Cael."

He nodded and grinned. "Yeah, you too, Mill."

"Alright, I'm heading out." I gave him one more swat on the head before he turned back to his dorm and, smiling, closed the door behind him.

Gods, it was like looking in a fucked-up twisted mirror. Charming, hilarious, happy—Caelum was everything I used to be. We were two chips off the same block, once upon a time. And now... I took a deep breath and calmed the rage of injustice in my gut. It would do no good to wonder why this had happened to me or how I could start feeling something...*anything*...again.

"You're sure...like doubley-triplely sure, you want to marry him?" Ava asked Sol, who stood at the full-length mirror, fussing with the corset on her gown. "Time's a ticking, and there's a getaway car out back."

Sol laughed and glanced at my twin with shimmering eyes, the ones that were suddenly so different than how I'd remembered them growing up. "Of course."

"But he's..." She trailed off, unsure of how to word it delicately.

"Evil?" I cut in, my hands on my hips. "Rotten? Our family's worst enemy in human form?"

"Evil and rotten?" Guin announced as she walked into the bridal suite. "You're not talking about little ole me, are you?"

"They're trying to talk me out of marrying Orion...*again.*" Sol shook her head, her ginger hair swaying with the movement.

"The ship's already sailed on that, I'm afraid." Guin sighed in dramatic exasperation. "Okay. Let's get this show on the road. We're already fashionably fifteen minutes late, and if we wait any longer, we'll rile up the president. As much as that normally thrills me, I'd prefer not to converse with him today of all days."

Sol rolled her eyes and grinned, but I looked at Ava, who wore the same expression of disbelief as I did. We still hadn't discovered their secret, but they would likely let it slip sooner or later. Sol, especially, had never been very good about hiding things.

We followed them through the corridor and down the grand staircase of the Vanderbilt mansion. When we stood at the French doors at the back of the house, Sol hid behind the curtains so the groom didn't see her before he was meant to. We took our spaces, Ava and me at the head of the line with Guin just before Sol. She didn't have a maid of honor because she said she couldn't choose between us. Our youngest brother, Galahad, and our eldest brother, Liam, stood ready to walk our sister down the aisle.

"You look wonderful," Liam said, grinning as he took one of Sol's elbows. "A vision."

"Exceptional," Galahad said. He wore a matching suit to Liam's but had opted to do his makeup just as glamorous as the brides-maids. I absolutely adored how he never adhered to any rules about fashion or gender norms.

"Is everyone ready?" the wedding planner asked, switching her clipboard to the other hip as she gave us a once-over. The orchestra started playing "The Wedding March," and the rows of guests turned to face us.

Ava walked out first, pacing herself like the planner told her to at rehearsal. When she hit the fifth row, I started walking. I didn't mind being on display in front of all these people. I presented my ideas in front of entire boardrooms full of rich parasites, most of them in this audience. But my hands shook and my feet wobbled on my heels. My knees turned to jelly, and for one horrifying moment, I thought my heart would stop again.

No. Not here. Not now.

I focused on Orion at the head of the aisle, his dark eyebrows furrowing as he no doubt wondered whether I would topple over. Kodiak stood directly in front of me, having been ordained by the state of Montana to perform marriages. To Orion's right were his groomsmen; only three were at the rehearsal yesterday. The fourth, the one standing second from the end, the one I would walk with, was Van.

He still stood six feet three with sandy blond hair and dark mahogany eyes, but he no longer seemed as full of life as he once had. Now, his posture was stiff, and he emanated a "don't fuck with me" vibe that most of the other Bastards carried, but not to this degree.

Our eyes connected.

My blood pulsed.

All the air whooshed out of my body.

Time seemed to slow down. In that one infinite moment, my consciousness shifted to an entirely new plane of existence, one without rules and land wars and family history. He'd filled out in the years since I'd last seen him, the old vestiges of his youth having given way to a man's strong, muscular lines. And wow, he looked terrific.

"Mae," came the hushed voice behind me. Guin had caught up to me and grabbed my shoulder to get my attention. "You have to keep walking."

Blinking back to reality, I realized I'd stopped in the middle of the aisle to stare at a Bastard, an objectively beautiful one, but my family's former-still-sort-of enemy all the same.

I cleared my throat, straightened my shoulders, and kept going, falling in line next to my twin.

Are you okay? Ava's expression asked.

Fine, I replied.

Sol walked down the aisle to her new husband, resplendent in her flowing white gown and perfectly groomed hair. Orion even got a little choked up, despite how happy he clearly was. They stared at each other, love and devotion in their gazes, but when I looked past them, Van stood on the other side, staring back at me.

No, not staring...*glaring.*

His eyebrows drooped into a scowl, his lips thin, his aura pulsing with menace and aggression. If this were anywhere else, I'd return the grimace and boldly demand to know what his problem was. But this was my sister's wedding, and I wouldn't ruin it by starting a fight before the champagne had been poured. That would be terrible form, indeed.

I quickly glanced away and spent the rest of the time avoiding him. This did not stop the pinpricks of awareness on my skin or the sheer certainty that he hadn't stopped looking at me.

What is going on?

Why did I have such a strong reaction to him? And why did being around him make my heart feel like it would pound out of my chest and flop around on the ground like a fish?

It's the shock of seeing him after all this time.

That's all.

Especially given how many times I'd fantasized about him and how deeply ingrained my crush had grown.

My attention caught on the tree line, where a fox sat with its hind legs tucked between its front. Its bushy copper-and-white tail happily thwapped against the ground, as if it could understand what was happening and approved. Amber eyes gleamed in the sunlight, shimmering with an awareness that seemed preternatural, almost intelligent.

I furrowed my brows and narrowed my gaze, wondering what it was doing so close to humans. Didn't it have a shred of self-preservation? Hell, most of the people in the audience would shoot it and stuff it as soon as let it be a spectator to the wedding event of the year.

It shifted its focus to me, blinking slowly, seeming to tell me things would be alright. I, of course, had never telepathically communicated with wildlife before, and some part of me wondered if I wasn't losing my mind. But this little fox's calming effect couldn't be ignored...almost as if I knew it, as if we'd met before, as if my soul recognized the same in it.

"I do," Sol said, drawing my attention back to the present.

"I now pronounce you husband and wife," Kodiak said. "You may kiss each other."

When I looked back, the fox had disappeared into the woods, and the strange moment had passed.

Sol and Orion held hands and cheered as the crowd erupted into applause. They led the procession down the aisle toward the house for pictures. Guin had been paired up with a tall guy named Moose with long brown hair. She wrapped her arm around his elbow and walked ahead. As I walked toward Van, I steeled myself, staring up at him with a parched throat and muscles trembling with nerves.

He held out an arm to me, I slipped my hand through his elbow, and together we strolled toward the house while Sol's guests cheered. But under my palm, Van's muscles were tensed like a coiled snake, like any second he might burst out of my hold and reprimand me for daring to touch him.

This was *not* the same guy who'd worked for our father years ago. That guy had an easy laugh and smile for everyone. He teased and joked around. He'd been more alive than anyone else I'd ever met. This guy seemed like he'd lived through every war known to humankind.

Once inside, the wedding planner tried to corral us toward the staircase for pictures, but Sol and Orion wanted a moment to themselves.

"Which means it's time for shots," shouted one of Orion's groomsmen, Lycan. Like the other Bastards, he was tall and muscular and had striking blue eyes that pierced anything they landed on. He had short blond hair several shades lighter than Van's, and despite my preference for lighter-toned men, he didn't hold nearly the same fascination.

"Don't get too rowdy, Lycan," Kodiak said, straightening his jacket as he followed us inside.

"Don't be a party pooper," Guin said, nodding toward the parlor. "A quick nip to take the edge off never hurt anyone."

"She's got a point, Prez," Lycan said before turning his attention to Van and me. "You two in?"

"Sure," I managed to squeak before clearing my throat and glancing at my escort. "Van?"

He pursed his lips and let out a heavy sigh. "Sure."

Lycan lined up the glasses while Guin smiled and poured whiskey into each, ensuring we all had one before raising hers high in the air.

"Cheers to the happy couple," she said, "and the people who support them along the way."

"Cheers!" we shouted in unison before slinging back the liquor. It burned on the way down, but not nearly as badly as Van's chilly attitude.

Of course, what did I honestly expect? It wasn't like we were friends when he worked here. Hell, he probably didn't even remember me, and the sentiment plucked at some self-deprecating guitar string in my heart. *Of course,* he didn't remember me. I was a little girl, barely out of pigtails. He'd been a man. Why would he have taken any notice of his girlfriend's slash friend with benefits' little sister?

"Come, come!" the wedding planner called, gesturing toward the foyer. I'd been just about to step in that direction when a hand wrapped around my bicep, stopping me. The touch rattled through my nerve endings, sending strange vibrations along my marrow and into my gut. I'd never felt anything like it, almost like he could reach inside me and pull out my insides.

I stared into his big brown eyes, marveling at the specks of gold around the rims. They sparkled in the late afternoon light, and a piece of hair fell on his forehead, making me itch to push it out of his face. When he said nothing, I raised my eyebrows and feigned impatience.

"Yes?"

"It's Vermillion now," he said.

"Excuse me?" I didn't understand what he was talking about.

"My name," he explained. "I haven't gone by Van since...well, it's been a while. Most people call me Mill."

Perhaps I expected him to say something more profound, maybe an explanation about why he seemed so pissed to see me. Did he not think I'd be at my sister's wedding? Why did I care? I was a silly girl with a stupid unrequited crush, and he was just a Bastard.

"Got it," I said, trying to leave again. He tightened his grip on me.

"You look..." He stopped and grimaced, his Adam's apple bobbing as he swallowed. "It's good to see you, Maeve."

I ignored the rush of relief that he *did,* in fact, remember me, and thought it was good to see me. Instead, I forced a tight grin and mocked his tone. "It's Mae."

"Mae," he purred as if testing the sound on his tongue. "I like Maeve better."

"Why?" I didn't understand why he had an opinion about my name. It had been nearly seventeen years since we'd seen each other.

He smiled for the first time that day, and it lit up his face, taking years off his features. But before he could explain, a loud screeching echoed through the atmosphere.

"Maeve! Vermillion!" The wedding planner skirted around the corner and balked at us. "Come on!"

"We'd better go." He didn't let go of me, just loosened his grip so he could walk us back to the group, his hand wrapped around my arm, softly guiding me like he was afraid of letting me go.

When we arrived in the foyer, Guin's eyes shifted between us, but she didn't say anything. I cut my attention to Sol and Orion, who looked so disgustingly adorable together, I almost couldn't stand it.

I'd been raised to see him as a threat, but in the six months since Sol had announced her shotgun engagement, I'd come to hesitantly accept her choice and Orion's role in her life. And when the RBMC started to work the ranch and turn things around, I tentatively came to terms with it, as much of a pill as it might have been.

Now, though...I was squeezed in between Lycan and Van...er, Mill, two Bastards on either side, and I couldn't help but feel suffocated, trapped on all sides by people I barely trusted and couldn't possibly understand.

"Mill, step closer to Maeve," the photographer said. He inched toward me. "Closer."

Finally, he pressed up against my spine, his chest connecting with my shoulder blades, his stomach at my lower back. My pulse thundered against my ribs, a tremendous hammering that almost had me doubling over. My muscles shivered, a chill skating down my torso and back up again, causing goose bumps on my flesh. Vermillion's fresh cedarwood scent rippled off him in decadent, intoxicating waves, and I wanted to bury my face in his chest to inhale it more fully. But it was more than that. Something in the way our bodies connected made me want to lean against him completely, as if electric sparks flicked between us in a magnetic field that required physical force to keep us separated. It entranced me, making me want to put my hands on every inch of his body to explore it more fully.

"Beautiful. Hold just like that," the photographer said before snapping off a few rounds. "Okay, just the couples now."

I didn't understand what he meant until he paired Ava with Lycan and had them stand in front of the marble staircase.

"What's wrong, little sister?" Liam asked, nudging me in the shoulder with his.

"Nothing," I squeaked and cleared my parched throat to try again. "Nothing. Why?"

"You look terrified." Liam, Ava, and I had inherited our father's black hair and bright blue eyes, nearly the color of the sky. But the stress of running the family business had taken its toll on my older brother. At thirty-one, he'd already started going gray around the temples, and I wondered if that was what I had to look forward to. Perhaps if I stayed at Vanderbilt Holdings, it might be. Of course, it made him look a little more devil-may-care. It would make me look like a wretched old hag. At least there was always hair dye.

I returned my attention to my twin and the Bastard, noticing how they looked strangely compelling together. His bright blond hair contrasted with her straight dark locks. It reminded me of a yin-yang situation, and based on how eager he was to do shots earlier, I suspected their looks weren't where that analogy might end.

"Mill, Maeve, you're up." The photographer urged us to take the spot where Lycan and Ava had vacated, and I held my flowers higher, forcing a smile. "Okay, get a little closer so I can get you in the same shot." I stepped toward Vermillion. "Closer." He moved toward me. "Closer. Okay, act like you actually like each other."

Vermillion put his hand on my lower back, and I stiffened, the warmth crackling through my molecules like lightning. I gulped and tried to smile wider.

"Relax," he whispered low enough for only me to hear. "You look like a scared horse."

"Well, what do you expect?" I retorted. "You've been glaring at me the entire ceremony."

"I'm not glaring," he snarled, his tone that of a lion having been chastised for chasing a gazelle.

"Hmm." I didn't say anything else, just suffered through the rest of the pictures before it was time for the other couples.

But when Vermillion took his hand away, a void opened under my skin, like the absence of his palm ached more than the sensation of it being there. I wanted to force him to touch me again. I wanted to have his skin on every inch of mine, and I didn't understand the compulsion.

Despite my girlhood crush on him, none of those desires made sense. And the strange rhythm in my heart when he was around only confused me further.

Stay away from him, my logical brain urged. *For the rest of the night, stay away from him.*

I just hoped I could rein in the part of me that lived for the adrenaline rush having him would cause.

CHAPTER 4

Vermillion

"**Y**ou okay, brother?" Moose asked from across the table, taking a sip of his beer.

I cleared my throat and shifted in my seat, realizing I'd been caught staring at Maeve. *Again.*

"Fine." The word came out more in a growl than a reassuring tone.

"You don't look fine."

"Yeah?" I gulped my beer. "What do I look like?"

"You look like you're about to tear into a Vanderbilt aorta." He raised his eyebrows and nodded toward the sisters dancing at the center of the party: Guin, Avalon, Sol...and *Maeve.*

Yes, crowed my inner wolf. *Bite her. Rip into her throat. Consume her.*

I shook off the voice and ignored the delicious aroma of her skin wafting over the dance floor, drifting toward me, reeling me in the more she sweated and laughed.

Back when I'd lived here, Guin and I had...something. It barely counted as a fling, but it was more than friendship. When she went through her transition, those agonizing few days when shifter magic took hold inside a human, I'd been the one to help her through it. But we weren't meant to be, and I'd made my peace with that. I would have been okay if the only Vanderbilt I ever interacted with was Sol… but today I saw *her*.

Maeve had been a child following her sister around in my ranch-hand days.

She wasn't a child anymore.

"Maybe I am," I murmured.

"Well, save it until after I leave, yeah?" Moose pulled his long hair back and twisted it into a bun at the base of his head with a bright pink scrunchie. "I don't want to have to whoop your ass on Orion's big day."

As sergeant at arms, it was Moose's responsibility to keep us all in line. If a Bastard started acting up, he and his inner wolf would smack us around until we fell in line. Moral and upstanding, Moose was easily the best of us.

"I've got no problems with the Vanderbilts." Not anymore. It was only their piece of shit father that had done any real damage to us, and that motherfucker was cold in the ground. Did the children inherit the sins of the father? I'd liked Guin when we were in our twenties, and I liked Sol now. If Orion and Kodiak believed we could heal the rift between our families, then I wanted to believe it, too.

"Really?" Moose whistled. "Then what's with the scowl?"

"Just ready to get out of here, I guess." The lie rolled off my tongue as easy as Sunday morning, but I doubted he believed it.

Everyone saw the stare-down between Maeve and me earlier today. I had no good explanations for it. She met my gaze, and I wanted to rip her to pieces, to hold her down and take, take, *take*. Touching her felt like sticking my hand in an electrical storm, like trying to grab a downed power line. It shocked me awake in the worst way, and I didn't like that shit one fucking bit.

"They already cut the cake," Moose said. "You can leave anytime you want."

I snorted and returned to watching Maeve dance, giggling and twirling her sisters around on the floor. She was beautiful. Her long, dark hair fell in soft waves to the center of her back, and her bright blue eyes mesmerized me the minute I'd connected with them, seemingly more intense now that she was a grown woman. She had an identical twin, and Avalon was gorgeous, too, but something about her specifically appealed to me.

I shifted in my seat again and took another drink of beer. Moose was right. I *could* leave. I probably *should* leave. But now that I was near her, I didn't want to be away from her, and that pissed me off even more.

Even before I died, I didn't have much experience with females. I used to wonder if it was because Guin was my mate and she'd rejected me. But that didn't make a ton of sense. How would I have been able to walk away from her? Wouldn't I have felt a bigger loss? The more time passed, the more I realized she and I weren't meant to be, and sleeping around wasn't my thing. Since being reborn, I said I didn't trust myself to be around anyone, but the truth was, no one had ever held much appeal.

I'd gone out of my way to drink the finest whiskey and smoke the rarest bud. I'd done it all in a foolish attempt to feel a semblance of what I had before those fucking vampires tore out my throat, only to lock gazes with a Vanderbilt and have my heart damn near skip a beat.

What is it about her?

I didn't want to know.

Not only was she Guin's younger sister, but now she was also in-laws with Orion. He'd be almost as territorial over her as he was his mate, and I had no desire to dance with the second.

"Woo!" Lycan said, plopping down into the spot next to me before taking a deep drink out of his flask. "That Guin's a lot of fun. I might try to ruffle up her hackles, if you know what I'm saying."

Moose rolled his eyes and chuckled. "Good luck with that."

"Don't need it, brother. But thank you all the same." Lycan tilted his head back and let out a howl.

"You go sniffing around Guin Vanderbilt, and you'll have to

answer to Kodiak," Moose explained. "The alpha's been...uh...*protective* of her."

Lycan pursed his lips and leaned forward. "Protective how?"

"She gives her updates to him directly," Moose said. "Anyone goes near her, and he has to know the reason why."

"You think he's into her?" Lycan grinned, seemingly happy our lonely alpha might have a lover.

The sarge shook his head. "I doubt Kodiak's into anyone, but that doesn't mean he wants you sinking your claws where they don't belong."

Lycan scoffed and rolled his eyes. I couldn't blame Kodiak for that. Lycan got around more than my brother, and that was saying something. He would fuck anyone with a pulse. Males, females, enbies, it didn't matter to him. If they were into it, so was he.

"What about the twins?" Lycan put his elbows on the table and twisted to face Moose and me. "Ava seems like she's wound tight. I bet I could—"

"How about you keep your hands to yourself for once in your fucking life?" I snapped, the words tumbling out of me before I could stop them. An image of Lycan rucking up Maeve's dress went through my head, and I wanted to rip his tongue out for even suggesting it.

"Temper, temper," Lycan said before slinging back another sip of whiskey. "I was just asking. Seeing as things worked out so well for Sol when she went through her transition, it's only a matter of time—"

"They're latent," I interrupted again. "It would have hit them by now if they weren't."

The longer Maeve went without transitioning, the more that meant she never would.

"You know I have a seventh sense about these things," Lycan said, his shit-eating grin so smug that I wanted to knock his teeth out. "I guessed it about Sol the first time I met her. I'm telling you..."

He pointed at Maeve and Avalon. "Those two are ticking time bombs."

I cracked my neck and rolled my shoulders to relieve the tension.

Moose raised an eyebrow and glanced between me and our drunk road captain. "How certain are you?"

Lycan shrugged. "Eighty...no, ninety percent."

I tried to pretend the thought of Maeve going through the change didn't delight my wolf.

Take her. Help her. It should be me.

The Bastard smiled again. "I can smell it on her. Maeve's going first. Then Ava. Probably around the time we're in Paris together." He snorted and laughed. "Maybe I'll take her to the Eiffel Tower, you know what I'm saying?"

"Don't be a prick," I said, rolling my eyes. Not that his sexual preferences were off-putting, but the casual way he talked about them infuriated me.

Lycan ignored me. "And probably that younger one, too. Galahad."

"And the older brother?" Moose asked.

Lycan tilted his head from side to side and frowned. "Now, he's latent. One hundred percent."

In our world, the shifter gene was dominant. Even if a human mated with a shifter, the children would most likely change. But every so often, the genes mutated and produced offspring who should have had the magic but didn't transition. We called them latent, but that didn't mean they were less than us, though some bigoted assholes in the pack would suggest otherwise. They were just as crucial to our healthy ecosystem, and Kodiak ensured everyone knew it. He wouldn't allow any talk of pure-breed or half-breed or latent. Everyone was pack, end of story.

"I think you're cut off, brother," Moose said, reaching for Lycan's flask. The blond pulled away and shoved Moose back.

"Bet me," he said.

"What? No." Moose laughed and went for the whiskey again.

"Go on, bet me." Lycan giggled and pushed to his feet. "Five hundred bucks and three perimeter rotations says that Maeve Vanderbilt transitions within a month, and an extra grand if Avalon goes after her."

"Fuck off, Lycan," Moose said.

"It's fucked-up to bet about someone going through the change," I added.

"Not to mention bad luck." Moose shook his head and rolled his eyes.

"Where's Poe, huh?" I glanced around. "Shouldn't you be trying to swallow his tongue by now?"

Poe was one of the newer members of our pack, and up until recently, Lycan's boyfriend…er, fuck buddy? I didn't know what they called themselves, only that they could regularly be found occupying each other's beds.

Lycan's features dropped, and he cleared his throat. "Poe and I… we're taking a break."

He said the B-word in the same tone he'd use to call someone a piece of shit.

"Uh-oh," Moose said. "Trouble in paradise?"

Lycan didn't answer, just tipped the flask over his lips for another huge gulp before screwing the lid back on and handing it over to Moose.

"I think you're right, brother," he said. "I'm toast, and I'm heading home."

"Hey, you alright?" Moose stood, holding out a hand to help him.

Lycan shook him off. "Just fine. Besides, we've got the prospects driving us home, right? I'll see you both when I get back from France."

He sauntered to the perimeter and sulked off into the night, his once playful aura now reduced to a dark, gloomy cloud at merely the mention of his former flame. Whatever happened there wasn't my business, but I did believe him when he said he had a knack for calling when someone might be about to transition. He'd been right about Sol; even Orion could admit that.

Is he right about Maeve?

I looked at her again, now slow dancing with some human jackass closer to her age. She laughed at whatever he said, and I swallowed down my completely inappropriate jealousy. I barely knew her. I had no reason to *get* to know her. And even if my history with her sister wasn't complicated, she was off-limits for a thousand different reasons.

"If Lycan's right, we need to have someone keep watch," Moose said.

"I'll be here with four other pack members," I said. "If she goes through it—" I'd been about to say someone would tell us, someone would help her. But that didn't sit right in my gut for reasons I didn't want to consider.

"You?" Moose raised his eyebrows and sipped his beer.

"Yeah, me," I growled. "But don't worry. I won't touch her. I'll send Columba or Aquila in there instead."

I tried to imagine anyone else in the pack giving her their magic, and I fisted my beer bottle so tight, I thought I might crack it.

"That isn't what I'm worried about," Moose said.

"Yeah, yeah," I grumbled and stood, deciding that enough was enough for one night. When I passed the dance floor, headed toward the ranch-hands' building on the other side of the farm, I ignored the way Maeve's eyes tracked me, telling myself it had nothing to do with me.

We were nothing. That immense pull I felt toward her was nothing.

All of this. All of life. All of it.

Nothing.

I drank well into the night and stumbled up to my bedroom much later than I had intended. I tried to get my bridesmaid dress off, but the zipper proved too complicated for my intoxicated state, so I collapsed face-first onto my mattress and passed out.

My skin would hate me in the morning, but who had time for a cleansing and moisturizing routine after a long night of consuming as much wine as possible and ignoring my childhood crush turned frenemy?

I dreamt that I ran through the forest behind my house. The thrill of the cool summer air whipped through my hair, coating my skin in dew and light from the full moon overhead. My bare feet hit the undergrowth, my toes digging into the soil before propelling me forward...faster...harder. A howl echoed behind me, sending a chill down my spine. I should be terrified. That sound meant wolves.

But I wasn't. I threw my head back and let out a roar of my own, something deep and primal. A snapped branch had me sprinting, and I laughed as I took off toward Bastard territory.

"You think you can run from me, baby?" The growl came from

right behind me, as if my chaser had leaned against my ear or whispered it inside my head.

"Only if you keep chasing me." I extended my stride, carrying myself as far as I could.

Just as I was about to break through the tree line and crash into the river, a thick, heavy body slammed into me from the right, taking me down to the ground. I squealed, half in delight, half in terror.

"Got you," the voice snarled, flipping me over onto my stomach. One hand held the back of my head down, burying my cheek in the dirt. The other grabbed my wrist, pinning it above my body. "Tsk, tsk, tsk. You should know better than to run from the big, bad wolf."

My heart pounded against my ribs, the ache in my legs matched only by the shudder between my thighs. The exhilaration of being hunted had turned me on, and when I arched my back into my attacker, rubbing my ass along the thick length trapped between us, he hissed in a breath and pressed it more firmly against me.

"You're a naughty girl, Maeve Vanderbilt," he said, trailing his nose down my neck to the space next to my shoulder blade. "What should I do with you?"

"Oh, no," I teased. "I guess you'll have to punish me."

He snickered. "You'd like that, wouldn't you?"

I brushed my ass against him again, rolling my hips, seeking out the part of him that I'd longed to have since I knew what desire was.

"Please," I said. "I've been so bad, and I need a strong, steady hand to put me in my place."

A loud, blaring noise infiltrated the dream, drowning out the sound of his hoarse reply. I jolted to life in my bedroom. When I snapped my eyes open, sunlight beamed through my windows, blinding me, spearing through my forehead like a jousting lance.

"Aw, fuck." I rolled onto my side and stuffed my face into the pillows.

My phone rang again, chirping the same annoying sound that had pulled me out of my dream. I glanced at the caller ID and sent it to voicemail.

Liam can fuck off.

A knock at the door startled me, and I lifted my head.

"Yes?" My throat felt like I'd swallowed an entire volcano.

"Miss," said Ellen, one of our family's staff who had worked for us since I was little. "Breakfast is ready. Shall I bring you a plate?"

"No." I groaned and collapsed back on my pillows, debating whether I wanted to get up and eat at the table like a normal person or starve until the hangover passed. Carbs would probably help soak up the drunk, so I got out of bed, changed into PJs, wrapped a robe around myself, and grimaced at the state of my reflection. My hair stuck out at odd angles; I hadn't bothered to remove the pins that held the top bits in place. My mascara had smudged on one side, and big, heavy bags hung under my eyes like saddlebags.

Well, screw it.

My family was already gone. I had no one to impress. Stuffing my feet into slippers, I opened the door and shuffled down the hallway toward the stairs, gripping the railing for dear life as I descended. My head spun and throbbed in time with my heart, and my stomach rolled with each step, like I might vomit if I jostled it too much.

Ugh, I'm never drinking again.

Rubbing my hands over my face, I lumbered into the dining room...only to freeze at the sight of the person sitting opposite my normal spot.

Van...

Er...Mill...

He glanced up at my approach, freshly showered and dressed for the day. He wore his leather cut, proudly announcing him as a member of the Royal Bastards Motorcycle Club, which matched the black cowboy hat sitting next to his silverware. Mill ran the length of me with his gaze, his features maintaining the same cold, stoic marble he'd had when I first saw him yesterday.

Great. Just freaking great.

This would be my luck to show up hungover, disheveled, looking like hell, and here he sat, as gorgeous as ever. Of course, his eyes held a sinister darkness, and his cheeks had sunken in, making him seem malicious, like a monster from a horror movie.

"Morning," he said with a hint of a growl.

Gulping, I stepped forward and cleared my throat to reply. "Good morning."

He sipped his coffee, and I zeroed in on his soft lips curled around the mug.

Stop that.

I quickly glanced away as Ellen entered the room to pour my coffee. She set a plate in front of me, the smell of eggs and fried tomatoes making my stomach churn. I lifted the creamer and poured a tiny bit into my coffee before using the spoon to stir it, purposely ignoring how Vermillion stared at me. The silence drifted on.

Typically, the ranch hands didn't eat breakfast with us, and since Orion had started, he and Sol had moved out to the manager's cabin near the bunks on the back property. They rarely joined us for meals anymore. Seeing Mill had startled me, and as the deafening quiet continued, I wondered why he was here. By the time I set in on my eggs, I was anxious for someone to join us and break the tension. I swallowed down the protein-rich food and sipped my caffeine.

When I couldn't take it anymore, I finally met his gaze and raised my eyebrows.

"What?" I asked.

"What?" He set his coffee down and leaned back in his chair.

"What are you doing here? Why are you staring at me?"

For a moment, he said nothing, just continued the glare that had me itching to squirm in my seat.

He cleared his throat and set his coffee mug down.

"I thought we should set a few things straight."

"Okay?" I stabbed another piece of egg with my fork and brought it to my lips, forcing it down, willing my stomach not to heave up everything I was putting in it. My headache had only worsened with all this talking, so I sipped my coffee.

"Sol didn't tell you?" He furrowed his brows, looking so damned confused and adorable, I nearly couldn't help myself from reaching over to smooth out the wrinkles.

"Tell me what?"

"I'm replacing Orion for the next two months while he's away," he explained.

"Yeah, she mentioned that." I rubbed my tired eyes, my mind struggling to keep up with the conversation and his frustratingly overwhelming presence. He took up every space he occupied. He sucked the air out of my lungs like he had a vacuum on my soul. "Why you?"

His eyes hardened, and the mahogany turned to a darker shade of brown, nearly matching his black coffee.

Realizing how mean that sounded, I shook my head and tried again. "No, I'm sorry. I mean...don't you have better things to do than run a ranch for people you hate?"

"Hate's a strong word." He glanced at the table where he fiddled with the corner of a silk napkin. "I'd do anything for Orion. He's family. So is Sol...after yesterday."

"And Guin?" I couldn't stop the words from tripping over my lips.

He met my gaze. "What about Guin?"

"Weren't you two like...together or something?"

"What's it matter to you?" His tone had dropped into a grumpy snarl, like he was annoyed at having to be around me and angry about the whole thing.

"It doesn't," I said.

"Fine," he said.

"Fine," I barked back.

Silence fell on us again, and heat bloomed across my cheeks at my outburst, spreading down my neck and into my chest. He continued to look at me, his stare burning holes through my skin like he could see all the way to my humiliation. I *didn't* care what it was between him and Guin, I really didn't. I'd seen them talking yesterday. She made him smile, and he made her laugh, and she'd touched his arm like she had a right to his entire body.

The way he'd held me surged back through my molecules, reminding me of the blazing electricity between us. I had wanted to devour every inch of him. I wanted him to do the same to me. In retrospect, that might have been the shot of whiskey going to my head.

I blinked back my shame and gulped my coffee, much too hot for my throat, burning down to my gut.

"I need you to look over the cattle rotation," he said, placing a folder on the desk. "And we've received a new stallion that needs to be broken. Do you want me to continue training him or sell him?" He explained a few other things that required my sign-off before pushing the paper stack across the table. I grabbed it with too much force, and my fingertips brushed against his at the center. That same zing of fireworks shot through my arm, into my chest, and settled at my heart. I gasped and yanked my hand back.

Mill didn't react, just raised an eyebrow. "You okay?"

"Yeah, just…static, I guess." I shifted my hips and opened the folder, glancing over the documents. I had only a passing under-standing of what needed to be done on the ranch. I'd spent most of my privileged life sheltered from the harsh realities of running one, always away at boarding schools or college. Now an adult, I worked in an office. Putting on denims and a cowboy hat and shearing sheep had never been a part of my plan.

But I trusted Sol, and she trusted Orion, who ultimately trusted Mill. Perhaps, deep down, if I were honest with myself, I had once trusted him, too, and wanted to again.

"This all looks…acceptable." I nodded and closed the folder again.

"Great," he said, pushing to his feet. "I'll get out of your hair."

He grabbed his hat and put it on his head, heading toward the door to leave. But the thought of being alone suddenly caught up to me. Ava had left for Paris early this morning. Guin had gone back to Bozeman last night. Sol and Orion were long gone on their honey-moon. Galahad had left early to return to school.

I was alone in this big old mansion.

"Mill," I said, stopping him.

He turned to face me.

The urge to ask him to dine with me tomorrow and every day until my family returned perched on the tip of my tongue. But that would be stupid, certainly one of the most ridiculous notions I'd ever had. He likely had better things to do than waste his time with me.

What? I couldn't suffer a few weeks of dining by myself? What would my father think? He didn't raise us to be happy. He raised us to be strong.

"Thank you," I said instead. "For doing this."

He nodded. "I'll see ya around, Maeve."

His boots heel-toeing across the hardwood echoed through my body long after he closed the door and went outside.

Ugh, I was such a mess. I couldn't even hold a civil conversation with the man. How in the world would I spend two months living in close proximity to him?

The nine-year-old girl inside me screamed in both mortification and delight as the twenty-six-year-old woman rubbed her hands over her bloated puffy face and internally screamed.

I didn't see Vermillion again that day. I showered, dressed, and meandered into my father's office to do the work Sol had left for me. I approved some invoices and replied to a few emails, but running the ranch didn't fill my soul the way it had my father.

He'd been a hard man, more likely to chastise his children in the name of discipline than to show us a kind word. I had only a few memories of my mother, but I didn't remember her being very happy. The only people the Vanderbilt siblings had were each other, and even that rested on shaky ground.

Percy had grown to be an evil maniac, Liam had a spine made out of Jell-O, and the jury was still out on Galahad. Though he did seem to be shaping up well enough. Guin, Sol, Ava, and I were the glue that held this family together, even if I still suspected Guin and Sol were keeping something important from the rest of us.

Once the bills were paid and I'd finished my meetings, I wandered around his office, admiring the ancient tomes on the bookshelves and reminiscing about the photos scattered around. Judging by these mementos, one might believe the old man cared about us. Perhaps he did, in his own way. He was never the touchy-feely type, made even colder by our mother's untimely death.

Some people shouldn't be allowed to have children, and he was one of them. Growing up, I often wondered what life would have been like had our mother survived. Would she have softened him? Would she have been a rock for him to break himself against? Or would this world have dimmed her light, too?

A few hours later, I forced myself to eat lunch on the veranda, sketching in my notebook and watching as the ranch hands worked the barn and corralled the horses. An unbroken stallion jumped in the training pen while two men circled it, trying to bring it to heel. Mill stood on the outside, arms over the metal barrier, his hat covering his eyes. But I could tell from his height and stature it was him.

I shouldn't stare. It was incredibly rude to watch someone while they worked, especially when that someone happened to be an employee. But something about him drew me in like a tractor beam. His broad shoulders gave way to a narrow waist and hips, his jeans complementing the muscular curve of his ass and legs. Almost as if he could feel my gaze, he turned and looked up at the balcony.

We were several hundred yards away from each other. There was no way he could have known I'd been looking or even that it was me eating all alone. But when our eyes connected, a shiver raced down my spine and landed between my legs, reminding me I'd once adored him and that young girl inside still did.

I'm ridiculous. Truly and utterly ridiculous.

Here I was, ogling some poor man while he was trying to do a favor for his buddy. He didn't want to be here any more than I did.

Feeling a strange pang of shame, I finished my iced tea, stood, and went back to work. Only after I sat at my desk and looked at my sketchbook did I realize I'd drawn a replica of his intense gaze at the breakfast table that morning. Disgusted, I ripped the page out, crumpled it into a ball, and started throwing it in the trash.

Just as I would have released it, something stopped me. I didn't *want* to throw it away. I wanted to keep working on it. I wanted to cherish it, even if I kept it in a deep, secret part of my notebook.

Hating myself for it, I smoothed the page out, stuffed it between the last page and the back cover, and told myself I'd get to it some other time.

At the end of the day, I ate dinner alone. Damn near at my wits' end with this quiet house, I begged Ellen to sit with me.

"Please." I gestured to the food and the empty seats around the obnoxiously long dinner table. "There's more than enough. Gather the rest of the staff. I'd love to get to know you all better."

Ellen only shook her head. "No, ma'am. I can't. It wouldn't be proper."

Whatever that means.

"We've already eaten," she explained, "and our shift is almost over."

I accepted her excuse and drummed my nails on the wood while I chewed the oven-roasted chicken she'd prepared. I'd never considered myself an extrovert. I'd lived alone in my apartment for several months, and some people could be entirely draining. But never had the ache in my chest been so impetuous as it was in this enormous house with no one to fill it.

One day in, and I wanted to jump out of my skin. How would I make it an entire two months?

My phone buzzed, and I glanced down at it, furrowing my brows when I saw a text message from an unknown number.

"Hey, Big Sis," it said.

"Who is this?" I wrote back.

"Your real brother-in-law." A chill went down my spine, but I ignored it.

It's probably someone playing a prank, or maybe a wrong number.

I reported the message as junk and deleted it from my inbox, feeling no less despondent that the only person blowing up my phone was someone I didn't even know.

When I went to bed, I left the French doors to my balcony open so the summer air could clear out the musky, stale atmosphere from the day.

Just as I'd been about to climb into bed, the sounds of jeering and country music echoed in from behind the house. Dressed in my silky white nightgown, I walked to the patio and glanced toward the ranchers' quarters.

Chris Stapleton blasted from the brightly lit windows, accentuating male laughter and the clinking of beer bottles hitting each other. The workers were gearing up for a party.

I tried to imagine Mill cutting loose. Years ago, maybe he'd have partaken. But now, it took all of my comedic chops just to get a smile. Was he out there now, carrying on with the rest of them?

It wasn't a huge dormitory, and the workers slept in bunks. Since Mill was lead and Orion had moved into a different house with Sol months ago, I suspected my favorite tall, blond, and grumpy biker was staying in a separate cabin afforded to someone in the head position.

Go out there with them, that reckless part of me whispered, the part that had died and come back to life and never wanted to waste another opportunity. *Go party and have fun.*

It would certainly be better than staying cooped up here with no one to talk to. But I had a lot of work to do tomorrow, and I didn't want to cross any boundaries. My father had been adamant about keeping the workers separate from the family for a reason. We were their employer. We were the Vanderbilts. Most of them were drifters, and more recently, members of the Royal Bastards.

Never the twain shall meet.

I snorted at that outdated elitist mentality and went back inside, settling into bed with a hot chamomile tea and a smutty romance novel before drifting off to sleep.

The next morning, I ate breakfast alone. Uncomfortable and wanting to fill the silence, I called Ava to see how her first day in Paris went. She reported that the conference was going well.

"It's just like we remember from boarding school," she said, recalling the class trip we'd taken overseas in eleventh year. She'd spent the whole time brooding in museums and visiting historical sites. I'd hooked up with as many French boys and girls as possible. "Artsy and beautiful, and the people?" She sighed. "The same."

I laughed. "Does this mean you're finally going to let someone between your legs?"

She gasped. "Maeve Eleanor Vanderbilt, I would never."

I shook my head. Sometimes, I couldn't believe we shared the same DNA.

"How are things there?" she asked. "Are you keeping everything afloat?"

"It's only been one day. I can't do that much damage."

"Uh-huh." I could almost see her eye roll from across the ocean. "And what about Vermillion?"

"What *about* Vermillion?" I stuffed a piece of strawberry into my mouth and choked it down. Despite not drinking last night, my hangover was taking its grand ole time in dissipating.

"Don't feign ignorance. Everyone saw how you two stared at each other at the wedding."

"It was nothing," I said. "Truly."

I meant it. Especially after breakfast yesterday. He'd been grumpy and distant, and even if I didn't remember him being that way seventeen years ago, a lot had changed for him in that time. A lot had changed for me, too.

Christ, get a grip.

He's just a man. A stupid, growly man.

She hummed, as if to suggest I could keep my secrets if I must. "Be good. Don't get into trouble."

We said our love and goodbyes before hanging up.

Three days went by like this. If I was feeling up to it, I rode Molly in the mornings, and if I happened to see Mill in the pastures, we ignored each other. I ate alone. I worked alone. Then I listened to the boys partying every night from my bedroom balcony, a solemn part of me working up the courage to join them. What would they do if I did? The Vanderbilts never mingled with the help...but weren't we about starting something new? Wasn't that what Sol and Guin were working toward?

On day seven in captivity, the dream came again.

I raced through the woods on the balls of my feet, exhilaration in my blood, the wind in my hair. I was running from something… *no,* someone. And they gained on me quicker than I'd thought they would. When they caught me, they tackled me to the ground face up, and I stared into fiendish crimson eyes. No, not crimson.

Vermillion.

He smiled, holding my wrists above my head, pressing his hips between my thighs. My nightgown had pooled around my waist, now soiled with sweat and undergrowth.

"You're such a bad girl. You need to be punished," he said, leaning closer to run his nose over the column of my throat. "Didn't you listen the last time? Running from me is the worst idea you've ever had."

"I like when you chase me," I whispered, barely able to get the words out over the drum of my beating heart. "I like it when you catch me."

"Tsk, tsk, tsk," he said, dragging his tongue up my neck to my jaw. His soft, warm tongue made me tremble as I imagined what it might feel like on other parts of my anatomy. "Don't tease the wolf, baby. You won't like what happens to you."

"Are you going to bite me?" I raised a playful eyebrow.

"Maybe," he said.

"Maybe I'd like it." I rocked my pelvis into his, gasping when my cunt pressed up against the long length of his erection behind his jeans. He was so hard, and he jerked at the contact, trailing his mouth down the side of my face to the spot where my throat met my shoulder.

"And what would you do if I did, huh?" he growled. "Would you scream? Would you cry?"

Vermillion kissed the tender skin, and I shook in anticipation.

"What if I drank every last drop of your blood?" He hummed and licked the spot, rolling his pelvis against me, dragging the hardest part of him over the softest, wettest part of me. I moaned, bucking into the connection. I wanted more. So much more. "You have no idea what I could do to you, baby girl...what I *want* to do to you."

"So do it." The quiver in my voice betrayed the terror in my chest. I should have been afraid of him. I should know better than to taunt someone as strong and dominant as him. But deep down, I knew he'd never hurt me. He *could* never hurt me. We were tethered on a molecular level, bound by fate and blood and magic. When the universe formed itself, we were one atom of stardust that had split apart to create our separate souls. Now that we'd found each other again, we would never be apart.

"Such things you say." He pulled his lips back over enormous fangs extending from his canines. His pupils had blown so wide, they eclipsed all of the red.

Then he struck.

On a gasp and a cry, my eyes snapped open to bright moonlight seeping in through the French doors. I wasn't in the forest, being attacked by my childhood crush. I was in my room. In my bed. And it had only been a dream.

CHAPTER 7

Vermillion

In my dreams, I chased her through the woods. It was sport between us. She liked to run, and I liked to catch her. Her riotous laughter echoed through the nighttime air, and when I got close enough, I tackled her to the ground.

"You have no idea what I could do to you, baby girl...what I *want* to do to you," I snarled.

She grinned like the devil and licked her lips, making me want to bite that smirk off her gorgeous face. "So do it."

My fangs extended, and my heart pounded through my body, my cock surging with evidence of my desire. But the thing that scared me, the thing that made me pause, was the sickening thirst pulsing through my molecules. I wanted more than her body. I wanted...*Fuck,* I didn't know. Everything about her. I wanted to devour her, and it made no Goddamned sense.

"Such things you say." I'd been just about to bite her when a grating sound from reality interrupted my fucked-up wet dream.

"Mill," Fenris shouted, pounding on the door to the boss's house. I blinked awake, having passed out on the couch shortly after eating dinner. The guys had wanted to play a few rounds of poker, but I had other things on my mind, and I wasn't much fun to be around these days.

The loud booming came again. "Vermillion! Wake up!"

I grabbed my gym shorts from the floor to slip them over my boxers before standing and going to the door. Fenris stared at me with wide blue eyes, his dark hair ruffled like he'd been running his fingers through it.

"What's wrong?" I grumbled, my throat scratchy and parched with sleep.

"Vampires." The word came out through a pant, like he'd spent the last hour running to get to me.

My heart dropped into my stomach, and I stepped back to shove my feet into my boots, tying them as quickly as my fingers could manage. We'd been here a week without a fucking problem. But of course, my luck wouldn't last forever.

"Where?" I took off after him as we stalked across the ranch and into the woods at the edge of the property.

"I was doing my perimeter rounds before I called it a night, and I caught the scent half a mile to the west," he explained. Fenris and I had grown up together, so I trusted him more than anyone else. If I was going to spend two months away from the homestead, I was happy he'd come with me. I didn't know how to live without him, and we'd become so close over the years, we could practically read each other's minds, even more than the pack bond already afforded.

"Shit, they're close." We walked for about three minutes before the rotten stench of vampires hit me in the face, reeking like a decayed corpse and coppery blood. It was fresh but fading, meaning someone had been here hours ago.

"It's Marx," Fenris said.

I nodded. I'd never be able to forget this particular odor. We'd taken out a lot of them the night we'd rescued Sol, but they'd almost returned the favor with yours truly. I owed Marx a couple of canines to the neck, and I intended to pay up.

"How many scents do you pick up?" Fenris asked.

I glanced around and closed my eyes, letting my inner wolf take over. When it came to tracking and hunting, the animal had the natural instinct. Enraged that someone had come so close to the house without anyone knowing it, my beast growled and tasted the air.

"Three. Maybe four, including Marx." My voice came out deep and grumbly.

"Me too," he said. "Should I tell the others?"

We were here with Holden, Poe, Columba, and Aquila. Holden was friends with my brother, and Poe was still relatively new to the pack. Despite this, he had become a trusted brother and friend. He always volunteered to take a shift at the Fiver when it was needed, and he didn't complain about any of the shit the MC put him through. He'd come to us from Baltimore a few years ago, which was how he'd gotten his road name. Columba and Aquila were twins, born in the pack a few years after me. They worked hard, and eventually, they had patched into the Royal Bastards. I outranked them all.

I didn't see how I could keep it from them or Kodiak. It would be in our best interest to have everyone on alert.

"Wake them up, bring them out here." I stalked back toward my cabin as Fenris followed closely behind me. "Quietly. I'll check the security footage."

He nodded and headed toward the ranchers' house while I went back to mine, going straight for my laptop. After Sol and Guin had been abducted, Orion had wasted no time setting up the most sophisticated alarm system Montana had to offer around Vanderbilt Ranch. If anyone trespassed on this territory, it should have gone off. It should have alerted me.

After clicking a few tabs, I pulled up the video footage of the surrounding woods and went back a few hours. I didn't have to go far.

Just after dinner time, Marx and his cronies came into view, dropping out of the trees like monkeys. I only saw four from this angle, but other cameras picked up at least five more. Nine in total.

The leader looked right into the camera with his disgusting, smug grin and raised an eyebrow like he knew exactly where our perimeter started. If he'd come any closer, he would have tripped the motion sensors. But he knew enough to stay out of range...which meant he knew more than I felt comfortable with.

He pulled out his phone and tapped on the screen before laughing and shoving it back into his pockets. Then, he climbed the tree holding the camera, bringing his face inches from the lens.

"Tell Big Sis that one Vanderbilt is as good as another. If I can't have the ginger bitch, I'll take a twin." He smiled, showing off his golden front tooth and his elongated fangs. "Hell, I'll take both of them. I don't give a fuck. A deal is a deal, especially with me."

My blood boiled. My canines extended. My claws threatened to shoot out of my fingertips.

"I'll take the twin."

Like fucking hell he would. I'd kill him before he ever got close to her. No one would touch her. No one.

Mine, my wolf howled.

But I squashed that down because *what the fuck?*

I barely knew her. Seventeen years ago, she'd been the girl who followed me around the ranch, and now that she was a fully grown, beautiful woman, she surely had better things to do. Hell, her attitude the morning I joined her for breakfast was enough for me to know she wanted nothing to do with me. Despite being hungover and wrecked, she was still the most gorgeous person I'd ever seen. I wanted to pull her across the table and spread her out to dine on *her* for breakfast. But that, too, I swallowed down and stuffed into a remote part of my consciousness.

Kodiak had said no touching the Vanderbilt, and the alpha's orders overrode everything. There was only one exception to that rule: when a shifter's mate was on the line. But that was a ridiculous notion. Maeve wasn't my mate, and I likely would never have one. Who the fuck would want to put up with my brooding ass? If I didn't find them before I died, I certainly had no hope of finding them now.

I switched through the rest of the camera angles, watching as the vampires retreated the way they'd come, climbed into the trees, and disappeared into nothingness. I'd have to organize a search party later today, and I grimaced as I thought about what wouldn't get done because I had to send people out to hunt for vampires.

Fuck.

My attention caught on footage of Maeve wandering through her house while the vampires were in the woods, her arms wrapped around her midsection, her eyes soft, and a frown on her lips. She looked almost...sad. All of the Vanderbilts were aware of the security cameras inside the hallways and common areas of their house; they'd been installed for their protection. For the sake of privacy and other obvious reasons, we didn't have any line of sight to their bedrooms. When Maeve entered her room and shut the door, I told myself to leave it alone. If she wasn't safe, we would have heard something.

But I couldn't resist. A clawing, nagging need to be sure urged me on. It took me no time to hack into her pathetically undefended laptop, which she'd left open on her desk in her bedroom, and hijack the camera.

It was dark, but when I switched the settings to night vision, I saw Maeve sitting up in bed. She rubbed her hands over her face and brushed them back through her hair.

"Stop dreaming about him, you stupid, silly girl." She clicked on her light and swung her legs to the side of the bed, hanging her head between her shoulders.

Sighing, she stood, the hem of her silky white nightgown barely reaching her mid-thighs. The top cut in a V down to her breasts, and I swallowed as a wave of desire surged through my chest and into my gut, pooling in my balls. Her wild black hair hung over her shoulders, and her icy-blue eyes were even more radiant at this time of night. She walked to the balcony and out of sight of the laptop camera, but she was still talking to herself.

"What are you doing, Vermillion?" she murmured. "Are you dreaming of me, too?"

Fuuucckkkk.

We were dreaming about each other?

That is not good.

Nope, not at all.

Taking a deep breath, I told myself to stay calm and stop spying on her like a fucked-up stalker. But when she walked back into the room and grabbed the laptop, I couldn't help but stare into her mesmerizing eyes.

What was she dreaming about? Did she imagine me the way I'd imagined her?

Fuck, what if we're sharing dreams?

Yes, my wolf grumbled, rolling his shoulders and wagging his tail. He wanted her for reasons I wouldn't...couldn't examine, and if we *were* sharing dreams, that could only mean one thing.

No, I wouldn't wander down that dark, windy road tonight...or any night. She was better off without me for a million different reasons. She deserved better.

Maeve took her computer to her bed and placed it on the empty side of the mattress while she lay down. She reached into the bottom drawer of her nightstand, and my pulse pounded when she returned with a bright pink vibr—

"Mill!" shouted Fenris as he knocked twice on the door before pushing it open.

Startled, I quickly exited out of the screen and went back to the security camera footage, adjusting my cock in my gym shorts to make it less obvious that I'd been spying on arguably the most fascinating Vanderbilt sister.

He walked into the main room with Poe, Columba, and Aquila behind him.

"Fenris took us out to the woods. I'm picking up at least six or seven different scents." Poe put his hands on his hips and pulled deep breaths, evidently trying to calm his racing heart.

Clearing my throat against how parched I'd suddenly become, I trained my features into the best poker face I could muster. "I think there were closer to ten. Come look."

"Fuck," Columba said. He ran his hands back through his dark hair and came to stand behind me.

At six-five, he was an inch taller than me and almost as big as Kodiak. He had bright green eyes and dark tawny skin, making him incredibly popular with the female shifters in the pack. I'd seen him hanging around Kodiak's youngest daughter more than once. Aquila was the same height as me, with dark hair and darker eyes, but still the same devastating good looks as his brother.

After I showed my packmates the footage, we watched it three more times before deciding to call Kodiak...which honestly should have been my first order of business. But I had to make sure Maeve was safe. I didn't like the thought of Marx having his target set on her, and now that I knew what she was doing up there in that big mansion all by herself, a small petulant (and perhaps overprotective) part of me wanted to burn this fucking house down so I'd have no other choice but to move into the mansion with her.

Do it, my wolf whispered. *Take her. Claim her.*

I ignored those thoughts and sighed when Kodiak answered the phone in his gruff, tired voice.

"We've got a problem, Prez," I said, explaining the situation to him. "He wants what he feels he's owed."

Kodiak growled. "He'll keep testing the boundaries until he finds a way through."

"This could be a ploy," I said. "Do we know where Guin and Ava are?"

"Yes," he said. "Guin's got her own bodyguards protecting her, and Ava is in France with Lycan."

"Do you think he'd follow her there?" Maybe we needed to call the RBMC in Paris and ask for a favor.

"He went after Guin last time, and he knows how much of a threat she is. I suspect he's coming after Maeve because he thinks she's more vulnerable." Kodiak took a deep breath, and I could picture him rubbing a hand over his bald head and pinching the bridge of his nose. "I'm sending Moose and Larentia and—"

"You can't spare them," I argued. "If you send them here, you risk leaving the homestead vulnerable."

"Are you questioning my decisions?"

"Yes," I said, knowing I could because I was a Bastard. I'd been patched into the council and sworn my blood and loyalty to the colors. We were brothers as much as packmates. Just because he was more dominant didn't mean he was unreasonable. "Look, let me figure it out. I'll keep her guarded. I'll move into the mansion. I'll..." The thought of staying down the hallway from her while she played with herself had me clenching my hand into a fist.

Focus. This is important. This is her safety.

"I'll call you if something else happens."

Kodiak grumbled low, muttering something to himself I couldn't make out.

"Okay, fine," he said. "But you will report to me every day, and if you get even a *whiff* of a vampire, I need to know first."

"Got it," I said. "I'll send you the footage."

"Good," he said. "I'll have Serpent and Ruby take a look."

We said our goodbyes and hung up. I ran a hand through my hair and blew a breath through my lips, debating the best way to tell Maeve she needed to give me a guest room in the main house.

"Move into the mansion?" Fenris raised his eyebrows and laughed. "Getting real cozy with the Vanderbilts, are we?"

"You got a better idea?" I glanced between him and the others. "She's alone in there. We can't leave her like that."

Poe winced. "Maybe I ought to, instead. I know Sol well. Maeve might feel more comfortable with me."

Neither I nor my beast liked the idea of Poe being that close to her, especially not with what Lycan had said at the wedding. If she really went into her transition within the month, I'd want every wolf within a mile radius of her to clear out.

But one step at a time. Tonight, I had to make sure she was secure. And if (BIG if) she started to change, I'd deal with it then.

"I outrank you," I told him. "And I know Guin."

Poe raised an eyebrow and ran a hand over his hair, seemingly weighing what I'd said with what he knew about the Vanderbilt sisters.

When no one said anything else, I dismissed them back to the dorm and tried not to think about what Maeve was doing in that big old house by herself or how much I wanted to join her. Fenris lingered by the door, his hands on his hips, his lips pursed.

"What?" I damn near growled.

"You sure it's a good idea?" He shrugged. "Your temper isn't exactly long and mild these days."

I ran my tongue over my canines and tsked through my teeth. "I don't trust anyone else to do it."

When I said the words, I realized that included him. I knew my best friend. If Maeve gave him an inch, he'd take a mile, even if Kodiak said to keep our hands off her. As we got closer to the moon, Fenris would turn all primal instinct.

He nodded. "What about the cattle drive?"

"You know what to do," I said. "You can lead it."

"And leave you here alone, knowing all those fucking blood-suckers are sniffing around?" Fenris scoffed. "I'd rather die."

"We'll deal with that when it comes to it," I said. "Just...go settle the guys, huh? I've got to call Guin."

Fenris laughed and opened the door. "Good luck."

Grumbling, I picked up my phone to call the eldest Vanderbilt. If I were going to be staying in her house with her sister, she'd want to know the reason why.

"Mill?" she asked, her voice groggy and scratchy like she'd just woken up.

"Hey," I said. "Something's happened." I explained the situation to her and what I planned to do about it. "I'll keep her safe, Guin. I promise."

"Yeah, I know," she said. "That's not the part I'm worried about. You and Maeve stuck together in the mansion all alone for weeks at a time? You can understand why that doesn't thrill me."

I snorted, admitting I had missed her sarcastic commentary. "You don't need to worry about that." *Right. I'm not watching her through her laptop like a creep or anything. Nothing to worry about.* "I'm just trying to keep her safe."

"Mill..." She sighed. "Maeve is not the same little girl you remember."

"I'm well aware." She'd grown into those long limbs and big ears.

"Okay, fine. Move into the house." Guin seemed resigned to knowing there was nothing else she could do about it. "You'll take care of her. And if anything happens to her, Mill, I'll kill you. Again."

"Don't I know it."

After she hung up, I sat back in my seat and told myself not to hack into Maeve's laptop again. No good would come from whatever I found there. But knowing that had never stopped me from destructive behavior before, and I figured, why change now?

As I watched her get herself off, I begrudgingly stuck my hand in my pants and wondered how the hell I'd keep myself away from her if I was only two doors down the next time.

The next morning, I showered and dressed before I went downstairs for breakfast. Which was fortunate because I rounded the corner to see Mill sitting in the same spot as the day after the wedding, his hat on the table, his hands around a mug of coffee.

"Morning," he drawled, raking his gaze over my jeans and boots and back up again.

I'd planned to go riding before my first appointment. My rides with Molly brought me the only solace I'd managed to find in the days stuck here. Despite being sober for over a week now, my head still pounded like I was hungover. I figured the fresh air and the wind in my hair would do me some good.

"Breakfast again? Lucky me." I blew out a pretentious whistle and sat at the place opposite him. "Should I plan to have you join me tomorrow, or do you enjoy the spontaneity of surprise intrusions?"

His stoic expression almost cracked as he took a drink of coffee.

I ignored the pang in my chest at the sight of his tousled dirty-blond hair and those dark eyes capable of piercing even my strongest attempt at apathy. This strange pitter-patter in my chest that always happened around him didn't mean anything. It was just some deranged holdover from childhood.

Ellen poured my coffee and asked what I wanted to eat. I ordered the same thing I always did before returning my attention to the Bastard on the other side of the table.

"To what do I owe the great honor of your dour presence?"

"Our perimeter was breached last night," he explained. "It seems your sister's former fiancé didn't appreciate being stood up."

That got my attention. "The Scorpions were here?"

He nodded and leaned forward, putting his elbows on the table. I glanced down at his hands—such strong hands, likely capable of terrible, delectable things.

"We picked them up on the security cameras around seven yesterday," he explained. "We need to take extra precautions."

"Such as?"

"Well, if you're planning on riding"—he gestured to my outfit—"you'll need to take an escort. And stay out of the woods."

"Volunteering for that position?" I grinned at his scowl.

"I'm supposed to be preparing the cattle drive next week," he said. "But your safety is a higher priority."

That surprised me, and a quick pang of alarm went down my spine. "My safety? What exactly is going on?"

Mill cleared his throat. "The president of the Bloody Scorpions threatened you. He seems to think he's owed a Vanderbilt daughter, and it doesn't matter which one."

The text.

Realization dawned on me, hitting me square in the chest.

"I got a random message from a number I don't know," I explained, reaching for my phone. I unlocked it, pulled up the message, and placed it on the table between us. "Do you think this is him?"

Mill read through the messages, his eyes darkening as his eyebrows dropped into a deeper scowl. "You shouldn't have responded to him."

"I didn't know who it was," I said. "I thought it might have been Sol or Galahad or…"

He made a noise that sounded like a growl before tapping the screen.

"Hey! Stop that. What are you doing?" I stood to snatch my phone, but he twisted away, causing me to nearly fall across the table. "Give it back."

"Who's Lennon?" he snarled.

I finally grabbed it and yanked it away from him. "Just some guy."

"Some guy?" He didn't sound pleased about that, and I wondered what else he'd seen when he'd been nonconsensually fingering my data. "Why does he think it's okay to ask you to send him nudes?"

I scoffed and locked my phone, placing it face down. "What's it matter to you?"

"I don't like the thought of random men traipsing through here," he said. "If you're going to have company, you need to let me know."

I balked like he'd slapped me, opening my mouth in shock. "That's none of your—"

"Your safety *is* my business," he said. "Do you plan to have company anytime soon?"

I hadn't seen Lennon in almost a year, and his incessant request for nudes said more about him as a fuckboy than it did about whether I'd actually sent him any. I was Maeve Vanderbilt. All it would take was one doxxing accident for those photos to be plastered all over the internet. I wasn't an idiot.

"No," I said, crossing my arms. Ellen chose that moment to return to the dining room with my breakfast, setting it down on the table in front of me. She glanced at Vermillion before looking back at me with a questioning glance, perhaps silently asking if I needed help. I shook my head and waved her away.

My confirmation that random men didn't just come *traipsing* through my house seemed to please him, and his features softened.

"I've already moved my things into the guest room next to your bedroom," he said. "Per Guin's insistence."

That astounded me, a surge of both exhilaration and frustration rattling through my nerves. "What?"

"We agree that you need protection," he said. "She can't make it up here for a while, and we can't have you alone in the house."

"Don't I get a say in this?" I didn't like that my sister had decided the best course of action for me without my agreement or involvement.

He tilted his head to the side and narrowed his eyes. "Is there a problem?"

I shifted my shoulders, ignoring the anticipation brewing in my gut. Part of me relished having him so close, all to myself, for the foreseeable future. The other part of me, the side very aware that he didn't like me the way I'd once adored him, revolted. When I couldn't sleep, I liked to *relieve* my anxiety in ways that would be very audible to someone in the next room.

I should have taken more time to argue with him. Instead, I wanted to show him up, to prove that I didn't care for him or any of this business, that it didn't impact me in the slightest. I was *above* it all.

"No," I said. "Fine."

"Fine," he agreed. "For now, you stay by my side. Or rather, I stay by yours."

"Don't you have work to do?" I gestured to the field out behind the house. "Aren't you supposed to be Orion's replacement?"

"Precisely. But Sol and Orion work side by side all the time." He nodded, stood, and put his hand on his head. "If you have business, I suggest you bring your laptop to the barn."

"The barn?" I couldn't believe what I was hearing. How did he expect me to get anything done out there? "I'm running an empire here. I can't have the sounds of bleating sheep and whining horses in the background of my meetings."

He licked his lips and grinned, a rare sight for someone normally so withdrawn and angry. "You're a smart girl. You'll figure it out, won't you?"

Mill rounded the table and headed toward the front door.

"Eat your breakfast," he said. "If you want to ride, I'll meet you in the stables in thirty minutes."

When the door shut behind him, I tried to ascertain if it was his audacity or his commands that bothered me more.

You're a smart girl.

You've been a naughty girl.

Baby girl, you deserve to be punished.

The versions of him bled together and, as I choked back my eggs and nursed my headache with caffeine, I told myself my subconscious was playing tricks on me. It was only because of the proximity that this sudden fascination with him had reemerged. I'd known him for nearly two decades, but he was a relative stranger now.

"Get yourself together, girl," I murmured, shaking my head as I finished eating. "He's just a man, just a stupid, stupid man."

Annoyed with the whole thing, I grabbed my phone to call Guin. She didn't answer, so I left her a voicemail.

"What the hell is this about Mill staying in the house with me?" I said. "Just because you and Sol have made nice with the local motorcycle gang doesn't mean I want him sleeping six feet away. Call me back."

I knew my sister. If she *deigned* to return the call, the argument likely wouldn't go in my favor. She'd inherited our father's stubborn, bullheaded attitude, and the rest of us had to live with the consequences.

But when I met him in the stables, I had difficulty reminding myself of that. He stood next to Molly, scratching her favorite spot behind her ears while she whinnied and chuffed in pure bliss.

No, I would not be jealous of my horse...even if I did want him to itch some of my most desperate scratches.

Enough.

He wore his Royal Bastards MC cut and a pair of denim jeans that rivaled the ones I'd seen him in while breaking the stallion. He had on a black flannel underneath with the sleeves rolled up to the elbows, exposing his muscular forearms and hands.

Such masculine arms—veiny and long and... I cleared my throat to stop that train of thought.

"Don't let it go to your head," I said. "She's an attention whore."

Vermillion turned to face me and smirked. "Like her favorite human?"

I put my hands on my hips and pretended to be offended. "How dare you? I'm an attention slut. There's an obvious difference."

He laughed and went to the stable next to Molly's, retrieving a gelding named Rusty, who had been rescued from a horrible human who left him alone to starve. My father may not have had many admirable qualities, but he did have a soft spot for animals, especially if he thought he could rehabilitate them and eventually make a profit. Fortunately for Rusty, my father had died before he could be sold, and now, the horse was a permanent fixture on Vanderbilt Ranch.

I hooked a foot in the stirrup and climbed into the saddle, adjusting my hips to sit the way I preferred.

"Hey, girl," I cooed to my horse, rubbing the same spot. "Don't go getting attached. He's a Bastard, and we only tolerate them, okay? We don't actively *like* them."

"Hmm," Vermillion said when he strolled out, already on top of Rusty. "After you."

I led Molly ahead of him, raising an eyebrow as I passed. I usually enjoyed taking these rides alone. It gave me time to think and enjoy the quiet. There was nothing like being under the big open sky with miles of land in front of me. Now, I had an *escort*...which was just a nice way of saying babysitter. Once we got into the back territory, I opened it up and let Molly stretch her legs. She loved to run, and I loved to go fast. Together, we were formidable. In another life, perhaps I'd been an equestrian, and we could have done tournaments. We both would have loved it.

Vermillion kept up with me, and it felt great to see Rusty in his element. No longer the starved, abused animal we'd adopted, he had the strength to match any other horse his size and stature. After twenty minutes, I slowed Molly down to let her catch her breath. Vermillion pulled up beside me with his lips split into a huge grin.

For half a heartbeat, he reminded me of the guy I'd used to know, the one with an easy smile and a quick joke for everyone he saw.

"You ride well," he said.

"Yeah, some guy I used to know taught me." I recalled the days when he would pick me up and prop me in a saddle, teaching me how to hold the reins and guide the animal with gentle cues.

"He must have known what he was doing." Vermillion smirked and looked away, avoiding my gaze. Even if he used to be (or still kind of was) my enemy, he looked really good.

"Sure," I said. "Until he disappeared and abandoned our family for a new one."

Vermillion glanced back at me. "There were things I had to take care of...things you don't understand."

"Uh-huh." I let the sardonic noise hang between us. "Whatever. It doesn't matter, anyway." He'd gone off to join the Bastards, and I'd gone to boarding school, and none of it had made a difference. My heart had stopped for five whole minutes, and none of that mattered, either.

"Why do you say it like that?" he asked, his tone surly and gruff, like the thought of it not mattering irritated him. "Like my leaving had anything to do with your life? You had your precious silver spoon and an abundance of caregivers. I'm sure twenty other people were waiting in line to teach you how to ride a horse."

"What do you know about it?" I spat. "You got your paycheck and left, and on life went."

He furrowed his brows, his mouth hanging open like I'd genuinely shocked him. "Why did my leaving make you so mad?"

I didn't know. I didn't understand where this reaction was coming from. My head ached, and my stomach rolled like my breakfast might project itself across the pasture. The little girl inside of me raged at having woken up one day to find a person she relied on had left. He'd been twenty-one at the time, barely a man himself.

"I had little siblings of my own to look after," he said. "And I don't know if you noticed, but our families have been enemies for decades. Working here pissed a lot of people off, my family and pac—" He cleared his throat as if he'd said something he didn't mean to. "My family and brothers included. The money was good, but eventually, my siblings needed me home. My parents were dead, and no one was looking after them."

That poured water on the fire in my belly. His parents were dead? I didn't know that. A heartbeat of silence passed between us, where I let my shame eat away at my pride. I didn't realize I'd been so angry at him, and for what? What did I honestly know about him?

"How did they die?" I asked. The words came out quiet and soft, my ire calmed.

"The attack on the Royal Bastards," he said. "Your father..."

Ahh. That one hurt. His family had supposedly killed my mother, though we never found her body. My father retaliated by hiring mercenaries from the Bloody Scorpions to infiltrate the Bastard homestead. It was a massacre, but my father had never been known to do things by halves.

"I'm sorry," I said, glancing at my hands to avoid his accusatory stare. "Father was cruel and heartless, not just to his enemies."

"It's not your fault. I only worked here to put food on my siblings' plates," he said, and something in his voice made it sound like he was still holding back a piece of the story. "But once a spot in the Bastards opened up, I took it. I couldn't stay."

"How does that work?" I asked. "More people are living at your homestead than seem to be in the Bastards."

He nodded. "That's right. We're more like a...commune, I guess."

I couldn't help the next thing that came out of my mouth. It shot out of me like a cannon. "Are you in a cult?"

Vermillion barked a laugh and shook his head, and the sound

warmed me. I *liked* his laugh, and I liked his smile...perhaps entirely too much.

"No," he said. "Though it does feel that way sometimes. No. We have a leader."

"Kodiak," I said.

He nodded. "And those closest to him, those he trusts the most, are part of his council. That's the RBMC. We ride together. We die together. We've sworn our loyalty to the colors and the club and each other."

I narrowed my eyes, partly in contemplation and partly to taunt him. "Sounds like a cult."

"What about you?" He raised an eyebrow. "Do you enjoy working for Vanderbilt Holdings?"

I sighed and shook my head. "I suppose I should. It put me through school. It's paying my bills."

"Does it feed your soul?"

I glanced at him and considered. "No. If I had my way, I'd ride every morning and draw in the afternoon."

"Draw?" His curiosity lit up his face, his eyebrows raised, and his eyes wide. "You can draw?"

"Some." I usually didn't like what I created, so I had an entire shelf of sketchbooks that would never see the light of day. Some even included portraits of him, though I'd never admit that.

"Don't be modest." He nudged my shoulder with his. "I'd like to see them."

"They're nothing really. My father used to tell me art was for the poor and foolish." I could still hear his voice in the back of my head. "'And you're neither,' he'd say. He made me drop my art classes in favor of a business degree. All of the Vanderbilt siblings were expected to join Vanderbilt Holdings after graduation. All except Ava, but that's only because she's a lawyer." My twin had been afforded the luxury of choosing a different path because it was more lucrative than the one I'd had thrust upon me. "I suppose if I had wanted to be pre-law instead, he might have allowed such a deviation from his plan."

"Well, he's dead now," Vermillion said. "So you can do whatever you want."

"There's a pretty thought." I snorted and shook my head. "Do you have a motorcycle?"

He nodded. "I do. I rode it up last week."

I pursed my lips, considering whether to ask the next question. If he turned me down, I'd be disappointed, so perhaps—

"Have you ever been on a bike before?"

I shook my head. "No. Father would have killed us if we'd even thought about it."

"I could..." He stopped himself. "Never mind."

"No, go on. Say it." I suspected he'd been about to offer what I wanted, and I yearned to hear it.

"I could take you out one day," he said. "If you want."

"Really?" I smiled, though I knew I shouldn't. Something about being on the back of his bike with my arms wrapped around him, all that internal combustion between my legs, seemed forbidden and salacious. I shouldn't want it, but heaven help me, the adrenaline junkie inside ached for it.

Ava would chastise me, I was sure. But what she didn't know wouldn't hurt her.

"Sure," he said. "Maybe this weekend sometime." Vermillion seemed like he'd been about to say more, but then he straightened and glanced around us like he'd heard something I hadn't. He sniffed the air and looked at the tree line on the other side of the stream.

"What is it?" I said. "Do you see something?"

He glanced back at me and nodded. "I think it's time we head back."

I'd barely gotten in the riding time I wanted, but I didn't argue. He turned Rusty around, and I followed with Molly. We took the path back home in silence, both of us perhaps having shared far too much with each other in such a short time.

CHAPTER 9

Vermillion

"They're back," I told Fenris when we returned to the ranchers' quarters. Maeve had gone ahead to the mansion while I made a pit stop to let my brothers know. I pulled Fenris, Poe, Columba, Aquila, and Holden to the side, away from the human ranchers, so they didn't overhear while they got ready for the day's work. "I smelled them out by Lot G, near the stream."

Columba jumped into action, grabbing his hat from the hook on his bunk before shoving his arms into his cut. "Let's fucking go."

"Wait, wait, wait," I said, holding a hand out to stop him.

We were two weeks from the full moon, and the dominant beast had started rearing its territorial head. It didn't like being told what to do. But I still outranked him, outranked them all, and both he and his wolf knew it.

"We can't go rushing in there all hotheaded," I said. "We have work to do, and the scent was a few hours old. They might be using it as a way in and out."

He snarled. "So we should set up shop to catch them the next time they come through."

"We know what they're after," I said, though I understood his bloodlust. I, too, wanted to tear some vampire heads from their rotten, bloodsucking bodies. But I wasn't just responsible for Maeve. While we were here, I was responsible for them, too. "We're protected here at the mansion."

"Not after we leave," Columba argued. "You still want us to move the cattle next weekend? Then we need to settle this before then."

"He's got a point," Poe said, crossing his arms.

Some of the other hired hands grabbed their hats and milled around, trying not to look like they were eavesdropping, though it was obvious that was what they were doing.

"If we move the cattle, that leaves only four guys here to protect the house," Fenris said, shooting a feeling down the pack bonds that suggested it wasn't enough...and I knew it. "We have to hunt them down before the moon."

I didn't have a good argument for that. When the call of the full moon took hold of our alter egos, we were incapacitated for at least five minutes. Our bodies broke down and rebuilt themselves as our animal side, and during that process, we were almost blind and completely undefended. Marx could strike then, when we were at our weakest, as they'd done in the past.

But what the fuck else were we supposed to do? I could call in backup from Kodiak, but then the homestead would be unprotected, and I didn't like the thought of that, either.

"Move the cattle," I told Fenris. "Be back in three days like we planned. That'll give us the rest of this week and two days when you get back before the shift."

"And if we can't find them before then?" Poe raised his eyebrows, clearly expecting a fully formed plan.

"We'll have to go home to shift with the pack." It would be our only option.

"And leave Maeve unprotected?" He balked and shook his head. "That's a stupid plan, brother."

"She'll come with us," I said.

Poe let out an incredulous laugh, perhaps not believing me at first. When he decided I was serious, he widened his eyes. "Wait... really? Bring Maeve Vanderbilt to the homestead on a full moon?"

"We have humans in the pack," I said. "They'll protect her while we shift."

"You better run that by Kodiak first," Fenris added. "You know he gets touchy when you start making plans without consulting him."

"I'll talk to him," I said. "In the meantime, let's get back to work." I glanced at Aquila, who had become our resident horse whisperer. I'd seen him get through to even the surliest of fillies. "You break that stallion yet?"

He shook his head. "The fucker is onery."

"Keep working on him." I gestured toward the big house. "I'll grab Maeve and meet you by the barn."

He balked. "She's working with us today?"

"Until we catch these fucking bloodsuckers, I want to keep an eye on her."

Fenris looked to Poe and Columba before pursing his lips and raising his eyebrows in disbelief.

"What?" I growled.

"How'd she take the news about you moving in?" Fenris asked, his hands on his hips, an eyebrow rose halfway up his forehead.

"Fine," I growled. "I didn't give her much of a choice."

"Vanderbilt women like that," Poe replied with a sarcastic smirk. "Sol *really* enjoyed being backed into a corner."

"She's alive, isn't she?" Orion had kept her safe up at that cabin. Poe and Lycan, too. If she'd listened to him from the start, she probably wouldn't have nearly gotten eaten by wolves either.

Poe put his hands out to either side in supplication. "I'm not arguing with you. I'm just saying...be careful."

I glared but didn't respond. I had to get back to the mansion. Neither I nor my wolf liked leaving her alone this long. The other guys jumped into action, going about their morning routine while I packed the rest of the things I'd need in the mansion. My best friend and resident pain in the ass stuck around. When I noticed him lingering, I raised my eyebrows and straightened.

"What?"

Fenris whistled. "Seems like you're *extremely* worried about her."

"What's that supposed to mean?"

"I mean...she's got an alarm system in the big house. If anyone comes after her, it won't take long for us to get there to help her."

I put my hands on my hips. "And?"

"Why do you need to have her by your side?" he asked.

I rolled my eyes, sensing where this was heading. "Knock it off."

"Look, if she's your—"

I didn't let him finish. Shaking my head, I headed out of the bunks toward the main house. Those idiots didn't know what the hell they were talking about. Maeve was too young, too stubborn, too...*human* to be anything more than a job duty.

But my wolf didn't like that insinuation. He reminded me of how hard my heart had stammered when I met eyes with her at the wedding. Touching her had set me on fire, and all my beast wanted to do was see how much of her he could consume in one bite.

I'd never felt like this about a female before. All of those encounters seemed mind-numbingly dull in comparison. Not Maeve. She made me laugh. She argued with me. She...was totally and completely off-limits.

When I got to the big house, I stomped my feet on the mat and wiped them off before shouting out for the Vanderbilt in question.

"Maeve!" I glanced toward the top of the grand staircase and waited to see if she'd respond. When she didn't, I followed her caramel and lilac scent up the stairs to the second floor, where it trailed into a room two doors down on the right.

"Exactly, Jonathan," Maeve said into her cellphone, pacing in front of an enormous desk in the study. "If we don't do it now, the window of opportunity could close, and then where will we be?"

She held up a finger to suggest I should wait for her to finish. While she negotiated with whomever was on the other end, I stood by the door and crossed my arms, letting my gaze roam over her. She'd taken off her riding boots and now stood barefoot, her perfect toes decorated with black nail paint to match the same on her fingers. She had long, strong legs that widened into hips just begging to be grabbed and squeezed. Her curves screamed for attention as they faded into her chest and a long, biteable neck.

My canines nearly extended at the thought of sinking into that delicate flesh and marking her as mine. And her eyes...*fuck,* her eyes were deep elegant pools of ice blue, and I wanted to stare into them while I made her scream. With pleasure. With agony. With the wanton yearning for both at the same time. But her scent — that sweet, floral decadence swirled around me, making me want to lap her up until neither of us could walk.

She hung up the phone and turned to face me.

"Vermillion?" She raised her eyebrows and smiled, and I shook my head before pushing upright, trying to tamp down the burn in my cheeks. "Are you okay?"

"Yeah, fine," I said, nodding toward the front door. "Let's go."

"Are you sure I have to come with you? I could keep all the alarms on and promise to check in."

Maybe my best friend, the big, stupid oaf, had a point. Maybe making her stay with me all day was too much. There was a security system here, like she'd said. And I didn't want to think of myself as a stalker, but when I'd gotten hold of her phone at breakfast, I'd installed a bug that alerted me if she suddenly dropped it or screamed for help. If I happened to also be able to track her movements, telephone calls, search history, and texts...well, that couldn't be avoided. It was for her safety, after all.

She grimaced and rubbed her temples. "It's just...after the ride this morning, my head is killing me. I think I'm getting sick."

Fuck.

Lycan's warning resurfaced in my mind, but I stuffed it down. Sometimes, a headache was just a headache.

"What time does the staff leave?" I figured she wasn't really alone, considering there were other people throughout. They wouldn't be that much help against a vampire, but perhaps I could keep tabs on her from the barn. It wasn't that far away, was it?

"Eight, after dinner," she explained.

My wolf grimaced and shook its hackles, clearly not liking the thought of letting her out of his sight.

"Please?" She stuck out her lower lip in a pout. "I promise I'll be good."

I ignored the effect her words had on me, instantly taking me back to the dream where I'd chased her through the woods and threatened to punish her. I took a deep breath and let it out on a sigh, berating my cock for its pathetic jerk. "Fine. But you will check in with me every half hour, and if I don't hear from you, I'll come looking."

She nodded and gave me a mock salute. "Will do."

"I'll be back for dinner." I adjusted my hat and straightened my cut as Maeve smiled. I pretended like the sight didn't melt my cold, dead heart.

"Looking forward to it."

Fuck me. I cleared my throat and forced my feet to head for the stairs. When I got back to the barn, Poe and Fenris teased me about caving to Maeve's wishes, but I snarled at them and we returned to work.

True to her word, Maeve sent me increasingly taunting texts every thirty minutes. I was checking the pregnant cows when the first one came through.

Maeve: I'm still working if you're still lurking.

I sent her back a thumbs-up.

Thirty minutes later, I had just finished documenting which cows were nearing their fertile period when the second one came through.

Maeve: What do you call sheep sliding down a hill?
Maeve: A lambslide.
Maeve: :-D

I rolled my eyes and chuckled, clicking into my app that would let me watch her through her laptop. She typed on the keyboard and grinned, her eyes glancing at her phone occasionally, like she was waiting for me to respond.

When the third check-in came through, I had to physically restrain myself from going into the house after her.

She sent a selfie worthy of being posted as a thirst trap. The top two buttons on her shirt were undone, and the camera angle was high enough to see right down the front. She had her hair down and her eyes wide, and fuck...her perfect lips pulled into a devastating smile.

Maeve: Proof of life.

I took a deep breath to calm my suddenly racing heart, the shock settling somewhere around my cock as it twitched to life with wanton expectation. My wolf howled at me to make her grin for other reasons, but I ignored that, too.

Me: Don't be a tease.

Maeve: A tease? If you want the full monty, you'll have to be nicer than that.

Me: I'm nice.

Maeve: You didn't laugh at my lamb joke.

"Hey, you working or texting?" Fenris put his hands on his hips and nodded toward the herd up ahead. "We only have a few more hours of sunlight left, and there's a shit ton to do to move them."

"Yeah, yeah," I mumbled, firing off one more text before locking my phone and putting it in my back pocket.

Me: Maybe a few more selfies would lighten my mood.

I was being facetious, but she sent one every thirty minutes for the rest of the day, practically taunting me with those baby blues and soft, delectable lips.

My inner beast wanted to bite them, to tear her apart to see what she was made of. I didn't understand that urge. I'd never felt anything like it, not with anyone I'd been interested in before.

Wait...am I interested in Maeve?

The dreams I'd been having...the possessive way I wanted to protect her...the stutter in my chest when I saw her at the wedding.

Aw, hell.

No. No, I refused that possibility.

She was off-limits, so pure and full of light, and I was a pitch dark void. I'd just drag her down. I blamed the time of the month for my wolf's wanton baser instincts. The full moon was closing in on us, and its magic brought out my feral side. It was no wonder Columba had gone head-to-head with me this morning. We were all more primal, our shifter sides closer to the surface.

"When we're done tagging the cattle, we'll move on to the sheep," I said.

Poe and Aquila nodded.

"Travers says most of the mommas are taking to their kids," Holden added. "Only a few need bottle feeding."

That was good. Sheep were notorious assholes when it came to twins or triplets. Sometimes, the mother would accept only one offspring and abandon the others. If we caught it fast enough, we could try to trick one of the other mothers into accepting it, but we didn't always get there in time.

After the day was done, I said good night to the guys and headed into the house, taking off my boots before crossing the foyer.

"Maeve?" I called out.

"In here," she said from the dining room to the left. I followed the sound of her voice but stopped in the entryway. The table had been set for two, candles glowing from the center with half-full wineglasses on either side. "I hope you're hungry."

My mouth watered, but cow shit seeped out of my pores in a rank plume, indicating my day spent in the pastures.

"I helped Ellen with most of it," she said with a slight wince. "I never learned how to cook. It's actually kind of fun."

Her adorable grin almost had me saying things I didn't mean, things that could never be forgotten between us. The intoxicating scent of her caramel pheromones wafted over, drowning out the chicken and roasted vegetables. It had been delicate and light at the wedding, but now it grew stronger, more potent. It dragged me under its spell, yanking me down into an uncontrollable fit of desperation. I swallowed against my dry, aching throat, one that no amount of water or wine could sate.

"It smells amazing," I said, grimacing as my wolf agreed. I meant the food. He meant the hormones signaling an available female. "I just need to take a quick shower." I pointed in the general direction of upstairs.

"Oh, of course." She smiled and shook her head. "Duh. Go ahead. I'll wait right here."

I tried not to scramble up the stairs like my ass was on fire, but the sooner I got away from her, the sooner I could convince myself this attraction had more to do with the proximity of my upcoming shift rather than anything unprofessional.

CHAPTER 10

Maeve

I rubbed my temples while I waited for Mill to return, my headache worsening throughout the day. It escalated into full-body chills by the time I asked Ellen to help with dinner. But it didn't wear me out the way the flu or a cold would. If anything, I wanted to do more. I had the sudden urge to straighten the place up, gather every pillow I could, and make a fort in the parlor, some place quiet and hidden and comfortable.

Maybe I could convince Vermillion to stay there with me tonight.

I sipped my wine, but it tasted like garbage. Perhaps it had turned, and despite how good the chicken smelled, the thought of eating it made me want to vomit. My stomach churned, and I scowled at the food.

It *had* been fun to help Ellen in the kitchen once I had finally convinced her to let me. She insisted it was her job, that I paid her to do it, and while I couldn't argue with that, I simply reframed the thought. Perhaps I was paying her to give me her wisdom.

Of course, now I suffered for it with pressure between my eyes and body aches that wouldn't go away.

I straightened when Vermillion's footsteps echoed down the stairs, and I forced a smile as he sat on the opposite side of the table.

His clean scent wafted over the space between us, reminding me of woods, rain, and *man*. There was something else there, too, something dark and inviting. I wanted to curl up in his lap, stuff my head in his chest, and inhale every last bit of him for the rest of the night.

"When you look at me like that," he said, scooting his chair in, "it's difficult to remember we're supposed to be enemies."

Warmth flooded my body, heating my cheeks, down into my neck. My skin burned with the memory of how he'd touched me at the wedding, how his rough fingers had electrified my nerves, bringing me to life. He'd flirted with me over text this afternoon. Did that mean something more? Or was he just being nice? He didn't seem like the playful type, but of course, how well did I truly know him?

"You're very nice to look at," I admitted. "And besides, we're not enemies anymore. Not really."

He chuckled and grabbed the wine to bring it to his nose.

"No, don't," I said. "It's soured."

Vermillion frowned and sipped anyway. "Tastes alright to me."

"Huh." I tried it again, only to shiver at the bitter taste sliding down my throat. "Maybe it's just me. God, I don't know what's wrong." Gripping my head, I ran circles on my scalp and sighed. "Go ahead and eat. I'm not sure I'm hungry."

Vermillion twisted his features into a worried frown before picking up the fork to stab into a piece of chicken, using the knife to slice it off. "Do you feel any better since this afternoon?"

"I don't know," I said. "I took some medicine, but it didn't help."

Vermillion gulped and glanced down at his dinner. "Is it just the headache?"

I shook my head. "It's body aches and chills. I think I have the flu. You should probably keep your distance."

"Hmm. I'm sorry to hear that," he murmured. "Thank you for dinner. This is amazing."

"You're welcome," I said. "I didn't do much, but learning was fun."

"What made you want to cook?" He narrowed his gaze on me and took another sip of wine.

I shrugged. "Not sure. Just felt like doing something, I guess."

"Uh-huh." He leaned back in his seat and tilted his head to the side, seeming to study me. "Are you noticing anything else? Like maybe the urge to clean or...other things?"

Snorting a laugh, I pushed the chicken around on my plate. "No. Why?"

"Never mind," he said. "How was your day?"

"Okay. Aside from having to check in with an annoying body-guard every thirty minutes."

Vermillion pulled his lips into a charming smile. "You didn't seem that annoyed in those pictures."

"Play your cards right and you could enjoy the same privileges as Lennon." I winked and bit into the chicken before deciding it tasted awful, too. Perhaps some bread.

He laughed and shook his head. "Don't tease me, sweetheart."

Sweetheart?

I liked the sound of that.

We bantered through our meal, and afterward, we sat and talked like old friends.

"Do you have a girlfriend?" I finally asked, emboldened by the few sips of alcohol and the cozy conversation.

"No." He scoffed like the idea was ridiculous. "I haven't been serious about anyone in a long time, and after I nearly died...it's easier to keep people at a distance."

That piqued my interest. "You nearly died?"

He nodded and explained how he'd been helping the MC with a raid, but things went wrong. He'd been clinically dead for five minutes.

"Me too," I said. "Some strange heart condition." I pointed to the spot on the floor where it'd happened. "Right there, in fact. About six months ago."

"Me too," he said. "So you're a day walker."

I chuckled. "A day walker?"

"You died and came back to life." He laughed, and a chill shot through me at the sound. "Did you see any white light? Any long-dead ancestors welcoming you into the great beyond?"

"Sadly, no," I admitted, taking another drink of wine.

"Yeah, same here. It's disappointing, isn't it?"

"Quite." I tried to ignore the contemplative way he looked at me, as if revealing the worst thing that had ever happened to me had changed the way he saw me.

"What about you?" He spun his empty wineglass around. "Any boyfriends?"

"Oh, tons," I said facetiously. "Yes, they're constantly blowing up my phone. I can hardly keep the men off me."

"Why say it like that?" He leaned forward on his elbows, studying me. "You're a beautiful woman. I would have thought you'd have them lining up around the block."

"I don't trust people," I said. "Especially men." I'd been broken-hearted too many times to count, and after a while, the risks didn't outweigh the benefits. "You think I'm beautiful?"

His cheeks turned an adorable shade of pink that echoed up to his ears and down his throat. "All of you Vanderbilts are."

The rush of cool, humiliating rejection splashed through my veins, calming down any hope that he might return my affections.

Then, he gulped the rest of his wine and stood. "I should go to bed. Thank you for dinner, Maeve."

"You're welcome," I said. "Will you join me for breakfast tomorrow?"

He nodded. "And another ride, if you're feeling up to it."

I waited for his footsteps to ascend the stairs before I grinned to myself, finished my wine, and retired to my own room.

This went on for three more days. In the mornings, we ate breakfast and talked about our plans. He updated me on the Bloody Scorpion sightings, pointing out where it was safe to go and where I should avoid. Anything within the bounds of the security perimeter was okay, but I should always have an escort. We took Molly and Rusty on rides, and I fell even more in love with his eyes in the sunshine. They were the kind of brown that had flecks of glistening gold, and when he smiled (which he rarely did), it lit up his entire face. I'd do anything to make him smile.

I told jokes and talked about my sisters, and we reminisced about his time on the ranch and what stupid kids we were. It was nice to have him around, to be in his company, and when he went to work during the day, I texted him every thirty minutes like he wanted.

On Friday, he finally took me out on his bike. It was a beautiful Harley, painted a deep red with sparkling flecks.

"It's Vermillion," he corrected when I pointed it out.

"Oh, like your name," I said, putting the helmet over my head and latching it under my chin.

"Uh-huh." He nodded and swung a leg over the seat, balancing it between his thighs as he fiddled with the buttons on the handlebars. Excitement bubbled in my stomach. Despite all my reckless behavior, I'd never been on a motorcycle before. My father would never have allowed me to surround myself with people who rode them. If he could only see me now. I couldn't contain my rebellious laughter.

"Now, listen," he said. "When we get going, you hold on tight, okay?"

The idea of wrapping my arms around his midsection and never letting go made my inner nine-year-old want to scream with both joy and mortification.

"Okay," I said with a grin as big as my entire face.

I climbed on the bike behind him, my knees on either side of his hips, and I put my hands on his waist.

"No. Like this, sweetheart." He grabbed my wrists and pulled them around his torso, forcing me closer to him, smushing my boobs up against his back. Completely embarrassing myself, I trembled at the contact, and I thought I heard him chuckle before he kicked the bike to life.

The loud rumble shot through me, and I forced myself to focus on my breathing to steady my heart rate. But after he took off, I couldn't contain the pure adrenaline-laced joy racing through my veins. I squealed as we went faster, the rush of the wind on my cheeks amping up the thrill in my blood. The combustion thundered under me, vibrating the soft spots between my legs, which was as scandalous as it was mesmerizing.

He kept it slow until we got to the main road, and then he let loose. We sped through the back-country streets, and when he took turns, I hugged him tighter to ensure I didn't fall. Tingles spun through my stomach, and my pulse pounded, but it was terrific.

Life was meant to be all about this: the heat of the moment, the unrestrained pleasures that stifled the monotonous boredom, the magic of the world whipping by. Minutes raced like seconds, and I enjoyed every single one to the fullest.

Mill drove us into the mountains, and when he finally stopped the bike, we were at an overlook that gazed down on all of Helena.

I climbed off the back, removed my helmet, and walked closer to the edge. The sun was nearly set in the distance, casting the town in vibrant blushes and tangerines. This was my favorite time of day, when everything was liminal. Not quite awake, but not quite asleep.

"This is beautiful," I said as Mill walked to stand next to me.

"Yeah, it is," he murmured, but when I glanced at him, he wasn't looking at the town. His gaze was set intently on me, his focus going to my mouth like he planned on leaning in to close the distance between us. I wanted him to. I wanted to push up on my toes, taste his mouth, and relieve some of the tension. But I hesitated. I didn't want to scare him off, and other than a few compliments and some chaste flirting, he hadn't given me any reason to think he'd welcome such a thing.

Cheeks burning, I looked back at the view and smiled.

"Thank you for this," I said. "It's easy to forget why we're alive, and then you see something like this and...it all makes sense." I closed my eyes and let the heat of the dying sun radiate across my skin, relishing the reinvigorating warmth. "Doesn't it?"

He didn't answer, and when I opened my eyes, he was still staring at me, his eyebrows furrowed, his lips pulled into a thin line.

"What's wrong?" I asked. He looked so forlorn and depressed, and after that amazing ride and this incredible view, I didn't understand what could possibly have made him so upset.

"Nothing," he said, finally turning his attention to the valley. "You're right. It's quite the view."

We stood there in comfortable silence until the urge to do something else...something reckless...finally took over.

"C'mon," I told him, nodding back toward his bike. "I've got an idea."

Holding on to him as best as I could, I directed him to a spot not too far away. This had been my refuge growing up, the secret I didn't share with anyone, not even Ava. Why I was sharing it with him, I didn't know. Maybe I had relaxed into an easier comfort in his presence than I ever could with my family. Maybe I felt like I owed him something for the bike ride.

He parked at the edge of the tree line, and we climbed off, removing our helmets.

"Where are we?" he asked. "I've never been this far up before."

I didn't answer, just grinned and nodded ahead. "Let's go."

He followed me for a bit, glancing around for any signs of danger, but when he decided things must have been okay, he walked by my side.

"Maeve, I don't like being in strange places without scoping them out first." He moved with a stiff, predatory gait, like he expected a Bloody Scorpion to jump out at us any second. True, that *could* happen, but no one ever came up here. Just me and my adrenaline-junkie self.

"Do you see any signs of them?" I asked, pausing to check in for reassurance.

He cleared his throat and raised an eyebrow. "No. I just..." Mill looked around again. "The sun is setting. We need to head back."

"We're okay, Mill. Besides, you're a big, strong motorcycle man. You'll protect me."

His cheeks turned a brilliant shade of rose, and I knew I had him.

"Hey," I said, giving him a quick nudge. "Race ya."

Then, I took off into the woods, the pads of my feet bouncing off the undergrowth like I was made for sprinting.

"Maeve, wait!" he called from behind me, but I'd done enough waiting. I'd been trapped in that mansion-sized prison for weeks. This was my first time off Vanderbilt property in almost a month, and I couldn't stand it. My skin felt too tight, my muscles yearning for more, almost like this ferocious energy was trying to burst from my skin. I knew these woods like my own mind, and I wouldn't be contained any longer.

The sounds of his boots behind me thundered off the trees, but I kept going, pumping my arms, giggling with delight. Joy burst in my chest as my heart pounded, and when we cleared the other side of the forest, I stopped only long enough for him to catch up.

"Goddamn it, Vanderbilt," he said. "Don't fucking do that."

"Such language." I pretended to be shocked. "But what about *this* view?"

We were at the edge of a cliff that stood atop Blackfoot River. The woods sprawled in either direction, the rocky basin beautiful this time of day, as if painted by the Gods. He caught his breath and moved forward, his hands on his hips as he took it all in.

"I used to come up here right after it happened." I didn't need to tell him what *it* was. Nearly dying could be the only *it* in my life. While his back was turned, I kicked off my shoes and peeled my shirt over my head. I shimmied my shorts down to my ankles and stepped out of them. "It's the best spot for cliff jumping."

"Wait, what?" He turned to me, but I'd already made up my mind.

I sprinted forward, digging my toes into the cliff's edge before throwing my body off the safety of land, free-falling into the abyss below. My stomach whirled, and wind rushed through my hair, every ounce of my soul weightless and boundless. Electricity shot through my veins, culminating in my fingertips and toes. When I hit the water, the cool, refreshing splash made me scream. It had been such a hot day, and riding in the sun on the back of Mill's bike offered a decadent contrast to the plunging caress of the river.

"Wooo!" I let out a tremendous shout when I surfaced, glancing up at Mill, who still stood on the top of the cliff.

"What the fuck is wrong with you?" He threw his hands up in the air.

"C'mon! It's fun!" I laughed and paddled around, treading water while I waited for him.

"There's no way I'm doing that," he said. "You're out of your mind."

"What good is life if you're stuck in one spot all the time?" I floated on my back, reveling in the comfort of the way the water cradled me. "Don't get shown up by little ole me!"

He seemed to consider that before turning around and walking away from the edge. I thought I'd lost him, that he'd left me alone to climb back up by myself, but a few moments later, his half-naked body hurled off the cliff, arms flailing, legs kicking. He landed in an enormous splash a few feet away, coming back up for air with a gasp.

"Yay!" I swam over to him. "You did it!"

"Fucking hell." His wide eyes hinted at how shocked he was.

"Not so bad, right?" I laughed and flicked water at him. "I told you."

He shifted his attention to me, his features twisting into a mischievous scowl. "*You* are a terrible influence, Maeve Vanderbilt."

Mill swam closer, reminding me of a shark that had smelled fresh blood.

Squealing with delight, I tried to get away from him, but it was too late. He grabbed me by the shoulders and dunked me under, but I tickled his ribs, and he dropped his elbows to try to cut me off. When I resurfaced, he shoved water at me, which caused me to push a giant wave back at him.

He laughed, *truly* laughed, and my entire body trembled at the sound. I *loved* that sound, almost as much as I loved his eyes and his lips and his generous soul. Ah hell, I'd crushed on him for so damned long, almost nothing about him disappointed me.

This time, when I splashed him, he grabbed my wrist and yanked me closer. I didn't know why I did what I did next. Maybe it was the welcoming look in his features. Perhaps it was the undeniable buzzing between us. Perhaps it was because I wanted to know if he felt the same way I did, or if he really thought of me as only Guin's little sister. He *had* called me beautiful. Regardless of the why, I couldn't help myself. I grabbed the back of his neck and pressed my mouth to his, colliding our lips in a glorious display of adoration.

They were soft and delicate, much more than I thought, given how gruff and insolent he pretended to be. I moaned into the contact, using my tongue to coax his lips apart. When he growled and pulled me closer, I smiled into the contact. God, I loved when a man took control. He twisted his fingers into my hair, holding me tight while I consumed him.

I licked and lapped, wrapping my legs around his waist so the softest part of me rubbed up his hardening cock, growing more prominent the longer we made out. I scraped my nails over his scalp, and he responded by dragging his fingers down my back to my hips, where I rolled against his pelvis, urging him on, frenzied for more contact.

It had been so long since I'd been with someone, weeks and weeks, and being pent up in my mansion made things worse. He needed only to give me one iota of consent, and I would pull my undies to the side, yank down his boxers, and impale myself on him right here in the Blackfoot.

Muscles trembling, I reached down in between us, stroking his impressive cock, and he hissed, moving his mouth down my jaw to my throat, nipping at my skin while I stroked him.

"Mill," I whimpered. "Fuck me."

Every reason not to still lingered between us, but coming off the adrenaline of the jump and the playful teasing, we both got caught up in the moment. He made a noise low and deep in his chest, half purr, half growl, and he moved one hand to my cunt, cupping me under the water, digging his strong masculine fingers under my panties.

"Fuck, you're soaked," he said. "Is this all for me?"

"Yes," I said, biting my way down the column of his windpipe. "Please. I want you. Please. Please."

With his free hand, he grabbed my throat and squeezed, causing me to startle and meet his gaze. I could have sworn flecks of red sparkled in his mahogany irises, but that was my imagination playing tricks on me.

"You promise not to run off the side of any more cliffs?" He dragged his decadent tongue across my mouth, sending shivers straight down my spine to my clit. "You promise to be a good girl?"

I nodded quickly. "Yes, I promise. I'll be your good girl. I swear."

He narrowed his increasingly obsidian eyes, and some small part of me screamed that I should be afraid. I should run for my life, but I didn't. I pressed closer to him, yanked his massive dick out of his boxers, and ran the tip over my vulva, sliding it through the wetness he'd been so proud of.

He inhaled, tension coiling in every part of his muscles, tightening his fist around my neck. He pulled his pelvis out of my grip and wrapped his palms around the back of my thighs, carrying me over to the shoreline, where he lay me down on the ground. I didn't care about the cool mud underneath me. Compared to the heat radiating off him, nothing else mattered.

I trembled when he kissed me again, working his way down my body to my breasts, yanking my wet bra cups down. When he sucked one nipple, I arched into the contact, bursts of pleasure-laced euphoria ricocheting through my nerves.

"Yes, more," I murmured, clamping my fingers in his hair, yanking and scratching to get him where I wanted him. He massaged my other nipple while he yanked my panties clean off my body with one powerful jerk.

I gasped, the sting of fabric slicing through my pelvis, but when he returned his fingers to my cunt, I quickly forgot all about that. He moved his mouth to the other nipple, lavishing that with the same affection as the first before sinking lower, kissing and licking his way down my midsection.

Staring up at me from between my legs, I almost had to pinch myself to make sure this was real, that this wasn't just another disappointing dream where I'd eventually wake up alone and cold in my bed.

"Tell me to stop," he said. "Tell me you don't want this."

"I want this," I said. "Please, Mill."

He sighed and hung his head, as if he was trying to think of a reason for him to end it on his own. He must have come to some resolution because he hissed a quiet, "Fuck it," and shifted his shoulders under my thighs so he could align his mouth with the part of me screaming for him.

When he speared his tongue through my sensitive skin, I bucked off the earth, surging upward with the jolt of ecstasy rolling through me. He moaned...*literally* moaned, and little vibrations rattled through me from the sound.

"Fuck, you taste delicious, better than I ever imagined." He latched on, sucking and flicking his talented tongue across my skin. Somewhere in my brain, I noticed he said he had imagined this, but that was quickly forgotten as he worked me like he owned me.

After teasing my entrance, he finally stuck one finger...two fingers...inside, and I almost came apart. The scruff of his five-o'clock shadow rubbed against the insides of my thighs, marking a rough contrast to the delicate way he cared for my pussy. He devoured me like a man starved, like he'd been waiting for this for eons, and I'd finally given him sustenance.

He took his time at first, licking and sucking in slow, agonizing pulls, curling his fingers to hit that decadent spot inside. I moaned louder, faster, fisting his hair, voracious to get as much of him as he would give. At my cues, he picked up speed, fucking me with his face and his fingers like this might be our first and only chance at such a connection.

I didn't last long, and my climax broke me in an embarrassingly short amount of time. He fucked me harder, greedy for everything I had, and when I came back down to earth, he didn't stop. He slowed down and stared up at me with eyes gone to lust.

"Come here," I whispered, clawing at his hair, his shoulders, anything I could get.

"No," he said, kissing along one thigh before going to the other. "No, I plan to take my time, sweetheart. You lay back and let me enjoy this, huh?"

Let *him* enjoy this?

What had I ever done to deserve that?

I didn't know, but I thanked my past self for whatever it was. If I had to die and come back to life again just to know I'd have this, I'd do it over and over. He increased his pace, licking me and sucking me, and soon, I was cresting again. My muscles tightened, and I screamed out my pleasure, apathetic to anyone else that might be in the vicinity. If the Scorpions were nearby, let them come. I didn't care. I only needed him. I only needed this.

After that, I was too sensitive for him to continue, and I pushed his face away, my muscles loose, my body riding waves of endorphins.

"No, no more," I said. "Please. Either fuck me or let me suck you off. I need a break."

He sat back on his haunches, his mouth and chin glistening with evidence of my orgasm, and he smiled that gorgeous grin he so rarely let anyone see.

"You wanna suck me off?"

I bit my bottom lip and pushed up on my elbows. "Would you let me? Please?"

He waved two fingers, gesturing for me to come closer. I scrambled up on my knees while he stood, and from this perspective, he was so tall and beautifully built—all tightly coiled muscles and chiseled features. His days riding a bike and working the ranch had certainly been good to him.

"Open your mouth," he said, hooking his thumbs into the waistband of his boxers.

I nearly tripped over myself to comply, sticking out my tongue in eager acquiescence. I wanted to be good for him. I wanted to do whatever he wanted. If I could make him feel a fraction of what he did to me, I'd consider myself privileged.

The space between my legs throbbed when he finally lowered his underwear and let his massive dick bounce free. I scooted closer, trying to latch onto it, but he was in a playful mood. He held the base and slapped it over my tongue a few times, delight in his eyes and mischief in his smile.

"You're an eager little thing," he teased.

I nodded. "I've wanted this a long time."

"Oh, yeah?" He seemed to like that. "Go on and show me how much."

I pulled him between my lips and sucked the tip, gently at first, working him up to it. I didn't want to go too fast, too soon, and show all my cards. No, I wanted to savor this, to take it slow and make him shake by the time it was over.

Gripping his boxers with one hand and the base of his dick with the other, I ran my tongue along the underside of him, swallowing down the salty taste of his precum. He leaned his head back on his shoulders, showcasing his broad chest and sculpted abs, and I thanked the heavens I got to see him like this. The sun was nearly under the horizon now, and up against the fading light, he looked like a God or maybe a fallen angel, something ethereal and eternal, come from heaven to save me from damnation.

"Fuck, your mouth is killing me, baby," he said, running a hand through my hair. He gripped it behind my head and used it to guide me how he wanted, sinking his cock deep into the back of my throat.

I relaxed my muscles and stuck out my tongue, rubbing it against his balls while I gagged around his thick length. He hissed and moaned in response, and that urged me on.

Nothing made me feel more powerful than turning a strong man weak. Was there any better way to do that than with his cock in my mouth and my teeth so close to his tender bits? Oh, how I loved it when he shivered and gave me praise.

"Fuck, just like that. Such a good girl. You take me so fucking well." He spewed countless other dirty thoughts, complimenting me on such a lecherous act. "You wanna drain my balls, baby? You want everything I have to give you?"

Not in a hundred years would I ever have thought Vermillion Alexander would talk like this *to me,* but I'd never been one to snub a gift, so I kept going. I gripped him tighter, worked him faster, took him deeper, even when my eyes watered and I started to drool.

My cunt aching with a fury, I pulled away and stroked him, staring up his body while he brushed hair out of my face.

"Don't you want to fuck me, Mill?" I asked, licking the taste of him from my lips.

"Oh, darlin', the first time I fuck you will be in a bed after I've feasted on you for as long as I want," he said, fisting a handful of hair on the back of my head so he could control me again. "Now get back to work. We're running out of daylight."

"Yes, sir," I said. I didn't need to be told twice.

I went back to sucking him, worshipping his cock like I might die without it. I inhaled him deep, relishing his clean musky pinewood scent...and something more, something richer and darker, something distinctly him. But hell, I loved that too. I'd bathe in it if I could. I'd wear it around all day like perfume.

When he got close to his orgasm, he held my head in place and fucked the back of my throat, hard and deep. I breathed through my nose to keep my gag reflex at bay, holding myself open for him, and when he came, he pulled out to stroke himself, spraying hot come across my lips and tongue.

I reveled in his salty-sweet depravity, swallowing down whatever landed in my mouth. I'd hardly been able to lick my lips before he grabbed my chin, held me in place, and leaned down to swipe his tongue across my mouth, kissing me to shove it inside. It was disgusting and obscene and absolutely one of the hottest things anyone had ever done to me.

"You're a good little cocksucker," he said.

"Thank you," I replied with a grin. "No one's ever made me come like that."

"No one? What an honor." He hummed his approval before giving me another kiss and pulling me to my feet. My knees ached, and my toes were numb, but I still managed to wrap my arms around his neck for a full-body hug.

"C'mon," he said, nodding toward the hill. "The sun's going down, and I wanna get you home before the Scorpions figure out where we are."

He grabbed my hand and led me up the side of the cliff, but as we got closer to the top, the harsh smack of reality descended upon us. One where he used to fuck my sister. One was where I was a Vanderbilt heir, and he was a Royal Bastard who worked for my family.

We weren't supposed to blur the lines between us. Sol and Orion aside, things were already complicated. How much more complicated had we just made them? That had been fun, but I feared that's all it would ever be. Fun. A quick break from the real world, one born out of adrenaline and the heat of an overwhelming moment.

He said nothing while we dressed, and neither did I. Maybe he also knew what had to happen next. Maybe he had also realized we shouldn't have done what we did. After I slipped on my shorts and pulled my shirt over my head, I stuffed my feet back into my shoes and started the trek into the woods.

"Maeve," he said, his tone soft and wary.

"It's okay, Mill," I said. "It was just a little fun, a way to blow off steam. It doesn't mean anything." Steeling myself against the dozens of other times this had happened to me, I smiled and nodded toward the trees. "No pressure, okay? No strings. No repercussions."

He nodded but furrowed his eyebrows, suggesting he didn't like that arrangement, even if he hesitantly agreed with it.

He didn't touch me again. Whatever we'd found on the banks of the Blackfoot River stayed there, even as we continued this tenuous dance between us.

Within the next few days, I'd gotten the hang of it. I worked the business side of things and helped Ellen cook dinner after I was done. (She cooked while I learned, and hey, I was getting better every day.) Vermillion came in just after sunset, and we ate like a proper family.

If I squinted just right, I could pretend this was our life. I could pretend we were married, and I played girlboss during the day while he ran the ranch, and at night, he'd whisk me upstairs and make love to me before falling asleep in each other's arms.

Of course, that was just a stupid pipe dream. He flirted with me, true, but our steamy, hot-blooded tryst ended almost as quickly as it began. If it bordered on anything too salacious, Mill excused himself to his room and left me embarrassed, rejected, and alone.

Things came to a raging halt the following Thursday night. My headaches had been getting worse, and the chills wouldn't quit. Admittedly, I thought I was pregnant, but that was impossible when I hadn't slept with anyone in months. My energy was abnormally high, and I didn't have a fever. I blamed it on allergies because I didn't know what else it could be.

"The guys are leaving for the cattle drive the day after tomorrow," Mill said from across the table, biting into his steak. "We need to be on high alert. We'll be less protected."

"Got it," I said. "So no late-afternoon cliff dives."

He smiled, heat passing behind his gaze for only a moment before he shut it down. "And no early-morning rides, unfortunately."

That sucked, but I understood. I hadn't gotten any more unsettling text messages, but that didn't mean Marx had gone away. According to Guin and Mill, he was biding his time, waiting for the moment when we were weakest. I had to stay vigilant.

"I'd like you to start coming with me to the barn," he said. "I can't protect you via text message."

My migraine pounded harder between my eyes, but I ignored it. "And here I thought you liked my selfies?" I sighed dramatically. "So demanding. Fine, Vermillion. I'll start sending you nudes. You only had to ask."

"Maeve, I'm serious," he said with an uncharacteristic blush spotting across his skin.

"Me too," I said. "We're close enough now. It's not unreasonable to ask for such things. I mean, I licked your cum off my—"

"Maeve—"

"Fine," I said. "But I demand topless shower pics in return. No, I won't explain why. Fair is fair."

"Maeve, listen to me," he said in that commanding no-nonsense tone. I was certain he hadn't meant it to be a turn-on, but heat sparked between my legs, and I clutched the tablecloth, remembering when he used the same voice to tell me to drop to my knees and open my mouth.

Stop that, stupid girl. That was a one-time thing, never to be repeated. A momentary lapse of judgment.

"Marx is not someone to let this slide. He *will* come for you, and he won't stop until he gets you." Mill ran his stern gaze over me. "Do you understand?"

"Yes, sir." I nodded and held his demanding stare with a timid one of my own. Of course, this was hardly the time or place for me to reignite filthy notions between us, but God. I had thought about him like that so many times, and the real thing had been infinitely better. And he had imagined it, too. He told me he did. How many times had he dreamt about going down on me? Did he want more? How much more?

Silence stretched between us as we both realized what I'd said.

Yes, sir.

He leaned forward, rested his elbows on the table, and softened his gaze.

"If you send *me* naked pictures of yourself, Maeve, I can assure you, sending you topless shower pics will be the *least* of what I'd do to you in response."

My blood ran hot as I sucked in a cool breath, my eyes widening in realization. This bordered too close to the line we'd drawn between us after that mistake on the river. But if he was game, so was I.

"Oh, yeah?" I bit my bottom lip. "And what *would* you do? Chase me through the woods? Tie me down to your bed and...how did you phrase it? Fuck me after you've feasted on me as long as you want?"

His gaze turned hungry, something dark dancing behind his irises.

"Don't tease me, sweetheart," he said in a low grumble.

"Why?" I licked my lips, and he dropped his focus to the movement before returning to my eyes. "Don't you like to be teased?"

My pulse pounded as I waited for his response, picking up a steady rhythm that thundered through my veins. And then I let the taunting drop as another wave of agony sliced through my head and down my spine. I clutched my chest as my heart banged against my ribs like doldrums, like it was trying to hammer out of my chest.

"I have to lie down."

Vermillion abruptly stood and walked around the table, coming to my side. "What's wrong? Here, I'll help you."

"Yeah, I just... I don't know what's going on." I pushed upright and dug my palms into my eyes as I headed toward the stairs.

Vermillion rushed toward me and grabbed one of my elbows, steadying me while I walked. I wanted to tell him I didn't need his help, I didn't need anyone's help, but having his hands on me again felt nice. It felt safe, like no one or nothing would ever hurt me.

Bring it on, you Bloody Scorpion fuckers. Vermillion will protect me.

When we got to my bedroom, he helped me to my bed, and I sat on the edge, taking a deep breath of his clean, masculine scent mixed with something richer and deeper, the same thing I'd smelled during our brief tryst. It soothed the headache, breaking up the tension with its heady notes and calm, steadying force.

"What can I do? Do you need anything?"

Mill knelt in front of me and slipped my house slippers off my feet, setting them to the right before looking up at me with mesmerizing eyes. Staring down at his big body in between my legs unwound the tension in my lower stomach, making me clench my thighs together to alleviate some of the strain. Being close to him evened out my pulse. It steadied the rhythm in my chest with confusing clarity.

"You're so beautiful," I said, running my knuckles down his cheek, memorizing the dip in his bone structure.

He stared at me like I was imaginary, like I might disintegrate any second.

"You're clearly having a fever hallucination."

I shook my head. "No. I've thought that ever since I've known you."

His features softened. He darted his eyes back and forth between mine, perhaps trying to see if I was lying. I wasn't.

Without thinking about it, I leaned forward and kissed him, chastely at first, simply testing to see if he would accept it. But he moaned and leaned into the touch, and it turned hungry. He opened his mouth, allowing my tongue to press inside, and when it brushed against his, a rush of excitement replaced the trepidation in my bones.

He growled and pushed me on the bed, crawling on top of me, his lips eager for as much as they could get. Like the time at the river, the energy quickly grew untamed, my fingers scraping into his hair as he bit my mouth, yanking and sucking like he wanted to consume as much of me as he could. My cunt clenched, suddenly so insatiable and wanton for more.

I spread my legs so he could settle his pelvis in between them, his body writhing on top of me, mine bucking in response. When I rubbed up against that hard strain in his jeans, I gasped into his mouth, fiery excitement bursting in my blood. I wanted to press myself against him until I came. I wanted him to break me apart and put me back together again, a new woman.

Long forgotten were the aches and pains of whatever sickness this was. He made it better. Being with him, touching him, kissing him made it all disappear. Suddenly, the world ceased to exist, it was just him and me and—

A sharp pain erupted through my lips and down my spine, a sharp metal taste coating my tongue.

Startled, I pulled away from him and touched my mouth. He'd bit me hard enough to draw blood, and I stared at my fingers when they came away crimson and wet.

Every survival instinct I had blared to life, urging me to get away from him as quickly as possible. The dream came back, the one where his eyes turned pitch and he used pointed fangs to tear my throat out, bleeding me dry.

Vermillion's wide eyes and stunned expression should have had me pushing him away. Instead, another instinct took over, more primal and inhuman than anything I'd ever experienced. I pushed my bloody fingers in between his lips as I licked the small wound on my mouth. He focused on the movement, wrapping his tongue around my digits to suck them clean.

Hot, needy arousal shot through me in a delicious display of molecular fireworks, straight down to the ache between my legs. I rocked against his pelvis, rubbing the apex of my pussy against the thick length of his cock. He was so perfect, so muscular and glorious, and I moaned at all the ricochets of nerves coursing through my body.

"Yes," I purred when he lapped at every drop of liquid, and when he went back to my mouth, he sucked the wound, drawing my essence out of me. It stung, but combined with the way he rolled against me, I wanted more. I wanted him to hold me down and—

"No." He snarled and shot off the bed, backing away from me until he was pinned up against the far wall. His eyes seemed to have turned that same dark shade of obsidian from my nightmares, but that must have been his dilated pupils.

"What?" I rushed to sit up, a cold void moving in to replace the vibrant warmth of his body. "What's wrong?"

He clenched his eyes shut, curled his fingers into fists, and shook with the fury of his restraint. He opened his mouth and shut it a few times before ultimately croaking, "I gotta go."

Then, he hustled out of my room and left me alone—shaking, bothered, and confused.

As soon as he shut the door behind him, my headache returned with a vengeance, and I shivered. But the ache between my legs hadn't gone away. No, if anything, it had gotten painstakingly worse. I stared at my ceiling and pressed my palms into my eyes, trying to breathe down the pounding behind them. Minutes ticked by like decades, but eventually, I couldn't stand it anymore.

I grabbed my laptop and vibrator, hoping that buzzing one out might alleviate the body aches. At least it would help me sleep.

The taste of her blood roared in my mouth like the first sip of water after a hard workout. I wanted to tear into her and devour every last drop of it. My wolf howled with delight, egging me on, and if I didn't get off her when I had, I probably would have slaughtered her right there on the mattress.

I *wanted* to. The urge to gorge myself on her still lingered on my tongue as I sat in my room next door, cowering in a corner with my knees to my chest and my hands curled into fists on the floor.

Take her, my inner monster growled. *Consume her. Mark her. Mine. Mine. Mine.*

I grabbed my hair and yanked as hard as I could, using the pain to bring myself back to reality.

Stop it. Stop it. Stop it.

After what happened on the cliff, I told myself I wouldn't touch her anymore. I couldn't. She deserved better than me, better than someone cold and lifeless inside. My monster railed against my restraint, and it had taken everything I had not to pound her into the dirt on the riverbank. Eating her delicious cunt had been enough to sate me, but now...fuck. I wanted so much more than I should.

We were five days out from the full moon, and my urges had

surpassed anything I'd ever lived through. My throat burned. My veins were dried up and shriveled. I could almost hear her heart pounding through the walls, a siren call beckoning me to come back to her, to finish what I'd started.

I pushed to my feet and sulked to the bathroom, turning the shower on as cold as it would go before tripping into it fully clothed. I sat under the spray and focused on my breath until the clawing need in my soul became a dying scream and finally a dull whimper.

Inhale...exhale...inhale...exhale.

When I could think straight again, I stripped out of my soaking clothes and dropped them on the bathroom floor before drying myself off. I dressed in sweats, purposely ignoring the muffled buzzing sound from her room.

Of course, I knew what that was, and I thought about the other night when I'd hacked into her computer to make sure she was okay. Licking my lips and telling myself I wasn't *that* much of a fucking creep, I eyed my laptop across the room.

No. If I did that, I'd cross the imaginary moral boundary I'd set for myself. I'd only done what I did before for her safety...to make sure that she hadn't become dinner for some bloodsucking Scorpion.

How about dinner for a Bastard?

Fuck! I pushed thoughts like those away, trying not to remember what Kodiak had said before I left.

"Fuck, brother. You died. You were brought back to life with magic. You're not an idiot. You know what that sounds like. Are you sucking blood?"

No. It wasn't like that. Not at all.

Morwyn should have let me die. They all should have let me die.

I didn't know what was wrong with me, but it was worse than death. Worse than anything else that could have happened.

My phone vibrated, and I glanced at the name scrolling across the top.

Wyn.

Speak of the devil.

"Shit." I took a deep breath to calm any tremor in my voice and answered. "Yeah?"

"Hello to you, too," she said. "Are you okay?"

"Fine." I came out in the same growl I'd used weeks ago. "What's going on? Is it Caelum? Is he—"

"He's okay," she said. "I'm good, too; thanks for asking."

I smirked. "Now, I know that's a lie. You're probably in your office, scribbling notes and looking at blood samples under a microscope."

She scoffed but didn't deny it, and her uncharacteristic silence told me everything I needed to know.

"You need a vacation," I said. "Tell Kodiak to let you have some time off."

"*You* need a vacation," she threw back. "You're the one whose heart stopped six months ago."

Something rattled in the back of my mind, some kind of recognition that my wolf had picked up and the human hadn't yet connected.

"This can't be why you called," I said. "What's going on? What did you find?"

"Can't a sister check in on her big brother?"

"Wyn." I tried to keep the annoyance from my tone but failed miserably.

"Mill, your blood…it's changing." She sighed. "Shifter cells take longer to decay than humans. Comparatively, we're practically immortal. I call it the magic ratio. Because of our other halves, we live longer, we age more slowly, we regenerate faster."

"Okay," I said, unsure where this was going.

"Two days ago, your blood looked the same as it did after you died." She'd explained this to me at the time. It contained higher amounts of magic, of that mystical essence that separated us from the rest of the world. She had attributed that to the amount of pack magic it took to bring me back from wherever I was. "But now…"

She went quiet.

"Now?" I asked, urging her on.

"Mill, do you feel any different? Are you still...you?"

"Where is this coming from?" I cleared my throat and shifted uncomfortably, perhaps already suspecting what she was about to tell me. "Am I...am I a fucking vampire?"

"No," she said quickly. "Heavens, no. They're diseased. Decayed and rotten. They need blood to regenerate or they'll shrivel up into dust."

"Then, what?" What was she trying to tell me?

Morwyn let out a tired sigh. "I don't know, Mill. It's like your blood is still attached to you, like it's changing as you change."

"I'm not changing," I said, more forcefully than intended. It came out like a roar, and I nearly scared myself. I cleared my throat and tried again. "How is that even possible? You drew it weeks ago."

"I don't know," she said, and I pictured her pinching the bridge of her nose the way our father used to do when he was tired and frustrated. "Look, I have a few theories, but I need to do some more research. Will you promise to let me know if anything happens? If any new symptoms pop up?"

I should have told her about wanting to drain Maeve dry, about going down on her a few days ago and feeling something for the first time in half a year. Hell, for the first time in over a decade.

I could have fucked Maeve into her mattress until the sun rose and set and rose again and still not have my fill of her. I could have sunk my fangs into her jugular and filled my gut with her blood while my cock filled her cunt with my cum. But those were just urges...sick, twisted, impulsive thoughts that had no basis in reality. I'd been able to pull myself away. I'd been able to stop.

Would I next time?

There wouldn't be a next time. No, I'd make sure of that. No more riverside blow jobs. No more bloody lip bites.

No more.

"Sure," I told my sister. "Of course."

"Good." She let out a deep exhale. "I've got to run. One of the cubs fell over a log and needs stitches."

"Okay," I said. "Thanks for checking in."

"Love you, big brother."

"Love you." I hung up and sat on my mattress, the buzzing from Maeve's room now gone. It chafed to know I could have...*should have*...been the one to satisfy her, to bring her whatever release she'd found at the end of a vibrator. But I was no good for her. I didn't know what I wanted, but it bordered too close to hurting her irreparably, and that repulsed both me and the wolf. Fuck, someone like Poe or Columba or any of my other packmates would be a better choice. I'd never be right for her. I'd never be good or whole again.

And yet...despite my reluctance and all the reasons not to, I stood, walked to my laptop, and opened a portal into her computer. She must have fallen asleep watching whatever got her off because the screen was still open and the camera was positioned right at her relaxed form. She looked angelic like that, all soft curves and delicate features. Her dark hair had fallen over her face, and my fingers itched to brush it away.

I closed my eyes and rubbed my palms into my tired lids, telling myself to shut this down and go to bed. It had been a long day, and tomorrow would be even longer. We had a lot to do to prepare the cattle for moving to a different pasture, and that didn't even consider the sheep, hogs, and horses. Still, I took some strange comfort in seeing her and knowing, *truly* knowing, she was safe and alive right there on the other side of the wall.

Telling myself it was part of the job, I also checked the security cameras for the day and any alerts on the motion sensors. Marx and his buddies hadn't shown up again, at least not within the perimeter of our alarms. Maybe we'd have to cast a wider net. Something in my gut told me that motherfucker was lurking out there, waiting for the right moment to strike. He would come during the full moon. He would come when we were at our weakest. He'd attack us like they did twenty years ago, taking as many of us out as they could.

We'd have to be ready. I'd have to talk to Kodiak tomorrow.

After I was sure we were safe, I returned to Maeve's screen. I must have dozed off watching her because I woke up just before dawn the next morning to the sound of my alarm. It took me a moment to realize where I was and why I was there, and when I glanced back at my computer, Maeve was still asleep in her nest of blankets and pillows. She moaned softly and rolled over, mumbling something soft in her sleep.

"Vermillion, come back," she said.

My heart sank, and I tried to remember what I'd been dreaming about. Had I been chasing her through the woods again? Had I held her down while I finished the job this time?

"Fuck," I grumbled, sliding my legs around to the side of the bed.

All of the signs were there, and unlike Orion, I wasn't in fucking denial about this. I couldn't be, not when it was plain as day. She'd been having headaches and body chills. She'd been cooking dinner for the first time in her life. She shoved her bloody fingers in my mouth, practically begging me to do my worst. I knew what this was.

Lycan had been right. She was close to her transition, and hell, the moon was only four days away. It made sense. I picked up my phone to call Guin, but what could she do about it? If she told me to stay away from Maeve and let Fenris or Columba help her through it, would I even listen? I doubted anything could keep me away, not after what we'd done together, not after last night.

I closed my eyes and shook my head. No, we weren't sharing dreams. I had to insist on that. The other stuff pointed to only one conclusion—Maeve was a shifter like her sisters. That wasn't a terrible fate, especially not since she had a dominant shifter to see her through it. But dreams? That would mean something awful, something neither of us would want, especially not her. That was the type of shit reserved for soul mates and bonded lovers, and I wasn't that for her.

Hell, I barely had my life together. Mating me would be the worst thing that could ever happen to her.

More certain of my conclusion, I dialed Kodiak's number and waited for his gruff answer.

"Hey, Mill," he said. "What's going on? More vampire bullshit?"

"No, uh…" I cleared my throat and told him the truth. "She's close. Today, maybe. Tomorrow."

"Fuck," Kodiak said. I could almost picture him rolling his eyes and running a hand over his bald head. "How certain are you?"

"I can smell it," I said. "Fenris can, too. She's got chills and terrible headaches."

I didn't mention the scent mark I was certain I'd left on her last night or the one I'd made her swallow at the river. Kodiak didn't need to know about that.

"Will you help her?" he asked. "Or should I send—"

"No," I cut in. "I'll do it."

"What about the work on the ranch? If you're down for three days, won't that put a damper on production?"

"Fenris can take over. He knows what needs to be done." He'd been lockstep with me for weeks, and he'd grown up on the homestead.

I did have an underlying concern about the impact of whatever was going on with me. What if my blood wasn't good enough? What if dying and coming back to life had changed me so much that I couldn't see her through to the other side of her change? But I was still a shifter, after all. And if Kodiak suspected there would be an issue, he would say something, right?

"Fine," the alpha conceded. "Call me when it's over."

"There's something else," I continued with a relieved sigh. "The moon. Changing leaves us open to attack, and the Scorpions know it."

"I've been working on that." He ran through his plan, including stationing pre-transition and human members of our pack at the border to protect us. "They've all volunteered, and they know what they're up against. It's only important for the ten minutes it takes to shift, and Marx isn't stupid enough to face us while we're in shifter form."

"Do you want me to bring Maeve to the homestead?"

"Stay there," he answered. "I'll send people to you. Protect Vanderbilt Ranch. After she changes, bring her here so I can make her pack."

"What about Guin?" I asked with a smile because I knew how much of a pain in the ass the eldest Vanderbilt had become to the alpha.

He sighed. "Let me handle her."

After we hung up, I showered and dressed for the day, choosing to skip breakfast this morning. I didn't want to have to look her in the eye, knowing I fell asleep watching her last night, and make excuses for why I ran out of there like some prepubescent virgin who'd never felt a girl up before.

I sent her a text.

Me: Check in every thirty minutes or I'll send someone looking for you.

Then, I stalked out of the mansion and across the pasture to the ranchers' bunks, where I came face-to-face with my best friend.

"Morning," he said with a big smile.

"Is everyone up and ready?" I glanced at the slow-moving bodies, some still brushing their teeth.

"What crawled up your ass and made you pissier than usual?" Fenris's smile faded as he took a deep inhale. "Sweet holy shit. You smell like bonding scent."

I ignored him while my inner wolf howled.

"Did something happen last night?" His shit-eating grin made me want to claw his eyes out.

"No," I snapped.

"Oh, just like nothing happened last week, too, huh? Did you take another bike ride with the Vanderbilt princess?" He clapped and hooted.

"Fuck off, Fenris."

"Whatever, dude. I can't wait to see the look on Orion's face when he finds out you're his new brother-in-law."

"It's not like that," I said. "I'm no good for her, and she's too young for me anyway."

He scowled. "Not any younger than Sol, and the mating bond doesn't care about that anyway."

In our world, the magic would pair shifters to their match based on compatibility. Things like age and gender didn't matter. If the magic believed two shifters would make good partners, it would force a bond. Then, it would be up to the animal side to accept it. I'd only heard of a rejected mate once or twice in my life, and in those cases, the shifter either went rabid or ultimately bonded to someone else years later.

"Can we get to work?" I suddenly felt too small for my skin, like I'd burst from the seams any moment and go screaming for the hills.

I sat in meetings with bureaucratic asshats all day, listening as they whined and complained about stock prices. I tried to pay attention, I really did. But the look in Vermillion's eyes when he climbed on top of me last night haunted me. I traced it on a piece of notebook paper while the corporate bootlickers argued among themselves. I was probably supposed to have an opinion about all this, but after the way he left me last night and his subsequent ghost act this morning, my headache had reached an all-time high. I almost took today off. I probably should have.

"Maeve?" came the sound of one of my directors. "Any concerns with moving forward?"

I came off mute to say, "No concerns," and returned to my drawing.

The day crept by at a glacial pace. I checked in with Ava, who was busy living her best Paris life, and I finally got a return call from Guin.

"I asked Mill to watch over you," she said. "It's for the best."

"You could have said something," I replied.

"Oh, so sorry I forgot to tell you my every waking move," she said. "I'm busy running a multimillion-dollar empire here."

I rolled my eyes and sighed.

"How is everything going?" she asked. "Any other signs of the Scorpions?"

"No," I replied and explained Mill's warning. "They're poking at the perimeter, waiting for the right moment to strike. We're playing it safe."

"Good," Guin said. "How are you? How are you feeling?"

"Fine, just stressed. I've had a headache for a few days, and I think I might be getting sick."

Guin stayed silent.

"It's nothing," I continued. "I'm sure I'll be okay in a few days. The ranch is fine. They're moving the cattle out to the far pasture tomorrow and—"

"You'll tell me if you're not feeling better by the day after tomorrow, right?" Guin sounded panicked, and for someone who typically presented a calm and bitchy front, that made me nervous.

"Of course," I said. "Guin, what's going on? I know you and Sol are keeping something from the rest of us."

"We're not," she said. "It's nothing you need to worry about. Just...get some rest, okay? I've got to go."

"No, wait!" But she'd already hung up, and I inhaled deeply to calm myself when I put the phone down.

"That bad, huh?" came a voice from the door to my office.

Startled, I glanced up at the tall, hulking form leaning against the entry. He was nearly as tall as Mill with dark hair and bright blue eyes, almost as light as mine.

"Relax," the man said, holding up his hands. "I'm Fenris. Mill sent me to check in on you. I guess you missed a text?"

"Oh," I grumbled and went back to my laptop. "Right."

"Are you okay?" Fenris pushed upright and crossed his arms, stepping into my office. "You don't look like you're getting assaulted by Scorpions."

"Completely Scorpion-free here." I raised an eyebrow. "Don't you have better things to do than be Vermillion's lackey?"

He snorted and shrugged. "Comes with the territory of being his friend, I'm afraid."

That got my attention. "Oh? I wasn't aware Mill had any friends. He seems like the quiet, loner type."

"He didn't always use to be," Fenris said, wandering around the space while he glanced at the mementos and books on the shelves. "He had a near-death experience about six months ago that stopped his heart. When he came to, he was...*different.*"

"Aren't we all," I said, under my breath, "but you don't see me ghosting people in the cold light of day."

"Ah, so something *did* happen last night." He laughed, which sparked some nascent hint of joy in my chest. "That explains his extra surly attitude this morning."

"No," I said, quickly realizing my mistake. "Nothing happened. I'm just a stupid, silly girl."

"Hmm." Fenris raised his eyebrows and walked back toward the door. "Well, seeing as you're still alive and in one piece, I'll head back to work. But do us both a favor and check in with him. He gets all agitated when you don't."

I shook my head. "I doubt he cares that much about me."

"More than he would ever admit," Fenris said before turning back to face me like an idea had suddenly occurred to him. "I can prove it to you."

I raised an eyebrow. "What? How?"

He flashed a devil's grin, mischief shimmering behind his eyes. "There's a party tonight at the ranchers' quarters. Stop by, and I'll show you."

"A party?" I didn't know if I was in the mood for a party, and it always dampened the mood when the boss tried to hang out with the workers.

Fenris nodded. "Yeah. It would be nice for the guys to see you. Maybe get to know you a little."

"I doubt Mill will be okay with that."

Fenris shrugged. "Who cares what he thinks?"

I hummed and remembered the sounds I'd heard from my balcony every few nights for the past three weeks. More than once, I'd almost put on my boots to crash it but decided against it because I didn't want to ruin their good time.

"I mean, it's your house," Fenris continued. "Your property. You hardly need an invite."

I shook my head. "I would never intrude on the ranchers' territory. I know I'm hardly welcomed."

"You're not intruding." Fenris furrowed his brows. "It'll be good for them...and for you."

"Are you sure?" I was still skeptical.

Fenris's smile widened. "Positive. Besides, we're family now. It's time we start acting like it."

I guessed that made sense. "Okay."

He gave me a friendly smile and a wink before turning to leave, shouting over his shoulder, "Text that bully, or I'll have to drag my sorry ass back up here."

After the door shut downstairs, I glanced at my phone and pulled up Vermillion's name. He'd given me the command this morning, and I'd only sent him one thumbs-up since. Now, I sent him an emoji with the eyebrow raised, suggesting I didn't enjoy being babysat.

He didn't respond.

I didn't forget about Fenris's invitation, and when Vermillion didn't show up for dinner, I pushed my food around my plate and made up my mind. We *were* family now, and it *was* time we started acting like it, so I went upstairs to put on my sluttiest pair of cut-off jeans and a white tank top. I stuffed my feet into cowboy boots and took my time doing my makeup.

By the time I was done, I looked hot. My headache had subsided enough that I figured it must have been allergies, so I grabbed a bottle of my father's most expensive scotch and headed across the backyard. Sounds of a party in full swing echoed from the windows, and when I knocked on the door, I fully expected whoever answered to tell me to fuck off. But when Fenris opened it with a big grin, he stepped aside and nodded.

"Glad you could make it," he said. "Is that Lagavulin?"

"Yep," I said, glancing around the space. Bunks lined the walls, one in front of me and two in the corner to my right. A kitchen area was in between the entrance and more bunk space in the back, and I rounded the corner to a central hangout spot with a card table set up in the middle and two long couches on either side. A flatscreen sat on top of a console at the far end of the wall, currently playing an old black-and-white movie. The conversation stopped when I got close enough, all eyes shooting in my direction.

Vermillion turned his head, my skin burning as he gazed down my body and back up again.

"Hey, now," Fenris said, pushing past me to take the empty seat next to Mill. "Y'all said you wouldn't deal until I got back."

The brunette opposite Vermillion raised an eyebrow at me. "Well, don't just stand there. If that's whiskey, get the shots going."

"It's scotch," I said, stepping toward them. Seven other men lingered around, three at the table and four more on the couches.

"Yeah, you uncultured swine," Fenris said, rubbing a hand over the brunette's mop of dark hair. "That's a sipping drink, not a shooting drink."

"It was my father's favorite." I snorted. "He was such a dick, and now he's dead. So I guess you can do whatever you want with it."

Everyone fell silent for a second before Fenris burst into laughter, causing the others to crack up as well. All except Mill, who had gone back to looking at everyone and everything except me.

"This is Columba," Fenris said, gesturing to the brunette.

"I'm Aquila," said the other person at the card table, a big man with hair the same color as Columba. They looked like they could be brothers.

"Poe," said the last person at the table. "I was at the cabin with your sister last winter."

"Right." Sol had said he was standoffish at first, but he became one of her favorite people. They were still close.

"This is Holden, Ricky, Travers, and Smalls." Fenris pointed to the guys sitting on the couches, who gave me a wave or a small salute.

I looked at the cards on the table. "What are we playing?"

"Hold'em," Poe said. "Twenty-dollar buy-in."

I loved poker. I remembered playing with my siblings during long summers, stuck here on the ranch. Being smack dab in the middle of the lineup meant I'd gotten good at swindling my siblings on either side out of their money.

"Can I play?" I walked to the table, grabbed an empty chair from the side, and pulled up next to Mill.

"Our table's full," he grumbled.

"Nonsense." Completely ignoring him, I reached into my pocket, grabbed a random bundle of cash, and plopped it down in the middle of the table. "Twenty dollars. Deal me in."

"Woo!" Fenris laughed and clapped Vermillion on the shoulder. "I like your style, Vanderbilt."

Smiling as I sat, I pretended the rush of being so close to the man who'd worked me up last night didn't affect me. His masculine scent hit me in the face, and it meant nothing. The warmth radiating off his body coiled around me, yanking me closer, and that, too, meant nothing. This preternatural pull in my gut, tugging me to him, was just a game. A farce.

He didn't want me.

Hell, more than that, I repulsed him, and there was proof. The minute I sat down and grabbed the tiny red cups to pour each of us a scotch, Vermillion scooted away from me. When I handed one to him, he grabbed it by the rim and set it on the table in front of him. And when I held mine up to say cheers and thanks for letting me crash their guys' night, he barely touched mine before downing his entire drink and getting back to the game.

"Aquila," Mill said. "Deal the cards."

The younger man did as commanded, and I sipped my scotch,

delighting in the burn that echoed down my throat and into my stomach. I hadn't eaten much today, so it hit me much harder than I thought. But I could see why my father liked it so much. This was as smooth as honey compared to the swill coming out of Kentucky.

Two cards landed in front of me, and I glanced at them, trying not to let my expression show how dismal I thought my odds were.

"So Vanderbilt," Columba said. "What brings you down to the trenches?"

I shrugged. "Fenris invited me."

Mill snapped his tumultuous gaze to his friend. "Did he?"

"Yeah, but I'd been thinking about crashing for a few weeks," I said. "Sol's gone. Ava's in Paris. Guin is off doing whatever it is she does. It's lonely in that big stupid house with no one else there."

"Poor you, huh?" Aquila said. "Must be rough, having all that money and no one to share it with."

"Hey!" Fenris cut in, smacking him on the shoulder. "Be nice or I'll have you shucking shit tomorrow."

Aquila lifted a pack of cigarettes to his mouth, bit into one, and lit it, inhaling before letting the smoke out on a sigh.

But I'd never let a taunt like that go unanswered. Perhaps it was this new wild side that Mill had awakened in me, or maybe I wanted to show them I wasn't afraid of them.

"Yeah, you know what? It is," I said. "But you get it, right? Must be rough for you, too. All those muscles and not a single brain cell to back them up."

Fenris balked and Mill straightened, but Columba laughed and gripped Aquila's shoulder.

"She fucking burned you, brother," Columba said. "Now say you're sorry and laugh at her joke."

Aquila chuckled and shook his head. "Alright. Sorry, Vanderbilt. Old prejudices die hard and all that."

"Hey, I get it," I said. "I'm literally sitting in a room full of Bastards. I thought you all were bloodthirsty monsters up until six months ago."

"Well," Columba added with a wink, "only on the full moon."

I giggled at his joke, and the night carried on with jovial conversation. Fenris won the first round, and Poe won the second, and by the time we were halfway through the bottle of scotch, both Columba and Aquila had lost all their money. But this hand...oh, this hand was going to me. I had a full house, and unless someone else had gotten incredibly lucky, no one had anything better.

"There!" Fenris flipped his cards over, revealing three of a kind. "Pay up, bitches!"

"Ugh, I got nothing," Poe said, pushing his cards toward the center of the table.

"Me neither," Mill grumbled.

"Aww, poor grumpy gills," I said, pouting at the guy on my right. "But it's okay. Because your money is mine." I flipped my cards over and reveled in how Fenris's features dropped.

"What? No!" He balked and widened his eyes at me. "You cheated!"

"I would never!" I pretended to be offended while I gathered my chips and stacked them in front of me. "You accuse me of this deception in my own house? In my own house?"

Mill laughed and sipped more scotch while Poe grumbled and rubbed his hands over his face.

"I'm out, guys," he said, pushing to his feet. "I'm broke and, between you and Vanderbilt, I'm a lost cause."

Suddenly, a song on the radio got the guys' attention.

"Hey, turn that up," Aquila said, wrapping an arm over Columba's shoulders while he started singing the bluesy country song at the top of his lungs.

"One more round?" I raised an eyebrow at the two men left sitting with me. "All or nothing?"

"Sure," Mill said, finally lowering himself to look at me with unfiltered heat. It must have been the alcohol. "Anything for you, sweetheart."

"Yeah, I'm in," Fenris said, drawing my attention back to him. He glanced between Mill and me before shuffling the cards and dealing them out. The liquor had gone to my head, making me woozy and warm and almost completely uninhibited. Mill drank the last little bit of scotch in his cup, and a drop spilled out of the side of his mouth, dribbling down his chin. I licked my lips, praying for the courage to lean in and lick it off myself. He looked down at me, and maybe he could read the urge in my gaze because he smirked and leaned closer.

"What are you thinking about?"

I bit my bottom lip between my teeth, rubbing over the tiny cut he'd made yesterday. "Nothing good."

"Alright, you two," Fenris said. "Since it's all or nothing, there are no blinds or calls. We're going right to the river." He flipped all five cards in the center of the table. "Reveal your hands."

Disappointingly, I had nothing. I flipped my cards over and pretended to pout. "Not my lucky day after all."

"I've got two pair," Fenris said. "What about you, Mill?"

"Flush," he said, smiling like the cat who'd absconded with the cream.

"Wow, you lucky son of a bitch." Fenris shook his head and gathered the cards, glancing at me with squinted eyes and a smirk. "Can you believe this guy? Death, Texas Hold'em, nothing beats him. Practically fucking Rasputin."

I sighed and held out a hand for Vermillion to take. "Good game."

He glanced at it before meeting my gaze again, gingerly taking my palm. "Good game, Maeve."

I tried to stand, deciding I wanted to join the guys in their sing-along, but Mill held on to my palm, placing his other one on top. He furrowed his brows like something was wrong.

"How are you feeling?"

"Tipsy," I said. "And rowdy. Now, if you'll excuse me." I tugged away from him and grabbed a beer from the fridge before standing next to Poe, who sang the Garth Brooks song at the top of his lungs. My older brothers used to listen to this, so the lyrics came to me from the depths of my subconscious. Our voices were off-tune and our words slurred, but it was the lightest I'd felt in a long time.

Here, in this den of cow shit and testosterone, it didn't matter what my last name was or where I grew up. It didn't matter who I'd been the day before or who had run out of my bed in disgust. We had shared a bottle of liquor and alleviated our troubles in each other's company, and wasn't that the point? Whether we had friends in low places or no friends at all, we had this one moment, this one night, together.

Poe put his arm over my shoulder, and Columba held me around the waist, and together, in one drunken entourage, we sang our stupid little hearts out to an endless night sky.

"Y ou've got a problem," Fenris said, nodding toward Maeve as she sang and swayed between Columba and Poe.

I nursed my beer. "Oh?"

"Oh's right." Fenris blew out a breath. "I could smell it the second I walked into the mansion."

I cracked my neck and straightened my shoulders, pretending I didn't know what he was talking about.

"She smells like shifter," he continued. "She smells like *you*."

Fuck.

I knew I released a bonding scent last night in her room, but I didn't think it would have lasted this long. He, of course, was right. I smelled it from here.

"She's got something carnal in her eyes." He shook his head. "She's close, brother. Real close."

"I know." I groaned and pinched the bridge of my nose before rubbing a hand over my face.

"Are you planning to—"

The glare I gave him shut him up. I'd already promised Kodiak I would, and even if I hadn't, my wolf wouldn't let me leave her alone. He wanted to give her the magic in my body and watch her transition into what she was truly meant to be. A small part of me was concerned about this new thirst for her blood, but I prayed the transition magic would keep me in line and prevent me from doing anything stupid.

"If you don't, you've got four other wolves here that will."

A low growl rumbled from my chest, and my fangs extended, my inner beast surging to the forefront.

Fenris let out a loud, mocking laugh and grabbed my shoulder. "You can't let her suffer alone. Poe went through the transition by himself. It nearly killed him, and he's a dominant. A submissive little thing like Maeve—"

"You think I don't fucking know that?" I snarled and glared at my buddy, malice radiating from my pores.

Fenris put his hands out to either side in a gesture of peace. "Brother, I'm just saying." He pointed to Maeve with his beer. "That female is exploding with pheromones. I can practically see it wafting off her. Those young shifters?" He blew out a teasing breath. "They're very male, and it's been a long three weeks up here on the ranch. The promise of a few days in a bed with her would make any of them feral."

The image of Columba, Aquila, and Poe taking turns with her churned through my mind, and my heart pumped erratically, sending raging fury through my veins. Neither I nor my wolf could stand the thought of it. I wouldn't let them touch her. I wouldn't let them anywhere near her.

Her sweet floral scent drifted over to me, enchanting and enticing, making my mouth water and my fingers tingle for the feel of her soft delicate skin. Resisting the urge to sweep her up and take her back to her room nearly brought me to my knees.

Take her. Claim her. Bite her. Mine.

My animal side hadn't stopped since I'd licked blood off her fingers, and now that I knew she'd likely go into her transition soon, I wanted to give in to those exciting demands.

We'd have so much fun with her, my wolf said. *We'll keep her forever.*

"I need some air." I turned away and stormed outside, bursting into the cool summer night. Fresh oxygen coated my tongue, slipping down my throat into my lungs, washing away her scent. I ran my hands back through my hair again, leaning against the side of the house as I struggled to maintain control of my inner beast.

Memories of taking her at the cliffside came back to my mind, how she'd gripped my hair, how delicious she'd tasted, how she responded to my touch. The sight of her climaxing on my tongue would stay with me for the rest of my life, and when she put me in her mouth and sucked me dry, I didn't think there was a greater pleasure on earth.

And all of it was a mistake. She'd said so herself. Just a one-time fling, done in the heat of the moment.

I struggled to understand how I had let it get that far in the first place. The alpha had said not to touch her. Hell, even Guin had threatened to rip my heart out if anything happened to her. There was only one thing more powerful than the alpha's word: when one's mate was involved. It was the way the species protected itself. I couldn't override the alpha's command, but if my mate was compromised, if my mate demanded something of me, the alpha could go fuck himself. That I'd ignored it, that I'd put my paws where they didn't belong last week and almost again last night—

No.

There was no way Maeve was my mate. Fuck, the girl hadn't even gone through her transition yet. She didn't know who or what she was, and after that was over, she deserved the time to understand her new life. She didn't need to be tied down to someone as despicable and rotten as me. I mean, hell. I'd wanted to *drink her fucking blood.* Like a Goddamned vampire. Like one of those fucking bloodsuckers we spent our lives tracking down. I'd died and come back to life as something unnatural and wretched.

I should go inside and beg Fenris to tear my head off, to drag me out into the woods and give me an Ole Yeller.

They should have let me die.

The door opened, and a mouthwatering scent of caramel and midnight dew preceded Maeve as she walked outside, laughing and yelling at someone behind her.

"Don't be such a brute, Columba," she said. Then she paused when she saw me and raised an eyebrow, slowly shutting the door behind her. "What are you doing out here all by your lonesy?"

She put her hands in the back pockets of those incredibly short cut-offs, her boots click-clacking across the wood of the tiny porch. Her skin seemed softer against her white tank top, her hair darker, her eyes brighter. The moonlight made them glow, and if I wasn't sure that her transition would hit her soon, I could have sworn she was already a shifter.

"Listening to the night," I said.

Cicadas and frogs sang loudly from the tree line, accenting the wind and squirrels and other members of the nocturnal orchestra. They grew louder with each step she took closer to me, as if they could sense the tension between us, and they, too, waited for it to boil over.

"Oh, yeah?" She bit her bottom lip between her teeth, and my focus dropped to that tiny cut, the one I'd made yesterday, the mark I'd left on her to let all those young shifters know she belonged to me.

Except she doesn't, and she never will.

"What's the night saying?" She tilted her head and moved closer, placing a hand on the porch railing so she could lean to the side.

"Nothing good," I said, sipping my beer.

She grabbed it from my hand and tilted it over her lips for a drink before placing it on the railing.

"You've been avoiding me." She moved to stand in front of me, clasping her hands behind her back so her chest arched out. "Was the kiss really that bad?"

"What?" I balked. "No."

"Then, why did you run out of there so quickly?" She raised an eyebrow. "Sorry about the blood thing. I don't know why I did that."

I gulped, the memory of her delicious taste making me salivate. "It's fine."

Maeve looked up at me, a hint of hope and playfulness in her gaze. "Fine?"

"I mean..." I winced and shook my head. "Maeve, I'm not good for you. If you knew me...the real me...you'd run away screaming."

"Do you want me to run from you?" Her teasing intonation and sparkling eyes set off the best kind of alarm bells in my mind. My wolf sat up at attention, howling and yipping.

Yes, he said. *Yes, run. Chase. Yes!*

"No."

She came closer, forcing me to spread my legs wider so she could move in between them. Now inches away, she peered up my torso with an adorable, beguiling grin, like she knew what I'd been dreaming about, had been dreaming about it herself. The inches between us sizzled with anticipation, crackling with how much I wanted to close them.

"What if I wanted to run from you?" she murmured. "What if I wanted you to chase me until you caught me and held me down while you took what you wanted?"

Fucking hell.

The mental image alone was enough to keep me hard for a month, and an electric shock of arousal ricocheted down my spine and into my balls. I *wanted* that more than I'd ever wanted anything in my life. For the first time in years...*literal years*...I lusted after a female with passionate abandon.

Maybe she read this in my eyes because she hooked her fingers into the belt loops of my jeans and pulled my hips forward, connecting my pelvis to hers.

"You're no good for me, Mill?" She scoffed. "I'm no good for you, either. But maybe we could be no good together for a little while and see where it goes."

Ohhh, what a tease. But I knew better. If I took her the way she wanted me to, if I let myself give in to it, I wouldn't be able to stop. She deserved better, that much was true, but there was more happening here than she knew about. She would transition, and fuck me, but I would help her through it because I didn't want anyone else to. And if we were bound to end up there anyway, what the hell was I waiting for?

"You enjoyed yourself at the cliffside; I know you did," she said. "And you told me you'd fuck me in my bed and taste me until you'd had your fill. Have you already gotten it? Your fill?"

The decadent feminine scent of her arousal plumed around me, pulling me under its spell, and the more I resisted, the more it yanked. I could give in. I could let it sweep me out to sea, releasing these years of pent-up sexual frustration. But I was terrified of what that meant. Four days from the moon, and I was clawing out of my skin. I wanted and I yearned and I...

Get your shit together, Vermillion.

She lost patience with me before I could give in and stepped back with a despondent smile and sad eyes. "Okay, Mill. I get the message, loud and clear."

My heart dropped as she turned and headed back into the house, closing the door behind her with a soft click.

Fuck!

What was wrong with me? If I wanted the female, I should take her. Now. While she could still say she wanted me back. The whiplash of swinging from knowing I shouldn't have her to being unable to resist her had my soul in shambles. I ran my hands over my face and took a deep breath before walking back into the cabin, steeling myself against the sight.

Fenris had one arm wrapped around Maeve's waist, the other holding her free hand up by their shoulders. She laughed as he spun her around, his movements crisp and clean, hers clumsy with mirth and alcohol. He leaned into her ear and whispered something that made her smile, such a quick reversal from the pout I'd gotten outside.

Last night, I'd made her grin like that. And last week, she looked at *me* with those fucking eyes and told me she wanted me.

This was the animal in her, trying to break loose. If I didn't give her what she needed, she'd find it from someone else. Even my best friend. Hell, out of all the monsters in this fucking place, he would be her next best bet—second only to me.

He slid his fingertips up the column of her spine, swaying her around to the beat of the slow music blaring over the radio. A hot wave of something dark and territorial flooded my veins, cascading from my chest down into my gut and fingers. I wanted to tear Fenris's head from his shoulders. I wanted to rip his hands off for touching her.

Fenris lifted his gaze to mine and raised an eyebrow.

I knew what he was doing, and fuck me for being such a stupid shit, but it was working.

I stalked over to the radio, slammed the power button, and glared at the two of them as they startled and glanced back at me.

"Party's over," I snarled, looking to the Vanderbilt. "Go home, Maeve."

"Mill," Fenris said. "Come on, buddy."

"No, it's okay." Maeve nodded and glanced around. "Thank you for the good time."

She walked toward the front door, brushing me with her shoulder as she passed. That one touch did me in. My beast yelped at the connection, electricity, and three weeks' worth of tension exploding. The door closed behind her. I glared at my best friend, sent a wave of *back off* down the pack bond, and turned to go after her.

By the time I stepped off the front porch, Maeve was a hundred yards ahead of me. She stalked across the backyard toward her house with her arms wrapped around her midsection, and I followed behind her like the obsessed psycho I was. Gods, what a fucking nightmare. I'd rejected her, pushed her away, and two minutes later gotten jealous that someone else had swooped in. My wolf cared about none of that. He simply wanted her and couldn't understand the human's reluctance.

When I got close enough for her to hear my footsteps, she rounded on me, her eyes blazing, her hands clamped into fists at her sides.

"What the hell is wrong with you?" She shoved my shoulders as hard as she could, but I outweighed her by at least a hundred pounds, so I barely moved.

"You know what he was doing." The words came out clipped and angry, almost as a roar.

"Of course." Maeve tilted her face to mine, staring me down, refusing to break eye contact. In my world, that meant a fight for dominance, but my wolf understood it as something else...something the human wouldn't put a name on. "But what business is it of yours? You want me, you don't want me. You eat me out, let me suck you off, you pretend it didn't happen. You kiss me, you ghost me. You flirt with me, you reject me. Make up your mind."

"I want you," I growled, surprised the words had come out. I shouldn't have confessed it, but we were well past insecurities now. I stepped closer to her, invading her space, towering over her. Despite how much she stood up to me, she seemed so small in comparison. "But I shouldn't."

"Says who?" Maeve waited for a response, but when I didn't continue, she rolled her eyes and scoffed, turning away again. I grabbed her wrist to stop her, whipping her back to face me.

My merciless half finally yanked free of its restraints, coming to the forefront of my willpower. I couldn't fight him anymore. I couldn't fight *this* anymore. Wrapping my hand around the back of her neck, I crashed my lips to hers, relishing in the surprised and satisfied moan that poured out of her mouth into mine. I swallowed it down, emboldened by it, aching to consume everything she'd let me have.

This was a dangerous game. Even now, I hungered for every last drop of her. The primal side of me called to something dark and powerful inside her, and I wanted to consume it, feast on it, let it live inside me forever, intertwined with my own depraved wickedness.

She melted under my touch, wrapping her hands in my hair, pressing her body firmly against mine. Just when I thought I had her, that we'd both finally succumb to the clawing thing between us, she pushed away from me and squared her jaw.

"No, you don't get it that easily," she said, voice trembling. "If you want me, you have to work for it."

I furrowed my brows, confused about what she meant, until she grinned and took off toward the cabin in a dead sprint. My heart nearly stopped (again), and I gave her exactly five seconds before I went after her. I knew what she wanted. This was part of the game, *our* game, the one I dreamt about for weeks.

I didn't want her to get too far ahead. There *were* vampires hiding out in the woods somewhere, but the thrill of the chase took me over. Her lovely scent left a trail for me to follow, and the sound of her feet on the grass amped up my excitement.

The beast inside me howled with delight as I pumped my legs to reach her. But I didn't want to make the game too easy. I let her think she had a lead as she veered toward the pastures.

The nighttime chorus grew louder, the frogs cheering us on, the crickets humming in approval. She howled at the nearly full moon, and I sprinted faster, my heart racing, my blood soaring. Joy filled my soul, the long-lost sensation of happiness overtaking both me and my wolf. It had been eons since the warm sparks of play had trickled through my veins, and I didn't know why I'd closed myself off to it.

Then again, I couldn't do this with anyone else. Maeve had a certain energy to her that complemented the void inside me. She was Persephone, the Goddess of spring and the queen of hell, bright and shining and ominous simultaneously. And I was the king of darkness, presiding over a paradise of death.

She vaulted over a fence, and I went after her, capturing her just as she landed. I took her down to the ground, rolling her onto her back, pinning her wrists above her head as I situated myself between her legs.

"The night is dangerous," I said. "You never know what could be lurking in the shadows."

She groaned and tried to break free. I held her tighter. "I like it when you chase me. I like when you catch me."

The words jogged a memory of a dream from a few weeks ago, right after I'd started working here.

"Don't tease the wolf, baby. You won't like what happens to you." It was the same reply I'd given her then.

She squinted at me, seemingly confused for a moment. "Are you going to bite me?"

Enough.

The call of her scent and her blood enticed me in ways I couldn't explain. My wolf knew what was happening, even if the male pushed back against the idea entirely. Mating her would be a terrible idea for a million different reasons, but a shifter couldn't always help it. What if...What if it was really happening? What if it had been happening all this time?

The scotch and the beer and the thrill of the night had caught up to me, and I shoved dangerous thoughts like that away. I leaned down and kissed her softly before pushing to my feet and taking her with me. When we were both standing, I lifted her into my arms, one under her shoulders, the other under her knees, and I carried her back toward my cabin since it was closer than the mansion, the smell of her heavenly scent buried deep in my nose.

By the time we got to his quarters, my body sang with the intimacy of being so close to him. Heat flooded my veins, the enticing blend of his arms around me combined with the gentle way he held me, and I trembled with anticipation.

The small house wasn't much more than a living room, kitchen, and bedroom, but I recognized the signs of him here. In the weeks since he'd moved in, he'd hung his hats up on the rack by the door, and one of his flannels lay across the back of the sofa.

He carried me to the room in the back, where he set me down on the bed and stood to kick off his boots. I did the same with mine, leaning back to unbutton my shorts and slide down the zipper. After I peeled them off my legs, I yanked up my shirt, struggling to get it over my head. Laughing, he leaned down to help me, brushing the hair out of my face afterward. He held my jaw in his massive calloused hands, and I let my gaze wander over his sculpted body.

Standing in only his boxers, he looked like a statue. His defined pecs gave way to shoulders and ab muscles that spoke of the manual labor he did daily. He had a deep scar on his neck that I hadn't noticed until now, and one on his lower stomach, disappearing into his Adonis belt. I traced over them and wondered how they'd happened. Had this been from when he'd died trying to save a pack-mate? Would he tell me even if I asked?

I glided my fingers along the top of his boxers, the erection behind the fabric protruding and nearly bouncing out at me. I licked my lips and lowered my hand, but he caught my wrist.

"No," he murmured, leaning down to kiss me. "You've had a lot to drink."

I balked. "So? I want this. I've wanted this for years."

He breathed out a soft laugh and shook his head. "You can't say things like that to me."

"Why not?" I nudged his forehead with mine. "The first time I ever masturbated, I thought of you."

He glanced back up at me, eyes seeming to glow with the weight of my confession. Or perhaps that was the moonlight drifting in through the windows. It would be full in only a few days, so it radiated with a proud bright illumination that lit us both beautifully.

"I know you heard me the other night," I said, rolling my hips against him, connecting me to his massive hard erection. He groaned and dropped his head, rocking his pelvis against mine. Pleasure burned through my molecules, amping up my excitement, causing more uninhibited words to tumble out of my mouth. "I was thinking about you then, too."

"Baby, you're killing me," he said, continuing to grind his cock against my clit.

I moaned, and he caught it in his mouth, licking my lips as if the sound tasted like ambrosia. He kissed my jaw and down my throat, alternating between sucking and nibbling my skin. I couldn't stand it, and I tilted my head to the side, granting him more access. I wanted him to bite me harder, to mark me, to show the world I belonged to him in every way imaginable, even if I didn't understand where that impulse had come from. When my hands drifted toward his boxers again, he grabbed my wrists and held them above my head.

"If you stay just like this, I'll get you off," he murmured. "Can you be a good girl?"

I quickly nodded, forcing myself to stay in place while he drifted down my body, teasing me with his mouth, sampling my skin like I was an amuse-bouche he had all night to try. When he got to my breasts, he glanced up at me, seeming to ask if it was okay.

Nodding, I arched my back, bringing them closer to his face. He pulled down the cup of my bra and lapped over my nipple, and oh, the inferno inside me grew to scalding. I burned everywhere, not just where he touched. My skin burst into flames.

"Please. More," I whimpered.

I didn't know what was happening. I'd had lovers do this to me before, certainly, but this was more intense. Lightning shot across my skin, burrowing under my muscles, electrifying my bones. My heart raced, beating against my ribs like a hammer. I couldn't think straight, and not just because of the alcohol, although that didn't help.

No, something else had taken over, something new and savage.

"Baby, you're burning up." He went to the other breast, giving it the same torturous attention, sending a rush of passion straight to the junction between my legs. "Are you sure you're okay?"

I writhed under him, trying to put more pressure between us. I wanted his cock inside me. No, I *needed* his cock inside me, and the urge became so overwhelming, I'd combust if it didn't happen. "Please, Mill. Please."

He continued his descent down my body, kissing my stomach, tucking his fingers under the waistband of my underwear, dragging them down my legs and off my feet. Then he sat back on his haunches and stared at me, his hands on his knees, his cheeks flushed with excitement. I pushed up on my elbows and watched as his gaze traveled down my body and back up again.

A small part of me grew self-conscious under his scrutiny, but this new side, the frenzied beast he'd unleashed in the woods, wouldn't let me shrink away. I preened for him, arching back, relishing in his predatory stare. He was the Mill from my dreams manifested. He was the monster hunting me down, staring at me like he wanted to eat me whole.

"I like you like this." I ran my foot up the center of his torso, stopping when I got to his shoulder so I could open my knees wider, giving him a better view. "Possessive. Unrestrained. Almost... hungry."

"Absolutely starving." He grinned and licked his lips, and I melted. He grabbed my ankle and kissed the inside of my calf, slowly working his way down my leg to my knee and the inside of my thigh. Every muscle shook, the weight of this reality finally taking its toll. After our brief rendezvous at the cliff, I never had any reason to think it would happen again. I thought it was just a fling, something he'd done to pass the time.

Now, I reveled in the truth: he wanted me. I wanted him. And nothing anyone could do would stop it. He took his time tasting me, kissing and worshipping the skin around my pussy, the inside of my thighs, the juncture at my hip bones, teasing me, drawing it out.

Something broke loose inside me, some previously fortified dam that finally crumbled under the stress of prolonged exposure. I bucked my pelvis toward him.

"Please," I groaned, and the word came out lower and more demanding than I'd meant it, but Mill didn't care. He placed his forearm over my hips, pinned me down, and speared through my skin with his tongue, lapping at my overheated skin.

"I told you last time that I planned to take my time," he said. "I meant it. Hold still. Be good."

The moan that poured over my lips came from the depths of my soul, and I relaxed against the mattress, curling into myself from the euphoria. This was beyond pleasure, even more intense than last week. This was sinful rapture. This was seventeen agonizing years culminating in one mind-blowing moment.

He nuzzled against me, sucking my clit like he was ravenous, like he couldn't get enough of me. I tunneled my fingers into his hair, panting against the sensations in my blood. My world spun around me, but none of that mattered anymore because something mystical was happening, something I couldn't explain.

My body burned, my skin shrank, and my blood boiled. The headache tormenting me for days now seemed close to nuclear, and as my ecstasy grew more intense, a new sensation took hold. That barbaric, animalistic part latched onto my heart and squeezed, surging up from deep down inside me.

I wanted to fight it, but I didn't have a choice.

"Mill," I managed to mutter, but he only intensified his ministrations, fucking me harder with his face, reaching up my body to massage one breast...and then the other. This added to the brutal outburst like a geyser at its breaking point, like a volcano pluming smoke in warning of its inevitable eruption. This was more than drunken sex with a man who had been such a massive part of my sexual awakening. This ran deeper, twisting around my soul, yanking something out of me that roared with ferocity.

I clenched my eyes shut and curled my fingers into fists around the blankets. My cunt seized with emptiness, painful in its want of Mill to fill it. It didn't make sense, but logic seemed to have no place here anymore.

My body screamed. I needed and I longed and I *wanted.* I yearned for *him* in ways I couldn't understand.

"Vermillion," I whined, clenching my legs together when the pain became too much. I was boiling, like every part of my skin had been singed, like I had a fever I might never come down from. The only person in the world who could help me was him. The only person in the world I wanted was him. "Please. Please make me come."

He sucked me harder, worked me faster, stuck one...then two fingers inside me to tip me over the edge. As my climax reached its pinnacle, all of my muscles seized, and anguished euphoria rushed through my veins. This wasn't like last time, not at all. This was worse and infinitely better. The world had shifted on its axis, righting all of the wrongs that had ever happened. My pulse thundered, my breathing came in sharp, heavy pants, and when I crashed back into my body, Mill looked up at me from between my legs with the most satisfied smile I'd ever seen.

"How you feeling, sweetheart?" he asked before crawling up my body to kiss me softly.

I hummed into the contact and reached between us, cupping his cock, ravenous to return the favor. He grabbed my wrist to stop me.

"No," he said. "I'm good."

"What?" I didn't like the sound of that. If he got to taste me, I wanted to taste him. "C'mon. You let me last time."

He chuckled and shook his head. "This was about you. Not me."

I pouted. "But I want to."

"Shh." He lay down next to me and wrapped an arm under my shoulders, tugging me close. The headache plaguing me for the last few days had subsided, and my body aches dulled to a tiny whimper. Whatever had been about to be unleashed in my molecules seemed to have dissipated, but a nervous energy still hummed in my blood like it might reappear before too long. "Go to sleep, darlin'. We have lots of time to play."

"Promise you won't leave me?"

"I won't leave you."

The confirmation made me relax. We fell silent, lying together in the simple comfort of a warm bed and a tight embrace. His heart beat steadily under my head, and in the aftermath of the night, it was the most beautiful sound I'd ever heard.

"Mill." I glanced up at him and grinned. "Thank you."

He narrowed his eyes but smiled and kissed my forehead. "Thank *you*, Maeve."

I closed my eyes, and unconsciousness pulled me under.

She didn't need to know I'd come in my boxers while going down on her, that tasting her had been as close to heaven as I'd ever come, even better the second time when I didn't have to worry about Scorpions breaking through the tree line.

Hell, seventeen years ago, I would have never thought I'd have Maeve Vanderbilt in my bed. Our twelve-year age gap would have been enough of a turnoff alone. But now, I regretted all the years I'd spent thinking she was too young for me, that I'd be better off on my own. I lamented leaving her last night and pretending what happened at the cliff was a mere hookup.

Holding her while she slept brought me a new level of peace I hadn't realized I would ever experience. Her features softened, and she breathed heavily. Knowing I had her in my arms, that I would protect her against any monster who came for her, made me the luckiest motherfucker in the world.

She was burning up. Her body had gotten ten degrees hotter than it should have been, and sweat beaded across her skin from more than alcohol detox. It wouldn't be long now. Her magic would tear through whatever scotch remained in her system, and when she opened those eyes again, she'd be in the middle of her transition.

I fell asleep for a moment, only a moment, and that was when it hit.

The initial blast of her magic launched me off the bed, shoving me sideways until I collapsed on the floor with a grunt.

"Fuck," I groaned, frozen in the shock wave of pheromones and magic pouring off her in a vibrant tangible cloud of energy. It forced me to hover there as it ricocheted through my molecules and roped me into its trance. My fangs extended on their own, my cock hardened, and the knot at the base pulsed, ready to lock me into place.

This was the magic of a transitioning shifter. A more submissive person would need a dominant to see them through it, and vice versa. Seventeen years ago, I had helped Guin. I'd been more dominant than her at the time, but she'd since grown to outrank me. I wouldn't stare her in the eyes for longer than five seconds now. But Maeve wasn't like her older sister.

My girl wanted to be cared for, wanted to cuddle up against someone more powerful than her, and know nothing would harm her again. I sensed her shiver every time I called her a good girl, and she responded with a determined, "Yes, sir."

The call of Maeve's primal side reached inside me, gripped my wolf by the tail, and yanked me to her. I'd known it was going to happen, so I stayed close. But if I hadn't, her magic would have expanded until it found a viable shifter to help her.

"Mill," came her pained moan. "Please. It hurts."

I pushed against the force of her energy, struggling to stand as it weighed me down. It was powerful, surging out of her in thick, potent waves. My wolf responded with a loud howl inside my mind, instinctively taking over the human part of me.

Give, he commanded. *Help her. Mine.*

She sprawled across the bedsheets, naked and coated in sweat, her features twisted in anguish.

"Ver...mil...lion," she murmured.

Finally, the magic ebbed, and I inhaled her scent like a drug — flowers, caramel, and sun in the springtime. It pulled me under its spell, wrapping me in its supernatural strength like an anvil blanket. I crawled on top of her, positioning myself between her legs.

"Shhh," I said, running my fingers down the side of her face. "Maeve, I'm here. It's okay. You're gonna be okay."

She turned toward my hand and sucked my finger into her mouth, the sensation surging down my spine and into my balls. My cock had been hard most of the night, but now it ached with heaviness. I had to get inside her. I had to spill my magic into her body and sate this rising tide in both of us.

"It hurts. Please." She opened her eyes and looked at me through the haze, her unfocused pupils glancing wildly around the room. "What's happening to me?"

"You're in transition, baby." I took a deep breath, recognizing my bonding scent in the air, notes of cologne and pine and something distinctly me. It would warn off other males in the area, including the four in the ranchers' quarters. They would sense her magic even though they were a hundred yards away. It would affect them, and if they wanted to keep their heads attached to their bodies, they'd stay the fuck away.

"Transition?" Her brows furrowed together. "I don't understand."

"Shh, relax. I'm going to help you." I kissed her lips, her cheeks, her eyes, anywhere I could get to mark her as mine.

Mine.

Mine, mine, mine.

Then I brought my wrist to my mouth and pierced my skin, the coppery rush of blood exploding across my tongue. I placed the wound against her lips and sighed as she started pulling, sucking down my life's energy, tugging my magic into her. I sensed it outside myself, swelling in her, starting to mingle with her own newly born instincts. She opened her legs wider, rocking her swollen wet cunt against my still-clothed cock, and while I let her drain my wrist, I pushed my boxers down to my knees and angled myself at her entrance, shoving inside with one hard thrust.

Maeve gasped and arched into the contact, digging her nails into my shoulders so hard, they left marks. I winced against the sharp pangs but kept going, unable to stop. Her pussy was so wet with slick, so warm and enticing, the rush of euphoria spread through my entire body, up my spine and over my scalp. Her mouth opened again, sharp little fangs now extended from her canines. She opened her eyes and they glowed a bright, luminous blue, like her human form but lighter, the color of the sky on a brilliant summer day.

God, she was fucking gorgeous, especially with all that crimson spread over her lips, trailing down her chin and neck.

"More," she moaned, and I didn't know whether she was talking about my blood or how hard I rutted into her. I brought my wrist back to her mouth so she could take more of my magic, and I thrust into her like a beast, like I was starved for touch and intimacy.

"Fuck, you're so good," I said. "You feel like bliss, like fucking heaven."

"Yes," she cried. "Please. More."

Between the pull of her mouth and the tight embrace of her cunt, I couldn't hold on for very long. Nor was I meant to. The point of the transition was to get as much of me into her as quickly as possible. When my orgasm threatened to take hold, I sank into it with a satisfying moan, burying myself as deeply into her as I could.

The muscle at the base of my cock expanded while I exploded, locking us together as undiluted pleasure pulsed through me. With my magic now coating the inside of her, the rush of her hormones subsided, and she relaxed against the mattress, her arms around my neck to keep me close.

"Mill," she whimpered before kissing me. "You're here."

"I'm here, baby," I said. "I'm not going anywhere. I'll see you through it. I'll help you."

That seemed to appease her, and she hummed before closing her eyes and succumbing to sleep again. I lay on top of her and brushed the hair out of her face, tracing the angles of her cheeks and lips with my fingertips, memorizing them, burning them into my retinas. I didn't want to forget a moment, not a fucking second.

I, too, had been caught up in the trance. The transition magic dulled reality and warped time, making me dizzy with intoxication. By the time my knot loosened, the preternatural energy swelled up in her again, launching out of her soul in a potent force. It pushed me into the air, and I hovered there for a moment, suspended in the grip of its fury, and when it finally let me go, I slid down her body, kissing and licking her skin, consuming the sweat on her precious body.

But the real prize was between her legs. When I spread my tongue through her, I moaned against the delicacy of her slick mixed with my cum. It tasted like both of us, and that amplified the heady arousal brewing inside me. Wetness streamed out of her, and I lapped it up, swirling my tongue around her clit the way that had made her moan earlier in the night. She pushed her hips up to meet my face, and I gripped her ass to hold her in place, feasting on her, reveling in being the one who got to see her so vulnerable, who got to protect her when no one else could.

"Fuck, baby," I groaned. "You taste amazing. I could stay down here all fucking night."

She sank her fingers into my hair, scratching my scalp and fisting handfuls to hold me where she wanted me. I gorged myself on her, gripping her thighs hard enough to leave marks, but that didn't matter. Maeve bucked against me, riding out the waves of her pleasure as they crested and ebbed, rose and fell again.

I crawled on top of her, and she calmed down when I kissed her lips, lining my cock up at her entrance before sliding home in one fluid motion.

Fuucckkk, the connection flamed through my body like sinking into a warm bath, and when she wrapped her legs around my hips, changing the angle of her pelvis to take me deeper, I melted against her. She needed more from me, more blood, more magic, so I tilted my head to the side to expose my neck, and I grabbed her head to bring her to it.

"Bite me, sweetheart," I said. "Go on. You need it."

She moaned and sank her new canines into my throat, which should have been painful and terrifying. But under the influence of the tether between us, it sent shock waves of pleasure zinging through my veins. I moaned and fucked her harder, shoving into her, using my knees to spread her wider, to go as deep as I possibly could. She drained me, and I relished it.

My magic sparked outside my body, deep within her, and our emotions combined into one gloriously tangled mess. I sensed when she was getting close to orgasm, and when she finally fell apart, it catapulted out of her, into me. Our souls merged in a mind-numbing tornado of sweat and sex and skin, her ecstasy mine, and mine hers. Our heartbeats synced up, trumpeting in time together, pounding out a rhythm that tied us to each other in ways only we could understand. I moaned as her climax pulsed into me, burning down my spine to my cock, where I spilled inside of her, my knot freezing us together.

My canines pushed out of my jaw, elongating and throbbing in time with my pulse. I ached for something I shouldn't want. I was supposed to be fueling her with my essence, but nothing made sense in the throes of the transition. I simply *had* to do it.

I leaned forward and bit her on the side of the neck, sinking my teeth into her flesh above her scent glands. It wasn't a mating bite, and it would probably heal after the full moon, but *fuck,* the taste of her blood rushing over my tongue and down my throat shoved us both into a different dimension. The exchange amplified what was already between us. I drew from her, sucking her back, and she screamed in a magnificent outburst of pleasure.

"Fuck," I said, swallowing down her moans and her cries of rapture. And when it was done, I collapsed on top of her, our torsos sticking together with evidence of the intimacy between us. I wanted to tell her so many things. I wanted to reassure her it would be over soon, but I didn't know when.

"Mill?" Her small voice had me lifting my head to glance down at her.

"Yeah, baby?"

"Am I dying?" She seemed oddly at peace with whatever the answer would be.

"No," I told her, pressing tiny kisses to her lips and nose, working my way to her eyes. "Once this is over, you'll be so very alive."

"Thank you," she said. "Thank you for helping me."

Her tenderness turned my insides into a big pile of mush. It hadn't been like this with Guin. That had only been about sex and blood. I didn't *feel* Guin the way I did with Maeve. The older Vanderbilt had transitioned within two days, and when we were done, I had only two bite marks to show for it. Even though I shared my magic with her, it hadn't resonated so deeply inside her. She left that experience smelling of herself and nothing more, nothing to indicate we had been together at all.

Now, my heart banged against my ribs in a staccato that was for my girl and her alone. I understood what it meant, even in the delirium of the fever, even if I didn't want to. We shared dreams, my territorial scent flared around her, and I couldn't stand the thought of anyone else touching her. I'd started to think of her as mine, and wasn't that a fucking shame?

I was cold and soulless. I had no room in my life or my heart for a mate. I didn't deserve her, and I never would.

Guin is going to kill me.

Kodiak is going to kill me.

I didn't care.

Maeve's transition went on well into the day and the following night. She bit into both sides of my neck until the skin was raw and destroyed from use. Then, she used the other wrist. I did the same to her. We shared everything about each other like we were made to do it. In between bouts of heat, we rested. When the magic reared up again, it plumed out of her in a debilitating wave that pulled me out of any sleep I managed to get.

It wouldn't always be like this. Shifters didn't usually drink each other's blood during sex, and there were only a few rituals that required cuts or consuming the stuff. But I could admit, sucking down her life force while I came made me want to whimper from the undiluted rapture. Pumping into her while she swallowed me down, the magic connected us in divine ways, like we were always meant to be one.

But those were thoughts for the future, when I could look at them with a clear head after ten to fifteen hours of sleep.

Days passed while we were in that bed. The sun rose and set and rose again; still, we remained enslaved to the pull of her change. By the end of the third day, I could barely hold my head up, and I didn't know if it was because of the nascent bond between us that I'd been so thoroughly wrung dry. I lay on the mattress next to Maeve when the last surge of energy pulsed from her. It was hardly a blip compared to how things started, but it pulled me to her nonetheless. I tried to lift my upper body, but a sharp wave of dizziness forced me down. I took a few steadying breaths before trying again, almost getting my shoulders up before realizing I couldn't do it.

I grabbed Maeve's waist and twisted her to the side, her chest to mine, one leg over my hips. I positioned myself at her entrance before sliding in as far as I could go, grimacing through the ache of it. The skin on my cock burned from overuse, but fuck, once she was fully seated, I exhaled in relief.

I'd fucked her at least twenty times in the last few days, probably more. But each time was a Godsend. She rolled her pelvis, her porcelain skin illuminated with vitality, her blue eyes glowing from under her hooded lids, her dainty canines extended between her lips, her dark hair in a tangled halo around her head. She was gorgeous... heavenly...and so full of my magic, she nearly burst at the seams.

"Mill," she moaned. "It's so fucking good. I can't stop myself. I'm sorry."

"Don't be sorry," I said, tucking her face under my chin so she could take my throat again. I winced when she speared through the raw bite, but it was what she needed, and I lived to serve her for however long this lasted.

Her orgasm crested in both of us, and when she sank into it, I went with her, moaning and cursing through the frenzied release. My cock sputtered, my knot expanded, and my muscles twitched with overuse. I held her to me, our chests rising and falling together, our pulses in perfect harmony.

The spell broke, finally letting go of its chokehold.

She sighed against me, relaxing against my torso, and I exhaled the weight of what we'd done together, knowing it was time to rest.

On the other side, it was a whole new start to a brand-new life.

Things would never be the same again, not for Maeve Vanderbilt, and certainly not for me.

CHAPTER 17

Maeve

The ache in my muscles woke me, and when I opened my eyes, I realized I wasn't alone in my bed. I wasn't in *my* bed at all, and a warm body lay next to me, breathing deeply in the depths of unconsciousness. I was in the lead worker's cabin— Vermillion's cabin—and I was *not* alright. Something had been fundamentally altered inside me, even if I couldn't determine precisely what that was.

A new licentiousness squirmed around in my head, urging me to wake Mill by crawling under the covers and wrapping my lips around his cock. The metallic scent of blood coated the air, and the sheets looked like someone had been murdered on them.

My canine teeth stung and, when I ran my tongue over them, I froze from how sharp and long they'd become.

What the hell?

I clenched my eyes shut, running through the last thing I remembered.

"You're in transition, baby," Vermillion had said.

What the hell was transition? I held my hands up to look at them, sensing something was different about my fingernails, even if they looked relatively the same. The sides of my neck twinged, and when I touched them, I winced at the puncture wounds.

"Hey," came the low grumble from my right. Vermillion rolled over and blinked up at me with dark bags under his eyes. His cheeks had sunken in on his face, and his torso looked gaunt, his ribs pronounced under his skin. Deep wounds had been carved into his throat on either side. Were those bite marks? Was that what ached on my neck?

"Holy shit, Mill." I gasped. "What the hell happened to you?"

He smirked and let out a little laugh, pushing himself upright so he could lean against the headboard. "How are you feeling?"

"Okay, I guess," I said, sitting beside him. "My muscles hurt. I feel like I ran a marathon, and there's something else...something inside. I'm different." I didn't know how to put it into words. "Are those bite marks on your neck?"

I had the sneaking suspicion I'd made them, that I was responsible for the entire way he looked.

Mill nodded and ran a hand back through his hair. "We should talk. But first...we both need to eat."

My stomach chose that moment to grumble as if agreeing with his assessment of the dietary situation. He sat up and swung his legs to the side of the bed to brace before standing. When he wobbled and put a hand out on the wall to steady himself, I scrambled after him to help, only realizing once I was fully upright that we both were naked. Vaguely, I understood we'd spent the last however long fucking and *doing other things* in the bed together, so I didn't know what I was so ashamed of, but I grabbed the top quilt and wrapped it around myself anyway while he slid his boxers up his legs.

Mill eyed my makeshift robe but said nothing as he walked to his kitchenette on the other side of the cabin. I followed him, wary about what had happened between us and what he might have done to me...or what I might have done to him.

Something was wrong. Smells hit stronger, and the world seemed more alive. As I sat at his dining room table, the scent of sweat and man drifted off him, an aroma distinctly his but *more*. When he opened the fridge, I caught the salty deliciousness of sliced turkey and Swiss cheese, even before he put the packages on the counter. There was leftover chicken in there and broccoli and ham, and...were those burgers?

My stomach made another loud rumble, and he glanced over his shoulder at me with a smile.

"I was starving after my transition, too. It's normal. The magic takes a lot out of you." He grabbed a plate and piled bits of meat and cheese in the center. I stood to help him, but he put a hand out. "Sit. It's my job to bring it to you."

"Your job?" I laughed. "What does that mean? Mill, what's going on? What's a transition?"

He sighed and stuffed a thick slice of ham into his mouth before nodding and plopping more down on the plate, clearly intended for me. He put more meat on top—chicken, burgers, turkey. He even grabbed an apple and sliced it into pieces while he talked.

"Maeve, I'm a werewolf. A shifter," he said, turning to bring the plate to the table. He sat down next to me and placed the food between us. "And as of yesterday, you're one, too."

He grabbed a piece of ham steak and held it out to me as if he wanted me to open my mouth so he could place it inside. I stared at him.

"What?"

"A shifter. Here, you need to eat."

I couldn't wrap my brain around what he was saying, and the whole thing seemed so ridiculous that I giggled.

Mill lowered the food and raised an eyebrow. "Why are you laughing?"

"I mean...you're joking, right?" I chuckled. "A shifter? And I'm one, too? What? Is some sparkly emo vampire going to burst through my window to watch me sleep?"

He furrowed his brows, his features dropping. "If he does, I'll tear his ass apart."

When I realized he wasn't joking, I straightened. "Wait...you're serious?"

"Yes," he said. "But I think you're maybe a fox." He stuffed ham into his mouth and held another bigger piece out for me. This time, I accepted it. "Like your sisters."

Like my what?

I paused mid-chew, the weight of surprise and shock hitting me square in the gut. I knew they'd been keeping something big from me and Ava. But no, it couldn't be. This wasn't real. This was ludicrous. Mill was fucking with me.

"Chew your food," he said, stabbing another piece of ham before holding it out.

I reluctantly obeyed, and then wondered why I had.

"I know this sounds like you went to sleep in one world and woke up in fantasy land, but I'm not lying to you," he said, feeding me when I finally swallowed and opened my mouth for more. "Humans don't know we exist, and we're forbidden from telling anyone who's not in the pack."

I tried to wrap my mind around what he said, but it all sounded unreal. Werewolves and fox shifters, these things didn't exist in the real world. But I couldn't deny what had happened in the last three days. The bed was covered in blood. His throat had been torn open on either side, and there were wounds on his wrists. I was the one who did it. I tongued my canines again.

"That's right," he said, pulling his lips back over his teeth. Sharp fangs elongated on either side of his mouth, pointed and fully capable of tearing muscle from bone. I gasped and leaned forward to touch them. He sucked in a hiss and pulled away. "They're sensitive. Touching them is...personal."

I tried to extend mine. When they twinged and grew in response, I nearly jumped out of the seat. Eyes wide, I glanced at Mill like he held all the answers in the world.

"What the hell?" I glanced down at my fingertips, where enormous claws had grown out of my nails, sharp and predatory. I bolted upright, and the chair went flying out from under me.

"Hey, it's okay," he said, rising and holding his hands to either side. "You're okay."

"Mill, what the fuck is going on?"

"I told you." He stepped closer to me and grabbed my palms, bringing them to his chest. "You've transitioned. You're a shifter, sweetheart."

"What does that mean?" I struggled to keep up with the words coming out of his mouth. A shifter? Werewolves? None of this was real. None of it... I touched the marks on his throat. "What happened to you?"

He grimaced and nodded back to the table. "I'll tell you if you sit and let me feed you."

Reluctant to accept this new reality, I lowered myself to the chair and opened my mouth so he could give me another slice of meat.

"This world isn't what you think it is. Most of the legends you've read about are true. Shifters, vampires, witches, they all exist."

"Vampires?" I balked, my eyes nearly bulging out of my head. "Like Anne Rice type of shit?"

"Worse," he said. "The vampires in this area all belong to the Bloody Scorpions MC." He explained that Marx was their leader, and being a vampire made his threat even more severe. "Shifter blood is an aphrodisiac to them. They'll spend days draining you...torturing you...*using* you. And that's if you're lucky. I shudder to think what he would have done with Sol if Orion hadn't gotten to her when he did."

My mind struggled to keep up with everything he said.

"There's a reason those stories have been passed down through the generations." He chewed and swallowed before sipping his water. "They used to be warnings, and when we went into hiding, they became fairy tales."

"How is this possible? What's wrong with me?" I asked, still trying to wrap my mind around it. "Did something happen to me to make me like...this?"

"No," he said. "There's nothing wrong with you, Maeve. You're perfect."

Some of my resistance melted away at his compliment. *Perfect. He thinks I'm perfect.*

"It's genetic," he continued. "One of your parents was a shifter. Guin and Sol think it was your mother."

"My sisters," I murmured. "They're like this, too."

He'd already said that, but it was only now that it clicked. They'd already transitioned and couldn't tell me. A slight pang of betrayal hit my heart at their deception, but I understood. If all this was real, if there really was a separate world of monsters and magic out there, there was no way for them to explain it to me so I'd understand. Hell, I had fangs and claws, and I still barely bought into Mill's explanation.

"Yes," he said. "They couldn't tell you, and you can't tell your other siblings."

"Why?" Not that they would believe me, even if I did, but I was curious why this was a forbidden topic.

"Humans are reckless and destructive," he said. "If they found out about us, they'd put us in zoos. We'd be their science experiments." Mill shook his head and sighed. "We can't change whenever we want, but we're stronger than normal humans even in this form."

"When do you change?" He seemed so sure in his answers that I couldn't help but be convinced this might be true.

"The part about the full moon is unfortunately accurate," he said. "We can't control it. Our magic comes from the earth. We're compelled by the strength of the cycle, and the closer we get to the moon, the more our animal sides come to the forefront."

I inhaled and ran my hands over my face, the weight of this information hitting me in the chest like a sledgehammer.

"What you just went through, the transition, usually hits a person in their early twenties. Sometimes sooner if they spend a lot of time around shifters. Guin...for example." He met my gaze hesitantly, like he expected me to freak out, but it took me a second to catch up. Guin would have transitioned around the time when he was working here. She was what... eighteen? And he would have been twenty-one.

"Oh my God," I said. "Did you help her the way you helped me?"

"Yes," he said. "But it was different, and whatever it was between me and her, it ended after it was over."

A small part of me sizzled with jealousy that they'd shared that level of intimacy. Had she sat at his table the next morning, wrapped in a sheet, while he fed her whatever meat was in his fridge? Had he had this same conversation with her?

That sensation washed over me, and I let it fade away. I had no reason to be possessive over him. She had needed his help, and he'd been there for her in a way no one else could. I was glad she had him in a moment of weakness, when she had no one else, when she was likely scared about what would happen next.

Then I caught on to what he'd actually said.

"Different?"

He sat back in his seat and nodded. "There's something about you, Maeve. I'm very...protective of you."

"Protective." I took a drink of water and focused on the coolness sliding down my throat as I waited for him to elaborate.

Mill grabbed my hand and wrapped his fingers around my palm, grounding me in his presence.

"You remind me what it means to live." He met my gaze and leaned closer to me, bringing his forehead to touch mine. Our lips were millimeters apart, and I inhaled his intoxicating scent. "No one's ever made me feel alive like you."

My heart nearly skipped, and a warm rush spread through my veins. I tilted my head so our lips touched. At the contact, he moaned and grabbed the back of my neck to hold me closer. His mouth was so soft and inviting, I couldn't contain myself. I dropped the sheet and crawled into his lap, my legs on either side of the chair, and I slung my arms around his neck to get as much of him as I could. My skin burned everywhere it touched his, and when I rocked my hips into his, we both hissed. Raw with use but desperate for more connection, my cunt protested the movement.

He broke away to look up at me, and I ran my hands over his face, brushing his hair back. Visions of the last seventy-two hours flashed through my mind. Most of it was a blur, but I did remember some things, especially the pain. I *had* to be filled by him, and the agony only got worse when he wasn't inside me. But after he was, oh, the pleasure became overwhelming. My teeth were tender, and I eyed the marks on his neck before softly running my fingers over them again.

"I did this." I looked back at his eyes in time to see them flash a deep crimson. I jumped, the surprise almost startling me off his lap, but he held me closer.

"It's okay," he said, wrapping his arms around my waist. "It's how it works. During the transition, you need shifter magic to activate the change. You need someone of the opposite dominance. Usually, that's someone of the opposite gender, but not always." He reached up to touch my neck, gently rubbing his fingers over my wounds. "I got you good here. I'm sorry about that. I tried to resist it, but...anyway. They'll heal after the moon. I promise."

"I remember..." I closed my eyes to think about it, the sensation of him being stuck inside of me lingering in my lower abdomen. "You couldn't move. You were inside of me and—"

"That's the knot," he explained with a chuckle.

"A knot?" I balked, both confused and amused.

He nodded and smiled, his grin sending warmth through my heart into my gut. "And you'll notice you get wetter than you used to." I raised my eyebrows, waiting for more explanation. "It's called slick."

"Slick?" I cringed, scrunching my nose before erupting into a fit of giggles. "That sounds gross."

He laughed harder. "It helps with the knot."

"I have no idea how I'm being so chill with all of this," I said. "I should be running for the hills. This doesn't make any sense."

Mill hummed and leaned in closer to kiss my lips. "It's my magic inside you. It'll be there for the next few days, just long enough for your own to develop."

"Your magic, huh?" I grinned. "What else does your magic do?"

He hummed. "Guess you'll have to wait and see."

I gasped, something having just occurred to me. "What about birth control? I'm on the pill, but we— Does the magic negate that?"

"Don't worry," he said. "You can't get pregnant unless you're in heat. The transition usually burns through any chance of that. The magic is too strong."

I relaxed, the relief in my chest palpable. Not that I didn't want a huge family someday, but with everything else going on, I'd like a few years to figure that out. "Thank you for helping me."

"You're welcome, baby." He kissed me again and put his hands on my hips to drag my pelvis closer. My blood sang, and he licked my lips, the touch rattling through my nerves. Granting him entrance, I wrestled his tongue with my own, the ache between my legs intensifying, now hungry for more contact. I rocked against him, urging it on, wanting more of him. Two quick knocks at the door stopped us, and he pulled away with a growl, narrowing his eyes at the entrance.

"Do *not* fucking open that," he yelled, before glancing back at me. "Go get cleaned up, darlin'. It's the full moon tonight, so we've got to get going."

"Tonight?" My heart nearly dropped into my stomach. "Where are we going?"

He grinned and grabbed his jeans off the floor, slipping them up his legs. "We change with the pack, and now that you're one of us, you're coming, too."

I still didn't know what to think about all of this, but how could I deny it? I had fangs. I had claws. I'd nearly bled Vermillion dry. I turned toward his bedroom, found my dirty clothes, and went to the bathroom to shower. I flipped on the light and caught my reflection in the mirror.

The person staring out at me was a stranger.

This girl had glowing blue eyes and luminous skin, the kind that supermodels had on the runway. Gasping, I stepped closer and leaned in close to get a better look.

Hello there, came the soft voice from inside my mind.

Startled, I stiffened and gasped, stepping back from my reflection. "Who are you?"

You, it said. *Me. Us.*

Us? How could it be us? Who *was* us?

God, how could any of this be fake? How could I conjure this up in a dream? I wanted to convince myself I'd wake up any second, but that didn't seem likely when this…being…seemed to come from the depths of my soul.

Vermillion said my sisters had gone through this, so until I talked to them, I decided to take things one step at a time. I turned on the water and got under the stream, determined to wash away who I was to make room for whoever I was going to be.

"You look like shit," Guin said from the other side of Kodiak's desk. After Maeve had showered and dressed in some of my old clothes, we drove to the homestead because Fenris said Kodiak needed to see me...*now*...in person. I hadn't been expecting an ambush from the eldest Vanderbilt sibling.

"No worse than when you went through your transition," I said, adjusting my hips.

"Definitely worse," Kodiak added with a wince.

"My little sister, Mill?" Guin crossed her arms, clearly displeased with the whole situation. "You told me things were fine, that you had a handle on it."

"I did," I said. "I do." I gestured to the office door, where Maeve sat on the other side and waited for her turn with these two overbearing dominants. "As you can see, she's alive."

Better than alive. She'd come out of my room, wearing one of my T-shirts, instinctively choosing to cover herself in my scent, something that pleased my wolf immensely. I didn't tell them that, though. It was just my magic in her making my wolf react like that.

So what if the transition had been different with her? So what if we were sharing dreams, if my emotions were in sync with hers? It didn't matter that being with her gave me a new lease on life. She was a newborn shifter in a sea of unmated males, and she deserved to find whoever made her happy. Even if it wasn't me.

The beast in my head growled at that idea, but I reminded him that fantasies dreamed up under the throes of the transition were simply that—dreams, works of fiction, idealized notions of romance that didn't exist. In reality, we were still as wrong for each other as before.

Guin sucked in air through her teeth and raised an eyebrow, looking from me to Kodiak.

"You said if one of my sisters went into their transition while I was in Bozeman, you would send someone *other* than Vermillion to help."

Kodiak smirked and leaned back in his seat. "I said I would *try*. You know how these dominant wolves get. Once they're in the haze, there's no pulling them out."

She rubbed a hand over her face and groaned. "You're the alpha, aren't you? The one keeping these Bastards in line? Can't you tell him to back off? She has bite marks on her neck, for Christ's sake."

"You can't get everything you want, Guin," he said. "You asked me to send someone I trusted to man *your ranch*, and I did. You asked me to keep your sisters safe while you handled your father's business, and I did. Making sure Mill happened to be outside of the blast radius when Maeve ultimately exploded wasn't part of the deal."

She put her hands on his desk and leaned in, holding eye contact with him. In our world, that was a threat, and no one could maintain it with the alpha for very long. I grimaced, anticipating his reaction.

"Deal?" She laughed. "Your piddly little homestead would still be a hovel if it weren't for our merger. You needed money, and I needed men. *That* was the deal."

I expected Kodiak to bare his teeth and rise to his full height, at least six inches over her, but he stayed seated, simply smiling while she read him the riot act.

"Now your Bastards probably think they can fuck any Vanderbilt who goes into transition."

"And who started that, huh?" Kodiak asked calmly, his steady voice betraying his rising temper. "Perhaps you're so upset because Mill helped you through yours, but you didn't carry his scent out of it?"

"Thank God for that," she continued. "I'd rather swim through hot vampire guts than be a part of your stupid little cult." She gave me a sidelong glance. "No offense."

How was I *not* supposed to be offended by that? But I didn't answer. Getting in the middle of two dominants when they were measuring their...*egos*...was never a bright idea.

"That can be arranged," Kodiak sneered.

Sensing the argument had ventured into dangerous territory, I started to push to my feet, yearning to make my way toward the door.

"Sit down," they both roared in unison.

Fucking. Yikes.

I planted my ass back in that seat so fast, but between me and God, I didn't know whose order I was following more. I had a healthy fear of Kodiak as my alpha, but Guin was downright terrifying.

She shook her head and rolled her eyes. "Just like a wolf. Arrogant and prideful."

"*If* Maeve wants to join the pack, she'll be given the invitation. The same as Sol. The same as you." Guin opened her mouth to speak, but Kodiak cut her off. "And if she chooses a Bastard as her mate...or chooses Mill as her mate, you'll have to make your peace with that."

"She's not my mate," I said, but the words tasted like venom.

Kodiak shifted his knowing gaze to me, and I resisted the urge to squirm. The alpha always knew more than he ever said. All of our connections ran through him. He was the lifeline, the literal spine, of this family. If the pack was a universe, he was the center, the proverbial black hole holding us all to him with his immense force of gravity.

"The moon is in four hours." He kept his tone unusually calm. If anyone else were to talk to him like this, he would have already snarled in their face and demanded their obedience. "We're making the trek to shifting territory, and our human packmates are on alert for any vampires that may try to test their luck."

"Is that supposed to make me feel better?" She scoffed. "Humans protected you the last time the Scorpions came in for a raid."

It was bold, perhaps a little cruel, to mention the time her father hired the Scorpions to invade our territory during a full moon and wipe half of us out while we were shifting. Even though the Bastards and the Vanderbilts had a tenuous truce now, old feuds died hard.

"We're better prepared this time," Kodiak said. "What happened then won't happen again."

"I hope you're right." She ran her tongue over a canine before straightening and walking toward the door. Guin swung it open with more force than was necessary, causing Maeve to shove to her feet on the other side. The younger Vanderbilt met my gaze with a hopeful one of her own before the entry closed again. I looked back at Kodiak.

"That female is testing every last bit of my patience," he sighed. "As for you, Morwyn filled me in on the research she's been doing."

"I haven't checked in with her in a few days," I admitted. Honestly, I didn't want to know.

"Your blood changed again after Maeve's transition. It's spawning and dying at rapidly increasing rates, almost like it's searching for something."

I swallowed against a suddenly dry throat. Morwyn still had my samples from before Orion's wedding, and I recalled her conversation about how they were still alive, still changing, still evolving.

"Oh? What does that mean?"

"You tell me," he said. "Notice anything different about this transition?"

Like the bite marks on her neck? Like the weeks of sharing dreams before it? Like the irresistible urge to drink her blood? Like how badly I want to yank her into my room and never let another wolf look at her?

"It was…more intense," I said. "Guin didn't need me the same way Maeve does."

Kodiak narrowed his eyes. "Did you drink from her during it?"

I gulped. "I know what you're thinking."

"You're not an idiot, Mill. Of course, you know what I'm thinking."

"I'm not a vampire," I said. "I'm not rotting from the inside out."

"But something *is* different." Kodiak raised his eyebrows, demanding an explanation.

"Yes," I said. "I drank from her. It was…" I shook my head, reliving the experience now that I was sober and (mostly) out of the haze. "Life-altering."

Kodiak pursed his lips and steepled his fingers in front of his face. "Are you a danger to the pack?"

"No more than I was a month ago," I said. "You weren't concerned about me then."

"I didn't know you were walking around with bloodlust."

"I'm not," I said. "It's just he—" I cut myself off before I said *her.*

He paused, letting the tension grow between us, making me more ashamed. Guin was right. Maeve would have been better off with Fenris or Poe or literally *anyone* else in that fucking rancher's cabin. I should have stayed as far away from her as possible.

Morwyn shouldn't have brought me back. She should have let me die.

But then, I remembered what Maeve had said when I took her out on my bike and we looked down on the valley.

"It's easy to forget why we're alive, and then you see something like this, and it all makes sense."

I had forgotten the meaning of life…until Maeve. And now, perhaps my existential crisis seemed dramatic. No one could have helped her like me. The thought of it boiled my blood.

"Guin tells me Maeve almost died about six months ago," Kodiak continued. "Her heart stopped while she was eating dinner. One second, she was fine. The next, she was on the ground."

"I know." Maeve had told me the story herself.

"Don't you find it strange that you *also* almost died roughly around the same time?"

"I didn't *almost* die, Kodiak. I *did* die. And magic brought me back to life. Maeve had her heart restarted by a crash cart." I didn't see what he was getting at. They were two totally different things.

"Uh-huh," he said, clearly not buying my bullshit. To be fair, I wasn't sure if I bought it myself.

I groaned and rubbed my eyes. "What are you trying to say?"

"I think there's more going on here than you're willing to admit."
Understatement.

"Do you think you'll be able to rein in your...*impulses* during the shift?" He raised his eyebrows, clearly demanding an affirmative answer.

I nodded.

"Words," he growled.

"Yes," I said. "I can."

"Good. Go see your sister. Let her get another sample to compare the old ones to."

Gritting my teeth and grumbling expletives, I stood and walked out of the office, making my way through the buildings to the infirmary.

When I arrived, Fenris and Morwyn were huddled together in her office, their heads tilted toward each other, whispering something I couldn't hear. At my approach, they quieted and looked up at me.

"There he is," Fenris said, patting my shoulder. "How are you feeling?"

I narrowed my gaze, wondering what he could have to talk to my sister about, but ultimately let it go.

"Fine," I said, wincing at the pull of the bite marks on my neck. "Kodiak said you wanted to see me?"

Morwyn nodded, her brown curls bouncing on top of her head. "Yes, I need to get new samples of your blood."

"Is everything at Vanderbilt Ranch squared away for tonight?" I'd been out of commission for the last three days, so I wasn't sure what had been done versus what hadn't. Columba and Aquila were supposed to move the cattle to a more secure location, but they should have been back by now for the moon.

"Everything's good, brother," he said, looking back at Morwyn one last time. "We'll talk later."

She nodded and gestured for me to follow her into an exam room. After Fenris left, I raised an eyebrow at my sister.

"What are you and Fenris talking about later?"

She tilted her head like I was asking a stupid question, but her cheeks flushed when she replied. "That's doctor-patient privilege only."

"Oh, is he your pincushion now, too?" I chuckled sardonically until she wrapped the tourniquet around my arm a little too tight. "Ouch."

"Don't be a baby." She stuck me with the needle before collecting her two vials of blood, and when she was done, she put a bandage over the puncture mark and let me off her table. "How are you feeling?"

"Why does everyone keep asking me that?" I groaned and rubbed my hands over my tired eyes. "I'm exhausted. Just like every other dominant when they come out of a transition."

She hummed and used a different needle to put some of my blood on a slide before placing it under a microscope on her desk and leaning down to glance in the eyepiece. "That's understandable. It's just that we're all so worri—" She cut herself off with a gasp and straightened, looking over her shoulder at me, her eyes wide, her mouth hanging open.

"What?" I stood and walked closer to her, but peering down the microscope would tell me nothing. I would have no idea what I was looking at.

"You're... What did you do?"

I furrowed my brows at her and shook my head. "Nothing. What's wrong?"

"Your red blood cells mutated. They look like..." My sister shook her head and blinked a few times before glancing into the scope again. "Well, I don't know. I need to run some more tests, maybe reach out to a colleague in Europe." She turned back to me and crossed her arms, tilting her head from side to side. "You went through a transition with Guin before. Was there anything different about this one? Are you noticing any new urges or anything you can't explain?"

I took a deep breath and debated being honest with her. She *was* my sister, after all. But I worried this might make her more anxious about all of it, and with the full moon in a few hours, what difference would it make? Still, she couldn't do her job if I kept things to myself. I opened my mouth to reply, but a knock at the door cut me off.

"Mill?" said Moose, ducking his head in the entryway. "We need you in the tech room."

I nodded and gave my sister a reassuring pat on the shoulder. "We'll talk after the moon, huh?"

Morwyn narrowed her eyes and nodded. "Yeah, okay. Just...be safe, alright?"

"See you at the shift."

I turned and followed Moose through the hallways leading to the tech room, where a few of our brothers and sisters sat around their computers, typing on their keyboards. Screens lit up one of the walls, sectioned into black-and-white video footage of the various security cameras set up around our property and Vanderbilt Ranch. Logistically, covering that much area would take more resources than we had, so we focused on the places we were more likely to occupy.

"We haven't been able to locate Marx since you got that whiff of him a few weeks ago," Moose explained. "But he couldn't have gone far."

"We've been searching all of the outer perimeter cams," one of the other pack members said. Channing was Lycan's youngest sister, and she'd been one of my mentees for the last few years. I was trying to teach her everything I knew about hacking, but being from a younger generation, she had a better mind for this than I did. She taught me as much as I did her. "But I can't get a read on him."

"They're good at hiding," I said. "Anything new at their old nest?" They'd once occupied the old sanitarium on the outskirts of town until we ambushed it and burned it to the ground.

She shook her head.

"What about the bar out near Preston?" The vampires used to hang out at a local dive. But they'd abducted one of our submissives, who later mated a fairy, and between the two of them, they'd torn that place apart.

"Nothing," she said. "I hope the rotation shifts we have going tonight will be enough, but I have no way of knowing."

"We have enough pre-transition and human pack to keep an eye out," Moose said. "But I didn't know if you had any better ideas?"

"Let me drive," I said, taking the keyboard to pull up a few other screens. Marx had texted Maeve weeks ago, and I'd been able to track him after that. If he were smart, he would have ditched that burner by now, so I was banking on him being an idiot vampire with nothing in his head. When I loaded the tracking software, nothing came up. But that could mean he didn't have the phone on. "Keep an eye on this. Let me know if anything changes."

"Ten-four," Channing said.

Head buzzing and nerves on fire, I switched through the feed from Vanderbilt Ranch, checking on the human day workers and the animals within the boundaries. All seemed okay, but something rolled around in my gut, warning me to pay more attention. Something was wrong, but I didn't know where it was coming from.

"C'mon," Moose said. "We're heading out to the shifting grounds."

Swallowing down my apprehension, I left the youths to their work and went with the sarge.

"It's true," Guin told me as we followed the group of Royal Bastards and their family through the woods to the shifting grounds. It was deep in their territory, surrounded by more fences and barriers than I would have considered possible. After all they'd been through, I understood why they took their security so seriously. "Everything Vermillion told you. The Bastards. Sol and me. The Bloody Scorpions. All of it."

I hugged my middle tighter while we walked. "Why didn't you say anything?"

"Would you have believed me?" She ran a hand over her forehead to brush her bangs out of her eyes. "Hell, I didn't until I went through my first moon."

"What's going to happen to me?" Vermillion had given me the highlights, but there had been so much to talk about, I didn't ask for details. Guin wouldn't sugarcoat it, and I appreciated that most about her.

"Your body will break down." She gave me a sideways glance before continuing. "The transformation takes about ten minutes. Your bones break and shift and reform, and your inner beast grows from inside you."

I stopped walking, my legs frozen in place. "What the fuck?"

Guin turned to face me and sighed. "I wouldn't wish this on anyone. You should know that."

"Does it hurt?" I clenched my hands into fists, my nails burrowing into my palms.

"At first, it's excruciating," she said as I caught up with her. "But then, once the moon takes over, it's…" Guin paused like she was trying to find the right words. "It's like a stiff drink after a long day. Or that first hit of a cigarette after a detox. It's life-changing."

She grabbed my jaw and tilted my head to the side, her gaze landing on the bite mark on my neck. Self-conscious, I instinctively covered it. She swatted my hand away.

"Fucking animal," she said. "He shouldn't have bitten you. I could kill him for that."

"It's fine," I said. "I actually—"

At her glare, I stopped talking before I admitted more than I should.

We stayed silent for a few moments while I digested what she said. She'd come out of Kodiak's office in a storming rage, but I thought that had more to do with the MC's president than with my transition.

I saw the back of Vermillion's head a few yards away, and it reminded me that he had helped Guin a decade ago. They both insisted there were no lingering feelings between them, that there hadn't been even after they came out of the haze. But their prior connection made things even more complicated. Did it make me some kind of deviant that I wanted *more* from Mill? That we'd hooked up before the transition hit, before the call of magic made us do it? Or had the pull always been there?

"I'm sorry," I told her, drawing her attention back to me. "About Mill."

She rolled her eyes and waved me off. "Please. He and I are ancient history. There's nothing to be sorry about." She narrowed her eyes. "Why? Are you thinking about taking things further?"

I thought about how he'd said I was different, that his pull to me was stronger than it was with Guin, and I tried to imagine a life where I came out the other side of this having no interaction with Mill whatsoever. Was my attraction to him simply because he'd played such a pivotal role in my pre-teen life? Or was there something more profound going on?

Guin had mentioned mates in our conversation earlier. Shifter magic would pair a person to their most compatible match, whether they liked it or not. Most of the time, they liked it very much. But she had heard of shifters matched with someone inconvenient, like a parent's friend or their sibling's spouse. Talk about awkward.

I looked at the back of Mill's head again. Was he my mate? And if he was, would I want that?

We finally reached a spot where the trees were so thick, I could barely see a hundred yards in either direction. The smell of undergrowth and summer air permeated the space, vibrant with the impending onset of nocturnal life. Members of Kodiak's pack stood around us, almost sixty in total, all in various states of undress. The energy between the pack members hummed with something electric and foreboding. A few people cracked their necks, tilting their heads from side to side, rolling their shoulders almost as if preparing for a fight.

She'd explained that we had to get naked to shift, but the reality of it didn't entirely set in until we were here...actually doing it. My nerves rattled under my skin, my stomach clenching and fluttering with anticipation. Perhaps some part of me still thought this wasn't real, that I would wake up in my bed at the mansion and realize this had all been a dream, some altered reality that had no basis in truth.

Guin yanked her blouse over her head and unbuttoned her trousers before kicking off her boots. I closed my eyes and shook my head, deciding I'd better go along with it. If it was as bloody and gruesome as she described, I didn't want to ruin my clothes.

"Fold them up and put them over there," she said, now naked as she carried her things to a rock near a big tree. Growing up in a house with seven siblings, I'd seen them all in their birthday suits at least once or twice when we were little kids. But the confidence with which Guin always held herself never ceased to make me jealous. She didn't care if anyone looked at her. She never hid from anything. Trying to don that same attitude, I shucked my shirt over my head and slid my jeans to the ground, stepping out of them before doing as she asked and placing them next to hers.

Shivering against the cool twilight air, I crossed my arms, half hiding my breasts and half trying to keep myself warm.

"Remember the rules," Kodiak said, his voice booming from the center of the space. "Stay within the bounds. And if you smell something, say something. I'll be in close contact with all of you."

He, too, was naked. Like many members of his pack, he was beautifully sculpted muscle, truly an exquisite example of the human form. But I wasn't supposed to notice those things. Guin had explained the shift was primal. It was a sacred ritual shared with one's pack, and the nudity was simply a part of it.

I wondered what they did in the winter. Certainly, they didn't come out here in the snow and freeze their bits off.

The thought made me laugh, and I covered my mouth to hide my childishness. Guin nudged me with her shoulder.

"Stop that," she said. "After the change, the people closest to you will be in your head. Mill, me, probably Kodiak and Fenris, too."

"In my head?" I furrowed my brow. "Like...telepathically?"

She nodded. "It's how we communicate in shifter form."

I wanted to ask more questions, but I caught sight of the moon trickling in through the trees overhead. Its shining luminosity stunned me into silence, so full in its splendor, so radiant and gorgeous. Had any moon ever been so beautiful before?

Groans and shouts of pain echoed from around me, and I'd started to wonder what was happening when a sharp pang yanked at my stomach, toppling me over.

"Fuck," I groaned, wilting at the knees. I dug my hands into the earth as fury erupted in my veins, spreading through my entire body. I was on fire. Every nerve ending burned with agony, and I clenched my eyes shut against it. Bile rose in the back of my throat. I was certain I would throw up, but I opened my mouth and the only thing that came out were my teeth.

I spat them on the ground, blood and saliva coating my tongue, and when I looked down, I saw my skin peeling back over my forearms, thick dark slices zigzagging across my wrists, up to my biceps, and dark obsidian fur poked out of the wounds. My fingernails pushed out of the ends of my fingers, replaced by tiny black claws. My spine cracked, and I arched into the pain, whimpering as something strong gripped my insides and yanked.

Like Guin said, it was pure anguish, and it seemed to go on and on. I grabbed my face, whining when my cheeks and jaw slid from the bone, my skull splintering, fracturing, taking on a new form. The pressure in my head built until my eyes popped out of the sockets with a disturbing crunch that made me believe I would never see again. But my vision did not darken. It was replaced with a stronger sight beyond anything I'd ever experienced as a human. My torso twisted and my knees bent the wrong way, and just when I was certain I would die, that this torture would be the end of me, a greater power took over.

It reshaped and reformed into a brilliant exhilaration, like that first leap off a cliff when the world gave way and there was nothing but the thrill in my blood and a great understanding that the ground would catch me. The urge to shake took over, and I landed on my paws, trembling until the last little bits of my flesh fell off my fur.

Fur!

It was the color of pitch, matching my human hair, and I inhaled through my nose...no, my snout, tasting the night. A thick musky cloud floated over the grass, remnants of the pack's blood around me, and when I tried to stand, I stumbled forward onto my face, collapsing on unsteady paws.

A weight behind me flopped onto the ground between my back legs. I looked over my shoulder at a thick, fluffy tail, wagging as I tried again to push upright.

"You're a fox," came the soft voice inside my head. My sister's voice. I glanced up to see her standing only a few yards away, her copper fur slick with blood and sweat. *"Like me."*

"This is incredible," I said as I panted. I tried again to stand, my body weak, my limbs barely able to hold me. They shook under my new form, muscles I had never used before, screaming with exertion. I stood there momentarily, terrified to try to walk again, but a cold wet nose nudged at my head, distracting me.

"You're okay," Mill said. He took the form of a massive chestnut wolf with dark crimson eyes, standing nearly as tall as his human half on all fours. I blinked, certain I would wake up from this dream any second, but when he was still standing there with his mouth open, tongue between his fangs, warm breath blowing on me in soft pants, I accepted this new reality. *"Try again."*

I pushed upright and took a tentative step, and when I didn't immediately fall over, I took another. Instinct guided me, like I was always meant to be in this form.

"There she is," he said. *"Come on. We hunt this way."*

Hunt?

No one had said anything about hunting, but my stomach grumbled, and the aroma of blood had awakened something beastly inside me. The part of me that was still human balked at the idea, seemingly repulsed by the notion of tracking and killing an animal. But the beast, the one that spoke for the feral side, came to life, excited by the idea.

Yes, it purred. *Yes, hunt.*

Guin trotted ahead, her fluffy ginger and white tail bouncing as she walked, and I followed her with Mill at my flank. We met up with Kodiak and Fenris, heading deeper into the woods, and I took a moment to glance around at the other shifters. Most were hulking wolves, bigger and more muscular than any wild animal. A few mountain lions roared in between, stretching and flexing their enormous claws. I saw deer and smaller animals like rabbits and eagles. I had no idea the pack was this varied, and I wondered how they got along so well living in such confined quarters.

CHAPTER 20

Vermillion

Maeve trotted next to me as Caelum approached my other side, nudging his massive shoulder against mine. I nipped at him in a playful greeting as he rubbed his head under my chin.

"*Good to see you,*" he said. "*I heard you helped another Vanderbilt through their transition.*"

I growled. Gossip spread through the homestead faster than a wildfire, so I wasn't surprised. Considering how I looked when I came home from the ranch, everyone probably knew by now. I glanced at Maeve to see if she'd overheard him, but she focused on her surroundings, seeming to take it all in.

Caelum ran his muzzle over my neck and ears.

"*You smell different, too,*" he said.

I ignored the unasked question in his tone and continued walking, watching as Fenris approached Maeve and lowered down onto his forearms, inviting her to play. She yipped and bounded toward him, causing him to take off ahead of her. He certainly could best her in a foot race, especially since he was a massive wolf, but he took a leisurely pace so she could keep up.

I kept a close eye on her as we followed Kodiak and the rest of the

Bastards toward our hunting grounds. Our animal urges often got the better of us when we were in shifter form. Some of the mates would sneak off to fuck, but the rest of us enjoyed the thrill of a good chase. We lived in harmony with the land. We only took down what we would eat, nothing more, and we never killed without purpose.

"I thought you'd be off with Lyra or Kai," I said, sniffing a decaying log. I picked up notes of rabbit and possum, but nothing exciting. It was just something to do as I kept an eye on Maeve and Fenris to ensure he didn't overstep any boundaries. Not that I thought he would, I just wanted to make sure she stayed safe. It was her first moon, after all.

"Lyra's with her friends," Caelum answered. *"We're still keeping that under wraps."*

I hopped over the fallen tree trunk and eyed the mountain lion group, picking out the female in question as she tackled a smaller cat for a wrestle.

"Are you okay?" Caelum ran the length of his body against me, trying to get my attention, and I pushed him back to let him know he had it.

"Fine. Why?"

"Just checking." He flashed me a big grin and took off like he wanted me to chase him. Usually, I'd indulge him. My wolf loved a good game of tag, but I didn't want to get too far away from my female. And besides, something felt different tonight. A violent hum thumped in my veins, and I didn't know where it was coming from. I was on high alert because of the threat of the Scorpions, but that happened anytime we shifted. No, this had to do with Maeve, and the insatiable urge to stay near her, to not let anything happen to her.

Caelum circled back to me and lowered his chest to the ground, wagging his bushy tail behind him. A bigger wolf came out of the woods to our right and slammed into him, taking him down in a playful taunt. *Kai.* And when two more jumped in on the madness, I left my brother to deal with his friends.

I found Maeve a few paces ahead, her snout to the ground. Fenris had left her to play with Morwyn, but she didn't seem to mind. She was more captivated by the new experience of her shifter form. I remembered the feeling.

"You doing okay?" I asked.

"This is amazing!" She blinked up at me with those crystal clear eyes, the color of the sky, and hung her tongue out of the side of her mouth, a big toothy fox grin from ear to ear. *"You were right. I've never felt more alive."*

I brushed along the side of her little body, reinforcing the remnants of my scent on her. *"C'mon. Let's go eat."*

She yipped and bit the scruff of my neck in response. Together, we joined the rest of the pack on our ritual hunt. Some shifters didn't like to eat in this form because of the hangover once we changed back into our human selves. A stuffed belly could lead to cramps or sluggishness the next day, but I enjoyed the ruthless call. It was the only time we got to be ourselves without the rules and expectations of human society.

The pack hunted efficiently, and once we were sated with elk meat, another urge took over, this one darker and hungrier. Most of the pack had peeled off to do their own thing. Fenris and Morwyn were gone. Caelum, Kai, and their friends had wandered back toward the other shifters in their age group. Kodiak had nipped Guin on the shoulder in play, causing her to growl and stomp after him to retaliate. After a while, it was just us, and that pleased both me and the wolf more than anything else the night could have offered.

She lay on her side, sated and belly full, her black tail lightly thwapping against the ground. I approached from behind her, watching as she enjoyed her after-dinner nap.

I took a step forward, and a branch snapped under my weight. She lifted her head and looked down her lithe little fox body, big blue eyes narrowing. When I took another step, she huffed and lay back down, letting out a deep sigh.

"Did you enjoy the hunt?" I asked, flopping on the ground next to

her, relishing in how her human caramel scent mingled with the woodsy undercurrent of her fox.

"I didn't like killing the elk," she said. *"But the meat was delicious."*

"Such a tender heart." I huffed out a laugh, and she rolled her eyes.

"All alone at last," she said and chirped.

"Just me and you, sweetheart," I replied, moving closer, rubbing my head over the side of her face.

"The moon is so beautiful," she said in a lazy, gratified tone. *"I could stay like this forever."*

I glanced toward the sky and marveled at the brilliant power of the ever-changing object hovering over us. Most humans thought it had no control over the beings here on Earth, but they didn't know about us. They didn't realize how loud its call could be, how its magic overwhelmed the pack every month, how it controlled the ebbs and flows of so many seasons.

"I thought I'd be scared," she said. *"I thought I would hate it. But life is so much better here...like this...with you."*

I froze and glanced at her, her sentiments clenching around my heart in a tight vice. Her emotions flooded through our bond, the squishy warmth of affection, the deep abiding attraction, her thirst for life that opposed my wretched hatred of it. I still didn't think I was any good for her, and even if we were destined to be mates, she could do so much better than me. *"Baby..."*

She must have sensed my hesitation because she hopped to her feet and nipped my ear in a mischievous bite.

"Stop being so grumpy," she said. *"The night is young, and I want to play."*

"Oh yeah?" I shot to my feet and jumped toward her, and she took off into the forest, screeching with delight. I let her have a head start. I was bigger and faster than her, and it would be an easy end to a fun game if I caught her too soon. She wound through the undergrowth like a missile, hardly a shadow darting through the thick cover of trees. But her intoxicating scent propelled me forward. I chased her nearly to the edge of our perimeter, heart

pounding, sucking in oxygen, all four legs extending to cover more ground.

I finally got her, snatching her much smaller body in my mouth before pinning her underneath my paws. She squealed, scratching at my face with her claws, nipping me on the jaw with her teeth.

"Shouldn't you know better than to run from the big, bad wolf?" The words came out instinctively, but she froze under me, blinking, her ears flattening like she was confused.

I took advantage of the hesitation and clamped my teeth around her neck, forcing her to admit defeat. She softened under me, her entire body relaxing into submission. It pleased both the man and the wolf in a way I didn't want to examine too closely. And when I let her go, she quickly got back to her feet and took off again.

For the rest of the night, I played with her, letting her run only so I could catch her. When the moon finally set, we shifted back into human form together, our bones cracking and reforming, our fur sliding off muscle like our skin had at the start. I remembered being terrified for my first shift, even though I'd grown up in this life and knew what to expect. I couldn't imagine having this thrust upon me the day before it took place. My skull pulled back on itself, taking its human shape, and my spine popped into alignment, painful and euphoric at the same time.

When it was over, I checked on Maeve to see that she had successfully changed into her human form, now lying on her side, facing away from me. I traced my gaze over the curve of her shoulders, her ribs, down to her waist and hips. Something in me snapped, like the moon's magic hadn't fully pushed my wolf into the farthest recesses of my mind.

I wrapped an arm over her torso and yanked her closer, bringing her back to my chest, rolling my hips against her delectable ass.

"How are you feeling?" I murmured, dragging my nose up her neck to her hair. Blood matted the ground, mixing with the dirt to cake our skin, but none of that mattered. Only her. Only this moment between us before we had to face the rest of the pack.

"Hmm." She turned her head to skim my lips with hers, kissing me softly. "Good."

Normally, the change took it out of me. I would have already been making the trek back to my room to sleep off the hangover. But having her so close to me, having spent the better part of my shift with her, altered my desires. My cock twitched against her, a low simmering heat building in my lower stomach.

She must have felt it because she smiled and rolled onto her back, leaning up to lick across my mouth. I opened for her, capturing her tongue with my teeth, gently holding it in place before sliding down over it, sucking it.

Maeve hummed in approval, and I rolled on top of her, positioning myself in between her legs, sliding my cock in between her sensitive skin. She moaned and wrapped her arms around my neck.

"Is it always like this?" she asked.

"What do you mean?" I moved down her jaw to her neck, alternating between gluttonous nibbles and hot open kisses.

"I want you so badly right now," she said. "More than I ever have. It's humiliating."

I grinned and pulled back to look down at her, raising an eyebrow. Fuck, she was so damned beautiful, even like this, after surviving such an ordeal.

"Do you want me to fuck you, sweetheart?" My muscles ached and my bones were sore, but nothing on this great earth could have stopped me from giving her what she wanted.

"Please," she said, scratching her nails down the side of my body. It stung on such fresh skin, but I liked that, too. Descending her body, I trailed worshipful kisses along her chest, pausing on her breasts to lick and suck her nipples. She arched into the touch, digging her hands into my hair. When she yanked and tried to get me to come back up, I grabbed her wrists to pin them at her sides.

"If I don't taste you, I will lose my Goddamned mind." I continued my downward trajectory, hooking one knee over my shoulder before paying the same attention to her inner thigh. I held the other leg out to the side, opening her glistening sex to me. Fuck, she was already wet and gleaming, and when I licked a long line up her slit, she made a sound that would replay in my greatest hits for the rest of my life. She tasted like heaven, like woman and Maeve and female, her pheromones hitting me in the gut to make me even harder.

My knot throbbed, wanting to get inside her, but I wouldn't let myself have that until she came on my face. I wanted to roll around in the sweet decadence of her arousal, wear it as a scent to announce I belonged to her and she belonged to me. At the thought, my own smell strengthened, propelling out of me like a fog to wrap around her. I wanted her doused in me so every other shifter in the whole world would know who'd come for them if they so much as looked at her the wrong way. It was an instinct that I didn't question, but on some fundamental level, I knew was more important than I gave it credit for.

She bucked against my face, rolling her pelvis, fucking me as much as I was tongue-fucking her. When all of her muscles tensed, her implosion imminent, I pulled back and watched her squirm.

"Mill, no," she whined, pushing up her hips to find me again, glaring down her beautiful body with fury in her eyes. "Please. I need to come."

"Oh, I know, baby," I said, slowly rubbing my thumb over her clit the way she liked. It was cruel to edge her like this so soon after the full moon. She must have been sensitive. My cock had only barely touched her and I nearly embarrassed myself, but fuck if I didn't love to see her so unbound and disheveled.

She reached for me, grabbing my shoulders and urging me up her body. I went and covered her in my torso, caging her shoulders and face with the protection of my arms.

"To answer your question, no," I said, positioning my cock at her entrance and glacially sliding into her soft, warm body. "It's not always like this. You bring it out in me. We bring it out in each other."

She mewled and relaxed under me, as if the connection brought her peace. A moan escaped my lips, the feeling of being sheathed in her, one with her, nearly overpowering all of my other senses. I rocked into her, pistoning my hips in a leisurely pace like we had all the time in the world. The sun rose on the horizon, capturing her soft alabaster skin in an otherworldly array of peaches and roses. She'd never looked so beautiful, heavenly, like my very own angel right here on earth.

After the animalistic nature of our night together, I expected it to be rougher. But it was sweet. I held her to me, our skin connecting from our chests to our hips and legs. She hooked her ankles behind my back and captured my lips with hers, rolling against me and taking me as deeply as she could. It slow and almost romantic until a darker impulse rose in me.

Shivers crept along my spine, up my neck, and over my scalp. My canines elongated, pulsing with ravenous gluttony, and I eyed her throat. The marks I'd left on her during her transition were now faded, the magic of the shift healing them. I, too, had been restored, but still, this newfound hunger rumbled through me like a freight train.

Bite her, my wolf commanded from the depths of my subconscious. *Take her. Consume her.*

Never in my thirty-eight years had an appetite like this gripped me so thoroughly, and maybe it was the exhaustion from the change or the way her blood still thrummed through my veins, but I couldn't stop myself.

She tilted her head to the side, giving me more access to her neck, and that should have been my first clue that something *was* incredibly wrong with me...with *this.* She wanted me to do it, and that wasn't normal.

I grabbed her jaw with one hand, held her in place, and struck, sinking my fangs into her throat with a violence that shocked me. But, oh, when her blood floated over my tongue and down my throat, I knew true ecstasy. The magic in her veins, *my* magic, *our* magic, pulsed in time with my heart, seeming to sync up.

"Yes," she cooed, gripping me tighter with her inner walls, and as I drank, she fell apart around me, her climax taking control, yanking me down into its abyss. It shot out of her like a nuclear blast, setting off my own, and I bottomed out inside her, my knot locking us in place, holding me still while I spilled everything I had.

I licked her wound, sealing over the bite marks as we both came to our senses, and then I rolled us so she was on top of me, her legs on either side of my hips.

"Fuck, that was amazing," she said. "You're so beautiful when you come."

I panted, my head woozy from both the exertion and the euphoria in her blood.

And then reality caught up to me.

I drank from her. I drank her blood.

Fuck.

What if Kodiak is right? What if I'm...

My knot shrank as if it, too, was disturbed by this thought. Panicked, I yanked her off me and sat up, examining her neck.

"Are you hurt?" I asked. "Did I hurt you?"

"No," she said, rubbing a hand over it. "It's fine. It's okay, Mill."

No, it wasn't okay. Shifters didn't drink blood. They didn't relish the sensation of coming and feeding at the same time.

What the fuck is wrong with me?

"C'mon." I stood and yanked her up. "We should get back to the others."

"Mill?" She furrowed her brows and made a sad attempt to cover herself with her arms, crossing them over her breasts. "What's wrong?"

I licked my lips, shame coiling deep in my gut when I tasted caramel and metal. I was a danger to her. One of these days, I wouldn't be able to stop. One of these days, I would drain her dry.

"Fuck, Maeve," I said. "You should stay away from me."

"What?" Her features broke, damn near crumbling right in front of me. "Why would you say that?"

"This can't happen again," I gestured between us, the anger boiling over, carrying words I didn't mean. "This is a new level of stupid, even for you."

She squared her jaw, widening her eyes with intensifying fury dancing behind them. "You're a fucking prick, you know that?"

Maeve shoved my shoulders and pushed past me, making her way down to where the pack had shifted. Once again, I gave her a head start before I followed from a safe distance, not wanting her to be left alone but knowing I couldn't get any closer.

I didn't know what was happening to me, but Maeve deserved better, and always had.

Fucking men.

I blinked back tears as I sat in the passenger seat of my sister's Range Rover. After returning to the clearing and shoving my clothes back on, I found Guin talking to Kodiak. She took one look at me, glared at Vermillion, and wrapped an arm around my shoulders to walk me back to the homestead. We wasted no time heading to the ranch. Mill, Fenris, and Columba said they'd meet us there, but I didn't care what happened to them.

How dare he? How dare he love my body so fully, so completely, and then dismiss me, telling me it was better for me to stay away from him? He didn't know what was suitable for himself half the damned time. Why should I listen to a thing he said?

My heart thumped in my chest, nearly breaking as I tried to hold myself together. I didn't know why I was so upset. We barely had anything. All that talk about me being different, about it being different between us, was just bullshit.

But I couldn't shake the feeling that there *was* something to it. Even now, his magic hummed in my veins, raw and potent, and the more distance I put between us, the more agitated this new side of me became.

Go back, it urged. *He didn't mean it. Can't you feel how he's breaking apart? Something's wrong. He needs you.*

"I can't believe he bit you again," Guin said. "That motherfucker. I swear, I'll tear his throat out with my claws."

"Just leave it," I said, skimming through the messages I'd missed from Ava while I'd been transitioning and changing. She'd called three times and sent over ten texts, threatening to notify the police if I didn't reply soon.

"You know you can't tell Ava, right?" Guin said. "You can't tell Liam or Galahad. None of them."

I swallowed against my dry throat and nodded, wondering how to lie to my best friend. Ava and I were two halves of the same whole, opposite sides of the same coin. I'd shared a womb with her, my DNA, my entire life. When I died, she'd been the one to bring me back to life.

This was the biggest thing that had ever happened to me, and I'd have to go through it without her. At least, I had Guin. At least, I had Sol when she returned.

"I know," I said. "How did you and Sol manage to keep it from us?"

Guin rubbed her fingers over her tired eyes and sighed. "She wanted to tell you, but I've been carrying the secret longer. Just try not to think about it when she's around. Sometimes, that helps."

Despite her advice, they hadn't been perfect about keeping it hush-hush. Ava and I knew they were hiding something.

Pressing dial on her contact, I brought the phone to my ear and waited for her to pick up.

"Finally," she said. "I've only been trying to reach you for days."

"Sorry," I said. "I've been busy."

She paused, and I could practically see her narrowing her eyes in suspicion. "What's wrong?"

"Nothing," I lied. *Everything.* "It's just this corporate hellhole I'm drowning in."

"Okay." She did not sound convinced.

"How are things with you?" I asked, trying to turn the focus from me. "How's Lycan?"

She tutted. "Things are fine with me. Lycan is perfectly professional."

"Uh-huh." I'd heard about him—a bona fide fuckboy. If he hadn't tried to get in her pants yet, it was only a matter of time. "Have you found a French lover?"

"Maeve," she said with a laugh, and the conversation moved on to how things were going at the ranch. I complained about work for the rest of the ride home, and at the end of the conversation, Ava still wasn't convinced. "Are you sure you're okay?"

"Yes," I said. "Don't worry about me. Just...do us both a favor and get laid, okay?"

She scoffed, and I imagined her rolling her eyes. "I'll move it right to the top of the priority list."

"Good. Love you!"

"Love you."

After I hung up, I glanced at Guin, who raised an eyebrow skeptically. "You need to work on your poker face."

"Yeah, no shit." I took a deep breath and texted Sol, asking her to call me when she had a moment. None of us had heard from her since she'd been on her honeymoon, but now that I was a shifter, there was an undercurrent of *her* that ran deep in my bones. It matched the same signature as Guin, so I figured this was what shifters called a packbond.

When I asked her about it, she confirmed my suspicions.

"I could tell when Sol transitioned," she explained. "The same as you. If you join Kodiak's pack, you'll make a blood pact with him. You'll start to sense everyone else, too."

"Are you in his pack?"

"God, no," she said with a tiny laugh. "I hardly need someone else telling me what to do. If I did, I would have already been married."

"So no mate then, either?" I raised my eyebrows, trying to

imagine the type of shifter it would take to stand next to Guin. Would she need someone more powerful than her? Did such a person even exist?

"No," she said stoically. "No mate."

I cleared my throat, debating whether I should ask the next question. After what happened today, it probably didn't matter anymore. "How do you know if someone's your mate?"

She licked her lips and looked at me, probably deducing why I was asking.

"I've heard it's like your entire world shifts. It becomes about them, about their survival, their happiness. You can feel them under your skin. Some people even have a telepathic bond. Sol and Orion can feel each other's pain."

That got my attention, and for some reason, the thought of Mill dying six months ago came to the forefront of my mind. *When* precisely had his heart stopped? I always found it strange we went through the same thing around the same time. But what if... No, that would be preposterous. We weren't mates. Hadn't he shown that today? If we were, he wouldn't have been able to hurt me like he did, push me away for the sake of his pride.

This was such a mess.

When we got to the ranch, Guin drove the Range Rover up the driveway, and I narrowed my focus to the front door, which was hanging open. A sinking weight of dread unfurled in my gut. Somehow, I already knew what had happened. I started to open the door, but Guin put her hand on my arm to stop me. The rotting stench of decay wafted inside the SUV, nearly making me retch.

"What is that?" I asked, turning to face my sister.

"Vampires." She put the vehicle in reverse and backed out of our property, grabbing her phone. Kodiak's voice filled the speakers.

"Guin, what's wrong?" he asked, as if he could tell we were in danger without us having to say it.

"Scorpions," she said, her voice stoically calm. I knew better than to think she was undisturbed. In the face of a threat, she either got angry or turned inward. In this case, it was the latter. "The front door was kicked down. We didn't go inside."

It was silent for a moment before he said. "Meet us at the corner of Lilac Drive and Dogwood. We're headed your way."

After she hung up, she opened the center console and pulled out a pistol, checking that it was loaded and one was in the chamber before she sped down the road to meet the Bastards.

Kodiak, Moose, and Vermillion escorted us back to the mansion, ten other Bastards following behind us on their bikes. They were heavily armed, each with handhelds on their waists and automatic rifles slung over their shoulders.

"Are you okay?" Mill asked, grabbing my shoulders as he ran his gaze over me.

"Fine," I snarled, breaking free of his hold. It had only been a few hours since he'd reprimanded me in the forest, and my ire had not dissipated. I deserved an apology. *He'd* bitten *me,* not the other way around. I wasn't stupid, not about him, and I wasn't sure how much I bought into us being wrong for each other. If we were, why did I feel so strongly about him?

"They're gone," Kodiak said when he emerged from the house, his heavy boots thumping down the stairs. "But...Guin, it's a massacre in there."

Mill's features dropped, and he ran inside.

"Massacre?" I glanced at Poe and Columba, reading the grief on their features. We had left the human workers here alone, trusting the security at the ranch to protect them. They were supposed to alert us if something terrible happened. How did they get through our perimeter? How had this happened?

It all caught up to me in one terrible moment of sinking dread in my stomach.

No.

I raced up the marble steps after Vermillion, ignoring Guin's call to stop me. I froze inside the foyer. Blood streaked the walls in a terrible display out of the worst true crime documentaries. I heaved at the sight of entrails decorating the crown molding like Christmas ribbons. In the parlor, human heads had been lined up on top of the fireplace mantel in a gory display, their faces twisted in horror and torment.

Heart thumping and legs unsteady, I walked through the rest of the mansion, where body parts were strewn about, having been ripped from their torsos with brutal force.

Monsters. These Scorpions were monsters out of the depths of hell.

Just as I ascended the stairs leading to my room, Mill walked out of the door and shook his head.

"Don't go in there, sweetheart," he said, his brows lowered in a scowl, his tone bordering on furious.

Of course, his saying that only made me want to go in more. I pushed past him, and my legs nearly gave out at the sight inside. Written on the wall were the words, "Give me my bitch or I start killing heirs."

Ellen lay on my bed, her throat torn, her chest ripped to pieces. My stomach rolled, and I turned to the side, vomiting right there in the doorway to my once safe space. I retched until nothing else came out, my nerves trembling, my pulse racing.

No. Not Ellen. Not her.

But when I opened my eyes again, she was still laying there, lifeless and still with rigor mortis. I couldn't look at it anymore.

Slowly and numbly, I walked back outside, overhearing Aquila reporting to Kodiak.

"The stables are empty, but the sheep...the cattle we just moved. All gone."

"Gone?" Guin asked. "What do you mean, gone?"

Dead, as it turned out. The Scorpions had mutilated the fields with them. Corpses spread as far as the eye could see, our entire herd decimated. I stared at the carnage, hardly able to look away, tears streaming down my face.

But my Molly was missing, adding salt to the already deep and infected wound. Where was she? Why were the stables empty? Had she escaped? Or was she, too, a casualty of this escalating violence?

"Where are the horses?" I asked Mill, who stood beside me with his hands on his hips. I sensed his anger, hot and fiery, mixing with a cold shame. He blamed himself. I blamed myself.

What were we thinking, leaving them like this, with Bastards on the homestead their only protection? The Scorpions had already proved they could get on our property. We should have stayed here. We should have done something, anything, to keep everyone safe. They had gotten through our defenses before, and they'd keep doing it until they had what they wanted.

"Poe and some of the others are tracking them into the woods. They might have gotten out." He turned to face me, wrapping his arms over my shoulders to pull me into a hug. "She might be okay, Maeve."

I accepted the comfort only because I needed someone to support my weight. This was the worst thing I'd ever seen.

"C'mon," Kodiak said, nodding back toward the mansion. "We'll regroup at the homestead, figure out our next steps."

"What do you think he means by killing the heirs? Are Galahad and Liam safe? What about Ava?" I wasn't stupid. If he planned to kill Vanderbilts, he'd go after my siblings. "Has anyone heard from them?"

"I've tried calling them," Guin said, wiping tears from her face. "Sol and Orion, too."

"I sent some people after them," Kodiak said. "We'll tell Orion and Sol to cut their trip short, to come back where it's safe. We'll need their strength. We can't do this shorthanded."

"And what about this?" I gestured to the bloody field. "What happens here?"

Kodiak shook his head and sighed. "We'll have to burn it."

Grief wrapped around my heart and yanked.

Burn it.

My compassion for the animals warred with the knowledge that we'd lost a fortune in one night. Our entire yield, everything we'd worked so hard to grow and maintain, all gone. And what was worse? These creatures had met such a vicious end. They deserved to live a happy life. They deserved to meet death humanely. Not this. Never like this.

I wrapped my arms around myself and walked next to my sister, steadily making our way to what remained of our home. But I couldn't go back in there, not even to get my stuff.

"We'll have someone clean the house," Kodiak said. "You both can stay with us for the time being."

"And what about the Scorpions?" Guin asked, her stoic voice unnerving with its intensity. Her rage simmered under the surface, radiating through the family bond, fueling my internal fire. "We can't let this stand."

"Of course we can't," Kodiak countered. "But we just came out of the moon. Half my pack is still sleeping off the hangover, and we're never as weak as we are right now. The shift's magic has retreated. We need to rest and recoup our strength."

"Rest and recoup?" Guin balked, her outrage now finally boiling over. "We need to find them. We need to tear Marx's head off and mount it out front as a warning."

Rationally, she must have understood that his plan made the most sense. But in her wrath, logic had taken a backseat. I didn't blame her.

In fact, I agreed with her.

"And I can't put my pack in danger," he said. "I understand your anger. Believe me, if anyone does, it's me. But I won't act until there's a plan."

Guin squared her jaw and stared him down. I didn't know much about pack politics, but the thought of doing that to someone as big and powerful as Kodiak made me shiver. She didn't even blink.

"What if it was *your* livelihood, huh? Your family at risk?"

"Your sister married my second, my VP. It *is* my family at risk." He glared down at her, unflinching, daring her to do anything about it. "I've already told you the plan. We'll regroup. We'll call in your siblings and keep them safe. I've got my best trackers out in the woods, looking for any sign of where they went. That's all I can do right now."

"I'll check the security feeds," Mill added. "See what we missed. I don't know how they got through without alerting Channing and the crew."

"One of our packmates, Nora, recently mated a fairy, Aoife," Kodiak added. "They live on the outskirts, out near Preston. They might have caught wind of any new vampires in the area."

A fairy? What good would a fairy do?

Again, I wasn't thinking clearly, not nearly enough to understand that fairies even existed. Guin clenched her eyes shut, more tears streaming down her cheeks. But I'd hit my breaking point. Between the shame rolling off Mill and the inferno deep in my gut, I couldn't handle it anymore. My cup had officially runneth over.

"That's not acceptable," I said, clenching my hands into fists, digging my nails into my palms to keep myself grounded. "We need to do something. Now. Before they strike again."

Kodiak focused on me, his eyes nearly obsidian, the pupils blown so wide. "And what would you suggest? That we tear off half-cocked to God knows where? We haven't found their nest, and until we have intel and backup, we don't know which direction to go. We're not strong enough yet."

It sent me over the edge. Enraged by what I'd witnessed and worried about my family, I launched at him, shoving at his chest and shoulders, punching whatever I could find. He was six-five and all muscle, so it was like hitting a brick wall, but I didn't care. I screamed and kicked until strong arms wrapped around my middle and yanked me back.

Mill.

"Let me go!" I scratched at his wrists, wiggling to get free.

"I understand you're upset," Kodiak said, his features dripping into a cool, calm level-headedness that infuriated me even more. How could he be so apathetic? How could he—

"Baby, it's okay," Mill cooed in my ear, and even though he'd broken my spirit earlier, the sound of it softened me. I relaxed into him, sobbing and wilting under his restraint. "This is a disaster, but we'll get them. I swear it. I swear."

"I'm not saying we won't go after them," Kodiak said. "Just give me time. Give *yourself* time. Nothing worthwhile was ever done with an emotional head."

"See that it happens," Guin said, standing between me and the alpha. "Or I'll take things into my own hands, Kodiak. I swear *that* to you."

"I have no doubt you will," he said, turning to leave us there in the clearing. Columba went after him, and I sagged in Mill's hold, my legs unable to hold me up anymore. Deep, heavy cries poured out of my chest.

Ellen.

The workers.

The animals.

My house. My safe haven.

All of it gone.

Digging my palms into my eyes, I let myself dissolve into the overwhelming grief of the morning. My body was exhausted from my first change, my mind reeling after the morning spent with Vermillion, and now this. It was too much for me to keep inside. Mill held me through it, even after Guin kissed me on the head and walked after the rest of the pack.

"I've got you," Mill cooed. "You're okay. Let it all out."

As angry as I was with him, I rested my head on his shoulder and gave over to the rumbling anguish inside. Eventually, he picked me up and carried me back to the SUV, placing me in the backseat so he could hold me while Poe drove us to the homestead.

Vermillion

urious didn't begin to describe the emotions raging inside my veins. This was all my fault. I was in charge of Vanderbilt Ranch while Orion was gone, and I'd let it all go to shit. I thought I'd set up the perimeter correctly. I thought our security was tight. I'd been a fucking idiot.

As we all stood in the meeting room, waiting for Kodiak to start church, my nerves frayed with the memory of watching Maeve fall apart in my arms. Kodiak didn't begrudge her for her outburst. Christ, he was lucky she hadn't drawn her claws. But if anyone deserved her wrath, it was me. I'd reacted poorly this morning, shoving her away when I should have pulled her closer, and now she'd lost everything.

"We found the horses a few miles in the woods," Poe said. "I don't know how they got out, but they're fine. We brought them to our stables to keep them safe."

Thank fucking fuck for that. Maeve didn't need any more heartbreak. When I'd gotten her back to the homestead, I put her in my bed, coaxed her to sleep, and left her to plan our next steps. The room was full of Bastards, the officers at the table around Kodiak, who sat at the head with one hand gripping the chair, the other fisted under his chin.

"They took off to the east," I said, detailing the footage I'd seen on the security cameras after we returned. They'd figured out how to loop the feeds closest to the house so it didn't set off any alarms to those watching from the homestead, but I'd caught them on the outer boundary, sneaking off to whatever fucking rock they'd crawled out from under. "I've contacted the fairies, but they're conveniently disinclined to get involved."

Nora and Aoife shifted in my peripheral vision. Aoife had been a member of the Montana fairy nest until mating Nora earlier this year. She spent most of her time here at the homestead, but that didn't mean she'd revoked her family.

"I'll talk to them," Aoife said, gripping the small axe on her waist.

"Thank you," Kodiak said with a nod. "What about the other Vanderbilts?"

"Orion and Sol are on their way home," Moose said, brushing his long dark hair behind his ears. "Liam hasn't returned our calls. I've sent three shifters out to pick up Galahad from college, and Lycan insists he and Ava are fine."

"The vampires in Europe are much more refined," Ruby said. As an enforcer, she held a high status in the pack. As Kodiak's sister, she was the only person who could hold his stare for more than a few seconds (aside from Guin). "They wouldn't start an international war without provocation, even to satisfy their American counterparts."

"So what do we do?" Talon asked. She ran her hands over her face and sighed. "We're not strong enough right now to go after them."

"But we can't afford to sit on our hands," Columba added. "They killed our friends. They killed the entire herd."

"We need to be strategic," Serpent said. "If we go after them when we're weak, we'll lose more pack members. If we wait, we risk more damage."

"We need to draw them out," Guin cut in from her spot next to Kodiak. "If we set a trap, we can pull them into our territory, where we know the odds are to our advantage."

"Are you offering yourself up as bait?" Ruby asked, giving Guin a toothy smile. Kodiak's sister had never liked the Vanderbilts, and last year, she'd been the most prominent opponent to us going after Sol and Guin when they'd been abducted. To her, the pack's safety always came first. I couldn't blame her for that mentality, especially since the Vanderbilts were responsible for the deaths of her parents and countless others.

"If needed," Guin said, baring her teeth back at the enforcer. "I'd do anything to end this war. Wouldn't you?"

Ruby scoffed and rolled her eyes, now tinged with the red of her wolf's namesake.

"This isn't up for negotiation." Kodiak leaned forward on the table, resting his elbows on the edge, clasping his hands in front of him. "We *will* retaliate, but we need to be smart."

"I like the idea of a trap," I said. "It allows us to control the circumstances."

"Perfect," Guin said. "Put me out in the open. I'll draw them in, you take them down."

"No," Kodiak said immediately.

"Why not?" She squared her jaw, hissing the word through clenched teeth. "It's the perfect plot. They want the heir, that's me."

"He wants Sol," I said. "And if not her, then Maeve."

"He wants a Vanderbilt," Guin countered, shifting her irate gaze to me. "And he's stupid enough to accept whichever one he gets."

"I'm not putting your life at risk," Kodiak said, which seemed to confuse her even more.

She furrowed her brows. "I'm not letting any of my siblings take that spot."

Kodiak held up a hand, and to my shock, she closed her mouth and pursed her lips.

"When Orion gets back, and *only* when Orion gets back, will we act. He's the second in the pack for a reason." Kodiak shifted his shoulders. "Moose and Larentia, gather our guns. Serpent, work with Ruby on a location." Kodiak barked orders at everyone else in the pack, seeming to cover all the bases, but he didn't say anything to me. "Fenris, the envoy from the Steel Roses MC, is here. Explain the situation to him, and see if he has any contacts in the immediate area who might be willing to help."

My best friend nodded. The Steel Roses were a national group, but we'd recently allied with their Madison County chapter out of Virginia. They needed help with supply lines to the West Coast, and we needed backup. Jameson, the president of the National Chapter, had approved the alliance weeks ago.

"I know the witches down in Asheville are always willing to hunt down a few monsters. I'll call Jameson and Duchess to see if any other chapters can come in," Kodiak continued. "We'll get back up. We can't do this alone, and it's time we stop acting like they're only a threat to us. The Scorpions are a danger to every Royal Bastard territory."

When he was finished, the rest of the pack cleared out, leaving me to sit in my chair, dumbfounded and pissed off that I hadn't been given anything to do.

I stared at him.

"Mill?" He raised his eyebrows once everyone had left.

"I didn't hear orders for me," I said. "I want to sink my fangs into Scorpion necks, too."

He sighed through his nose. "I saw the marks on Maeve's neck today."

I froze. "And?"

"That *isn't* a mating bite."

Crossing my arms, I shifted my hips uncomfortably.

"What happened? And don't you dare lie to me."

"Kodiak, I'm..." How exactly was I supposed to confess this to him? If I said I craved her blood, that I had been since that night in her room when she ran her fingers over my lips, covering them in the delicious stuff, he'd confine me to quarters until Morwyn figured out what was wrong with me. But fuck, hadn't I been the one to push Maeve away? Hadn't I been the one to recognize there was something distinctly messed up about my attraction to her? "There's something wrong with me."

"Oh, I am well aware," he said. "I'm glad you're finally admitting it."

"Taking her blood during her transition was bad enough," I said, running my hands over my jeans. "But this morning, I couldn't stop myself. I fucked her and then I drank from her and I..."

I loved it. *She* loved it.

Kodiak ran his hands over his face and head before planting them on the table to lean toward me.

"Listen, it's not your fault, okay?" He adopted his gentle voice, the one he usually reserved for cubs. "You didn't ask to die and be brought back to life. You didn't make the call to leave the ranch unprotected. And you can't help whatever's going on with Maeve."

I blinked back tears, the weight on my chest nearly suffocating me despite Kodiak's words.

"I need to kill them," I said. "It's a fire inside me. I *have* to take them out."

"Which is why you will take Maeve to Morwyn as soon as she's awake. I want a full workup on both of you."

That confused me. "You think it's biological?"

"I think something happened to you when you worked on the ranch seventeen years ago."

I heard what he wasn't saying. My heart stammered, my hands balling into fists. "No, she's not my—"

Despite being hazy from the change, my wolf yipped in my head, perking its ears and wagging its tail. It agreed with Kodiak, and maybe deep down inside, I'd known all along. It was why Guin didn't smell like me after her transition, why our connection faded so quickly afterward.

I thought of the first time I'd seen Maeve, brace-faced and

wearing her hair in pigtails. She'd been a child, and my instincts then were more protective than anything else. After I left, I tried to move on with my life, but no one else satisfied me the way simply being in her presence could. When I saw her again at Orion's wedding, my entire body reacted like I'd suddenly been catapulted to life.

"Being alpha means I have a connection to all of you," he said. "When you join the pack, you make a blood bond with me, and it is through me that our magic is unified. What no one else knows, what only another alpha *can* know, is that I *feel* you all. I see you in my mind like a web, interconnected by relationships and friendships and genetics. For a long time, you've had a faint line trailing from you, disappearing off the map."

I drew in deep breaths while he continued, my pulse thundering in my veins as his explanation started to ring true.

"I thought it was Guin, but once I met her, once I met *Maeve,* my hypothesis changed."

"What is it?" I asked the question, but I didn't need to because I already knew the answer.

"You tell me," he said, his eyes imploring me to come to my own conclusions.

"Do you think that's why I crave her blood? Do you think I'm..." I couldn't say the words, but I had to. I fucking *had* to. "Do you think I'm a vampire, Kodiak?"

"No," he said. "And I remain convinced you're not a threat to the rest of the pack, but something else is going on here, something you've been trying to avoid for a long time."

The human side of me couldn't wrap my mind around it. Kodiak was implying I was mated to Maeve, that I had been since the first time I met her, but if that was the case, how could I have helped Guin through her transition? Fuck, how could I even stand to be apart from her?

A small voice spoke in the back of my mind.

But what if he's right?

What if I had formed a mating bond to her all those years ago?

Would my wolf understand I had to wait until she was old enough? That I would have to be with others until she transitioned? The more I thought about it, the more it made sense. She made me feel alive. As much as I'd told myself to keep my hands off her, I couldn't resist her. Being near her was like bathing in the light of the full moon, radiant and beaming and beautiful.

"What if I kill her?" I asked. "What if I can't control myself next time? What if I drain her dry?"

"That's why I need you to go to Morwyn," he said. "My wolf is telling me to be wary, to tread carefully around whatever magic brought you back to us." Kodiak let out a breath and leaned back in his seat. "And that beast is never wrong."

He dismissed me from the meeting room, and I stalked through the homestead to my cabin. I opened the door and walked into the living room and kitchen combo, stomping my feet to shake off the mud.

The running water from the shower echoed in the distance, and I walked through my bedroom to the bathroom, pushing open the door enough to see Maeve in the mirror's reflection. She ran her hands through her dark hair, wringing it out as she moaned under the water's stream. I didn't deserve to join her. The last time we were alone together, I'd disparaged her for letting me bite her, for even being interested in me in the first place. But like always, when it came to her, I couldn't stop myself.

I yanked my shirt over my head, shucked my pants to the ground, and kicked off my boots before stepping out of the denim. I closed the door behind me as I walked in. She turned when she heard my footsteps, staring at me with desire and reticence.

I gazed back at her, willing her to kick me out, to hit and scream at me, anything.

Instead, she squared her jaw and inhaled, letting it out in a deep sigh.

"I'm sorry," I said. "For what I said this morning."

She raised an eyebrow and covered the bite mark on her neck. I pushed her hand away and ran my fingers over it. I didn't bite her in the marking spot, where my saliva would mix with her scent glands, and she'd smell like me for the rest of her life. That would indicate a claim. This was pure lust, plain and simple.

"I understand that you shouldn't have done this," she said, glancing between us. "But I didn't hate it, and I don't think I'm putting myself at risk by being with you."

She was wrong. So very wrong. But so was I. There was no slowing this train down now that we were barreling off this cliff. Being conflicted about it didn't help.

Maeve lifted a hand to my cheek, forcing my gaze to hers. "You've kept me safe, Mill. You'd never hurt me."

"I died and came back to life," I explained. "There's something darker about me, something I'm afraid of."

"You're not like them," she said. "You're not like the monsters that tore my house apart, that killed all those..." She trailed off, seemingly unable to mutter the words.

"I'm scared that you're wrong." It took a lot for me to confess that, to be that vulnerable in the face of all we'd been through so far.

But she lifted on her toes and pressed her lips to mine, and I melted into the touch. When she wrapped her arms around my neck and pulled me closer, I licked my way into her mouth, wrestling her tongue for control. She easily submitted to me, and I turned her toward the wall, pressing her up against it while I ran my hands down her wet, warm body. Her breasts were so soft, and she moaned when I rubbed my fingers over her nipples, arching into the touch.

The bloodlust usually reared up after I fucked her, and I should stop this until my sister ran her tests, but my aching cock and the knot at the base urged me forward. Wasting little time, I speared my fingers through her sensitive skin and, finding her already wet for me, I kissed my way down her jaw and neck, lapping at my bite wounds.

I wanted to mark her for real. I wanted to sink my canines into that special spot where her neck met her shoulders and make sure everyone knew she belonged to me. But I wouldn't do that to her, not until I was certain she would always be safe with me.

Dropping to my knees, I descended her body, pressing delicate kisses onto her stomach and hips before lifting one leg to bring it over my shoulder. Fuck, there was no greater taste in the world than the slick between her thighs. She was already soaked, and not because of the shower. I speared my tongue through her, licking and lapping, paying attention to the areas that made her sink her nails into my scalp.

"Yes," she whimpered. "Please, Mill. I need you."

"Are you going to come for me, baby?" I murmured against her, and she rolled her pelvis against my face, fucking me harder. I loved it when she was like this, so uninhibited and untamed, so very *mine.*

"I'm so close." She gripped my hair in tight fistfuls, holding me where she wanted me, and I stuck two fingers inside her to massage the spot that sent her over the edge. Her muscles tensed, her climax dragging her down into sweet oblivion. I sensed it through our magic as it tingled up my spine and down into my cock.

I was already rock hard for her, my knot aching with need, ready to expand. After that, I couldn't control myself. I stood, twisted her around, and lined myself up at her center, pushing myself to the hilt.

Fuuccckkk, she felt amazing, so tight and warm, like a dream come to life. I'd never experienced anything like Maeve Vanderbilt, and as I gripped her hips to hold her in place, I decided I'd never want anyone else. I wrapped my arms around her waist to pull her upright, keeping myself buried to the hilt. She leaned back against my chest, her head on my shoulder, and she turned to face me so I could take her mouth.

I loved how she responded to my touch, and my wolf roared at the delight of being with her, of being like *this* with her.

"We're meant to be together, Mill," she whispered. "It's the only thing that makes sense."

"Even if it's dangerous?"

Her answering grin was all the explanation I needed. "What's life without a little risk?"

After my death, I'd closed up. I didn't see the point in going on. But maybe she was right. Maybe there was something about taking a big gamble for a big payoff.

"Fuck me hard," she whimpered. "Let me show you I'm not made of glass."

I pushed her face into the tile with one hand and held her waist with the other, rutting into her, bottoming out with a roar. The human side of me gave over to the beast, and I slammed our bodies together like it might be the end of the fucking world. She gave it back to me, meeting me thrust for thrust, and when she broke apart again, I went with her.

My orgasm surged out of me in a mind-blowing explosion, and combined with hers, every nerve ending came to life. I groaned and panted, my canines extending, the urge to bite her again nearly over-whelming me. My knot expanded, locking us into place, and I held her there while the rush of hormones subsided, circling my arms around her, pulling her to me in a compassionate embrace.

"Shhh, it's okay," she said, rubbing her palms over my hands and forearms. "You're shaking."

Am I?

Son of bitch, I was. Tremors rocketed through my body like I was freezing instead of standing under a hot spray of water. Aftershocks of fantastic sex had me nearly on the edge of tears.

"I'm not sure I can live without you," I said, tucking my forehead against the base of her head. "I think...I think I need you, Maeve, and it scares the shit out of me."

"Sometimes, the things that scare us the most are what's best for us." She sighed and twisted her upper body so she could kiss me much sweeter than I deserved. "We just need to agree this life is worth living. Me and you. You and me. Together."

"Together," I agreed, but I didn't feel better about it. The words I said next slipped out of me with no restraint, like our time together in the shower and her forgiveness had unleashed a barrier from my heart to my mouth. "I think I might be in love with you, Maeve."

She leaned back to look me in the eyes, a cold shock slipping through our bond followed quickly by a potent warm relief.

"Is that okay?" I asked, horrified that she might say no. After what I'd done this morning and the way I'd just handled her, she'd be well within her rights to slap me and tell me to get out of her sight. Instead, she leaned in to press her soft lips to mine in a delicate embrace.

"I think I might be in love with you, too, you big stupid wolf."

My heart pounded, and I smiled as I kissed her again. Yes, mating me...loving me... might turn out to be the worst thing for her, and the bastard that I was didn't care.

He loved me.
He really loved me.
And fuck, I loved him.

It had been only a month, but I knew in my bones that I adored him with a ferocity I'd never experienced. I had for a long time. Was that love? I didn't have other words for it, and I couldn't explain it any other way.

Despite this rare moment of honesty, I knew he still craved me in ways he thought were deplorable. According to Guin and Kodiak, drinking blood wasn't normal for shifters. Some enjoyed a good blood kink, but that wasn't what was going on with Mill. He said he couldn't control it, that the urge nearly overwhelmed him. We hadn't had sex since the morning in the shower three days ago. He hadn't outright said it was because he wanted to drink from me, but we were still connected on a metaphysical level. I felt his urges like they were my own.

It had been four days since the full moon, and we still hadn't done anything about the vampires who attacked Vanderbilt Ranch. They'd brought what remained of our livestock to the homestead, but knowing they were safe did not erase the memories of the count-less more we'd lost.

Guin had insisted they would call in reinforcements before we went after the Scorpions, but it didn't make me feel better. In the meantime, we tended to the people who had died on the ranch. We paid our respects to Ellen and the others, even if we couldn't attend their memorials. Her loss ached in the pit of my stomach like a void, one I would never get over.

When I felt up to it, Mill and I went to his sister, the pack's healer, for blood tests. She wanted to find out why he was reacting this way. Even still, I felt like he was keeping something from me, holding something back.

After all these days cooped up in the homestead, I felt like a zoo animal, poked, prodded, and stared at by everyone who passed me. They whispered to themselves, giggling and pointing at the strange new thing. I was sitting in the cafeteria, minding my own business as I picked at a bagel and ignored the gossip, when someone plopped down onto the bench in front of me.

"Cheer up," came the familiar voice. "It's not that bad."

I glanced up at the big emerald eyes of my sister, Sol. She looked tanned and bright, her ginger hair pulled back into a ponytail. Relief flooded my body, and I stood, sprinting around the table so I could pull her into a hug.

"God, I missed you," I said.

"Yeah, I bet." She let me go so she could grab my shoulders and run her gaze over the length of me. "Well, you look like you made it through the transition and the full moon in one piece."

"Barely." I sighed and shook my head. "I should be furious you kept this from me, but I'm just so damned happy to see you, I could cry."

She laughed and ran her fingers over the bite on my neck, which had turned into a pink mark that would heal in a few days.

"So Mill, huh?" She raised her eyebrows.

I returned to my side of the table and sat, continuing my breakfast. "It's a mess."

"Go on." She sat opposite me and crossed her hands, seemingly ready for the entire tale. I glanced around at all the other packmates in the cafeteria, all the other ears and eyes ready to spread more gossip.

"I'll tell you later," I said. "How was your honeymoon?"

"Much shorter than I planned," she answered. "But completely amazing."

"That's wonderful." I grabbed her palm and squeezed, hoping to send reassurance her way. I was happy for her. She and Orion seemed good for each other, and now that I was a shifter, I sensed her joy through the bond between us.

"There you are," said another voice from our side. I looked up at a girl with brown curly hair and sandy skin, her big hazel eyes kind as they landed on me.

"You mind if I sit here?" she asked with a smile.

"Please," Sol said, scooting over so the other person could sit. "It's good to see you, Ginny."

"You too." Ginny looked at me and held out her hand. "You must be the newest member of the pack."

"I am." I gave it a firm squeeze. "Though I haven't been officially inducted yet."

"Soon enough," she said. "My dad won't let you hang out for long without a pact."

Her dad.

Kodiak.

"You're the alpha's daughter?" Now that she said it, I could see the resemblance in her bone structure. She had the same nose, eye shape, and mouth as her father.

"One of them. My sister's Henny. She's at school." She pointed over her shoulder, suggesting it was across the hall. Two people walked by, giggling and talking in hushed tones while they looked at me. Ginny glared at them, baring her teeth with a loud hiss. "Fuck off, Amelia."

Amelia and her friend averted their gazes and scurried away.

"Sorry about them." She tilted her head and assessed me. "We're not used to newcomers, especially not Vanderbilts. You'd think they would have gotten over it after Sol mated Orion."

"People are always going to talk," Sol said with a small smile. "They're not so bad after a while."

"Of course." I rubbed the bite on my neck and noticed a similar mark on Sol, lower, near her shoulder. It had turned into a scar, its bright white lines standing out against her skin. It must have been her mating mark, which claimed her as Orion's. Mill hadn't done the same to me, not like that, and despite saying he loved me, I doubted he ever would. Over the past four days, he'd barely touched me, too afraid he'd start craving again.

Did I even want to be mated to him? My inner fox purred at the idea, thwapping her tail against the barriers of my mind. She ached for that kind of connection. The one we'd created during my transition had started to fade; it would probably be entirely gone by tomorrow.

Ginny and Sol discussed their plans for the day, but I went silent, retreating into my own navel-gazing ruminations.

"What about you, Maeve?" Ginny asked. "Wanna get out of this place and go for a walk with me?"

I perked up at the mention of going outside. Mill barely let me leave his room, and according to Kodiak, I wasn't allowed to go anywhere unsupervised. Not that I gave much thought to his permission, but with the Scorpions on the run and us still waiting for reinforcements, I had to agree that walking around alone wasn't the best idea.

"I would love to," I said. "But I'd better check with Mill first. With the Scorpions running around, he's been...*territorial.*"

Sol snorted. "Yeah, I bet."

"They get like that, those alpha males. You're probably lucky he lets you out of his sight." Ginny grinned, and I admired how it lit up her entire face. "Are you sure you don't want to come, Sol?"

"I promised Orion I would help him with the animals this morning," she said. "You two go. I'll catch up when I can."

"Okay." Ginny stood and nodded toward the door. "C'mon. Let's find your male, and then I'll give you the homestead tour no one else knows about."

I hugged my sister goodbye and followed Ginny out of the cafeteria and down the hallway. I thought it might take longer to find Mill, but I followed my intuition through the underground tunnels of the connected buildings, sensing his presence running through my veins. It was faint but still a thrumming mystical shimmer that exploded whenever I approached him. He was in the tech room with the other IT pack members, flicking through computer screens and chattering around, upgrading the cameras.

At first, he was happy to see me, but his grin quickly disappeared into a scowl after I explained that I wanted to explore with Ginny.

"No," he said. "Absolutely not. We don't know where the Scorpions are, and I don't have time to go with you, not right now."

"Mill, I'm dying in here. I have to get some fresh air." I put on my best pout while Ginny talked to Channing a few feet away. "It's not like I need your permission. I just want to be safe."

He took a deep breath and ran his hands over his face, and a thick wave of anxiety poured out of him, coating my lungs with dread as heavy as steel.

"Fine," he finally said, glancing over his shoulder. "Holden!"

The younger wolf walked over and raised his eyebrows. "Yeah, boss?"

"Take the girls out for a walk, will you?" Mill grabbed Holden's shoulder in a friendly pat.

"Oh, thank fuck," Holden said. "I need to get out of this place. These early curfews are making me antsy."

"See?" I said with a smug indignant look. "Even your own pack mates are getting cabin fever."

Mill snorted and shook his head. "Keep an eye on your six, got it? And if anything strange happens, call it in. I don't care if it's a squirrel that smells funny."

"Ten-four," Holden said, giving a mock salute before turning to me. "C'mon. Let's stretch our legs."

"Thank you!" I pushed up on my toes and kissed Mill before yelling for Ginny.

Feeling better now that I had a bodyguard, I followed Ginny and Holden down the corridors and out a side door that led to the courtyard. It was a gorgeous morning, the sun bright against clear blue skies, and the scorching heat of summer hadn't yet taken over the day. Holden led the way, and Ginny stepped beside me as we wandered toward a path in the tree line.

"Hey, Ginny," someone called, "Where ya going with the Vanderbilt girl?"

Ginny turned to the older guy and waved. "Just walking the trails. We'll be back in an hour."

The guy looked like he wanted to say something else, but ultimately let it go. "Be careful out there, okay?"

"You got it, Polar," she said, "Holden's going with us."

"Alright," Polar shouted back, but his tone made it sound like it was anything *but* alright.

Mill's trepidation mixed with Polar's half-warning caused a brief sting of anxiety to swell in my gut. "Are you sure this is okay?"

Holden flashed me a pistol on his belt and nodded. "We're not going outside of the perimeter. Trust me. No one's getting past our patrols."

I figured Holden and Ginny knew what they were doing, and I was practically crawling the walls.

Once we were far enough into the woods so that no one in the pack could overhear us, Ginny gave me a sidelong look. "So, how are things going?"

"Great," I added in a sarcastic tone. "Amelia and the others have been super welcoming. I'm practically family already."

Holden glanced over his shoulder and raised an eyebrow. "Don't let her get to you. She's jealous."

"Jealous?" I scoffed. "Of what?"

"You're all new and interesting," Holden continued. "And she's used to being the center of attention."

Ginny sighed and nodded. "He's right, unfortunately. I'm sorry about them. We're a pretty close-knit pack."

"It's not your fault," I admitted. "Thank you for inviting me out."

"I know what it's like for everyone to talk shit about you behind your back," she explained. "Being the alpha's daughter means everyone either wants to use you or hate you. There is no in-between."

I understood. I had a similar problem as a Vanderbilt heir. Making friends was hard to come by, and even if I found someone interesting, they were just as likely to be only interested in what connections I could make for them.

"My mom died when I was eight," she said. "Not to trauma dump on you, but after that, everyone got weird around me. No one knew how to act."

I thought about my own mother. Ginny and I had more in common than I would have initially thought. "I get it."

"Yeah, Sol told me," she said. "I'm sorry for your loss."

"Same to you," I said.

We walked for a while and talked about our lives up until now. She'd applied for a college in Hawaii, much to Kodiak's chagrin, and now that she'd been accepted, she had been trying to convince her father to let her go.

"There's a Bastards MC out there," she explained. "Most of the world doesn't know about shifters, and it's illegal to tell regular humans, but we make special allowances for other clubs. I'd be protected."

"So, what's his problem?" I stepped on a log to hop over it, waiting for her to do the same before we continued. The under-growth crunched under my feet, and the birds chirped in the woods around me, the sounds of summer filling me with a new sense of life.

"He's just overprotective," she said. "Like most of the dominant males in the pack."

Mill had talked about that before, dominant shifters and submissives. "Are all shifters either dominant or submissive?"

It was Holden who answered me.

"There's a hierarchy and a place for everyone," he explained. "We need submissives just as much as dominants."

"The submissives are the nurturers," Ginny added. "The proverbial mother bears, no matter their gender. And the dominants are the protectors, the ones on the front line. Everyone has a mix of both, but most usually fall on one side or the other."

She pointed out a camping ground off to our left where I could come with Mill if we ever wanted to escape. After that, we kept walking, and she explained more about the dynamics of the pack. "We have a variety of different species. We're the biggest one in the United States, and my dad takes great pride in keeping everything running smoothly."

I had noticed that during the change at the full moon. I assumed it would all be wolves, and I had no idea so many different types of shifters could live together harmoniously. When I told Ginny that, she chuckled.

"Well, it's not always a bundle of laughs." She rolled her eyes. "Old prejudices die hard, ya know. It used to be that we didn't mingle with humans, and if a shifter mated one, it was very taboo. Half-breeds used to face an incredible amount of stigma. Most of that has stopped, but you might still hear it around the pack. Especially since..." She trailed off, but I understood what she meant.

My father was a human. My mother was (likely) a shifter. Which made me and my sisters half-breeds. I opened my mouth to ask more questions, but Holden froze in front of us as a rotten stench made my stomach sour. My knees locked into place. I grabbed Ginny's shoulder to stop her.

"What's wrong?" she asked, glancing in the same direction as me and Holden. It was coming from the south, super close, much closer than I would have expected.

"Do you smell that?" I swallowed, my throat suddenly dry, my heart pounding. The scent nearly made me retch; it was so overwhelming and disgusting. It could only be one thing...one terrible thing.

Vampires.

"Yeah," Holden said, reaching for his pistol.

"How far away are we from the perimeter?" I glanced at Ginny, her features tightening as she read the panicked look on my face.

"A mile...maybe half a mile."

"Holden, call it in," I said. "We need to—" My words died as snapping twigs to my right caught my attention. I whipped my gaze in that direction, gasping at six vampires dropping out of the trees like they weighed nothing.

"Well, well, well," said the big one at the head of the group. "Isn't this a feast for the senses?"

I recognized him from the photos Sol had shown me. She'd once been engaged to him, but thank heavens that hadn't gone forward. This guy reeked of sulfur and decomposition, his hair graying at the temples. He wore a leather cut with *Marx* on one side and *Bloody Scorpions* on the other. But what shocked me, what had me rooted to the spot, was the man standing to his left, a few feet behind him.

Percy.

My eldest brother. His skin had turned gray, and his cheeks were sunken in, like he'd lost twenty pounds he didn't have in the first place. His eyes were dark and menacing, and he, too, wore a leather vest, labeling him as a Scorpion.

"Percy?" I whispered.

"Hey, little sister," he said, tilting his head to the side. "It's been a while."

"What happened to you?" My heart broke. He'd always been a spoiled bratty shit, but he was my brother. I grew up with him, and even if we spent most of our time in separate boarding schools, we'd been together in the summers. We were family. Blood.

But now, we were on opposite sides of a war. I was a shifter, and he'd been made into a vampire.

How did this happen?

"I could ask you the same thing," he said. "But it doesn't matter anymore. Nothing matters."

"Enough," Marx cut in, holding up a hand.

Holden had reached his limit and fired his gun at Marx's chest, but the vampire only stumbled back as the other vampires attacked, launching themselves at our would-be protector. Holden went down under their weight as I took off in the other direction, back toward the homestead.

"Take them," Marx commanded, and footsteps stomped behind us as they descended. We made it a few feet before a heavy weight landed on my back, and I dropped, screaming at the top of my lungs.

The magic pulsed inside me, and I sent a surge of panic down the bonds, hoping Mill or Guin would feel it. But the connection was stretched thin this far away from the rest of the pack. I prayed Ginny had a stronger tether. I prayed Holden was okay and that he'd gotten a message to the pack in time. I scrambled and kicked, trying to get away, but the vampire on my torso grabbed my hair and yanked my head back.

I saw myself hurdling toward the ground, the sound of a gunshot ringing out before everything went black.

The sun had nearly set by the time all of our reinforcements arrived. Dozer, Apollo, Grinder, and Jagger from the Royal Bastards MC chapter in Montreal made the trip as soon as Kodiak put out the call for help. Captain Pink and Odin from St. Louis got settled in yesterday. They were supposedly the sons of Gods, which said things about the afterlife I'd never considered. I could spend hours talking philosophy with them and never get any real answers.

The guys from Montreal didn't know about vampires or shifters, but what were a few secrets among Bastards? They didn't believe us until Kodiak showed them his fangs.

"What the fuck?" Dozer said, taking a step back.

"Fucking awesome," Jagger replied, moving closer, squinting in wonder.

"Amateurs," muttered Captain Pink with an eye roll from Odin.

All had agreed to go after these Scorpion motherfuckers with everything we had. Even the Steel Roses MC envoy had been willing to throw down. Lore was human and wore an eyepatch over one eye, but that didn't stop him from being a badass.

"If you need help, the Roses always have your back," he'd said, running a hand through his dark hair.

The problem was the resounding ache in my chest that only got worse as time went on. I hadn't seen Maeve since she went hiking with Holden and Ginny, but things hadn't exactly been great between us. I was still scared to touch her, and she was still testing her boundaries. Until Morwyn got the results of our blood tests, I didn't want to get too close, which had only created more distance between us. Now, though, something else was wrong, and I didn't know what it was. Panic surged in my veins, my heart pounding, the magic connecting me and Maeve barely a whisper of what it was immediately after the transition. If I focused hard enough, I worried I might not feel her anymore.

We were standing in Kodiak's office, waiting for him and Orion to deliver the final plan, while I called her phone to check in. When it went straight to voicemail, I pulled up the app I used to track her, ignoring how fucked-up it was that I'd started doing it to begin with, and my blood iced over when I found no signal. Even if it was off, it should have thrown out a location—something my tracking software ensured.

"Anyone seen Holden?" Kodiak shouted, rubbing his chest while his gaze swept the floor.

Fuck.

Anxiety gripping my heart, I pushed through the crowd to the head table.

"He went with Ginny and Maeve earlier today, just out on the trails," I explained. "They should have been back by now."

"Ginny was supposed to report to patrol a half an hour ago," Talon said. "She didn't show."

"Fuck." Orion glanced around the place, waving Guin over when he found her across the room.

"Can you feel Holden?" I asked. "Through the pack bonds?"

I couldn't, but I wasn't very close with him. As alpha, Kodiak was connected to us all. Instead of answering, he grabbed his phone and dialed Ginny, only to get the same result as I did. Ginny's voicemail message rang through his speaker while Orion told Guin what had happened. Kodiak tried Holden next, but it only rang and rang.

Something's wrong, my wolf urged. *Go to her. Run. Now!*

"I'm heading down to the trail," I said, my beast growling with rage and anticipation.

"Moose, Serpent, and Larentia, you're with Mill. Orion, take four others around the other direction. I'll take Guin, Ruby, and Fenris up the middle. Reach out if you find anything." His voice stayed steady, which was worse because it meant he'd gone into reaction mode.

I didn't know how his bonds worked with his own family before they transitioned, but I could imagine he still felt them. Maeve hadn't officially been blooded yet, but that didn't mean he couldn't sense her. Whatever he felt (or didn't) had startled him, and I tried not to let that send me into a tailspin.

The pack took off into the woods, and I followed the path from the stables where Polar said he'd last seen them. We made it about two miles before I stopped. The rotten stench of vampires permeated the atmosphere, a couple of hours old but no less potent. Maeve's scent mingled with Holden's and Ginny's. They'd come this way, but hadn't gotten farther than this, and when I noticed a few broken plants on the undergrowth, I found Maeve's busted cellphone against a tree. Signs of a struggle lined the ground—displayed dirt, limp grass, and a small puddle of blood.

"Fuck," Moose said, stepping in next to me.

I tried to stay calm, but my inner animal was already bucking at my restraint. He wanted to sprint toward the vampire smell and hunt them down. He wanted to tear their throats out with his teeth. We were only a few days on the other side of the moon, so I wasn't as powerful as I'd need to be. It didn't matter to him. A shifter was never as strong as when its mate was on the line.

Fuck, I'd been such an idiot. I should have taken the time to go with her today. I should have made our bond official when I had the chance. What the hell had I been waiting for? Why had I been in such denial? Of course, she was my mate. Her absence and the threat of harm coming to her only made that more glaringly obvious.

"Is that what I think it is?" Larentia said. "Is that her phone?"

"Yeah," I replied, but it came out in a growl.

"They're not here anymore," Pink said. He'd tagged along because he said he could sense when the Scorpions were near, perhaps even anticipate their moves. But none of that helped us now that they were off our property.

"Guys!" Moose called from a few meters ahead, squatting over a prone body—one of our own. I recognized the scent immediately.

Holden.

"No," Larentia said, running over to him. "No, no, no."

Moose pulled out his phone to call Kodiak, but my world narrowed, darkening into one focus, one predatory drive. I would find the fuckers that took them. I would tear into Marx's neck and rip his head from his body. And when I was done, I would hunt down every last Scorpion that dared touch her, that dared take one of our own.

Holden.

This was my fault. I'd asked him to go with her. I put him in danger. His blood was on my hands. Hot fiery anguish shot through my body, making my knees weak, and I bent over, dry heaving into the dirt.

"You alright, man?" Pink asked.

I sucked in lungfuls of air, trying to catch my breath, but it was no use. The pain wasn't mine. It raced down the bond between me and Maeve, sending waves of terror and pain barreling at my molecules.

"She's hurt," I said. "And she's scared."

"C'mon." Moose wrapped an arm around my shoulders and pulled me upright. "We've got to get back."

I clenched my eyes shut and tried to walk, making it only a few steps before I fell against a tree and crumbled to the ground.

"Help!" came her scream inside my head. They were torturing her, burning her, and there was nothing I could do.

"I have to go after her," I roared. "Now!"

She was mine. *Mine.* And I needed to protect her, to get to her, to keep her safe.

"We will," Larentia said, wiping tears from her cheeks. "We have to regroup. You can't do it alone."

Somehow, I returned to the homestead, my feet reluctantly dragging me forward. Both the wolf inside and the human ached to follow her cries until I located her, but Larentia was right. I couldn't fight them alone. Hell, the pack had called in reinforcements for a reason, and nothing could be done until we had a solid plan.

When we got back to headquarters, Kodiak was already in a fit. He barked orders at everyone, somehow still maintaining his composure despite Ginny being taken, but the signs of panic were written into the tight muscles around his lips and the rigid way he stood. My body coiled with tension, boiling in my veins like poison, and when Larentia loaded people up with guns, I trembled with the first signs of a battle.

We'll find you, I tried to tell her through our bond. *We're coming for you.*

Help, was all I got in return. *Help! Mill, I need you!*

I'd never felt more trapped and useless. I *had* to get to her, and standing here while everyone got ready only made it worse. No one moved fast enough, though the logical side of my brain said they were going as fast as they could.

A wail rang out in the hallway, and everyone quieted down, showing respect for our fallen packmate. Holden's parents had just been informed of his death, and though an undercurrent of grief gripped all of us severely, we couldn't give in to it yet. There would be time to mourn his loss, and we would. But we had to get Ginny and Maeve first. He'd want us to do that. He'd want us to save them before tending to his last rites. It was the price we paid to be in the pack. If I were him, I would have insisted on the same thing.

"Serpent, did you perfect that special mist?" Ruby finally asked when Holden's mother's sobs died down, bringing us back to the present.

"It's fucking diabolical," he answered. "It mimics the sedative effect of shifter blood on vampires. They'll get high as fucking kites and drop like flies. Then, we'll move in."

"What about bullets?" Orion asked. "How much iron do we have?"

"Enough to bring down a small army," Larentia replied. Some of the old wives' tales were true. For example, iron brought down a vampire quicker than tearing its head off. On the other hand, silver burned shifters like a hot poker. It would take a large quantity to kill us, but even small amounts slowed us down.

"Channing," Orion called out. "Is there any way to trace them? A phone or—"

"What about Ginny's fitness tracker?" Talon asked. "She never takes it off."

Channing opened her mouth and shook her head. "I don't know—"

I grabbed the laptop and set it on the table, hunching over it to tap away at the keyboard. I had a few tricks up my sleeve that weren't exactly legal, but who the fuck cared? My mind raced faster than my fingers could type, but I could use the same back door method to hack Ginny's tracker as I did to get into Maeve's laptop. Of course, fitness trackers didn't give off the same signal as laptops and phones, but that didn't mean they were untraceable. You just had to know what you were looking for.

First, I hacked into Ginny's laptop to get the IP address for her tracker. That took longer than I wanted, and by the time I had it, the excruciating pain rattling through me had started to make my eyes water. My head splintered like a spear had been shoved between my temples, but I blinked against it and kept going. Slowing down now would do neither of them any favors.

"C'moonnnn," I snarled, bouncing my leg as the laptop took its sweet fucking time. Finally, I got the information to bounce a signal off a government satellite and narrow it down to a ten-mile radius. "There. Are there any abandoned buildings in this area?"

Channing brought something up on a different computer, rattling off the names of several buildings for sale: a pub, a few houses, an old lumberyard, and a slaughterhouse.

"That's it," I said. I didn't know how I knew it, but my intuition and my inner beast were sure. A pub wouldn't have enough space, and they wouldn't risk a real estate agent or local youths finding them in an abandoned house. Besides, there was something poetic about vampires in a slaughterhouse, wasn't there?

"Take me," Pink said. "If you get me within a mile of it, I'll know whether they're in there or not."

I glanced at Kodiak, whose wide, angry gaze shifted to Orion. Pink was a Bastard. He had no reason to betray us, but this was putting my mate and the alpha's daughter at risk. If he was wrong...

"Trust me," Pink said. "I'm here to help."

After only another moment's hesitation, Kodiak nodded and cleared his throat, clearly swallowing down the myriad of emotions that must have been bubbling in his chest.

"We have to consider the possibility that this is a trap," Moose said. Ever the pragmatist, our sergeant at arms would ensure we considered all options.

"Of course it's a trap," Poe added, rubbing a hand over his face. "But we can't stand around and do nothing."

"Weapons?" Kodiak growled.

"We're ready," Larentia replied.

"Meds?" he asked.

"I'm ready," Morwyn said, pulling at her bulletproof vest, the few packmates around her nodding in agreement.

"Serpent?" Kodiak asked.

"Locked and loaded," our enforcer answered.

"Listen, everyone." Kodiak crossed his arms and took a deep breath. "This is a fight we've been preparing for. We know what to do, but the stakes are higher because of Ginny and Maeve. Don't be stupid, and don't waste your shots, you understand? You aim to kill, and you keep in touch."

Orion went over the plan again, pairing us off into teams. I would go with Fenris, Larentia, and Pink. After everyone else was split up, we headed out, hopping on our bikes with Morwyn following in the medivan behind us. It might have been smarter to go in something quieter, but we wanted the Scorpions to know we were coming. They'd infiltrated our home and taken our family. They had to know we'd retaliate.

Even if this was a trap, we were ready for them, and this time, Marx wouldn't slither away like the fucking snake he was. This time, we'd make sure to take him down for good.

CHAPTER 25

Maeve

I woke up to the sound of clanking metal and the smell of old death. My head pounded, and my eyes burned. I brought my hand up to touch the ache, and my fingers came away crusted with blood. I remembered a vampire taking me down from behind, slamming my forehead on the ground. Chains lined the space, hanging from the wall in an ominous display of gruesome intent. They were attached to the ceiling with thick metal hooks, amping up my fear. My hands were in cuffs, hooked to the wall behind me with a thick tether, and my ankles had been tied together with a zip tie. That seemed like lazy work compared to the other options surrounding me.

Glancing around the dark space, I tried not to let the sinking dread consume me. My muscles burned, my veins coated in fire like I was having an allergic reaction to everything. They must have dosed me with pure agony.

I reached out through the weak bond to Mill, something that faded faster the longer I stayed down here.

"Help!" I called. *"Help me!"*

"We'll find you," he replied. *"We're coming for you."*

Terror seized my heart, shooting adrenaline through my body, but I reminded myself to stay calm. Getting panicked would only do the vampires a favor. I took a deep breath, inhaling and exhaling through my nose, praying the pain would disappear.

A slumped body sat in the corner opposite me, its head leaning up against the wall. I recognized Ginny's scent, but a heavy metallic smell permeating off her told me she'd lost a lot of blood. I had no idea how injured she was.

"Pssttt!" I hissed. "Ginny! Ginny, wake up."

When she didn't move, I banged my cuffs on the cement floor. I didn't know where the vampires were or if they'd be able to hear us, so I didn't want to make too much noise, but if there was any way to get out of this, I'd need her help. I wouldn't leave without her.

"Ginny!" I called again. This time, she groaned and lifted her head, wincing as she looked around.

"Fucking hell," she mumbled and touched the wound on her temple. She, likewise, had been knocked unconscious. "Where are we?"

"The vampire house of horrors," I said. "We have to get out of here."

She clenched her eyes shut and blinked a few times. "I think I have a concussion."

I opened my mouth to ask her if she could get out of her cuffs, but a door on the far end of the room opened and several people entered. The disgusting scent of rotten eggs filled my nose, and I nearly heaved. Vampires were horrendous creatures. How could Mill ever think he was like them?

"Welcome back to reality," said the big one in the front. When he stepped into the light, I recognized him as the leader, Marx. He clapped his hands and rubbed them together, flashing a wicked grin that made my skin crawl. "You two wouldn't have been plotting an escape, would you?"

I squared my jaw and glared at him.

"That wouldn't be very well behaved for someone with your upbringing, would it?"

Percy moved to his left, and I shifted my focus to my brother. I hadn't seen him in months. Guin and Sol had led us to believe he'd moved away after his fall from grace, leaving his pregnant wife behind. But now, I knew the truth. He'd been turned into a vampire by the piece of shit standing in front of me.

"How can you stand this?" I asked Percy. "How can you let him do this to me? To your family?"

Percy shifted and rubbed his neck, glancing at the ground.

"Fucking spineless—"

A sharp slap twisted my head to the side, amplifying the headache blossoming behind my eyes, making the anguish in my muscles worse. Torment radiated down my cheek and into my jaw, and I spat blood on the floor in front of me, the result of biting my tongue.

"That's enough," Marx said. "Percy is a good little soldier, aren't you?"

Again, Percy remained quiet.

"I was owed a Vanderbilt daughter," Marx continued, holding up a hand to his goons. "I mean to take what's mine."

He waved his fingers, and they moved forward, three on either side of me. One unbuckled my cuffs on either wrist while the other held my feet down, but as soon as my hands were free, I lunged. Claws jutting out, I scraped a female on the cheek and tore into another's throat, who gasped and clutched at the wound.

The sound of a cocked pistol halted my fury, and I looked at Ginny, who had a vampire standing in front of her, barrel aimed at her head.

"Come willingly or I'll put a bullet in her brain," Marx said.

"Don't listen to them," Ginny said.

But I didn't have a choice. They would kill her if I didn't do what they said, and I would rather die than watch her brains paint the wall.

"Okay," I said, holding my hands to either side. "Okay."

The vampire I'd scratched grabbed my upper arm and dragged

me to my feet, whispering in my ear. "You'll pay for that, you filthy fucking animal."

I grinned a predatory response. My heart raced and my muscles trembled, but I wouldn't show these walking corpses any of that. If I went down, at least I could say I went down swinging. The big guy next to Percy bent to lift me from the waist, slinging me over his shoulder in a fireman's hold. Marx told one of the vampires to stay and guard Ginny while the rest went with us. I scrambled for what to do next. I was sure they planned to take me to some dark, dingy room to do dark, horrible things. Mill's words ricocheted in my head.

They'll spend days draining you…torturing you…using you. And that's if you're lucky. I shudder to think what he would have done with Sol if Orion hadn't gotten to her when he did.

I swallowed down another wave of terror, knowing if I put up a fight, they would hurt Ginny in response.

Think, Maeve! Think!

We rounded a corner, and the sounds of shuffling feet made me perk my head up. Over thirty other vampires stood in a circle. The room reeked of death, and my terror started to take over.

"Calm," urged my inner fox, but I didn't know how to do that when the threat of being dinner became abundantly clear.

The guy holding me dropped me to the ground in the middle of the group, and I landed hard on my ass, nearly spraining my wrists as I tried to right myself. The horde laughed and hissed, staring down at me with dead, lifeless eyes and sharp, intimidating fangs. I took slow breaths to slow my thudding pulse, but it echoed in my head. I shivered, clenching my jaw to keep my teeth from chattering.

"Show no fear," my fox urged, bucking at the confines of my mind. She wanted to take over. She wanted to go rabid and tear as many of them apart as she could. *"Fight as hard as you can."*

I found my brother in the fray and peered at him with pleading eyes. When he glanced away, I figured he must have found a new family. I was nothing more than a name to him, and that betrayal cut the deepest.

"Ladies and gentlemen," Marx shouted, raising his arms high above his head in a grandstanding gesture of performance. "Esteemed children. Behold! My new bride!"

Shock consumed me, filling my chest and gut with dread. Shouts of joy echoed around me, more terrifying than waking up in a cold dungeon.

"She's not the one I was promised," Marx continued, grabbing Percy's shoulder. "We have our newest pledge to thank for that, but she'll have to do."

I scrambled for a plan. They hadn't bound my wrists (*fucking idiots*), and I hadn't been gagged, so I could scream if I needed to. I didn't know what to do about my feet, which were still tied together at the ankles. Even if I fought, I wouldn't be able to run. And whatever they'd dosed me with had made me sluggish and woozy, almost like I was drunk without the thrill. The room spun, and my eyes struggled to focus.

"Get her up," Marx said, and one of his cronies pulled me to my feet. The vile leader walked toward me, stopping inches from my face. His breath was rank, like cigarettes and old compost, and I nearly recoiled away from it, but the vampire behind me held me in place. "What do you think, little shifter bitch? You wanna be my wife for the rest of eternity?"

"I'd rather die," I said, grimacing and turning my head away.

He gripped my chin, forcing my face back to his. "Oh, don't worry. We'll make sure that happens. It's all part of the process."

The group laughed, some even shouting their enjoyment.

"Kill her! Kill her," they chanted.

"Tear her throat out," said the one behind me.

Marx turned back to me with his slimy grin. "And once we're done with you, we'll set in on the cub."

Ginny.

I pictured these fiends sinking their fangs into her body and tearing her apart. Rage simmered through my veins, and I couldn't contain it. It flowed through me, so overpowering and all-consuming. I didn't think; I just reacted.

"No!" I struggled against the vampire's hold, throwing an elbow behind me so it hit him in the solar plexus. He let out a loud "Oomph" and wilted, letting me go. I curled my hand into a fist and pummeled Marx in the throat as four more of his goons descended on me, grabbing my arms, yanking my head back to expose my neck. I wasn't as strong as I used to be, and I tried again to focus.

"You fucking cunt," Marx wheezed, raising a hand to bring it down on my face again. I whipped my head to the side, pain ricocheting down that side of my body. But this time, he didn't stop. He hit me again and again, hard enough that my vision darkened into shimmering stars, my ears rang, my jaw crunched. A hard knock to the stomach pushed all the air out of my body, and I keened forward, gasping for oxygen, coughing, and struggling against the force.

"Is that enough?" Marx taunted. "Or do I need to bring in your friend?"

"No," I managed to mutter. "Don't hurt her."

"I bet she tastes like sin. I bet she tastes like little virgin alpha slut."

I widened my eyes at the realization. They knew who she was. They knew Kodiak was her father, and they'd taken her anyway.

"Her daddy's gonna be pissed when he finds out what we're gonna do to her."

My head hung limp on my shoulders, blood seeping out of my nose and mouth, dribbling on the floor. A sharp tug on my hair had me looking up again, staring down the vampire president with an unfocused gaze.

He stuck his tongue out and licked up the center of my face, scooping crimson into his mouth with a soft, masculine groan.

"My, you *are* delicious." He tsked through his teeth and shook his head before leaning in to lick more blood from my chin, swallowing it down with a look of pure rapture. "Are you gonna scream for me?"

Knowing he liked his victims to struggle made me more resolute to keep calm. I wouldn't give him what he wanted. I wouldn't—

He yanked me to the side and bared his fangs, striking as quick as a viper. His pointed teeth sank into my throat, right where Vermillion had bitten me twice, and the pain reverberated through my entire body. It stung like poison, like venom coating my veins, and I jerked against the fuckers holding me, thrashing, trying to break free.

Tears bubbled in the corners of my eyes, spilling down my cheeks, and all I could do was wilt against him while he sucked and gulped and slurped it down.

Mill had often compared himself to these beasts. He was terrified he had become one. But I knew differently. He'd never be so cruel to me, so heartless and callous. He still had his soul, and this piece of shit had none.

Dizziness clouded my brain like a wave, tugging me under its enthralling spell. I wanted to let it. I wanted to fade into the darkest recesses of my mind and never resurface. It would be easier to give in, to just let them take me, but if they were going to hurt Ginny, I had to fight until the last moment.

Marx pulled away with a satisfied smirk, his fangs and lips sparkling with red liquid, his pupils dilated.

"Well, I'll be Goddamned," he said, leaning in closer so he could take a deep inhale. "You've got some of us in you already."

What?

He tapped the end of my nose with his finger and winked.

"Have you been sucking vampire blood?" He raised his eyebrows. "Hmm? Or maybe vampire dick?"

I didn't know what to say. I'd never been around a vampire before. Unless...could Marx sense whatever magic was in Mill? Could he tell that Mill had died and been brought back to life?

"A little of both?" He chuckled again and shook his head, stepping away with a dazed swagger that must have indicated how drinking from me had impacted him. "Whew! What a fucking rush."

"Let us have a taste?" the vampire on my right said, leaning in to sniff the wound.

"Hang in there, baby," came Mill's voice again. *"We're almost there."*

I sobbed at hearing it, my knees turning to jelly, nearly giving out. But the small flicker of connection between us grew stronger, and if I focused hard enough, I could almost see it like a rope in my mind, glowing brighter the closer he got. My wails turned to laughter.

Marx tilted his head and looked at me, grabbing my chin to lift my face. I burst into hysterics at his stupid, perplexed expression. Maybe it was the blood loss, but everything seemed so hilarious. Mill would come for me, and the pack would tear Marx's limbs from his body, and I would watch it all happen with glee.

"What's so funny?" He leaned in and smirked. "Do you think your silly pack is coming for you? Do you think they stand a chance against us?" He nodded to his group. "I could have them kill you right now, and then what? Your little boyfriend would show up to find you dead, and there'd be nothing he could do about it."

"He's gonna gut you," I said. "They're going to kill you...*again.*" It made me giggle harder, my sides nearly splitting from how much it entertained me.

"C'mon, Marx," one of the vampires said. "Let's turn her and end this, once and for all."

Marx held up a hand to silence him, narrowing his gaze on me.

"You know we infiltrated Kodiak's pack and killed them. I even killed that little bitch in your bedroom. It's not hard to get on Bastard turf, and I won't stop coming until I get what's mine."

My heart clenched again for Ellen, but I ignored it, shoving it down until I could fully process it.

"God, all the fucking monologuing." I rolled my eyes. "You know what I think?"

Marx peeled his lips back from his fangs.

"I think you *want* them to come. I think you want a fight. If you didn't, you would have killed me or whatever the fuck you're planning to do." I shook my head, hardly able to hold it up anymore.

"I think you've yet to give me a scream," he said, nodding to the guy on my right. "Go ahead, Jollies. You and the rest of the nest can have her. Once her heart gives out, I'll give her my blood, and we'll see how much fight she has in her then."

Jollies exhaled in pure excitement before sinking into my throat, just below Marx's bite. I winced at the sharp lance of agony but didn't make a noise. Another bite came on the other side, and then another, and a fourth. All the while, I stared at Marx, determined to hold out. I wouldn't give him what he wanted. I wouldn't—

One of them sank into my left thigh so hard, he hit bone. The anguish that surged up my body crippled me, so deep and paralyzing, it took over my soul. They were killing me. Truly and utterly destroying me. And there was nothing I could do. There would be no paramedics to rescue me this time, and I wasn't sure if the pack would make it.

When one of them sank into my stomach, I lost my composure.

And then I screamed.

Vermillion

I t took too long for us to get to her. Her pain echoed through our bond like razors under my skin, like they were scraping me apart from the inside out.

"They're here," Pink said, staring at the crumbling slaughterhouse with an intense focus.

"You're sure?" Kodiak asked, his eyes already gone red to his wolf.

Understandably, my beast was also close to the surface. He couldn't retreat or let me rest until we had her again. The human, too, had a vengeful streak that wouldn't be calmed.

"I'm sure," Pink said. "I can sense those motherfuckers like a plague."

Kodiak nodded and turned to the group. "Split up. You know your groups. Stay tight. Keep an eye on your six."

Fenris gripped my shoulder in a reassuring squeeze, but it didn't help. I knew I had my pack behind me, but it was my fault she had a target on her in the first place. I should have kept my distance from her. If I had, she might not have transitioned. As soon as I thought it, I remembered Lycan telling me she was close at Orion's wedding, and I chastised myself for my shame.

This would have happened anyway. I couldn't have stopped it.

I pushed thoughts like that out of my mind and focused on the task. We had to get in there and find her. With two pistols on my waist and an assault rifle in my arms, I snuck around the corner of the building toward the side entrance. I'd been able to pull up blueprints, and I knew this led to the basement. The last time we'd raided a vampire nest, they'd kept Sol and Guin tied up in the darkest room, so I suspected they'd do the same here.

Just as we approached the door, Larentia held up a fist to stop us, narrowing her gaze at the entry. I smelled them before I saw them, the decrepit decay of rotting flesh. It hit me in the nose, and I recoiled, forcing my legs to stay still so I didn't rush into an ambush.

One heartbeat went by before the thick metal doors burst open, five vampires pouring out. They launched at us, two taking Larentia down before Fenris fired bullets into their brains. I rained hellfire down on them, shooting before thinking, but the biggest one in the back jumped on me, knees to my chest, forcing me to the ground before I could stop him.

I landed with a loud grunt, and pain rattled through my sternum, but I managed to get my pistol and aim it at his temple. He grabbed my neck and bared his fangs like he meant to tear into my jugular. I shot before he could. Cold, disgusting brains splattered my face, and I winced to keep from getting it in my eyes, pushing to my feet so I could help my teammates.

Pink had ripped a vampire in half and thrown its carcass to the side, while Fenris shot at three more that piled out of the door before they could attack. Larentia stood and brushed herself off before checking in.

"Everyone okay?" she asked, her observant gaze trailing the length of each of us.

"Let's go," I snarled, taking the lead this time. I sensed my girl somewhere inside, and when we emerged into a long hallway, my wolf told me to head straight, even though we were meant to take the stairs on the left and go to the basement. The ceiling was falling apart, thick pieces hanging in scattered spots, the musky scent of mold nearly masking the overwhelming aroma of death. The floors were littered with garbage and peeling wallpaper. This place hadn't been operational for years.

"This way," Larentia said, nodding toward the stairs, but I resisted. Maeve wasn't down there. My instincts told me to go forward, that I would find her up ahead.

I didn't respond, just continued treading lightly as I went in the direction of my girl.

"Mill," Fenris hissed. "C'mon. What are you doing?"

"Maeve's up this way." I kept going, ignoring the protests of my packmates behind me.

"Go," Pink said. "I'll take the basement."

"Not alone," Larentia said. "Vermillion, stop."

I didn't. I couldn't. My wolf and I were laser-focused on one thing: getting to Maeve as quickly as possible. Her torment and fear raced through my veins, and the most vicious part of me urged me forward. As I moved, I stepped on something that sounded like broken glass, but as soon as I moved my foot, a loud blast went off to my left, and a slicing pain shot down my right side.

I wilted and dropped to the ground, crumpling onto one knee.

"Goddamn it, Mill!" Fenris grabbed my shirt and hauled me up, yanking me into the room on the right as more blasts sounded up and down the hall. I'd triggered a trip wire, setting off a string of rifles positioned in the corridor.

"Fuck," I groaned, grabbing at the wound on my ribs. My fingers came away wet with blood, but it wasn't serious. It was barely a cut. "I'm okay."

"Hell," Fenris said, running his hands back through his hair. "What are you doing? We have orders."

"My *mate* is down there, Fen," I said. "You'd do the same fucking thing."

When the guns stopped shooting, I peeked my head out into the hallway to make sure we were alone. Once I verified we were, I stepped out and stared at the ground so I didn't set off anything else.

My rifle held high, I continued, checking each door as I walked. Fenris fell into step behind me, Pink and Larentia behind him, begrudgingly staying with me despite the breach in orders.

"Mill," came Kodiak's voice in my head. *"Stick to the plan."*

I ignored him, pushing his frustrated voice away. Technically, I would have to answer for this, but I didn't care. Only one thing mattered.

"Goddamn it, Mill," Larentia said. "Fine. Lead the way."

Just as we walked into the opening at the end of the hall, a group of vampires appeared out of the shadows, snarling and hissing, blood dripping from their chins.

I recognized the scent. It was Maeve's, and that infuriated me. A roar ripped out of my chest as I raised my gun to shoot them, but Fenris and Pink reacted quicker. My buddy pulled the pin from one of Serpents' gas grenades and launched it, tugging me back into the corridor as it exploded. Crimson vapor filled the space, reeking like shifter blood and chemicals. The vampires recoiled at first, but it made them woozy, and they dropped to the floor one at a time until all of them were incapacitated.

"That was Maeve's blood," I roared, feeling sick. My wolf bucked at what little restraint I had on him, begging to take over, pleading to have his revenge.

"I know, brother," Fenris said.

"We're with you," Larentia added. "Let's kill these fuckers, and we'll keep going."

We went around the room and fired bullets into their heads, but I knew we'd have to come back and cut them to pieces to keep them down forever. Their brains splattered on the floor, and when some of it hit me in the face, I winced and wiped the wretched stuff away. Fuck, I'd be covered in the slime by the time I got to her, but I didn't care. I couldn't think of how I looked right now.

After we put these fuckers down, I sensed Maeve was off to the right, so we entered another long corridor, checking each door as we passed it. My pulse thundered, her energy getting stronger under my skin as we drew closer. We'd just reached the end when the door on our left flew open, bodies piling out of it faster than I could count. Two became four became six, and I stumbled back, the vile scent nearly blinding me. I fired my rifle, but there were too many, and the weight of them took me down to the ground.

I swung my arm, nailing one in the face before twisting to hold another by the neck. Its enormous fangs chomped two inches from my face, and I snarled, shoving it to the side. A sharp pinching slice tore through my calf, another through my forearm, and I screamed.

"Vermillion!" came the anguished sound of my best friend, mere feet from me.

Even I was brave enough to admit things weren't going well, and I reached for my knife, stabbing it into the eye of the Scorpion on top of me. It wilted to the side, and I went for my pistol, aiming it at the monsters by my leg.

"Die, you fucking bloodsucking bitches!" Rage exploded from me as I shot them, but then my gun clicked and went lifeless. I'd run out of bullets, my rifle had fallen out of reach, and there were still more coming. I scrambled backward, and Pink grabbed my shirt to pull me to my feet.

"We're fucked," he said. "Let's fall back."

I couldn't swallow that. I could only go forward. She was just on the other side of—

A blinding white light cut off my train of thought, and I clenched my eyes shut, holding up a hand to block it out. A vibrant magical plume permeated the space behind me and the hallway up ahead. The rotten decay of vampires quickly turned to a burning smell, ash filling my nose and throat. I coughed, and when the light finally died, I focused on a silhouette behind me. Boots echoed off the cement floor as the person came closer, and I recognized the leather cut before I saw her face.

The Royal Harlots MC: Asheville, NC, read the patch on one side. On the other side, her nametag said Marta—*Prospect.*

"Hiya, boys," she said, tilting her head to one side. "Need some help?"

The Royal Harlots in Asheville were witches, and they'd been tasked with keeping America safe against rogue monsters. Kodiak had called them in for help, but we didn't think they'd make it in time. Marta had long dark hair that she'd piled into a ponytail, and for being as powerful as she was, she wasn't much taller than five feet.

"Thank you," I said, grimacing through the bite on my leg.

"For real," Larentia added. "We would have been vampire feed without you."

"Let's go," I said, picking up my rifle before nodding toward the end of the hallway. I stepped and fell to the side, my leg refusing to work. Hot, sticky liquid pooled in my sock, and I winced. But my wolf came to the front of my consciousness, taking the pain, dulling it to the point where I could keep going.

"You okay?" Marta said, glancing down at the wound.

"Fine," I growled and forced myself forward. "My mate's in there."

We pushed through the door on the end, and I held my gun up, Marta on my right, Fenris on my left, Larentia and Pink guarding our backs. The entire ride here, I'd prepared myself for what I might find. Maeve was still alive, I sensed it in my bones, but she'd been tortured. I expected her to have been beaten up and bruised, but the sight that greeted us stopped me. My muscles froze, my heart sank, and wrath boiled through my blood.

Maeve lay on the floor in the middle of a circle of lit candles, vampires chanting all around her. Marx kneeled at her side, his wrist pressed against her mouth while her body writhed and spasmed. At our arrival, he lifted his head, bloody streaks down his chin, his obsidian gaze unfocused.

"Well, well, well," he said, ignoring us to return to his sick, twisted work. "It's about time you showed up."

The other vampires continued speaking in tongues as if we were mere annoyances rather than their death sentences.

"Let her go," I shouted, holding my rifle up before taking another step forward.

Marx clucked through his teeth, his fangs gleaming in the dim light. Giant hooks hung from the ceiling, fixed from thick metal chains, and dilapidated machinery lined the walls. This must have been the room where they dressed the animals after they slaughtered them, and I prayed to whatever fucking fates listening that they hadn't used any of this shit on my girl. This fucked-up ritual was bad enough.

The sinking weight of dread coiled in my stomach. I knew what they were doing, and I hoped to God we weren't too late.

"Now, why would I do that?" Marx said with a laugh. He sauntered closer to the edge of the circle, and I aimed the barrel of my rifle right at his head before pulling the trigger. Nothing happened. I tried again. My nerves seized as I got the same result.

Fucking jammed.

I tossed the damned thing to the side and roared, launching myself into the fray. Marta held her hands out to either side, smoky wisps of magic streaking from her fingertips, while Fenris grabbed a pistol and fired at the onlookers. I raced toward the circle but hit an invisible wall at the edge, forcing me back.

"Stupid, arrogant shifter," Marx said with a cruel laugh. "You think you're the only ones with magic?"

Limbs shaking and panic racing in my molecules, I shoved to my feet and tried again, pounding against the barrier, throwing my body at it, trying to break through.

"Maeve!" I shouted telepathically. *"Maeve, come back to me."*

The sounds of metal doors bursting open nearly distracted me, and thick, heavy boots came closer, breaking Marx's concentration. He glanced behind me, but I sensed the pack had joined us. Marta continued to chant spells in the background, Pink hauled vampires over his head like they weighed nothing, and Orion tore through them like a juggernaut, like they were nothing. But even once the last vampire had been dismembered, the veil still held firm.

I reached down inside, sensing the tether between me and my mate, and I yanked. I pushed against the magical wall while I tugged Maeve toward my soul. My vision blackened, my head going dizzy, either from blood loss or the weight of my tie to her, but I ignored it. My wolf reached out to her fox, curling around her, coating her with the supernatural protection of pack, covering her in everything that was mine. Kodiak gave me his energy through the bonds, shoving it toward me and through me, into her. She wasn't officially a member of his family yet, but that didn't seem to matter, not when my beast had already decided it would have her.

She opened her eyes and gasped, looking at me with that crystal clear gaze. Was she still in there? Was it still her...or had she been perverted by him?

"Mill," she whimpered.

"I'm here, sweetheart. I'm here." I threw energy into her. I gave her everything I had, pouring my fury through our bond. I'd never had a mate before. And despite not having officially sealed it with Maeve, something felt different about this. It was bolder, brighter, stronger. I imagined it like a bolt of lightning, a bright shimmering electric string tying my soul to hers, my blood to her blood. I fed it with my entire soul.

"This all could have been avoided if you had just given me what I asked for at the beginning." Marx circled to stand in my view, his filthy boots blocking her from me, and when I glanced up at him, the scalding power of my hatred overtook my senses. I sent that to Maeve, too. I gave her my forcefulness, my will, my dominance. I turned it all over to her, knowing it would weaken me. But if it saved her, I would die happily. I would give her anything to see her live through this as the shifter she'd been when she entered it.

"Mill," Orion said, coming to stand next to me. "Mill, we can't get through to her. We can't—"

A cold spray of blood hit us both in the face, halting his words. I blinked and watched as Marx choked, spewing up black liquid, his body convulsing. A hand protruded from his chest, his putrid heart gripped in between claws as it gave two final beats. Maeve yanked it back, ripping the damn thing from his body.

Marx collapsed and dropped to his knees, revealing a menacing, pissed-off female behind him. Her eyes glowed ice blue, her wild dark hair in bloody mats around her head, her canines exposed over red, furious lips as she dropped his putrid heart. Then she gripped the top of his mouth in one hand, curling her fingers under his teeth, before putting a foot on his shoulder. With one terrible yank, she separated the top part of his jaw from the rest of his body and tossed it to the side.

I had one final moment to memorize her in all of her bloodthirsty raging beauty before my consciousness gave out on me.

I rolled onto my side and snuggled into Vermillion, resting my head on his chest. We were on the cliff in the woods near my house, the same one I'd taken him to all those weeks ago. The sun had set on the horizon, painting the sky in beautiful peaches and tangerines. The heat of summer coated our skin in a thick blanket of warmth and security. We were safe here together. Nothing could harm us.

"It's a beautiful day," I said, wrapping an arm over his stomach while he lazily ran his fingers up and down my spine.

We'd taken each other four times already, but ever the insatiable slut, I wanted more. I'd always want more. My heart kicked as he laughed and kissed the top of my head.

"We could go swimming," he said. "Would you like that?"

I hummed a noncommittal noise and glanced up at him, resting my chin on his sternum. "I feel like there's something more important we're supposed to do."

"There's nothing more important than this," he murmured, leaning down to take my mouth. I sighed into the contact, relishing how soft his lips always were.

"Stay with me, Maeve," came the sound of a familiar woman on

the wind. It sounded like Guin, but that couldn't be. What the hell was she doing here? She didn't know about this place. It was mine. Mine and his.

"Goddamn it, Mill," said a deep baritone. *"Don't do this to me again. You don't fucking do this to me."*

Fenris?

I furrowed my brow and glanced down at Mill, who shared my look of confusion.

"What is that?" I asked. "Do you hear that?"

He nodded.

Flashes of a bright room and a woman with curly brown hair blurred through my mind, almost like memories trying to yank me out of paradise.

"It sounded like Fenris," Mill said. He sat up and glanced around.

More memories burst through my mind's eye—the stink of vampires, the stab of sharp fangs in my neck, the taste of rotten blood in my mouth. And then...Mill. Blood-soaked and limping. The sensation of strength suddenly filled my bones, lifting me off the cold cement floor, forcing away the darkness in my soul. It had been so cold, so desolate. I was sure I was dying. But there he was, burning it clean with his vitality. It had ripped through me like an inferno, and whatever had been done to me was suddenly *un*done.

"Mill...I think we died," I said.

He narrowed his eyes and chuckled. "Again?"

I laughed and glanced around. Even though this was a perfect replica of my cliff, something was off. The sun had been setting for hours...days. The wind hadn't blown, not once. And the birds were chirping gleefully, not a predator in sight save for us.

"Where are we?" I asked. "Is this a memory?"

He shrugged. "I don't care one way or the other."

"Vermillion, keep her here," Morwyn said. *"You both stay here, understand me? I'm not losing you again. I'm not—"*

"We have to go back," I said.

He shrugged. "It's nice here, isn't it? We could stay."

"We agreed that life was worth living," I said. "Me and you. You and me. Together."

The sound of Mill's chuckle filled me with joy, and his amazing smile lit up his face. "I guess you're right."

I remembered most of what happened, the tumult of images assaulting me. I should have panicked. I'd been drained and fed vampire blood. I'd been beaten and abused. But I'd also had my revenge. I tore Marx's heart from his chest and ripped his head off his body, and he wouldn't be able to hurt my family any longer. Up until Mill found me, I'd been so weak, sure that I would die, sure that Marx would turn me into one of them. Could a shifter even turn into a vampire? I didn't know. But that sudden surge of strength...that wave of fire...

"Did you save me?" I asked.

"You saved me, baby girl," he said. "We saved each other."

"Maeve, Goddamn it!" Guin's anxious voice filled my senses, lighting a sense of urgency in my soul. Something powerful overtook me, like pack magic but stronger, more furious, and overbearing. It demanded I respond. *Kodiak.*

Mill lay back down, and I rested my head on his chest again, listening to the steady beat of his heart.

"So we agree, then?" I said. "We'll go back?"

He tangled his hands in my hair and sighed. "Whatever you say, sweetheart. I'll go anywhere with you."

"On the count of three." I held him tight, refusing to let him go. "One... Two... Three..." I closed my eyes, and our Eden drifted away.

I'd never given much thought to dying.

My mother passed when I was six, and though I understood all things must come to an end, I didn't fully comprehend the precarious tightrope upon which we mortals walked until the Grim Reaper gave mine a good shake.

But I'd looked that fucker in the eyes twice now and told him to beat feet.

When I opened my eyes again, a wave of pain and nausea hit me so fiercely, I immediately rolled to the side and heaved up whatever was in my gut. It tasted awful, and I kept going until it was all purged. My body ached, and my head pounded between my eyes. Every muscle protested my movements, but a cool hand greeted my forehead, and a calming energy floated through my nerves, soothing the anguish back into dormancy.

"There she is," said a familiar voice. *Guin.*

"Decided to rejoin us among the living?" Sol asked, squeezing my hand.

"Where's Mill?" I croaked. Someone had taken a sandblaster to my throat, but none of that was as urgent as locating my mate...my Mill.

"He's right here," Morwyn said, touching my neck to check my pulse. "We couldn't get you two apart. You've been clinging to him since we brought you in."

I blinked to my left and found Mill squinting at me through bleary, tired eyes. He looked like shit. His cheeks were sunken, and his skin had turned a deathly pallor that made me want to cry. I imagined I looked worse.

"What happened?" I tried to say.

"Shh." Morwyn held a straw to my lips, and I sucked back the most delicious water I'd ever tasted.

"You ripped a vampire's heart out," Sol said with a laugh. "And then tore off his head."

"You're a regular badass," Fenris added.

I started to smile, but then the thought of who had been abducted with me hit me like a freight train. I started to struggle, trying to sit up. "Ginny!"

"She's okay," Guin said, holding me down, forcing me against the hospital bed. "She's just fine. Kodiak found her before anything serious happened."

"You're the one with the injuries," Morwyn said. "You need to rest."

I relaxed at hearing she had survived and held up my hand to wipe my face. I had bite marks up and down my forearm in deep red circles. A sob poured out of my chest before I could stop it, and I glanced down at my body, where even more wounds marred my skin.

"You'll heal," Morwyn said. "I promise. They'll fade."

"Am I a vampire now?" I asked through broken cries. The last thing I remembered was those sick fuckers casting some spell and Marx forcing his blood down my throat.

"No," Morwyn said. "No, Maeve. We got there in time."

"Mill saved you," Kodiak said, suddenly appearing in the doorway to the room. "Whatever was being done to you, he pushed it out."

"I think it was the...blood sharing...that made your connection so strong," Morwyn explained. "But, we'll talk about that later, okay?" She turned to my family. "Everyone out. They need to rest."

I let my eyes close, and I drifted back into unconsciousness.

Days passed like centuries after that. It was a long road to heal-ing, and not just because I'd been drained of blood and forced into some vampiric ritual. Mill had given me so much of his strength that we'd yet to find an equilibrium between us again. The connection between us had been ripped open, turning a rope into a tunnel, making each of our bodies weaker. He would get better and try to send it to me. I would feel better and send it back to him.

There was a particular kind of intimacy in that, I supposed. No other set of mates so strongly shared magic, but Morwyn warned us that it could be detrimental. She wouldn't leave us alone until we were back to a more typical homeostasis. We were released from the infirmary once we both could walk, but it could be weeks or months until we returned to normal.

I spent my days sketching and sleeping...sleeping and sketching. I did portraits of anyone I could, trying to heal the neural pathways between my fingers and brain. My hands didn't work like before, but Morwyn assured me they would get there. I just had to keep trying. My favorite was when Mill was relaxed in his post-climax glow with a slight smile on his lips, his hair tussled, and that sated look in his eyes.

"That's creepy, you know," he said, looking down at my drawing of him. "You sketching me all the time."

I raised an eyebrow. "This coming from the guy who tracked my phone and hijacked my computer?"

He'd told me how he found us, that he'd been running surveillance on my electronics and eventually hacked into Ginny's computer to track her smartwatch. I probably should have been upset about the invasion of privacy, but after everything, I didn't mind so much. Secretly, I kind of liked the idea of him watching me, especially during those more intimate moments. That conversation had led to this most recent round of lovemaking, and there was no greater pleasure than being in his bed...*our* bed.

Mill chuckled and kissed my temple.

"You're my favorite muse, big bad wolf."

We tried to move on. But the nightmares came almost every night. Vampires ripped me to pieces. Fangs pierced my skin. I screamed and sobbed and tried to get away, only to wake up crying in Vermillion's arms.

"It's okay," he said, kissing the tears from my cheeks, pulling me tighter to his body. "You're here. It was just a dream."

I was thankful we weren't sharing those. I'd come to rely on him to bring me out of them. More than once, he'd roll on top of me and slot himself between my legs and bring me such intense pleasure that the bad memories drifted away to ancient history.

But all was not well with my knight in shining armor. He struggled to regain what he lost, and in the days immediately afterward, he could hardly lift anything over fifty pounds.

"I'll be back to normal after the next moon," he insisted. "The moon always heals."

I worried he might not even survive it. In the heat of the attack, Mill had given me all of his strength and magic. It was what gave me the power to get to my feet and kill Marx. But in doing so, Mill had made himself vulnerable. If I could return the favor, I would.

"Do you need to feed from me?" I asked him one night after an intense orgasm. He'd collapsed on top of me and shook so badly, I thought he might be having a seizure.

He lifted his head and stared at me with eyes nearly as red as his wolf's. "No."

"It's okay," I told him. "I know it's you."

Maybe I should have been more scared of him drinking my blood, especially given the trauma I survived, but the difference between my mate and the Scorpions was so vast, I could clearly distinguish between them. Mill would never hurt me like them. He would never make me feel powerless. If anything, the blood tie between us strengthened us both, and I adored that part of our relationship.

"I won't ever do that to you again," he said, kissing me. "Not ever."

I didn't like his answer, but I didn't push him. He'd come around when he was ready.

"There's something else bothering you," I said. There was an undercurrent of shame rattling around in his soul, and until he let it out, I worried it might eat him alive. "What is it?"

"It's nothing," he said.

"Come on, I can feel it." I brushed hair away from his face, resting my hand on his cheek.

He gave me a sad smile and shook his head. "It's just...I sent you three out there that day. I should have gone with you. I should have stopped you from going. Now, Holden is dead. Marx got on our turf because our alarms failed. You were taken because...because I didn't stop it."

"That's not your fault," I said. "You couldn't have known. And if you were there…" I didn't want to think about what would have happened to him in Holden's place. "We still don't know why the alarms failed. Marx was coming for me no matter what."

It didn't matter what I said. Mill took his job as the head of tech seriously and blamed himself for not being better equipped to deal with such an attack. We'd been blindsided, and in his mind, he should have done better.

"No one blames you, Mill. You're the only one doing that."

He nodded and kissed me again before rolling off me to head to the bathroom.

When I saw Ginny for the first time since the attack, she rushed into my arms and squeezed me tight, and we both broke into tears, sobbing until we could have a coherent conversation. Steadfast and strong, we'd survived the worst together and come out the other side.

"I'm so glad you're okay," she said. "I thought they'd kill you. I thought—"

"We're okay," I told her. "We survived, and we're okay."

A few days later, I had to face the music. Ava had been calling me nonstop since it happened, and I suspected I knew why.

"I felt it," she said, concern in her voice. "Something happened to you. I swear it."

"It's nothing," I said. "It was just a…blip."

Guin stood anxiously in the corner of the room while Sol paced and chewed her lip. I'd been sworn to secrecy, even from my twin, my other half, but that didn't mean I liked it. They were both sure I'd slip and spill my guts. After all, Ava was the only sister who didn't know now, and according to Lycan, she'd be next. Since he was still in Paris with her, I figured he'd be the first to know.

"A blip?" Ava scoffed. "What the hell is that supposed to mean?"

"It means I'm alive, and you don't need to worry about it," I told her.

"So what? You're keeping secrets now, too?"

I sighed. "Would you believe me if I told you I'm in love with a Bastard?"

That distracted her long enough to have her squealing. "Is it Mill?"

I chuckled and admitted it was. We talked for a few more minutes before she had to run to a work meeting.

"I'll be home in five more weeks," she said. "And then you're going to confess whatever you're keeping from me."

"I'm not keeping anything," I said, but she knew better. Twin telepathy had always been strong between us, and this new shift in my character would only make her more suspicious. After we hung up, I looked at Sol and Guin and raised an eyebrow. "I hate lying to her."

"It's for the best," Sol said, standing next to me so she could hold my hand. "Once she transitions, she'll know."

"Why can some of the other Bastard clubs know but she can't?" I didn't see the logic in it. One way or the other, this secret was too big. It was a wonder the rest of the world hadn't found out already.

"They're sworn to the club," Guin explained. "Loyalty or death. Everyone knows that."

"Besides, *you* need to start worrying about your initiation and mating ceremony." Sol smiled that classic Vanderbilt grin, and I tried not to let the pressure get to me. Was it idiotic to mate myself to a man I'd only admitted to loving a week ago?

Maybe.

But he did save my life, and the nine-year-old girl inside of me screamed with excitement. She'd been in love with him for years, and if I was honest with myself, it had only been a matter of time between us. I'd wanted him from the first time I saw him, and now I'd have him for the rest of my life.

"Yeah, maybe you're right," I said. "But first, I have to go see Morwyn. She's got the results of the blood test back."

"Want me to come with you?" Sol asked.

"No." I waved her away. "It's fine. If I was going to turn into a vampire, I'm sure I'd already be stinking up the place."

I hadn't forgotten what Marx said when he drank from me.

"You've got some of us in you already. Have you been sucking vampire blood?"

Why would he say that? What did he taste? What magic did he sense that no one else could?

Sol glanced sideways at Guin, who shrugged and pursed her lips in some kind of silent communication.

"Hey, none of that," I said. "I'm fine. I'll join the pack and mate my lover, and on the world spins." I grabbed my phone and shoved it into my back pocket before turning to my eldest sister. "Don't you have a meeting with His Highness, the almighty alpha?"

Guin rolled her eyes and crossed her arms. "He can wait."

"He hasn't convinced you to join the pack, yet?" Sol asked with a girlish giggle.

"He fucking wishes I'd sink so low as to acquiesce to his every whim," she said.

"It's not *exactly* like that," Sol said. "I mean, I still have free choice and everything. It's more like...family. And he's the patriarch. He wants the best for us."

"Hmm." Guin didn't dignify that with more of a response, just headed toward the door and opened it for me so I could go ahead of her.

"Are you sleeping?" Morwyn asked, her wide eyes inquisitive and compassionate. I blushed when I realized how much she looked like her brother. But she resembled Caelum, too, and I wondered what their parents must have been like.

"Yes," I answered. "But the nightmares are intense." I paused for a moment, trying to decide if I should bring it up or not. Ultimately, his sister had known him longer. Maybe she could get through to him in a way I couldn't. "I'm worried about Mill."

"I know. Me too." She grabbed her stethoscope and put the ends in her ears. "Do you mind if I listen to your heart?"

I nodded, and she moved behind me, pressing the circular part to my back. After a few moments of the inhale-exhale gig, she removed the earpieces and wrapped them around her neck.

"It all sounds fine." She scribbled down some notes. "If there were any lingering magical effects, they would have shown up by now."

I rubbed the side of my neck, absently hiding the scars from where Marx had bitten me. "Do you think he was trying to turn me?"

"I don't know." She sighed. "Marta, the witch from the Royal Harlots, said she would do some research on her end. It was an ancient ritual, not one they normally use to create vampires."

"I don't feel any different."

"That's good," she said. "Marta thinks they didn't get to finish."

"Did she already head back to Asheville?" I would have liked to thank her for her help. Mill and Fenris would have died without her. I probably would have died without her.

Morwyn nodded. "The Asheville Witches are monster hunters. You don't get to be a Harlot until you've paid your dues. I imagine she had other fish to fry."

I hummed in disappointment and made a mental note to send her a fruit basket or something.

"The blood tests came back with some anomalies. I'm still trying to work through it. You said you have a history of cardiac arrest?" Morwyn asked, flipping through pages on her clipboard.

I explained what happened to me, making sure to include the medications I'd been on and what specialists I'd seen in the aftermath.

"When was this?"

"November 10th," I said.

She froze and glanced up at me, raising her eyebrows. "November 10th? Are you certain?"

I nodded. "7:05 p.m. They used an AED to revive me."

Her features dropped like she'd come upon some dawning realization that would solve all our problems.

"When did you first meet Mill?" she asked.

"When I was nine," I said. "He worked on the ranch for a summer. Why? What's that got to do with my heart?"

Morwyn blinked and shook her head, turning back to her computer and clicking through screens faster than I could see them.

"Christ, Kodiak was right," she mumbled to herself. "I didn't believe it. How could he have lived that long—so long without—"

"What?" I tried to look over her shoulder, but she closed her laptop before I could catch anything worthwhile. "What's wrong?"

"Maeve, I think I know what happened," she said. "But I need to get Vermillion for this conversation."

"Okay."

She left in a hurry, and I waited in the exam room, trying not to let my anxiety get the best of me. A small voice in the back of my mind warned me that what she had to say wouldn't make Mill any happier. Maybe I already knew what the solution was based on her line of questioning. I mean, hell, it wasn't that hard to figure out. If Mill was my mate, exactly *how long* had we been connected like this? And if she thought my meeting him as a kid had anything to do with my heart, maybe we had been more mated than we initially thought.

When she returned, Mill was right behind her, his features drawn tight, his eyes stoic but alert.

"What is it?" he asked. "Is she okay?"

"Yes, she's fine," Morwyn said, gesturing to the chair next to the examination table. "Sit down."

"Kodiak told me what he suspected, but I didn't know how it could be true," Morwyn said once I sat. I squeezed Maeve's hand, hoping to show that I supported her no matter what my sister said. "Most of the time, a mating bond doesn't happen until a shifter transitions. But not always."

Maeve furrowed her brows and glanced at me.

"What does that mean?" Maeve asked.

"November 10th is when Vermillion was attacked by vampires and died. His heart stopped for five minutes." Wyn looked between us, her gaze imploring us to catch on. "At exactly 7:05 p.m."

Maeve's features dropped, realization dawning on her. "Oh my God."

"I don't understand," I said. "What does that mean?"

"That's exactly when Maeve's heart stopped," Wyn explained. "There was no reason for her to have gone through that, not unless..."

"We were already mated," I finished for her. Fucking hell, that was precisely what Kodiak had hinted at weeks ago. "Is that possible?"

Wyn shrugged. "Anything's possible. We don't fully understand magic and never will, as much as I might try."

"So what?" Maeve said, tightening her hold on my fingers. "We've been mated since I was a child? I thought shifters couldn't live without their mates."

"The mating bond wasn't sealed," Wyn replied. "It still isn't, but I suspect Mill's wolf had already chosen you, and the tiny bit of you that was a shifter, the part that was lying in wait until you turned, it selected him, as well."

"But he helped Guin through her transition," Maeve continued. "How could he have done that if his wolf was already dedicated to me?"

"The transition is a compulsion," Wyn explained. "And since the mating bond wasn't official, he could go through with it. But, they came out of the other side no more connected than they were when they entered it."

"Which is why we're different," Maeve said.

"Exactly," Wyn continued. "I think you crave her life force because you spent so long without it. Dying and coming back to life changed you both, but it was this connection that ultimately saved you."

"Will it go away?" I asked, my voice hoarse with shock and surprise. "Will I ever stop...wanting that?"

Wyn shrugged. "Maybe. But if not, and Maeve is willing..."

"You need me," she said, lifting my hand to her mouth so she could kiss my knuckles. "And I need you."

This explained everything, and I felt like an idiot for not realizing it sooner. Kodiak had been right. My inner beast purred with contentment, as if he were adding his two cents in.

"And I can't hurt her, right? I'm not—we're not—" I didn't want the pack or anyone else thinking we had been turned into our enemies. Despite whatever Marx had done to her, she still smelled like her. The ritual, or whatever it was, hadn't been completed. But magic like that lingered, and it terrified me.

"No, Mill," Wyn said. "I've studied the difference between vampire and shifter blood. If that were true, the vampires in that nest would have recognized you as one of their own."

"Marx said—" Maeve cut in. "He said I already had some of them inside me. He asked if I'd been drinking vampire blood."

Wyn bit the side of her lip. "Maybe he tasted the magic. There's a difference between being brought back to life and becoming a vampire. I'll keep digging, but in the meantime, I'm not worried about either of you. You're pack, and you're safe."

The confidence my sister had in her assessment dissipated the heavy weight I'd been carrying in my stomach since the attack.

"The more time you spend around each other, the more comfortable you get, the easier the cravings will be." Wyn smiled in that reassuring way that made her a wonderful healer and an even better friend. "When you're apart, your blood changes. When I put the samples together, they attract like magnets. It makes you both stronger."

I sighed, feeling a tremendous burden shift off my shoulders. I wanted her. Some part of me had always wanted her, and that was okay. It was all okay.

After leaving Wyn's office, we went to my room, where Maeve shut the door and locked it with a mischievous glint.

"How are you feeling about all this?" She put her arms behind her back and strolled toward me, grinning and biting her bottom lip in an adorable tease. I loved her like this...playful and pretending to be innocent. I knew the truth. My girl liked to roll around in the filth with me, and based on the way she stared at me now, combined with the luscious aroma of her arousal, I suspected she wanted to get dirty.

"Better. Much better," I said, returning her haughty expression as I sat on the bed at the far end of the room. "If things weren't the way they used to be between our families, we might have noticed it sooner."

She tilted her head to the side and stepped closer. "And now that you know you're safe, will you finally do what you need?"

"Hmm." My cock kicked at the thought of being buried in her while I took what I craved. Wyn said it made us stronger, and I didn't see any reason not to believe her, especially given everything that had happened. I held up two fingers and waved her closer, opening my knees for her to stand in between them.

She put her hands on my shoulders as I grabbed her hips and leaned my forehead against her chest. Her scent intoxicated me, her skin so delicately soft and inviting. I guided her into my lap, her knees on either side of my thighs, and I slowly drifted my hands under her shirt, inching it up her body.

"We'll plan to do the mating ceremony at the new moon," she said, running her hands through my hair. "Then there's no going back."

I laughed and leaned up to kiss her precious mouth. "There's no going back now, sweetheart."

"Oh, I'm sure I could run from you if I wanted."

"You wouldn't get far." I preened for her, a deep rumble pouring out of my chest as she raked her nails over my scalp. Now that I knew the truth, this seemed inevitable. The vibrant pull to her had always existed, and I'd never been able to resist it. She was mine before I knew she was, and now she would be forever. It pleased both man and beast, and deep down, my soul shifted with the unbearable weight of her adoration.

We took our time undressing, worshipping each other with a reverent gentleness that soothed any lingering hesitations. I called her mine, and she called me hers, and we proclaimed our love in moans and cries and heated pants.

When I finally gave in to the impulse to rut into her like a feral beast, I let my instincts take control. She tilted her head to the side, showing me her neck, willing me to do it—to do the one thing I'd been embarrassed about since I reconnected with her. My canines extended, and I latched onto her throat, piercing her skin right as she broke apart around me. The carnal taste of her blood filled my mouth, coating my body and soul as I swallowed.

The intimacy in it pushed me over the edge. I erupted inside her, spilling everything I had left to give. Ecstasy and euphoria pulled me into a never-ending abyss of paradise, my entire body quaking by the time it was through.

The craving passed. I worshipped her for hours. And when we finally came up for air, I decided marking her would be the best thing I could ever do.

She was mine. I was hers. And everyone would know it.

Despite how well things were going with Maeve, I couldn't shake the guilt and the shame coursing through my soul. Holden had died because I was too distracted to keep a better eye on my mate and the security perimeters. Channing and my team had been beating themselves up since. We later found out they'd been able to dismantle the alarms, but we still didn't know how. It kept me up at night.

Maeve was the one having nightmares, but insomnia had started to eat away at me.

Kodiak told me it wasn't my fault; it wasn't anyone's fault. That did not change Holden's demise. It didn't change Marx's ability to abduct Maeve right off our territory. We weren't safe anymore, not like this, and that needed to change. I made a plan to upgrade the defenses around our territory. It would be an expensive undertaking, but we might pull it off with the new influx of cash we received from our stake in Vanderbilt Holdings.

A few days later, Kodiak called the entire club for church. We needed to regroup and plan our next steps. Even though we suffered injuries to save both Maeve and Ginny, we got lucky in the rescue. The only person who died was Holden, and we planned his memorial for the upcoming weekend.

I sat next to Orion and Moose while Serpent smoked a cigarette across from me. Ruby, Larentia, and Talon rounded out the officers.

"Marx is gone," Kodiak said from the head of the RBMC table. The rest of the club members clapped and whooped from their spots around us. "I watched his body burn myself."

The amount of relief that brought me should have been illegal. I'd been passed out when they turned that slaughterhouse to ashes, but knowing the ringleader was gone (as well as all the other vampires inside) made the future seem brighter. None of the other Vanderbilts would have to worry about Marx coming for them, and the pack would never have to wonder when he'd try to invade our territory again.

"But there are more Scorpions out there," Kodiak continued. "At least ten in that nest got away, including Percy Vanderbilt. They'll be back."

"Do we know if Marx has any relatives?" Moose asked. "Any close family that might come looking for him?"

"He's been undead for at least three decades," Larentia explained, twisting her curly blond hair into a ponytail. "All his real family are probably long gone, but who knows how many vampires he created in that time?"

"More will come," Kodiak reiterated, drumming his fingers on the table. "They always come."

Ruby rolled her eyes and scoffed.

"Have something to say, Rubes?" Kodiak raised his eyebrows as he looked at his sibling.

She took a deep breath and leaned forward on the table. "All due respect, brother, but you must end this treaty with the Vanderbilts."

Some members murmured among themselves. A few even cleared their throats, seeming uncomfortable. I glanced at Orion, who immediately looked at me with a knowing glimmer in his eyes. Any dissenters would have to pry our mates from our cold, dead hands. It was true, I took an oath to be loyal to the pack and the MC, but that only went so far. My girl would always come first. Always.

"They are the reason this is happening," Ruby continued. "Their father killed our parents. If not for them, Holden would still be alive."

"So we should punish the children for the actions of their father?" Kodiak asked. "We should blame Maeve and Sol for Marx's behavior?"

Ruby leaned back in her seat and hesitantly shifted her stare to both Orion and me. "No, of course not. But we shouldn't associate with known enemies of the—"

"Sol is a member of this pack," Orion said.

"And in one more week, Maeve will be as well," I added.

"Guin has signed over the territory that Uther Vanderbilt stole from us," Kodiak explained. "We have an interest in Vanderbilt Holdings, and if things continue to go as they have, we'll have made enough money this year to run as many guns as we want."

"Not to mention other things," Talon continued. "We'll never have to worry about cleaning our money again. Financially, this deal has been very advantageous."

"Just because you want to fuck Guin Vanderbilt doesn't mean—"

Kodiak slammed his hand down on the table and stood, his eyes shifting red, his canines elongating. "Enough, Ruby."

She quickly diverted her gaze to the ground. Kodiak was alpha of the pack for a reason. He was the biggest, strongest shifter in the room.

"Listen very closely. All of you." Kodiak glared, his tone dropping into a growl. "If anyone knows the pain Uther Vanderbilt caused, it's me. I lost my parents, my wife, and my predecessor because of him. If he weren't already dead, I'd be doing everything in my power to make that happen. But he *is* dead." The alpha directed that last bit at his sister. "Instead of fighting two enemies, we now only have one. It makes no sense to continue this useless rivalry, especially not when we have benefited from it."

Kodiak straightened and crossed his arms, emanating all the power of a rightful president. The crowd fell silent, and a few members shifted.

"We are safer now because of our truce with the Vanderbilts. Our children, our elders, *the pack,* is safer now." He raised an eyebrow and tongued a canine. "But this is not a dictatorship. If anyone wants to challenge me for the top spot, you are more than welcome to try."

He paused and waited for someone to come forward, but not even Ruby moved. A threatened alpha was truly a sight to behold. With his wolf in his eyes and dominance radiating off him, none of us even breathed loudly.

"No takers?" Kodiak nodded. "So be it. Any talk of breaking the alliance will cease immediately. Am I clear?"

"Yes," came the chorus.

"Good," he said. "In three days, we will mourn our dead and give Holden the send-off he deserves. He died to protect my daughter and a fellow packmate. He went down like a soldier, and for that, we will never forget his sacrifice."

"We will never forget his sacrifice," I murmured as the chant echoed around me.

"We'll resume operations." Kodiak sat and looked at Orion, giving him the go-ahead to read off the run schedule. The veep went through the upcoming trades and planned visits from our brother clubs.

"Lore went back to Virginia," Orion said. "But he'll be our envoy from the Steel Roses from here on out."

"Do we think he'll talk?" Larentia asked.

"No," Orion said. "He knows what will happen if he does. He's still processing everything he saw."

"What about our friends from the other chapters?" Poe added.

"We're good," Orion continued. "Everyone runs a tight ship. And you know what they say about loose lips."

"There's one more thing," Larentia added, leaning forward on the table to rest her elbows on the wood. "Before she left, Marta warned us about some strange reports the witches have been getting from the Canadian border."

This piqued my interest.

"She says there's a big pack moving closer to our territory," Larentia explained.

"Is it Zion?" Kodiak asked.

"She wasn't sure, and the Harlots risked enough by sending her out here. They've got their own shit to deal with and can't spare the extra eyes."

We weren't the only shifter pack in North America, nor were we the only ones of our kind. There were others out there, ones that could change form at will, that weren't enthralled to the moon. But we were the biggest, except for our neighbors to the north. In Calgary, Alberta, a pack of other moon shifters had been forming for years, led by a bear named Zion. He'd once been a member of the Helena pack, a patched and blooded Bastard. But after our former alpha, Kerrick, went rabid and died, Zion had disappeared. We later learned he'd started his own pack, one that only took in predator animals—wolves, wild cats, bears, and the like.

This, by itself, wasn't unusual. It happened anytime a new alpha was born and grew strong enough to lead on its own. One day, it would happen with Kai, and as long as he remained amicable with Kodiak, there was no reason for us to treat him any differently than we did now. We could go on as allies and friends.

But Zion hadn't been born an alpha, and he had no right to go MIA. It should have been enough for us to take off after him and deal our personal brand of justice. But Kodiak had forbidden it. We had our hands full with the Vanderbilts and the Scorpions, and chasing after a deserter hadn't been high on our list of security risks.

Until now.

"Mill." Kodiak said only my name, but I understood the assignment. Find him. Figure out what he's doing. Report back.

"On it," I replied.

"Thank you," the alpha said, "and try to get a lead on Percy Vanderbilt. That little prick is well past his expiration date."

"Agreed." I could have Channing and my team expand our search area. With more eyes and some upgrades to our systems, we could keep track of every threat that got even a millimeter too close. What happened with my mate wouldn't occur again. I'd swear to it if I had to.

"Anything else?" Kodiak asked.

"I think that's enough for one day," Orion said. Everyone else agreed, and Kodiak called an end to the meeting, but when I stood to leave, he raised a hand in my direction.

"Mill, a quick word." He leaned back in his seat and crossed his arms.

I sat and waited until everyone else left before raising an eyebrow at the prez.

"Finally going to take my patch?"

He snorted and shook his head. "No, of course not. I wanted to check in."

"Christ, here we go." I sighed. "I take it Morwyn sent you her findings."

"She did," he said. "I'll perform the mating at the next new moon. But that's not what I was talking about."

"I have a few ideas to upgrade our perimeter." I laid out my plan, relieved at his appreciative look as he nodded.

"I like it," he said. "Get Talon on board so you have the funds. I want weekly progress reports, and let me know if you need anything."

"Thanks, Kodiak." I eyed him with a more scrutinizing gaze. Bags hung under his eyes, and he rubbed his palm over his face like he needed the friction to stay awake. "How are you doing?"

"Fine," he said, but both my wolf and I sensed it was a lie.

"Maeve says Ginny was a badass," I continued. "She refused to back down from those fuckers, holding her ground at every step of the way."

Kodiak smirked and went eerily still. "She gets that from her mother."

Fond memories of Kendra floated to the forefront of my mind.

She and Kodiak had been a power couple, and when their girls had been born, I'd never seen Kodiak so happy.

"I think the apple doesn't fall far from either tree," I said.

"Fair enough." He chuckled and nodded. "Listen, I know you've been feeling some things since the attack, and I need to reiterate that it wasn't your fault. I ordered you to run tech and come to the office that day. I was the one who pulled in all our strongest shifters. If the blame lies on anyone's shoulders, it's mine."

"No," I started to say, but Kodiak held up a hand to stop me.

"When I give you an order, I expect you to follow it. You hand that control over to me, and my duty as alpha is to keep everyone safe." He tilted his head to the side. "Do you understand?"

"Yes," I said, swallowing down the tension and guilt that bubbled up my esophagus. I didn't want to be rid of my shame. I deserved it. But hearing Kodiak say that was like a balm to my soul. My wolf stopped riding me so hard. My conscience let loose of the reins. I breathed easier.

"Thank you," he said. "Now get out of here. Your brother's been looking for you, and your new mate is probably bereft without you."

I couldn't imagine Maeve being bereft about anything, but I didn't argue. I nodded, stood, and held my hand out to him. He grabbed it and shook.

"You deserve forgiveness and grace, too, Kodiak," I said. "I remember Kendra; she wouldn't want you to be lonely."

"Who says I am?" He furrowed his brows, but I raised an eyebrow, saying so much without words. The man looked like he wasn't sleeping, and I barely saw him in the cafeteria these days, which made me wonder how much he was eating. Much more of this, and he might crumple under the weight of all he took on.

But that's what they said about kings and alphas—uneasy lies the head that wears a crown.

Caelum looked terrible, and I didn't blame him. He and Holden had been friends since they were cubs, and losing him in such a horrific way had left its mark on all of us. I'd seen him since the attack. He'd come to check in on me in the infirmary, and he'd even brought Lyra once or twice, though I got the sense they were still trying to keep their relationship a secret.

Now, he looked like someone had ripped his heart from his chest. His eyes were red-rimmed and heavy, his cheeks sunken, his features drawn and stoic.

I rubbed a hand over his hair and pulled him into a hug. He clung to me like he did when he was a boy, after our parents died and he didn't have anyone else except for me and Wyn.

"Hey, it's okay, kid," I said, holding him tighter. "It's okay."

"I swear I'm going to track down every last one of those fuckers and rip their throats out," he mumbled against my shoulder.

"And I'll help you." Pulling back, I grabbed his shoulders and stared into his eyes. "But first, we have to lay Holden to rest, okay?"

He nodded and sniffed.

"You need to be strong for his parents, you got it?" I barely got the words out without breaking down myself. I didn't like seeing anyone in pain, much less my little brother. Fuck, I'd basically raised him as my own. His agony was my agony, and I felt this as much as he did.

"Got it," he said, forcing a smile up at me. "Kai, Nyx, and some of the others are planning a get-together out in the woods after the memorial. You wanna come?"

I shook my head. "No, you take your time together. You need it."

Caelum smirked, a knowing look dancing behind his gaze. "You need to get back to your mate?"

Rolling my eyes, I shook my head and shoved his shoulder playfully. "Leave it."

"Hey, I'm not judging," he said. "Isn't she my age?"

"Shifter magic doesn't care about age," I said.

"Unless she's nine."

His teasing made me feel a little better. It made me hopeful that he would heal from this. Even though he would never forget his friend, he wouldn't let Holden's death keep him from being who he was.

"I didn't *mate* her when she was nine," I said. "It's just...ya know...it's complicated."

"Uh-huh," he said.

"What about you? You still with Fenris's little sister?"

"Hey." Caelum shook his head and tsked through his teeth. "Lyra and I aren't together. It's just..." He cleared his throat and shifted his shoulders. "Complicated."

"Right." I laughed and wrapped an arm around his neck, pulling him into a teasing headlock, which he wrestled out of by elbowing me in the gut. We smacked each other around for a bit before collapsing on the couch in his dorm, side by side. I thought of our parents and how they might feel about the situation we'd both found ourselves in. I'd like to think they'd be proud of us both for the males we were turning out to be. I'd like to think they'd approve of Maeve, even if she was a Vanderbilt, and they'd be happy with how Caelum had grown up. I'd done my best. Looking at his profile, I noticed how much he looked like our mother, especially as he got older, and a pang shot through my heart at how much I missed both of them.

Six months ago, I wished I'd died. Hell, I'd almost given in to the temptation of staying in that dreamy paradise with Maeve after the attack. But she was right, as she so often was. I had so much to live for. My family needed me, and I needed them.

"I'm glad you didn't die...again," Caelum said, turning to face me, catching me staring at him.

"Yeah, me too."

He squinted at what he must have seen on my face. "What's that look?"

"There's no look."

"There was definitely a look," he said. "Come on. Out with it."

I shook my head. "Just thinking about Mom and Dad."

"I thought you were trying to cheer me up," he said, clutching his chest. "Fucking Debbie Downer."

"I think they'd be proud of you, Cae," I said.

He smiled and nudged me with his shoulder. "Yeah, I think they'd be proud of you, too, Mill."

Two days later, we buried Holden's ashes in the woods in the memorial gardens where all the pack's ancestors rested. Kodiak made a speech about how those who came before us still lived within us, in the blood and magic of the pack. Holden may be gone from this realm, but we could still find him in the ties that bound us together.

"We're a chosen family for a reason," he said. "We're blood bound for a reason. Fate, destiny, magic, it brought us together, and we will always be together. May he never be forgotten."

"May he never be forgotten," we all repeated.

Maeve held my hand through the entire ceremony, gripping me for strength and sending me her own in return. Watching Holden's parents place his remains in the tiny grave sent tears down my cheeks, shattering my heart all over again. I made a vow then and there that I would never wish for death again. There were those who deserved to be here and weren't. And if they couldn't live, then God fucking damn it, I would do the living for them.

"Hold still," Sol said, swirling a tiny brush over my arm to complete a spiral design she said was traditional in pack-mating ceremonies. "Almost done."

"Here." Ginny came closer and finished a dark streak on my cheek before stepping back to admire her work. "Perfect."

It wouldn't last long. Once we got this formality over with, Mill would take me back to his room and do his best to smear it into streaks. I shook with anticipation.

"Are you nervous?" Sol asked.

My stomach had been in knots all day (not the good sexy-time kind), and I trembled with the knowledge that everything would be different after the ceremony. Kodiak would officially make me a part of the pack, and Mill would mark me in the proper spot so we would be joined forever. Maybe some part of me should have been more concerned about that, but I saw how my sister was with her mate, and I wanted that with a wretched passion.

"A little," I admitted.

"You'll do great," Ginny said. "Trust me, I've been to dozens of these things. Everyone's always anxious at the beginning, but Mill loves you, and he'll be with you the whole time."

"Unless you've changed your mind?" Guin raised her eyebrows and inhaled on a cigarette, tapping ash into the tray on the windowsill.

"Not a chance," I said.

"Well, the safeword is Cowabunga, so if you get up there and it all starts going sideways, work that into your vows and I'll rescue you," Guin said with a snort.

"Do you think you'll ever get mated?" I asked Ginny.

She shrugged. "Maybe one day. I'm only nineteen, so I still have a long way to go. My transition will hit sometime, but I want to go to college and all that before."

I nodded. That was reasonable. Ginny had a good head on her shoulders.

"My father says he and my mother would have been mated if she had lived," Ginny continued. "But I think if it was going to happen, it would have while she was alive." She dipped her paintbrush again and finished the triskelion on the back of my hand. "We go rabid if our mate dies and we survive. It's what happened to Kerrick, and why my father had to put him down. Better that mates die together than one survive the other."

It was a somber thought, and I again wondered if I was making the right call. The sinking weight of realization settled in my gut, but there was no other way. Mill and I were already so connected. We'd died *twice* and returned together. So long as he walked this earth, I would be by his side. There existed no other reality for me.

"So Kodiak could still mate?" The thought almost made me laugh. He'd need someone willing to stand up to his dominance, someone who could put him in his place. Was there anyone in the pack capable of that? They all seemed to wilt under his commanding presence, even Orion.

"I hope so," Ginny said with a small smile. "Not that I spend much time thinking about it, but he needs to get laid."

"Ginny!" Sol laughed and smacked her arm.

"What?" Ginny said. "It's true. He's all pent up and repressed, and it's been over a decade since my mother died. I hate to think of him so secluded all the time."

When they'd finished their paintings, I looked at my reflection in the mirror and took a deep breath. I wore a black knee-length dress with a sweetheart neckline and spaghetti straps across the shoulders. My hair fell in soft ringlets down my back, the top half pulled into a cute bun. Designs sparkled across my skin, each representing a different part of shifter lore and history. I hardly recognized myself, but my inner fox yipped with delight and wagged her tail in my mind. My eyes glowed, my canines tingling with anticipation of what the night would bring.

I missed my twin, and once again, I prayed that Ava would go through her transition soon. I wanted her here. It was like missing half of my body, and I didn't know how much longer I could go on like this.

"Wow," came the voice from the doorway. We turned to see Fenris leaning against the jamb with a huge smile. "You look amazing. Mill is going to lose his shit."

I laughed and smoothed my hands over my dress. "You think?"

"Oh, I know." He nodded toward the hallway. "C'mon. It's time."

Guin took one hand, and Sol took the other. Together, we walked outside, following the torch-lit trail that led into the sacred grounds where all the mating ceremonies occurred. The humid night air clung to my skin, but the sky was beautifully starry. Cicadas and frogs chirped in the distance, and I trembled again. When we got to the clearing, my focus narrowed to the male standing next to a cement column with a dark chalice on top.

Kodiak stood on the other side, but I only had eyes for Mill. He was dressed in dark trousers, his naked chest and arms bearing the same spirals and dots as mine. Guin placed my hand in his, and the moment our skin connected, a rush of magic danced down our bond, warming me, wrapping around my soul with a gentle caress.

"Hiya, sweetheart," he said telepathically, his grin stretching wide. His bright eyes flashed red, indicating his wolf was close to the

surface. I returned the look with a glowing response of my own, my fox entirely too pleased with the whole experience.

"Hi there, my big bad wolf," I replied.

"Friends, brothers, sisters, and pack," Kodiak said, opening a small leather-bound book that had seen better days. "We've come tonight to celebrate the mating of Maeve and Vermillion."

He continued talking, explaining the intricacies of mating and how it has been in our history for millennia, but I didn't have the attention span for that. I stared at Mill and willed time to go faster. I wanted to get this over with so I could steal him back to our bedroom and have my filthy way with him.

"Maeve," Kodiak said. "You are about to swear a blood oath to the pack. You will become family in both name and spirit. Do you so agree?"

"Yes," I replied, almost too eagerly. Mill laughed as the crowd chuckled around me. I didn't care what they thought. I was ready to do this.

Kodiak held up a knife with a handle carved with intricate and beautiful designs. He sliced a tiny clean line across his palm before holding it out to me, palm up. Mill put my left hand in Kodiak's before the alpha turned the handle of the knife around to me. I had to do the same, and it had to be of my own will.

I hardly felt it as I cut my palm open, knowing it would be temporary. Once I sealed the blood pact with the alpha, I'd be tied to him forever, almost like the mating bond, but not as intimate. Mill would always have access to my mind and magic, but Kodiak would only use it if needed. He'd explained it like a computer network. He *could* hack in if he wanted, but he only did it if circumstances required.

When blood pooled on my skin, I turned my hand around and placed it in the alpha's, mixing my blood with his as Kodiak covered our embrace with his free hand.

"I recognize you as one of my family, Maeve," Kodiak murmured, maintaining eye contact with me. "And my wolf recognizes you as one of my pack. You have the strength of the Royal Bastards behind you, should you need it. And should the Royal Bastards need your strength, you will be required to give it. Are you willing?"

"I am," I replied. The alpha's magic poured into me, tightening the tiny tether between us. I gasped as it coated my molecules, reinvigorating me with the energy of those around us. I sensed Sol's magnetic vitality and Fenris's warm spirit. I felt Poe's mysterious power and Morwyn's calm determination. Moose, Larentia, Lycan, and Serpent all filled my bones. There were more, some I hadn't even met yet, some I didn't know very well. They were all there. I had been tied to them and them to me. But the most powerful of all was Kodiak, who shone like a sun at the center of a vast solar system of love, respect, and loyalty.

"The bonds of pack and mating are not to be taken lightly," he said. "Once you are family, the only way out is death."

It didn't scare me as much as it might have once. I'd greeted death on multiple occasions. That sucker would have to fight a lot harder if he wanted to snatch me into his terrible embrace.

"Last chance to back out," Mill said, giving me a wink while pushing adoration and reverence down our connection.

"Not a chance," I replied as my cheeks burned with desire.

"Vermillion, once you complete the bond," Kodiak continued, "there will be no others. You will use your body, blood, and soul to protect Maeve. Do you agree?"

"Yes," Mill said, holding my stare so I knew he meant it.

"Maeve, once you complete the bond, there will be no others. You will use your body, blood, and soul to protect Vermillion. Do you agree?"

"Yes," I said.

The crowd erupted into cheers, clapping as they stood to greet the new couple.

"It's my honor to announce Vermillion and Maeve mated in the eyes of the pack and the traditions of our ancestors," Kodiak said, his voice booming over the onlookers. "May you know great joy. May you never be torn apart."

I stepped closer to Mill, threw my arms around his neck, and kissed the hell out of him. It had taken us such a long and winding road to get here, but we'd made it. With him, I could do anything. With him, I could touch the sky. And as long as we were together, I'd help him do the same.

I stepped back and grabbed his hand, but my attention caught on a shape near the tree line behind us.

A burnt-orange fox sat with its tail wrapped around its front legs, a curious, pleasant expression on its tiny face. My inner fox immediately recognized it as family, as someone close to me. But who? Shifters only transitioned on the full moon, which was weeks away. I'd just been about to get Mill's attention so he could see, so I could ask what it was, but the fox stood and sauntered back into the woods. And the night carried on.

The party was still going by the time we left. The pack had been through a lot recently, and everyone needed the revelry. Music blared through the speakers, and mirth echoed through the pack bonds, adding an intoxicating coat to an already dreamy experience.

We burst into our room in a tangle of kisses and desperate embraces. I clawed at his linen trousers, desperate to tear them from his body, but he chuckled and pulled my hands away.

"Mill," I whined, trying to get at them again.

He leaned back and stared down at me with an eyebrow raised. "Patience, baby."

Patience?

I'd been patient for seventeen years.

At my indignant pout, he ran his thumb over my bottom lip and stuck it in my mouth. I wrapped my tongue around it, sucking it the way I wanted to do to his dick.

"Tsk, tsk, tsk," he said, shaking his head. "Such insolence."

"Yeah?" I bit down on his finger, enough to make him hiss in a sharp breath. "What are you going to do about it?"

He paused long enough to send a quiver down my spine before bending to haul me over his shoulder. I squealed with delight as he walked me to the bed and plopped me unceremoniously in the center. I bounced and rolled onto my knees, waiting for his next move. Mill stared down at me like a disapproving teacher who couldn't wait to take a ruler to my ass. I wanted him to. I wanted every deliciously vile thing he planned to do to me. And then I wanted him to mark me in the way only a dominant shifter could.

"That depends entirely on you," he said as he put his hands on his hips. "If you're a good girl, I'll make you come on my face before I bite you."

My lower belly tightened and sent a hot surge to my cunt. "And if I'm bad?"

His wolfish grin gave him away. "I'll make you come twenty times before I bite you."

"Twenty?" I balked. "That doesn't sound like a punishment."

He let out a condescending laugh and shook his head. "Oh, you sweet girl."

Mill held up two fingers and waved them, gesturing me closer. I crawled to him, and when I got within arm's reach, he grabbed the bottom of my dress and hoisted it over my head. The cool bite of air rushed in around me, my skin pebbling, but the heat of my desire for him burned through my blood. He nodded toward the mattress.

"Lie down," he said.

I nearly tripped over myself to do as he asked, another wave of his affection shooting down the bond as I stretched out on the duvet. The mattress dipped as he crawled over me, running his hands up my shins to my knees and thighs.

"You are the most miraculous thing that's ever happened to me," he murmured. "Do you know that?"

"That's saying something for someone who's died and come back to life twice," I admitted with a small laugh.

"Hmm." He pulled one of my legs up to his shoulder and kissed the inside of my calf, alternating soft pecks with open-mouthed bites. "That smart mouth of yours will get you in trouble."

"I thought my mouth was one of your favorite things about me." I couldn't help being a brat. It was in my nature, after all.

He struck like a snake, leaning over me to wrap a hand around my throat, his pupils dilating with a small crimson ring around the edges.

"And if you don't shut it, I'll give you something else to do with it."

I bit my bottom lip, excited about the prospect. Everything Mill and I did together was amazing, but if there was one thing I loved the most, it was sucking him off. I liked to watch him fall apart because of what I could do to him. I loved his little moans and how he grasped my hair to position me where he wanted.

He worked his way down my body, nibbling at my neck before lapping over a nipple with a tiny nibble. I arched toward him, rolling my pelvis against the growing tent in his pants. Mill laughed and pulled away from me, grabbing his cock as he slid down the bed. Then he speared his tongue through my cunt and grinned.

"Hmm, already so wet?" He did it again, and I threw my head back with a moan. I couldn't help it. Being a shifter came with the added benefit of slick, and it now dripped down the side of my legs, puddling underneath me as he continued to suck.

Nearly five orgasms later, after he'd had his fill, he finally resurfaced and prowled up my body with a slow easy grin. Evidence of his handiwork dripped down his chin, and when he kissed me, I tasted the combination of us in all of its resplendent earthy notes.

Not breaking eye contact, he reached between us and positioned himself at my entrance, sliding all the way in on one hard thrust. I surged off the mattress, but he held me still with his massive weight, dark eyes trained on my face. The first few thrusts were easy, and then he slammed against me, pounding me into the mattress, filling every inch of my cunt and soul. I sensed he was getting close to his own climax, the heavy weight of sensations rattling between us like unhinged fireworks.

"Are you ready?" he said, pulling his lips back over his canines.

"Yes, do it." I tilted my head to the side, giving him more room, and when he bit me, I blasted into another reality. His teeth sank into the spot between my shoulder and neck, right on the scent glands, and our magic pulsed, cementing into place. It wasn't like any other time he'd pierced my skin. This permeated with magnificent brilliance, like my entire life had been leading me to this one moment, like everything was suddenly so right and free and perfect.

When he pulled away, his lips bloody and teeth gleaming, my instincts took over. I leaned up and sank my canines into the same spot on his shoulder, impregnating my saliva into his body. His scent flared, his body convulsing as he emptied into my cunt, his knot expanding into place.

"Fuck, fuck, that's amazing," he groaned, his breathy sighs adding to my own ecstasy. Was there anything better than turning a powerful man to mush? I didn't think so.

The tether between us snapped taut like a tightening guitar string. I sensed it pulsing, twisting around my soul and extending into his. He collapsed on top of me, his heavy weight like a blanket, making me feel secure and loved and precious.

"I'll never stop wanting this," I said, running my fingers up and down his spine. "I'll never get over how amazing we are together."

He leaned up and brushed hair out of my face before pressing tender kisses to my mouth and nose. "Thank you for saving me, Maeve."

I smiled and shook my head as an untenable wave of adoration crashed into my heart. "No, Mill. Thank you."

I'd grown so much since he first came back into my world. I'd once been reckless and rash. I'd once thrown myself into dangerous situations just to feel the rush of life under my skin. And while I wouldn't necessarily give up some of my favorite pastimes, I had to admit—Mill had a point. I needed to care for myself as much as he needed to do the same. That girl who clung to life had found a reason to pause...to slow down and take things one at a time. I hated what had been done to me, but with time, I hoped I'd become grateful for it. I appreciated life in a whole different way now.

We fell asleep wrapped in each other, our legs and arms tangled, our bonding scents thick and heavy with sex. I didn't have any nightmares that night, thank God, but something pulsed inside my chest around two a.m. that had me sitting up with a gasp.

At first, I thought it was just aftershocks of what we'd done together. The mating magic lingered like a shot of good whiskey, making my limbs tingle and my head dizzy. But no, this was different. This was an ancient knowledge pulling in my gut, something rare and primal.

Ava.

I reached for my phone to check my messages, but I didn't have any from her. And just when I started to call her, my fox told me to stop. Something was happening, but it wasn't bad.

No, I sensed her the way I did Guin or Sol, deep in my bones, wrapped in my magic.

"Maeve?" Mill asked, sitting up next to me so he could kiss my shoulder. "What is it?"

"It's Ava," I said. "I think she just went into transition."

Mill met my eyes with a serious gaze, and together we came to the same realization. She was in Paris.

And the only one with her, the only one who could help her, was Lycan.

Epilogue

MAEVE

November 10

Five Years Later

I sat on the patio of our cabin at the homestead with a cup of coffee on the table next to me, my sketchbook in my lap, wrapped in a blanket. The sun rose over the horizon, painting the sky in beautiful roses and mandarins, accenting the burnt oranges and crimsons on the dying leaves. My mate and our children were still asleep in our bed, but I didn't want to miss this. It had been five years since my heart stopped, and I was still here.

Death had tried to come for me, but I was a tough bitch to kill.

Since Mill and I had been mated, I'd pulled back from the corporate life at Vanderbilt Holdings. I still had my seat on the board, of course, but I didn't want the day-to-day. I focused on my art, even setting up a little studio in downtown Helena to sell my pieces and feature those of other local artists. When I wasn't at the shop, I spent time with my kids or helped around the homestead. Life was too short to spend it doing things I didn't want to do, and nothing pleased me more than being around my family.

I slowed down. I listened to the instinct telling me not to go so fast, that life was worth living in the present. It had been a hard lesson to learn, but I'd finally accepted it.

"Hmm, here you are," Mill said, walking outside. He wrapped his arms around me from behind and leaned in to kiss the mating scar on my shoulder. "Why are you up so early?"

He circled to stand in front of me before lifting me off the porch swing, holding me in his arms, and sitting so I nestled in his lap.

"Just wanted to watch the sunrise," I said. "It's been five years."

He smiled and kissed me, nuzzling his head into my neck. "Has it? Feels like only yesterday."

"Are the cubs awake?" I murmured, trying to keep my voice low.

"No," he replied with that characteristic taunt in his tone. "I've got you all alone for once."

"Oh?" I chuckled and licked my lips. His focus immediately dropped to the movement, and I knew what he had on his mind. "And what, pray tell, do you plan to do with such spoils?"

He ducked his hand in the blanket, coasting it up my inner thigh until he reached my underwear, dancing his fingers over the increasingly soaked fabric.

"Anything I want," he said.

I feigned offense. "Such arrogance."

"Are you going to be a good girl?" he said. "Or am I going to have to—"

He cut himself off and leaned in, taking a deep inhale. I raised an eyebrow and looked down at him, waiting for him to finish.

"What?" I finally asked.

"Baby, you're pregnant again," he said.

"No, I'm not," I said. I'd gone into heat two weeks ago, and I hadn't bled yet, but that didn't mean anything. The last time this happened, it took almost a month before my body indicated I wasn't with a cub.

"Yes, you are," he said. "I can smell it. I can *sense* it."

The last two times he'd knocked me up, he had known before I did. He said the dominant always knew first. I opened my mouth, preparing to tell him how wrong he was, but he put his hand on my stomach, and a tiny flutter stirred inside me.

We already had three kids, a set of twin girls and a younger son, but the thought of another brought joyful tears to my eyes. We had both lost our parents way too young and, as a result, wanted a huge family to nurture. In five years together, our connection had only grown stronger. I thanked whatever fates had brought us for each moment we got to share, for each child, for each remarkable day alive.

He wrapped his arms around me to pull me closer, and we watched the sun rise together.

"Happy five years," I murmured to him.

"Happy five years, my sweet girl." He kissed my temple and held me close, and when our children rose for the day, we kissed them too, determined not to let anything take us from them. It was a good life, and I was determined to keep it.

VERMILLION

"Another one?" Fenris said when I told him. "Jesus Christ, my man. You're just raising your own little Alexander-Vanderbilt army, huh?"

"Your kids said they wanted more cousins," I replied. "I'm just fulfilling my promises."

He laughed and pulled me into a congratulatory hug.

It had been five years since I'd died and come back to life, and I had so much to live for. My siblings were doing great, my pack was thriving, and my mate...well, nothing brought me more joy than waking up to her beautiful smile every day. Watching her with my cubs, loving them, holding them, and raising them with uncondi-tional acceptance filled my heart nearly to bursting.

Once, a long time ago, I wished I'd died. I wished I hadn't been brought back to life by pack magic. I was scared of what it meant. Now, I couldn't believe I ever thought that. I had so many blessings, and when I let myself dwell on them, I almost broke down in tears.

The blood cravings eventually went away. Once my magic understood that she wasn't going anywhere, that we wouldn't be separated again, it stopped being such a sharp, piercing ache. Every now and then, she'd beg me to do it, and I would give her whatever she wanted. Yes, I lived to spoil my girl, but she lived to please me back. And on and on our love went.

I could have stayed with her all day, and I wanted to, but duty called, and she urged me to go.

"Did you tell Caelum and Morwyn yet?" Fenris asked.

"No." I shook my head. "We'll break it to them at the same time as the rest of the pack."

We headed toward the clubhouse office for church, and when we arrived, most of the officers were already in attendance. Kodiak sat at the head of the table with Orion at his right and Lycan at his left. Moose, Serpent, Larentia, and Ruby surrounded him, brightening when we walked in.

"There he is," Kodiak said, tugging his mate close to his side. She'd started joining our sessions shortly after they made it all official, and it had taken some getting used to by everyone else, but now she was a fixture at the head of the table, providing that delicate balance of intense determination and fierce protection that was indicative of an alpha's other half.

It pleased me to see Kodiak so happy. He deserved it, and even if it had taken a long time to get there, I was delighted he'd finally allowed himself to have it.

"Now that everyone's here," Kodiak continued as I sat in my usual seat. "I have an update."

"Oh?" Moose said. "Are we expecting a couple of new little alpha cubs to start running around?"

"Shut up, Moose," Kodiak said. "No. We've gotten word from the Royal Harlots. Another pack is on the move."

"Fucking great," Orion said, rolling his eyes. "Who is it this time?"

As we all set about planning and scheming, I let contentment fill my heart. I was right where I wanted to be with the people I'd chosen as family. And no matter what came for us, I'd stand up and fight to protect them, even if it meant I'd have to die...*again.*

I'd sworn my loyalty to these Bastards in blood, and they'd sworn the same to me. Together, we were stronger for it.

Five years ago, I wanted it all to end, and now, I'd grasp at life with everything I had, and may the Gods curse anyone who tried to take it from me.

The End

Want More?

Thank you for reading! If you enjoyed this book, please consider leaving a review. They help other readers find my work and enable me to keep writing. (Seriously, I am a sucker for validation and have a praise kink. Plz love me.)

The next book in the series is *Blood and Trouble,* featuring Ava, Lycan, and Poe. Coming September 8, 2026. I've included the first chapter, just for you.

I've also included a sneak peek at the first book in the Royal Harlots MC: Asheville, NC series, *Filthy Little Witch.*

You can stay up to date by joining my newsletter. ANNNDDD you get free smut just for signing up.

https://jenadoyle.com/join/

(No spam, only smut. I promise.)

I'm also @thejenadoyle on all the socials. Be sure to follow me for book recs, pictures of my cute dog, and all the news about upcoming releases.

Blood AND
TROUBLE
ROYAL BASTARDS MC
HELENA, MT
JENA DOYLE

Blood and Trouble

Three hearts. Two months in Europe. One trip that changes everything.

<u>Ava</u>

I don't trust easily, and I never give control to anyone.

But Lycan isn't a man I can say no to. He's dangerous and dominant and knows exactly how to break me into pieces. What's more shocking is how much I like it.

Then his gorgeous, infuriating ex shows up and, together, they shatter every line I've ever drawn. I thought I knew who I was, but I never expected this.

<u>Lycan</u>

I've never been in love. Ever. Not even with the one man I desperately wanted for my own.

But Ava Vanderbilt is a temptation that I yearn to claim and corrupt. She's the best kind of innocent, the kind that makes me want to dirty her up just to see how it feels.

Then Poe crashes back into my life, and the three of us ignite a dangerous inferno, scalding and impossible to resist.

<u>Poe</u>

I don't want him. And worse, he doesn't want me. I only came to protect them and follow the President's orders.

But the two of them awaken something in me, something I never thought possible. Lycan knows how to force me to my knees, and Ava's the perfect good girl with a filthy soul. Together, they make me weak.

In Europe, passion has teeth, and none of us will walk away unmarked. Desire isn't a game; it's a hunt. And the three of us are its perfect prey.

Blood and Trouble

Ava

I stood on the balcony overlooking the Paris skyline below, ignoring the tightness in my chest and dread in my gut. Lights twinkled in the distance while a gentle summertime drizzle coated the landscape. Laughter and the low, dulcet tones of business-like chatter echoed from the open doors behind me, beckoning me to get my tail back in there. My absence would be noted and questioned, but I needed a moment to collect myself.

I'd been on this networking tour for three weeks now, and the long days had started to catch up to me. I thought I was ready for this. I thought I was prepared to face him. But nothing I could have done would have been good enough.

Such a stupid girl.

Bringing my cigarette to my lips, I took a slow inhale and blew it out with a deep sigh.

"Those things will kill you," said a familiar voice as footsteps drew closer to me.

I smirked and turned to face my bodyguard, Lycan, as he leaned against the metal railing next to me.

"We all have to die someday," I replied, taking another relaxing draw.

"That's bleak." He held his hand out and waved two fingers, gesturing for me to hand it over. Amused, I raised an eyebrow and held the cigarette out. He took it, inhaled, and turned to face the beautiful skyline, leaning his elbows against the railing. "What's got you all morose and chain-smoking by yourself?"

"One cigarette hardly counts as chain-smoking." I brushed hair out of my face and straightened, steeling myself against what I needed to do.

Lycan shifted his grey-blue eyes to me and pulled his lips into an incredulous grin, and I ignored the girlish pitter-patter in my heart. Yes, he was beautiful, and he knew it. At six-three with pale silver-blond hair, Lycan could bring even the most conservative puritan to their knees. He flirted relentlessly with everyone, even the other security detail we'd hired. All he had to do was flash that killer grin, and people tripped over themselves to do whatever he asked. My twin sister, Maeve, and my younger sister, Sol, had warned me about him. Unabashed Playboy. Ruthlessly singleminded.

"He'll fuck anything that moves," Sol had said.

He'd been the consummate professional, at least to me. I probably should have been thankful. I didn't have the time or the patience for all that. Not now. Maybe not ever.

When he'd first shown up for the flight to Europe, he'd been dressed in cowboy boots, dirty denim jeans, and a leather cut that said "Royal Bastards MC: Helena, MT." My first task had been to take him shopping when we landed in Paris. I'd be lying if I said he didn't clean up well. A bespoke suit and a pair of custom-made leather shoes would make anyone shine, but on Lycan, it rattled some long-forgotten cage inside my heart. Regardless, I wouldn't have someone representing Vanderbilt Holdings who looked like they just walked off the ranch or climbed off a motorcycle. He needed to embody the part of a boardroom executive, and I was surprised that he could play it just as well.

"You're avoiding the question," Lycan said, handing the cigarette back to me. I finished it down to the filter and stabbed it out in the ashtray next to me.

"What makes you think something's wrong?" I forced my voice to stay steady as I drew my mental shields up, reinforcing my armor, stuffing my emotions way down inside where they belonged.

"For three weeks, I've watched you walk into these ridiculous soirees and sweet-talk rich assholes into turning out their pockets." He narrowed his icy gaze on me. "Tonight, you're quiet. Nervous."

"Nervous?" I laughed. "Me? Never."

"I can smell it," he said.

I raised an eyebrow and cast a disbelieving glance at him.

"If I can, they can, too." He nodded toward the party inside, the one with said rich-assholes mingling around, congratulating each other on their magnificent displays of capitalism and wealth. "So, go on then. Out with it."

In the time we'd been shuttling around Paris, we'd developed a hesitant friendship...as much as I could say *anyone* was my friend besides my sisters. The Vanderbilts were the richest family in Montana. We owned an immensely successful cattle ranch that my father had turned into an energy empire. We supplied and controlled most of the clean energy on the Eastern side of the United States, and if I was successful here, we'd expand our enterprise internationally. All I had to do was walk in there and demand it. *Sweet-talk* it out of the men who could make it happen.

Except...

I took a deep breath and decided to trust Lycan. Last year, Vanderbilt Holdings had formed a tentative alliance with Royal Unlimited, the official incorporation of the Royal Bastards Motorcycle Club. Our families had been enemies for years, but when Sol fell in love with their Vice President, Orion, we'd become family. So far, the agreement had been profitable for both sides. Old bad blood had been washed away, and when my eldest sister and current CEO, Guin, had asked me to come represent our interests globally, Lycan had been elected as the representative for Royal Unlimited.

We were in this together. So if there was a problem, he deserved to know about it.

Turning to face the party, I found the source of my anxiety towering over the crowd. Scott Fitzgerald. Tall, blond, and just as handsome as I remembered. Current Chief Financial Officer for Fitz Global, one of the most prestigious energy organizations in the world. His smile still gave me butterflies, and even though things had ended in devastating heartbreak between us, I couldn't help the swell of emotion rising in my gut.

"You see that man over there?" I nodded, and Lycan turned to the side, following my gaze.

"The balding dude with glasses?" He scoffed. "You could have him calling you Mommy in twenty minutes."

I laughed and playfully smacked his arm. "No, the one standing next to him. The one closer to my age."

"Hmm." Lycan tsked through his teeth. "What about him?"

"His name is Scott Fitzgerald IV, Seventh Earl of Pembrook," I explained. "He and I... well... it's been over for a long time, but there's still... I'm still..."

I didn't know how to describe the desperation clawing at my chest. I didn't have a long list of ex-lovers like Maeve, nor did I routinely let other people into my heart. I had too much to do — law school and the family business and millions of things to accomplish. Scott had wanted something more serious than I was willing to give. And when he showed up tonight with his pregnant wife and the big shiny ring on her finger, I lost my nerve.

"He looks like a douche," Lycan said, dismissing Scott to turn back toward the skyline. He grabbed two glasses of champagne off a tray as a server passed by and handed one to me.

I sighed and turned toward him, exhaling the weight of the long evening ahead.

"I don't have many exes," I confessed, "even less who I would say I loved...or came close to loving."

Lycan glanced at me with commiseration behind his eyes, his lips twisted into a kind smile. "I can relate."

"But Scott..." I shook my head and sipped the bubbly, relishing the tender heat as it settled in my gut. "Well, anyway. I knew I would see him tonight. I knew I would have to get him to turn out his pockets, as you say. Knowing that does not make it easier."

"Is that his wife next to him?" Lycan asked.

"The one currently forty months pregnant with their fourth child? Yes. Bea. She was friends with Maeve and me at boarding school." I gulped another big swallow of alcohol and thanked God for liquid courage. I'd need all the help I could get.

"She looks like you," he said.

Up until this point, I had purposely ignored that glaringly obvious fact. She had the same long black hair, the same bright blue eyes, the same curvaceous figure. I hadn't wanted to admit it to myself, that there might still be something there on his part, too. What did it matter if there was? He'd gone off and married the heiress to some massive oil fortune, and I'd gone to law school, and we'd left the past where it was, no matter how bad it hurt.

"You're prettier," he whispered, but quickly added, "Not that it's a competition. I'm a girl's girl, after all, and cutting down other women for the sake of male attention is beneath someone of my caliber."

A chuckle raced up my throat before I could stop it.

"But you're also smarter," he added, "and sharper. And if you wanted, you could probably have Scott Fitzgerald IV, Seventh Earl of Douchebags, calling you Mommy, too."

"Stop it," I hissed, trying to compose myself.

"C'mon." He nudged me with his shoulder. "You're Avalon Vanderbilt the First. Queen bitch of Helena, Montana. You've walked into boardrooms with guys more powerful than him and had them eating out of the palm of your hand."

"Yes, but this is personal," I said. "This is...He was my first."

"Well, you never get over your first," he teased, hints of sarcasm in his tone, and he leaned closer to whisper, "Who cares?"

"A sizeable deal with his company would be advantageous," I said. "We need his influence."

He raised a disbelieving eyebrow and tilted his head to look over his shoulder one last time before standing up.

"If you say so." He finished his champagne and placed the glass on an end table before reaching out to take mine. "Just play along, right?"

I furrowed my brows, but before I could ask any clarifying questions, he straightened his jacket and nodded toward the doors, gesturing for me to go ahead of him. I smoothed my hands down my little black dress and walked inside, trying not to stiffen as his hand landed on my lower back. Since we'd been here, I could count the number of times he'd touched me on one hand, and all of those had been accidental.

This was intentional. A claiming. A territory grab.

"Ava!" Bea beamed and pulled me into a hug over her baby bump, leaning in to kiss my cheeks. "You look lovely."

"Bea," I said and returned the greeting. "Good to see you. Pregnancy agrees with you."

She rubbed her belly and smiled. "After three boys, Scott's aching for a girl."

I forced my grin tighter and turned to my ex, the man who'd crushed my heart and married my childhood friend. "Scott. It's wonderful to see you."

"You, too, Lonnie." He opened his arms for a hug, and I leaned in, wincing at the nickname. I used to love it, but now I despised every wretched syllable for the memories they conjured. "You remember Pierre?"

Scott gestured to the older man next to him, the CEO of Joyeaux International.

"Of course," I said, shaking Pierre's hand. "We met with Pierre last week."

"Made quite the deal," Pierre said. "I'm still reeling over the details. But what else can I expect from the daughter of Uther Vanderbilt? The man was notoriously cunning, and the apple hasn't fallen far from the tree."

"Pierre!" someone called from across the room. "You need to hear this."

The older man nodded at both of us before politely excusing himself to make his rounds.

"And who's this?" Scott gestured to Lycan, standing beside me, his hand still possessively on my waist.

"Lycan Mitchell." My bodyguard held his hand out for Scott to shake, and my ex took it in his firm grip. "Head of Global Strategy and Partnerships for Royal Unlimited."

"Right," Scott said. His gaze dropped to Lycan's curling fingers on my hip, and I struggled not to move, not to seem like this was the first time I'd ever felt them there. I caught onto the game quickly. Lycan was pretending to be intimate, acting as if there might be something more between us, so Scott wouldn't have the upper hand. I bit back a grin. "I heard you'd made peace with your father's old nemesis."

"Well, you know what they say about keeping your friends close and your enemies closer." Lycan tightened his fingers around my waist.

"I think that's fabulous," Bea said. "Let bygones be bygones."

"It's been incredible," I started, explaining how we've managed to combine our resources to make both companies even more reputable. But as I talked, Lycan ran his fingers up my ribs to my bare shoulder before sweeping them over my arm. I tried to ignore the shiver down my spine. No one had touched me like this in years, and the sensation crept into my nerves, coiling around my soul, puddling between my legs. I ignored that, too.

"Ava's brilliant, you know," Lycan said. "And with our sights set globally, we're on track to diversify our offerings."

"The European market is expanding quite rapidly," Scott added. "Now's the time."

"Exactly," I said. "I heard your father turned over most of the control of Fitz to your sister when he retired."

Scott tried, unsuccessfully, to hide his wince and murmured under his breath. "She's made a grand mess of things."

"Oh?" I raised my eyebrows, pretending to be ignorant of their current financial status. They needed our investment. We needed the global expansion. It was a win-win.

"Scott's being facetious," Bea said, trying to soothe her husband's sour mood. "Liv's been a breath of fresh air."

"Quiet, Beatrice," Scott snapped.

Sufficiently chastised, Bea trained her features into a calm facade and sipped her bubble water.

I pursed my lips and settled tighter into Lycan's side. It probably gut-punched his ego when his younger sister took over, after he'd been trained and prepped for the position his entire life.

"Well, we've been looking for a place to invest our considerable assets. I'd be open to a conversation." I forced a tight smile as Lycan leaned into my ear, intimately brushing my hair over my shoulder.

"Very good. Now smile and drive it home," he whispered.

"Vanderbilt Holdings and Royal Unlimited are always looking for bold ideas and powerful partnerships." I tried to keep my face neutral, acting like we weren't as desperate for them as they probably were for us. Both stayed silent for a few moments, long enough for me to add, "Or perhaps I should reach out to Olivia. She and I were such good friends all those years ago."

That was a stretch. Olivia barely tolerated her brother's girlfriends, even less those who came from families less well off than hers. But for the two years Scott and I were together, she'd been agreeable, certainly enough to entertain the idea of sitting down with me if Scott proved uncooperative.

"You always did know how to go for the throat," Scott replied.

"Consider it." I tried to sound congenial rather than threatening, but Lycan's tightened grip on my waist suggested it was the latter. "We're going to Denmark in the next few weeks, but our trip ends in London. I'll have my assistant reach out."

"Hmm." Scott sipped his champagne and smirked. "It was good to see you again, Lonnie." He shifted his attention to Lycan as he wrapped an arm around Bea. "Mr. Mitchell."

As they turned to disappear into the party, Lycan smiled and shook his head. "You're ruthless."

I sighed. "Securing a deal with them would open our way into the British market. We could own them in five years."

My attention caught on a blonde woman eyeing me from the back corner of the room. She was tall and lithe, with chin-length hair cropped at a lethal angle. I didn't know her, but the gleaming and mildly threatening look in her eye suggested she knew me...or perhaps my family.

"Do you know that woman over there?" I asked, leaning into Lycan.

He furrowed his brows and followed my gaze, but in the time I'd spared to look away, she'd disappeared. I glanced around to find her, but she'd already gotten lost in the crowd.

"Who?" Lycan stretched his neck and looked to my right.

"Never mind." I shook my head. "Maybe too much champagne. I'm going to hit the bathroom, freshen up."

"You want me to come with you?"

"No," I said. "No, it's okay. I'll be right back."

I walked to the washroom, did my business, and washed my hands, fighting the churn in my stomach and the vibration in my nerves.

God, what is happening to me?

Maybe I was coming down with the flu.

Another toilet flushed, and the stall next to the one I used opened, revealing the haunting woman from earlier. She stepped out, and I met eyes with her in the mirror as she grinned and went to the sink on my left.

"Ava Vanderbilt," she said.

"I'm sorry, I don't believe we've met." I grabbed a towel to dry my hands.

"No, I don't believe we have," she said. "I knew your mother. From before."

"My mother?" The words fell out of my mouth before I could stop them. Priscilla Kennedy-Vanderbilt had disappeared twenty years ago when I was six. We'd only ever found a bloody patch in the snow. "How?"

The stranger didn't answer, just dried her hands and smiled, something sinister and foreboding flashing behind eyes so dark, they were almost black. "You look just like her."

Then, she turned and left me there with my open mouth and wide eyes.

What the hell?

My mother had strawberry-blond hair and green eyes. My sisters, Sol and Guin, were spitting images of her. Me? I'd inherited my father's dark coloring and bright blue eyes. Aside from similar facial structure, I didn't resemble her at all.

I hesitated for only a moment before I rushed out of the bathroom after the woman, wanting to ask her more, but she was already gone. I didn't find her in the ballroom, either.

"Are you okay?" Lycan asked when I found him near the bar.

"Yeah, just...I met someone in the bathroom who said they knew my mother. That I looked just like her."

Lycan blinked and glanced around. "Who?"

"I don't know," I said, belatedly realizing one important fact. "She never told me her name."

"I'll have Bow pull the guest list," he said. "Whoever she is, she got in somehow."

The night went on around us, and by midnight, my feet ached, and my eyelids stuck together anytime I blinked. We left before the party ended, escorted back to our hotel suites on the penthouse floor by a team of security. Locust, a member of the Royal Bastards MC and the leader of the squad, unlocked my door and headed inside while Lycan and I waited in the hallway next to Bow.

"Thank you," I said, sheepishly looking up at Lycan. "For saving me back there...with Scott."

He scoffed and stuck his hands in his pockets. "You had nothing to worry about."

"Still. I appreciate you having my back." I raked my gaze down his disheveled attire. He'd untied the bow around his neck, now hanging unevenly down his chest, and his hair stuck out at odd angles, evidence that he had run his hands through it on the way home. In my semi-drunken state, the urge to tunnel my own fingers through it nearly overwhelmed me. I clenched them to my side to keep them in place.

"You dodged a bullet with him," he said. "I hope you know that."

I nodded and breathed a small laugh, pitying the younger version of me that had allowed myself to be heartbroken over what could have been.

"No man should talk to a woman like that, especially not one carrying his fucking child."

"Such language." I balked and feigned offense. "Careful not to upset my delicate sensibilities."

Lycan chuckled, his storm gray eyes narrowing on me. "You did good, Ava. You should be proud of yourself."

"Well, he didn't agree to discuss my proposition any further, so I suppose that remains to be seen."

Locust returned and nodded at both of us, holding open the door. "All clear."

"Thank you, Locust," I said and took a few steps forward.

Maybe it was the champagne catching up to me, or maybe it was the lingering sensation of Lycan's fingers on my waist, but a sharp pang echoed through my chest at the thought of being alone for the rest of the night. Our security detail walked down to the end of the hallway, taking up their posts on either side of the elevator while Lycan lingered in the same spot.

"Do you want to come in for a nightcap?" I nodded inside my room.

Lycan lifted his eyebrows, a brief look of surprise parting his lips before he quickly returned to his default casual demeanor. "I should get some sleep. We've got an early start tomorrow."

I pretended the ice-cold rejection racing through my veins was nothing. Our earlier closeness had been a ruse, a farce. He wasn't interested in me, not like that. We were business partners. Barely friends. What the hell was I thinking?

I'm such an idiot.

"Of course. Right." I pulled up my iron shield, ignored the stab in my chest, and forced a smile.

"Raincheck, though," he said, but I knew he was only being polite.

"Sure," I said, trying to maintain what little remained of my pride. "Good night, Lycan."

"Good night, Ava."

I shut the door, turned to my cavernous suite, and rubbed my hands over my face.

Preorder Now!

ROYAL HARLOTS MC
ASHEVILLE, NC
FILTHY LITTLE WITCH
JENA DOYLE

It's **The Craft** meets **Supernatural** in this enemies to lovers, why choose witchy romance.

Marta

I joined the Royal Harlots MC to hunt monsters—not to fall in love.

Atlas and Wesson Colt are chaos wrapped in leather and sin. Brothers bound in blood and violence.

When a ritual goes wrong, the three of us are dragged into a liminal world where desire has teeth, pain tastes like pleasure, and every boundary we once held sacred melts into hunger.

Atlas

I've spent years fighting monsters and keeping my brother alive. I can handle blood, curses, and death, but not the way this bond twists through the three of us, tightening until I can feel Wesson's breath in my chest and Marta's heartbeat in my veins.

The liminal exposes everything—every craving, every flaw, every memory I buried to survive. In this place, hate and hunger blur until I can't tell where mine ends and theirs begins…and whether any of us can survive the pull of our worst impulses.

<u>Wesson</u>
I wasn't made for this life. Not the Harlots, not the warriors, not her. Atlas carries rage; I carry shame. The kind of damage you don't come back from.

But being in the liminal forces it all to the surface. Every thought I shouldn't think. Every desire I shouldn't feel. For her. For him. For the darkness strangling the three of us with every breath.

If we don't escape this realm soon, it won't just claim us. It'll consume us.

Three enemies. One cursed bond. A darkness that feeds on love and fear alike.
When the only way out is each other, survival might cost them their souls.

MMF • Witches & warriors • Enemies to lovers • Forced proximity • Liminal world • Why choose

Filthy Little Witch

CHAPTER ONE

MARTA

I was used to existing in liminal spaces. Half witch, half biker. Both Catholic and pagan. Attracted to both men and women. A proverbial pie chart of ancestry that included Mexican, Scottish, and Indigenous roots. In many ways, this was what pushed me where I stood today. I existed everywhere, so I belonged nowhere. And in that desperate struggle, I forced myself to be better, to be smarter, and to work harder than everyone around me.

"Are you nervous?" my cousin, Bridge, asked from behind me. I glanced up at the mirror and looked at her, smiling as I shook my head. "Good. You're ready. You'll do great."

Tonight, I would be given my warrior, a partner supernaturally bonded to me whose sole mission was to keep me safe. I didn't take this privilege lightly. Looking at the leather vest on my shoulders proclaiming me a member of the Royal Harlots MC, I thought about how much it had taken me to get here.

Years of training. Years of learning from the elders. Decades of service dedicated to the coven. All of it would culminate tonight when the president, Lilith, finally announced the person who would stand at my side while I enacted my life's work. Getting patched in was one thing; getting bonded to a warrior sealed the deal.

"Was it painful?" I asked Bridge. She'd been inducted years ago, right around the same age as me, and had already completed several missions.

"Nah." She waved me off and winked, brushing her flaming red hair behind an ear, a blush on her alabaster cheeks. "It's over before you know it."

The Asheville chapter of the Royal Harlots wasn't like any other chapter in America. We were the most powerful witches this side of the Atlantic, and it took a lot even to be considered a prospect, much less welcomed into the club with a patch.

The Royal Harlots MC had only recently been recognized by Duchess, the president of the founding chapter, four years ago, but it was the local coven that had made it possible. Formalizing ourselves as Harlots gave us access to a nationwide network of empowered women, something that had been difficult to manage until recently. Since we all swore our blood and loyalty to the MC, we had their strength behind us, and it had made all the difference when we needed it. They looked out for us, and we looked out for them.

"C'mon," she said. "We're going to be late."

We left my bedroom, where my abuelita sat at her kitchen table with a steaming cup of tea in her hands.

"Oh, look at you!" She stood and held her arms out, gesturing me into her embrace.

I tried to hide the burning in my cheeks as I went to her and wrapped my arms around her midsection. When my parents died, Tita took me in without hesitation. I'd been a child, young and terrified of the world. But Tita had loved me through it all, through the nightmares and the rebellious teenage years, through the prospecting of my early twenties. She'd been a motorcycle-riding witch once upon a time, as had my mother. As much as she would rather see me off to college, doing anything other than what took her son and daughter-in-law from her, she also recognized that magic ran in my veins and I had always been destined for tonight.

"You look so beautiful," she said, pushing a piece of dark hair behind my ear. "How do you feel?"

"Okay." I smiled and tried not to shake. I'd heard the ritual could be taxing, sometimes deadly, but the club wouldn't have recommended me if they didn't think I could handle it.

"Remember," Tita said, "you are the strongest of us all. Your grandmothers are rooting for you." She touched the cross and the locket I always wore around my neck and grinned. For being well into her sixties, she didn't look a day over forty, which was a testament to the strength of the magic in our family. From her, I had inherited a long line of Mexican and Spanish ancestry, all powerful witches and healers. On my mother's side, I traced my roots back to the first settlers of Appalachia, equally strong and rooted in the natural energy of the world.

"I'll take good care of her," Bridge said as she grabbed my shoulders in a comforting squeeze.

"I know you will." Tita smiled at Bridge and kissed each side of my cheeks, cupping my jaw in a tender embrace before she touched her forehead to mine. She muttered a whisper to Saint Marta for strength and another to the Virgin Mary to look out for me. I closed my eyes and envisioned a shield of my abuelita's love coating my skin. Even if I had my disagreements with God, Mary, and most of the saints, I did believe in the force of my grandmother's love. It had gotten me this far.

When she was done, she let me go and hugged Bridge. Then she went back to her tea.

"Make sure you're back before supper," she said. "I'm making tamales and roasted chicken. The entire club better come, including your warrior."

"Okay, Tita." I waved goodbye to her and walked out of the front door, descending the stairs with knots in my stomach. I wiped my hands on my black jeans and adjusted my cut before kicking a leg over my bike and lifting it upright. Bridge got on her bike next to me and reached out to tug on my braid.

"It's gonna be fine, Marts," she said, using her nickname for me. "Trust me."

I wanted to. I really did. But Tita's mention of my warrior reminded me that this was real. This was happening. I'd been born into this family of witches, and despite what aspirations my parents might have had for me, there was never any other choice.

In my world, women were the most powerful practitioners. *All* women, even those who were misgendered at birth. We were the ones with the deepest connection to the earth, the ones chosen to wield magic to defend it. There were a lot of monsters out there— rabid shifters, chaotic vampires, ruthless demons. It was a Harlot's job to keep the rest of the world safe.

Normies didn't know we existed, not in any real sense. Even if some humans could tap into the unique reservoir of preternatural energy in their blood and the elements, they could not manipulate these forces the way we could. We worked our entire lives to perfect it, and once we came into our power, we spent most of the time fighting the real evil in the world.

But magic always came with a cost, and there was a downside to casting. It left the witch vulnerable to attack, especially if she used too much magic too quickly. She needed someone to defend her, to protect her, to channel energy into her if she got injured—hence the warrior.

A warrior bond wasn't inherently sexual, nor was it based on compatibility or mutual attraction. It was based on strength, on the ability to fight together with complementary skills. A witch could survive the death of her warrior, but a warrior would never survive the death of his witch.

I'd get mine tonight, and I tried not to think about who it would be on the long drive to the meeting grounds. There were dozens of unbonded warriors in the Harlot community. I prayed it was someone I got along with, someone I could put up with on long missions and even longer nights.

Instead, I focused on the weight of my bike between my legs, the wind in my hair, the brilliant blushes and pinks in the sky as the sun set over the horizon. God and I may have our differences, but I couldn't help but marvel at His creative splendor when the world came to life like this.

When we got to the mansion-turned-clubhouse way up in the mountains, we parked the bikes in the long row of motorcycles belonging to my sisters and walked to the treeline on the right. Rituals like this always happened outside during a full moon in our ancestral forest, one that had belonged to the witches in the Harlots for over a hundred years. Some could trace their lineage through Indigenous roots; their families had been practicing here for even longer.

I paused at the entrance to the woods and took a deep breath, wiping my sweaty palms on my jeans as I stared at the lit torches lining the trail deeper into the trees.

"It's too late to back out now," Bridge said, coming to stand on my right. She nudged me with her shoulder and smiled. "Your mom would be proud of you, ya know? So would your dad."

I thought of my parents and blinked back tears as I envisioned younger versions of them standing at this very spot, walking this path, making the same vow to pledge themselves to their coven. They had lived and died by that promise, and while some part of me resented that they'd been taken from me so young, I also understood that they'd died heroes. They'd gone down fighting, protecting the world, saving people, and I was proud to call myself their daughter.

"There you are," came a voice from in front of us. "We've been looking for you."

Our resident nomad, Valkyrie, walked forward, her dark hair pulled back in a braid, her leather cut firmly on her shoulders. She flashed a friendly smile and glanced between me and my cousin.

"All set?" Valkyrie asked.

"Just nerves," Bridge answered.

I scoffed and bumped my hip into hers. "I'm fine."

"Don't worry," Valkyrie said with a roll of her bright blue eyes. "We won't go easy on you. It'll be better that way."

I snorted and followed as Val led Bridge and me through the woods. The birds chirped in the distance, settling in for the night, and the cicadas buzzed through the pines and cedars. Lightning bugs had just started flashing around us, waking up for the night, and the frogs bellowed out their own version of a mating call, adding the perfect chorus to the September night. Our boots crunched on the dirt as we made the walk, and the closer we got, the more my heart pounded against my ribs.

No, wait.

That drumming sound wasn't coming from inside my body. It was up ahead, the riotous orchestra of voices chanting in time with each other, accompanied by the rhythmic *dum-dum-dum* of mallets on drums. We paused when we got to the clearing, and I forced myself to pull my shoulders back, to stand up straight, to not let the sight overwhelm me.

The entirety of the patched Harlots stood in a circle, singing to welcome the land spirits, to ask them for their grace as we performed our ceremony. Though the official members of the coven totaled thirty, another fifty stood around them on the outskirts of the clearing, near the trees. Some banged on drums, some clapped and danced to raise the energy of the spell, and others stood stoically in contemplation.

The warriors.

I recognized some of them as being bonded to Harlots, here to lend their energy should they need to. But a lot of them were unbonded. Any unbounded warrior was obliged to attend in case the magic selected them. I gulped and stepped closer to the circle, knowing I had to wait until Lilith called me forth to join.

I eyed the crowd, picking out a few people I'd known most of my life. Off to the left stood Leander, brother to the Harlots' secretary,

Isobel. Next to him was his best friend, Lyr, twin brother to the treasurer, Lorelei. A few other family members milled around, but my attention caught on the Colt brothers in the far corner, standing in the darkness, shrouded by the trees and the impending twilight.

Atlas Colt stood on the end, dressed in a black jacket, matching jeans, and boots. He was the eldest at thirty-two, standing nearly six-three with broad shoulders and a strong jaw that gave way to lips permanently etched in a sneer. His dirty blond hair complemented his bright green eyes that sparkled in the firelight.

Wesson, his younger brother, stood next to him. He wasn't related to Atlas by blood, but he'd been the only child of Atlas's father's second wife, and when she died, he'd taken the boy on as his own. Wesson was taller than Atlas, nearly six-five, with dark, curly hair he kept cut short and skin almost as tawny as mine.

Neither of the Colts liked me, and truth be said, I didn't like them, either. Their father had been my mother's warrior, and three of them had been with my parents when they died. I didn't trust that they had nothing to do with it. They said my father died protecting my mother, and once he was gone, my mother went quickly after him. But if the brothers were close enough to see it, why hadn't they stopped it? Of course, they'd been new to missions at the time, but that mattered little when the result was the same.

Rage simmered in my blood for one heartbeat before I swallowed it back, remembering they had no other choice but to be here. Atlas and Wesson worked for the Harlots. Even if they weren't bonded warriors, they were family, whether I liked it or not.

The chanting stopped, and the sudden silence brought me back to the present, refocusing my attention on the witches around the fire. Circe, the vice president and second in command, walked to the center and held her arms above her head, her black hair tumbling down to her waist.

"On this night, we have gathered on sacred land to protect one of our sisters. She will complete her patching ceremony by bonding a warrior chosen for her." She turned in the direction opposite to me to call in the elements: North, East, South, and West, respectively.

Once the witches had finished their chant, the atmosphere changed. A chilling vibrancy now floated above us like an invisible mist, coating our skin and giving us an ethereal link to the world. Circe turned to Lilith, our president, and nodded, indicating she was done.

Lilith came to the center and took her place, looking toward the heavens, her deep umber skin shimmering in the firelight, her eyes completely white with the power of trance, the irises and pupils gone. "Great ancestors, grandmothers, grandfathers, all those who lived like us, loved like us, and thought like us, hear our call. Be with us tonight. Give us your wisdom and your strength as we seal an ancient rite. Hail and welcome."

The moon had fully risen now, shining in the sky like a heavenly beacon, illuminating us in a divine glow. A whoosh went through the air, lifting the hairs on my arms and the back of my neck as a loving warmth sank into my gut. I'd grown up with magic. My tita was powerful, and I'd learned to control my own energy from the very women in this circle. But this...This was the most potent and electrifying experience I'd ever felt. It was the ancestors letting me know they were here. It was the hundreds that came before me, whose blood still lived in my veins, and they would bear witness to my induction.

I thought again of my parents and chewed my lip, wondering if they'd made the journey. Were they here in the astral realm? Were they just beyond the veil, waiting with smiles and joyful expressions, hoping my bonding went according to plan?

Of course, I'd never heard of anyone *not* surviving the bond, but as with any magic, your mileage may vary.

"Elizabeta Marta Maria McDonnell-Ruiz, come forward." Lilith held her hand out to me, waving her fingers to gesture me toward her.

I took a deep breath and stepped closer, sensing the increased vibration from the circle as I did. It hummed against my skin and coated my tongue as I breathed, and when I reached the magical boundary, it rattled through my heart, twisting my stomach with excitement and anticipation. It wasn't evil, but it wasn't altogether good, either. It felt like the unknown, like a dark shape in the woods on a new moon.

"Marta, being patched in is an honor, not a right. You have earned that place, and so tonight, we pair you with a protector," Lilith said, bowing to kiss the back of my hand.

When she stood, I did the same to her, following the proper protocol of honoring the president of the Harlots and the high priestess of the coven. Lilith smiled and cupped my cheek, winking before breaking our connection and turning to the crowd.

"Our sister cannot stand alone," the high priestess said. "Every witch requires a warrior. Who is called to this position?"

Shouts of "I" and "Me" came from the onlookers, all the various men who had come to witness my induction and bond themselves to my sacred power.

"Brave Marta, you have heard those who are called," Lilith said as Circe came forward, holding the chalice. Lilith took her time pricking her finger with a ceremonial knife, holding it over the goblet so a drop fell inside. She handed the knife to me, and I held back a wince as I repeated the motion. Our combined blood sizzled as it handed inside, and I swallowed back my anticipation. The time had come, and now I would know.

"Place your hand over the cup and ask the ancestors for guidance," Lilith said.

I did, closing my eyes and whispering a prayer to the universe that it provide me with someone capable and strong, worthy and loyal. *Find me the right person. Mother, father, ancestors, help me.*

The cup grew hot, burning under my touch, and when I couldn't stand it anymore, I ripped my hand away and held it to my chest, grimacing through the pain.

A piece of paper flew out of the top, landing in Lilith's outstretched hand. She opened it, read it, and furrowed her brows.

"Colt," she murmured.

Colt?

No, that couldn't be. There were only two Colts in attendance. My heart sank, and my overheated blood suddenly froze like I'd mainlined ice water. A shiver raced down my spine.

"A.W. Colt," Lilith called, louder this time. She glanced around until her focus landed on the two men standing in the far corner. I couldn't bear to look at them, too terrified of what I'd see.

Wait...

A.W?

Which one was that? Was that Atlas's entire name? Were his initials A.W.?

"Atlas, Wesson, step forward," Circe said, waving her hand in their direction.

Boots echoed on the earth, breaking twigs and stomping through grass, and I felt their presence on either side of me.

"Which Colt?" Wesson asked, and the sound of his deep baritone ricocheted down my spine.

Circe looked at Lilith, who crumpled the paper in her palm before closing her eyes and leaning her head back toward the sky.

I sensed it before she said it. The weight of the energy in the atmosphere settled around me, and my intuition picked it up as if it were flashing a bright neon sign.

Both of them, it said. *Both of them.*

"Atlas...*and* Wesson," Lilith answered.

"Two warriors?" hissed someone close to me.

A chorus of murmurs repeated the surprise.

"I thought she was only supposed to get one?"

"Why two?"

"Both Colts?"

"That can't be right."

"Silence!" Lilith's voice rang out into the night, booming and deafening. "There has never been a Harlot with two warriors, but we do not question the ancestors. We do not question the magic."

I did. I had *loads* of questions, starting with, *"How fucking dare you!"*

The Colts were there when my parents died. I'd heard the rumors. Atlas and Wesson had stood by while some vicious demon tore my family apart. And now, I was supposed to bond with them? Rely on them for protection? I hadn't said more than two words to them in years.

"Lilith," I tried to say. "High Priestess, please. There must be—"

"Do you not accept this gift the ancestors have bestowed upon you?" Lilith asked, her tone suggesting I better not argue.

Once upon a time, she'd been bonded to her father's best friend, who eventually died protecting her. She hadn't been given another warrior since. And here I was, bestowed with two? Why two? Why *these* two?

In all the years I'd lived, I had more than enough reasons to be mad at God. Now, I had beef with the ancestors, too? Would the horrors never cease to persist?

I swallowed against my suddenly dry throat and licked my lips, hesitantly looking at Atlas on my right and his stepbrother on my left. Atlas glared at me, his emerald gaze and tight pursed lips radiating with the years of animosity between us. Wesson, on the other hand, looked destroyed, his jaw hanging open, his brows pinched together, his eyes nearly shimmering with hot, angry tears.

Even if I said I wouldn't accept the gift, nothing would happen. I'd never heard of them pulling another name from the chalice. In fact, I'd never heard of a Harlot rejecting their warrior at all. To be patched and blooded as a Harlot was an honor; to be given a warrior was the cherry on top.

"Yes, Lilith," I said, returning my focus to the ground in front of me. "I accept this gift."

"Good, all is well." She held out her hand, the same one she'd cut earlier, and waved her fingers for me to place mine in it. I did, and I shivered when Atlas put his on top of mine. Wesson moved to stand across from me, holding our fists under me. Lilith placed a red ceremonial ribbon on top of Atlas's knuckles before wrapping it over and around our combined embrace. Over and around. Over and around.

"I bind you together in the tradition of our beloved dead," she said. "Warrior to witch, witch to warrior. You will share your energy, your strength, and your magic. What the ancestors have bound, let no one tear asunder."

"What the ancestors have bound," the three of us repeated, "let no one tear asunder."

Lilith dragged her knife down the sides of our palms, scorching a hot cut along the outside of our hands, deep and fiery. It ached more than my blooding, and when Atlas's blood dripped down into my cut, I winced as a tether opened up between us. Circe brought the chalice over to us, catching the dripping liquid as it pooled under our bound fists. Normally, the warrior and witch drank of each other, and the ceremony concluded. But I didn't know how this would work with *two* warriors. Would they then be bound to each other? Would they have the same connection that a witch typically had with her warrior?

Circe handed the cup to Wesson, who took it with his free hand and held it up.

"Marta, witch of the Royal Harlots," he said, his voice trembling. He cleared his throat and stared up at me with dark mahogany eyes, holding my gaze as he said the next part of the oath. "I swear my allegiance and fealty to you as your blooded warrior." He drank, and my connection to him soared. His energy rushed into me like a warm campfire, like autumn bursting in my veins. He hadn't wanted to be selected because of how *I* might feel about it. He reeked of shame and guilt.

It wasn't like I could feel his emotions or read his thoughts; more like I got the energetic imprint of them. I understood them, even if they weren't my own.

"Marta," Atlas said when Wesson passed the cup to him. He

sighed and shook his head, hanging it over his chest like the words took every bit of his energy to say. "Witch of the Royal Harlots. I swear my allegiance and fealty to you as your blooded warrior." When he drank, I gasped as his life force barreled into my chest, hot and fiery and reckless. It boiled with indignation and resentment. He *hated* me, almost as much as I hated him.

No, no, no.

This would not be a good match, not at all. How the hell was I supposed to run missions with them when we couldn't even stand to look at each other?

Atlas handed the cup to me with a squared jaw and hardened eyes; the green having almost disappeared around dilated pupils.

"Atlas Colt, Wesson Colt, warriors of a sacred line. I accept your allegiance and fealty as my blooded warriors. I swear to honor, respect, and protect you until the end may come."

"Until the end may come," the Colts repeated.

I drank from the cup, swallowing down the rich metallic taste, wincing as all three pathways snapped into place. Atlas groaned and Wesson winced, but undoubtedly, they now knew I hadn't wanted this, that I wished it had been anyone else. They knew I blamed them for every rotten thing in my life. They knew I hated them.

A small, vindictive voice spoke up from inside me.

Good.

Acknowledgments

Dear Reader,

Thank you for reading this little shifter romance. My lore started in paranormal, and it is such an honor to take all my favorite werewolf tropes and combine them into one world. I hope you enjoyed Maeve and Vermillion's story. Also, if you're a Steel Roses MC reader, stay tuned — we will definitely see more of Lore in the RBMC universe.

Next up, we'll hear from Ava, Lycan, and Poe. The idea of a three shifter mating bond has always appealed to me, so I look forward to creating that synergy and seeing where it goes. Plus, who doesn't love a sword crossing why-choose?

There are so many people to thank for their help on this —

First, to the lovely, Crimson Syn. Thank you for welcoming in to the Royal Bastard world with open arms. This has been an amazing experience, and I am thankful every day that I got to sit next to you at SmutLovers.

To my amazing editor, Misha Robinson, who has put up with my reluctant muse this entire year. Through pushed deadlines to amazing line-editing wisdom, I am incredibly grateful to have you on my team.

To my beta-readers: Leslie and Maggie, I appreciate all you do. This story wouldn't have been what it was without you.

To my wonderful partner and spouse, Mr. Doyle, thank you for giving me the time, space, and means to keep up with this hobby.

And to you, dear reader. If you've just joined or if you've been here since the start, I am eternally humbled and grateful for you. It is because of your support that I continue to publish.

Cheers!

-Jena

Also by Jena Doyle

<u>MIDSUMMER</u>

We Wild Things (Prequel Novella)

Midsummer

Samhain

Solstice

Beltane

<u>STEEL ROSES MC</u>

They Called Him Saint (Prequel Novella)

Crimson Chaos

Savage Saint

Oleander Oaths

Mischief Mayhem

Ruthless Reign

<u>ROYAL BASTARDS MC: HELENA, MT</u>

Blood and Whiskey

Blood and Magic

Heats and Holidays (Novella)

Blood and Trouble

<u>ROYAL HARLOTS MC: ASHEVILLE, NC</u>

Filthy Little Witch

www.ingramcontent.com/pod-product-compliance
Lightning Source LLC
Chambersburg PA
CBHW020246010826
48973CB00006B/1680